LINES
IN THE
WATER

LINES
IN THE
WATER

David Scott McVey

atmosphere press

Published by Atmosphere Press

Cover design by Ronaldo Alves
Lines in the Water artwork by Jordan Thatcher

atmospherepress.com

*I am grateful to all encouragers and supporters,
thank you, as always...*

Foreword

This book is completely a work of fiction. The community of Fair Creek, Georgia does not exist. While Hawkinsville and Pulaski County are certainly real places, I have completely created a map of the town to suite the story. The characters are not real people. They are not representative of any specific individuals but they are representative of people of their respective times. Some events in the story do come from similar life experiences in my life, but they have been changed and usually sensationalized for the sake of the fiction. I hope I have done justice to these good people and communities. I mean nothing but respect.

The 8th Infantry Regiment of the Confederate States Army was indeed a real unit that fought with valor in the Civil War. Company G was comprised of soldiers from the Pulaski County area. I based the events in this story on the very real history of the 8th Infantry Regiment. The 8th Infantry Battalion was also a real unit in the War Between the States. I have changed the history of the units in minor ways to fit the story. However, I tried to do so in a way that does not diminish from the sacrifice and service of any of the soldiers.

I have always been intrigued by two things that are important to this story. The first is the incredible bravery of the soldiers on both sides of the lines in the U.S. Civil War. When I visit the many battlefields of this war, I must choke back tears thinking of the fear, agony and despair experienced by so many men and boys (and horses). To avoid future wars we must understand the true human costs of war.

The second matter is the long term struggle between races in the history of the United States. It is certainly easy to understand why there was and is strife. It is far less easy to understand why the struggle has remained so intense. Legal slavery and even discrimination have been removed from our society as a matter of law, but they have not been removed from many hearts as a matter of principle. Changing hearts requires that we understand the human costs of hate and anger.

Some fights are as old as the first disagreement among brothers. At the center of the reason to fight is a belief that I am right and that I am willing to destroy and kill to prove it. There is also an inherent need to compete and to dominate, be it football, checkers, music competitions or war. However, in the case of war, the risks and potential costs are unlike no other competition. It is amazing that soldiers of war, after seeing the horrible deaths and destruction, will continue through a battle or a series of battles or even multiple wars. But they do, and human kind seems destined to fight the same battles over and over.

When the United States of America was just over four score, these battles in the form of our Civil War tore the ground and hearts of our young nation. So desperate were the struggles and so deep was the hatred that the wounds have not completely healed. Some remain. Uncle Sam is now very dignified middle-aged gentleman, but he is a veteran of many battles that have left wounds that are very slow to heal.

Some of the wounds that will not heal quickly are often reopened over and over again by the sharp edge of bigotry and hatred. While the battles that tore the ground ended in 1865, the battles that tear the heart continue to this day. But victories also occur. Unlike war, where a conquering army controls the ground and takes the objective, the victory may be a smile or a friendship earned, or maybe even a life saved.

DSM
29 May 2021

TABLE OF CONTENTS

PART 1
CHANGE ARRIVES

The Vision of Spirits

We believe that the past is gone – now just buried in a history book or a memory that will fade to a distant place in our minds. But the past is always with us – never far away. There are old souls near us – good and bad, sometimes merciful and sometimes vengeful. They watch with keen interest. They have purposes. They direct the players on the stage of the living to their purposes. The old souls begin the first act the drama with the innocent players, our children.

∞

FISHING IN FAIR CREEK

Fair Creek, Georgia, is a small community of good people just west of Hawkinsville, Georgia, in Pulaski County. Pulaski County is located along the belt buckle of the state on the widest east-to-west stretch. The county was named after the Polish count Casmir Pulaski, who died a hero in the Revolutionary War while retaking Savannah from the British in 1779. At that time, the land around Fair Creek was lush and held abundant wildlife. The area had been the home of Native Americans long before any colonial settlement.

Fair Creek was a clear stream that ran towards Hawkinsville. It emptied into the mighty Ocmulgee River. Many fiercely independent farming families had settled this land (as had the Creeks and Mississippians). They established their homes with hard work and had little personal wealth. It's no surprise that during the Civil War their support for states' rights was deep and passionate—no Northern Republican president was going to tell them what to do and when to do it. Right or wrong, they were good, strong people. That strength allowed them to endure the war's tragedy and atrocity, but their strife and suffering didn't end with the war. Forgiveness, acceptance, and peace would come very slowly. For some, it would never come at all.

In the early 1960s, blacks and whites throughout the country struggled to find ways to live together. The people of

3

Fair Creek were no exception. The fight against inequality, while necessary, sometimes complicated the process of just getting along. Adults frequently had difficulty establishing even simple relationships with neighbors of other races.

This was not the case with children. Curiosity on both sides often led to friendship.

Such a friendship was born one day in 1965 between two ten-year-old boys. This happened along Fair Creek, along the same paths on which young men had left home to march to war a hundred years earlier. It happened along the same creek banks where young couples held hands and old folks sat in the sun and smiled. On a warm fall afternoon, a little boy named Mike Thomas was fishing in a good hole. It had been a good hole for many years: several generations of his family had fished these same waters. He had wandered away from his mother and her good friend Larry Wayne, a state trooper who had been a friend of Mike's dad. The trio often went fishing together on Saturdays. Mike had snagged his hook on a log and had broken the line. He was trying to tie on a new hook, but fumbled with it. He did not want to go to Larry for help - again.

As Mike struggled with the stubborn line, another boy was working his way towards him from downstream. Lee Sanderson was intently focused on working his doll fly through the good spots. Lee loved fishing—he was good at it, and always smiled as he fished. Like Mike's, his family had fished these waters for generations.

Mike was so focused on his knot that he didn't notice Lee. Lee was mesmerized by this curious white boy. He had never seen anyone have so much trouble tying on a hook. Lee had also never spoken directly to a white person.

But he gathered a little courage and said, "Boy, you sho' got a funny way of tyin' on a hook!"

Mike was startled, and stared at Lee. Finally, he replied, "It's the only way I know how."

"Well, you gonna do a lot more tyin' than fishin'."

For the better part of the minute Lee watched Mike struggle with the hook, then said, "Let me show you something."

Lee cast his doll fly downstream and brought the doll fly slowly into the deep pool, near a sunken log. Lee had fished this old hole many times and had lost many flies on that log. He was slowly bringing it along with a few delicate twitches.

"Want a bluegill?" Lee asked. He smiled as Mike nodded in wonder.

Bang! Suddenly the little rod bowed and the fight was on. A few seconds later Lee pulled out a slab-sized bluegill.

Mike's mouth dropped open. "That's the biggest one I've ever seen out of here!"

Lee laughed softly. It was the biggest he had ever seen, too, but he wasn't going to admit it.

Over the next few minutes the boys discussed the art of catching fish. Lee gave Mike two doll flies and some instruction.

Mike would never forget this kindness. The mighty racial tensions of the South were absent from this stretch of the creek, at least for today.

Near sundown, Lee's older brother approached from downstream. When he saw Lee talking to a tall white kid, he felt a flash of anger and said, with force, "Lee, get yo' dumb butt over here and let's get home!"

Lee gave Mike a parting wink, Mike smiled, and the boys separated. As Mike walked back to his mom and Larry, he felt good. It didn't even cross his mind that some would think it wrong for him to fish with this black boy. But he also realized he didn't know his new friend's name.

Neither Lee nor Mike knew about the old black man, almost a shadow, who had been watching them from the trees across the creek. With a big smile, he had softly muttered to himself, "That's good, boys. Uh huh."

5

He began to fade as the sun set; first his smile, then the softly glowing eyes. But he would be around a while longer; he, and others like him, had been on this creek for many, many years, living in the shadows. These spirits remained on this earth as a result of the immense and violent tragedies of life and war. These ghosts from the past worked, for evil or good, through the living.

Both Lee and Mike began to seek each other out along the creek, sharing good times with their lines in the water. Their friendship grew strong as they discovered they had much in common. But Mike would always struggle to tie a good knot on a hook, no matter how many times Lee showed him how to do it.

Always, the old man watched - and smiled.

BREAKFAST—1970
FIVE YEARS LATER

Even by Georgia standards it was a very warm morning for late August on this first day of class for Hawkinsville High School. But it wasn't Hawkinsville High School anymore: it was Pulaski County Consolidated High School, and all of the county's students would be in attendance, including the black children.

Sure, thought Mike as he dressed. Like many teenagers, Mike had perfected the art of conversation through the liberal use of sarcasm.

He couldn't help but think how warm it was going to be in pads and helmets at football practice. Mike had woken with a nagging worry about practice already. Starting today, with the new school year, the freshmen and sophomores would practice with the varsity. Mike couldn't help but think, We'll be fresh meat!

But that wasn't the biggest change on this day in 1970. For the first time ever, Mike would find himself in classrooms with black students and black teachers.

Mike's mother called up the stairs from the kitchen." Let's not be late today! And I need to talk to you before school."

Mike laughed to himself coming down the stairs. "Mom, you've never let me be late to anything, ever!" he said. "I doubt we start today."

Mike entered the kitchen and smelled coffee, as well as cinnamon toast, which was usually reserved for birthdays and holidays. It seemed almost wrong for the first day of school. Mike poured a big glass of milk and wolfed two pieces of the cinnamon toast. The kitchen was not large, just room enough for the small stove and the refrigerator on one side, the sink and the counter on the other. The equally small dining room was separated from the kitchen by only a bar, which served as an extra counter. The dining room had just enough space for a table and four chairs. There wasn't much counter space or shelving, but Mike's mother, Ruth Anne, made it very cozy and special, setting out flowers underneath the family pictures that hung on the walls. One very old photograph was a black-and-white of Mike's great-great-grandmother Susannah Thomas and an elderly black woman Mike knew only as Miss Ellie; the pair sat in rocking chairs on the front porch of a long-gone house. They wore soft smiles reflecting lives that had seen both happiness and heartbreak.

Mike switched on the big transistor box radio and tuned it to WHPR. As the sound of "American Woman" filled the room, he reached for a third piece of toast.

"Mike, for goodness' sake, do you have to turn the radio up so loud?"

"Sorry, Mom. I like this song." He sang along, "Momma let me be...ee!"

Ruth Anne, prim and proper and beautiful in her nurse's uniform, turned off the radio, ending Mike's guest performance as the lead singer of The Guess Who.

"Mike, we need to talk, right now!"

Because of her tone, Mike knew that meant that mom needed to talk and he needed to be quiet and listen.

"Mike, there will be Negro children in your school today," she said.

Mike already knew this, but resisted the urge to smart off to his mother.

"Many of the children come from very poor homes, so their clothes may not be as nice as yours are," she continued. "But I want you to understand something—and this is very important: you are never to make fun of them, ridicule them or show disrespect in any way. Ever! If you treat people with respect, they will respect you. These children have as much right to be in school as you do."

"Okay, Mom."

"I'm serious about this, Mike!"

"I know, Mom. I wonder if Lee Sanderson and his brother Arthur will be at school?"

"Probably so, Mike. There's one more thing I need to say."

Mike took this opportunity to go for the fourth piece of toast, although number four turned out not to be as good as numbers one, two and three were.

"Mike, you must be careful," Ruth Anne said. "Some people are very angry that the Negro children are in your school. Please try to avoid any ugliness. There will be some hate towards white people who show respect and kindness to the Negro children. So please, Mike, be careful!"

Mike promised to be careful, and respectful. He had heard the talk among his teammates and others about the arrival of the black students. Some of it made him very uncomfortable. But he was eager to see Lee. A few minutes later, Mike was out the door and walking to school.

There were two things Mike did not yet realize about his mother's warning. One was that she was speaking from experience. She and Dr. Ed Roberts, her employer, had been providing medical care for black families for several years. More than a few white people regarded Ruth Anne and Dr. Ed as white trash because of this work. Dr. Ed had been denied membership at the country club, and neither he nor his wife was invited to the important parties thrown by the town's "upper crust."

The second thing Mike didn't realize was that his mother's

before-school lesson would forever be one of his strongest memories of his mother and her goodness.

First Class

Before you can have a first day of school, you have to get to school. Usually Mike walked: the school was only about three-quarters of a mile from his Fair Creek community on the west side of Hawkinsville. As he walked, alone, he usually was singing some song from his many favorites. Today he belted out, "I got sunshine, on a cloudy day."

I would take a few clouds today, he thought. Especially during football practice.

Mike's route to school took him down Scenic Drive towards Fair Creek Park, past the Civil War Veterans marker, then along a short trail through the woods that led into the parking lot of the Lilac Road Baptist Tabernacle, in an area that many referred to as "Colored Town." Mike would then head up Lilac Road and slip through the hole in the fence of the baseball field at Hawkinsville High School (the old name would die slowly). Mike rarely saw anyone on this route—he had discovered it as a freshman while seeking the quietest, most desolate path so that he could sing without being heard.

The only person Mike regularly came across was Reverend Amos Ross at the church. They always exchanged greetings and had developed a unique acquaintanceship in this unusual way. Mike didn't know that Reverend Ross was the contact and go-between for Dr. Ed and Ruth Anne when people needed medical care.

11

No other white kids walked through this corner of Colored Town, but it didn't surprise Reverend Ross that Mike was the exception. Mike wasn't a crusader—he simply didn't concern himself with such issues. Many of the black folks would smile and laugh about "Singing Mike." Mike had a lot of friends he didn't even know about.

He also had some enemies—not everyone was as accepting as Reverend Ross and his flock, and Mike's secret route was not as much of a secret as he thought. Reverend Ross had even told Mike's mother about his path by the church, and promised Ruth Anne he would watch over for Mike.

This simple acquaintanceship would one day save Mike's life.

But on this day, the first day of school, Reverend Ross was escorting several black children to the now-integrated East Side Elementary School, which was near the high school. One did not see a parade like this every day. Revered Ross and the children, with Mike as the caboose about twenty yards behind, marched up Lilac Road. A few people noticed this odd parade, and so did some of the town's spirits. As the reverend and children proceeded up the road, the spirits gathered. But today was not the day for action. Not here, not now.

Mike already knew his class schedule. First period was geometry. He entered the school from the back door by the cafeteria. Mike had gotten to know the cafeteria staff informally by passing through this way almost every day. Sometimes Isaiah James, the kitchen boss, would give Mike a jelly biscuit.

The hallways were alive with noise and excitement as friends saw each other for the first time in weeks. Raymond Cary, teammate and friend, caught up with Mike as he walked along. "Mike, where are you going? Geometry, maybe?"

"Yep. At least I get it over with early."

"Me, too!"

"Ray, only three hours until lunch!"

Ray was a big boy, but not fat. He was every bit of six-foot-three and just about two cheeseburgers short of 250. He was probably the best center in the state, even as a sophomore and only sixteen years old. His family had money and his father was an attorney and district judge.

The bell was ringing as they walked into class. The first thing Mike noticed was Lee Sanderson sitting alone in the back corner. Without a second thought, Mike walked over and took a seat beside Lee. Once he settled in, he noticed that many of his classmates were staring at him. Even the teacher, Miss Majors, was surprised. Without speaking a single word, they had all sent Lee and Mike a very sad message: "You are not supposed to sit beside one another. You are not supposed to speak to one another."

Mike saw this as a test of his friendship with Lee: it would either break or become stronger. He stayed in his seat, ignoring the stares and the facial expressions of disgust.

Oblivious to this tension, Anthony Joseph (A.J. to all) came in and sat down by Mike and Lee. A.J. and Mike were also longtime friends.

They were an unusual pair. Mike was tall, lean, very athletic, handsome and popular, though he did have a very shy streak. A.J. was short and not athletic. A.J. loved sports and fishing, but he was never going to make a long run carrying a football or beat out an infield single. Mike and A.J. were just natural buddies. They had bonded over common interests such as electronics, rocketry and airplanes. They both liked technical gadgets and science. A.J. and Mike could chat comfortably while building a rocket, though to most of their classmates these interests were weird or boring or both.

Mike and A.J. sat together in classes and at lunch, with Ray usually close by, protecting his geeky friends. Ray and A.J. often engaged in insult contests, with Mike would have to be the referee and sometimes tell them to shut up. These three musketeers were about to add a fourth person to the gang, Lee

Sanderson. These three friends made up Mike's circle of confidents. This fraternal circle was about to be shaken by a new person in Mike's young life, and she had blond hair.

One person that had not stared at Mike was a new girl in class. Setting across the room at the front of the class, the new girl thumbed through her textbook while everyone else gawked and glared at Mike. When he noticed her, he instantly forgot Lee, his mother, geometry and most everything else, including his own name. This angel from heaven had very long strawberry-blonde hair. Suddenly first period became the highlight of Mike's day, and it had nothing to do with the axioms of Euclidean Geometry.

Finally, Miss Majors broke the classroom tension by taking roll. Mike didn't answer when she called his name. The boy was smitten.

THE CAFETERIA—
COLORED FOLK ALLOWED TO EAT NOW

This first day of the new school year had been interesting, but not sensational so far. Sure, there were black students in many classes. But segregation was still alive and well—the black students tended to be relegated to the back corners of the classrooms. A few teachers assigned seats alphabetically, but that just created isolated, lonely students, and it especially isolated the black students.

There were very few of the black students that were in the advanced, or so-called college prep classes. Only the persuasive arguments of Mr. Elbert Penner, now the interim assistant principal, allowed for a few really good students from the old J. L. Bozeman High School to gain admission to the advanced classes. J. L. Bozeman had been the all-black, or "colored," high school. Very few of the black teachers were retained after the integration, Mr. Penner being one of the few. He was a professional, a talented no-nonsense teacher who knew trigonometry and calculus as well as anyone in Pulaski County. Mr. Sam Bob Ellis, the principal of Hawkinsville High, realized that Mr. Elbert, as he called Mr. Penner, was an incredibly valuable asset, and allowed him to teach freshman math. Most of his students quickly realized that Mr. Penner was perhaps the best teacher they would ever have. If nothing else, his amazing dexterity with a pointer at the blackboard

15

was entertaining, even for those who would never comprehend multiplying or dividing fractions.

Two gifted students in the advanced classes were Amanda Ross, or Mandy, the daughter of Reverend Ross, and Lee Sanderson. On that first day, both Mandy and Lee were sitting with other black students on a back-corner table in the cafeteria at lunch time. This informal segregation would remain in force for some time. It was members of school bands, clubs and athletic teams that finally broke this form of segregation. But even that would take time and did not happen on the first day of school after court-ordered integration.

As Mike, A.J. and Ray entered the cafeteria, Mike saw Lee across the room and nodded. He wanted to go talk to Lee about fishing on Saturday, but thought better of the idea. Mike was aware of the tension in the air that formed a very thin and fragile line of separation between the blacks and whites. He sensed that Lee was feeling uncomfortable and strained, not the Lee he knew down at Fair Creek. Mike was torn between wanting to sit with Lee and not wanting to create more tension for his friend.

This cafeteria was one of the few places Mike and other white kids had frequent contact with the black people of Fair Creek or Hawkinsville, who comprised most of the cafeteria's workforce. Mike recalled the smiles from the cooks and servers, and thought of how they were always laughing and enjoying life. He always looked forward to his morning journey through the cafeteria. And the food was good, especially the biscuits and fried chicken and apple pie and pumpkin pie and turkey and dressing. It was just burgers today, but that was okay. It made no sense to Mike that these kind people were good enough to cook for the faculty and students but not good enough to go to school as fellow students. One small step forward, he thought. Maybe we will be sitting together soon.

Ray and Mike sat down at a table beside some fellow

football players—but only after Mike had quickly scanned the room for the strawberry blonde.

Ray laughed and asked, "Who you lookin' for?" It was clear he had a pretty good idea, as he had watched Mike staring across the room at the girl during geometry.

"Nobody!" Mike replied, too quickly.

Ray laughed again and said, "Yeah, right."

The table's conversation was dominated by the older guys, and based mostly on making fun of the younger players. One of the leaders of this intimidating group was Bobby Willet, the son of the local sheriff. Most of the guys had heard that Mike had sat by Lee in geometry, and versions of the story had circulated around school already, even among the teachers. After Mike, A.J. and Ray sat down at the table, Bobby yelled toward Mike, making sure everyone heard: "Ain't you gonna go sit with your buddy over there? He might be missin' you."

This resulted in loud laughter, as if it were the funniest joke ever told. Mike found it a stupid comment that deserved no response. He was willing to let it go. But he looked at Lee and felt embarrassed.

Most of the boys were intimidated by Bobby. He was loud, had a violent streak, and was followed by a small gang of stupid, equally violent boys who would do anything he said. He was also a decent tailback looking forward to a good senior year. Mike really wanted no confrontation with Bobby. Ray, however, had no fear of Bobby, or any other human. Ray could whip most bears; in fact, most pairs of bears. Deciding to intervene before Bobby got really ugly, Ray winked at Mike as if to say, Watch this!

Ray stood up, pointed at Bobby, grinned and said, "Maybe you should go over and make friends, 'cause there's a couple of guys over there that are going to kick your white ass all over the field this afternoon! I'm looking forward to it myself!"

This silenced the Willet gang, and Bobby's face looked like a version of the original face of anger and hate. Smoke was

17

coming from his ears and his eyes were locked on Ray.

Oh shit, Mike thought as goose bumps formed on his arms.

A.J. laughed and elbowed Mike as he said, "Our Neanderthal colleague is poking the bear with a big stick!"

Ray kept going. "Hey Bobby," he said, "Can you play guard, or some other spot? I hear that Arthur Sanderson is the best running back around. Maybe you can block for him."

Arthur Sanderson, Lee's older brother, was one of the new black players the team would meet on the practice field that afternoon. But most people called him by his nickname— "Gone." He earned that moniker because at J. L. Bozeman, as soon as he touched the ball, he was quite often "gone". During long touchdown runs, the public address announcer would say, "Ball carrier was Sanderson, an' he be gone!"

The "name" stuck.

Bobby stood up and threw a milk carton at Ray, but he missed. Bobby screamed, his voice shaking with anger, "Nobody in this cafeteria will take my spot! And you should shut up before I make you pay, fat boy!" With that, Bobby stormed out of the cafeteria, his gang following like a string of baby chicks.

Mike looked at Ray and said, "Well, at least practice will be interesting today."

Ray just smiled and asked, "Are you gonna finish those fries?"

A.J. laughed and added, "Ray, are you ever not hungry? I have a banana left for your big gorilla ass if you want it."

"Okay, smart boy, how much will it increase the mass of your brain if I stuff it in your ear?"

Mike stopped this exchange of intelligent ideas. "Both of you shut the hell up," he said. "Let's clean this milk up. Ray, you made Bobby mad enough to sling the milk at us."

"Yeah, but it was fun."

A.J. laughed. "Ray, you are good for some entertainment! That was funny. Willet was pissed."

The tall black cafeteria boss, Isaiah James, Mike's morning friend, came over to assist with the cleanup. Isaiah had been cleaning the cafeteria for many years. He was also the choir leader at the Lilac Road church - most of the time he whistled or hummed old spirituals. This was far from the first time he'd had to deal with the results of a prank. With a big smile, he said, "Y'all don't have to do this. But I thank you boys."

Mike again felt embarrassed—he seemed to be the cause of problems for others today. He also thought this might be the strangest day of his life. But the day was not over yet. More strangeness and goodness were to come.

SCIENCE CLASS WITH THE WIZARD

Science, the last class of the afternoon, started with a bang. Once again Mike was with Lee, although they didn't speak before class started. The cute girl from geometry also came in, took a seat by Mike and smiled at him. Once again Mike lost brain function. He couldn't think of anything clever to say while he floated between heaven and stupid. Again he didn't even hear his name when Mr. Paul Foss called roll. Mike came back to reality with the class laughing at him, very loudly. Mr. Foss smiled, just a little.

A.J., sitting behind Mike, also was laughing, and poking Mike with the eraser end of a pencil.

"Mike Thomas, are you present now?"

"Yes, sir... I mean... here, sir!"

Ray was laughing the hardest. Even Lee looked down at the floor and giggled softly. In a few seconds, Mike had gone from floating in heaven to sinking in hell. He also realized that this pretty girl, whose name he didn't really even know yet, was blushing and that his staring at her was the reason. It would now probably be at least several days before Mike would work up the courage to talk to her.

A.J. leaned forward and said lowly to Mike, "You really impressed her, Romeo!"

Mr. Foss called the class to order. He was a very good teacher but he had one weakness. Lee Sanderson was one of the first black pupils to ever sit in his classroom, and Mr. Foss was looking for any opportunity to flunk or expel this boy he saw as an upstart and disrespectful. Lee was none of those things, of course, but he represented everything Mr. Foss hated about forced integration and a slowly changing culture. The man still firmly believed "separate but equal" was the way to go. After all, he was a wizard.

Just not in science. Mr. Paul Foss, like his father before him, was a Grand Dragon and wizard of the local Ku Klux Klan. He was often visited by spirits of anger. They would be calling again soon.

Mr. Foss wasted no time getting into the class material. As he began to speak about the physical properties of water, he looked around at his pupils. He was surprised to see that Lee was listening and taking notes. This was more than most of his students. He also saw that Mike still had his head down, seemingly not paying attention. Mr. Foss chose not to embarrass him again.

"Please turn your books to page thirty-seven."

Mr. Foss watched as students turned the pages. He noticed that Lee had a puzzled look on his face, which he interpreted as confusion. Actually, Lee's expression was concentration: he was already on page thirty-seven and was reading the caption of a figure on that page. But Mr. Foss just had to say something sarcastic, with a condescending smile: "Mr. Sanderson, page thirty-seven comes after thirty-six."

Most of the students in the class laughed softly and quickly glanced at one another.

Lee felt a quick flash of anger, but let it go. He knew who Mr. Foss was and what he believed and what he could do. Few of the white kids knew these things about Mr. Foss, but within a few weeks, that would all change.

Lee replied, "Yes, sir, and right before thirty-eight, and there is a diagram of the Kelvin temperature scale at the top of the page, if that helps you find it."

Every jaw in the classroom had dropped and was hanging open, and Mike thought, Oh Lord, will my friends ever stop doing dumb things today?

A.J. was the only person who laughed, but he quickly stifled it. Leaning forward, he whispered to Mike, "Lee is very good—I knew I would like him!"

Lee was known by family and finds to have a quick mouth and also to not back down from direct challenges. He wasn't going to start doing so today, even though his grandmother, who had raised him, had begged him to be careful.

Mr. Foss was very practiced at hiding anger and hate. He had other ways to express these feelings. The look he gave Lee would burn rock. "I am glad you found the page, Mr. Sanderson," he said – his anger oozing out through the sarcasm.

When class ended, the students left quickly to go share their new stories and gossip. Holy cow, there were new stories to tell and the gossip did fly forth.

Later that day, Mr. Foss drove home in his Chevy pickup alone. Alone, but yet he had a passenger. This particular spirit had visited Paul Foss often, and many like him. Currently visible to Mr. Foss alone, the shadow was dressed in a dirty butternut uniform. This spirit really had no cause or mission other than to use self-doubt and mistrust to provoke anger and hatred, and in so doing be the voice of evil. There was no right or wrong, no fairness or injustice—there was only anger and violence.

As Mr. Foss drove, the spirit whispered, "You must teach this boy respect. He spat in your eye today."

Mr. Foss would do his best to teach this boy, all right. But science was not the subject he had in mind.

Bobby shut down

After science Becky, the girl that had smitten Mike, walked towards the music hall with her books stacked in her arms and carrying her clarinet case. It was quite a load, and she went at a fast pace to get to band practice on time.

This had been an interesting day to say the least. Though she liked many of these new kids, she wondered how long it would be until she'd feel like she belonged at this new school. She thought, I wonder if I can ever get Mike to speak to me?

She liked that shy boy. But there were other boys she instinctively knew were nothing but trouble. Like Bobby Willet, who suddenly stepped out of a classroom door and blocked her path, causing Becky to stumble and her books to tumble.

Bobby laughed, and as he knelt to help pick up the books he said, "You better watch where you're going!"

Becky didn't like being startled, and she was angry. "Bobby, you stepped in front of me on purpose!"

"Sorry," he said with a grin and a snicker. His ever-present posse giggled and laughed. They moved into a loose circle, blocking Becky's exit.

Worried, she said in a shaky voice, "Okay, Bobby, I need to go."

"Can I carry the books for you?"

"Nope."

"Well, maybe we can get together at the Circle tonight?"

"Nope, I don't think so. Now please let me move on, I don't want to be late."

"Well, okay, I'll be seeing you."

With that, Bobby slammed the last book on top of the stack in her arms. Becky almost dropped them again. Then each member of Bobby's gang bumped her against the lockers lining the wall.

As Becky walked on, she thought, Suspicions confirmed—that boy and his rat pack are trouble.

As she hustled down the hallway, she smiled as she thought about the cute, goofy and very shy boy who blushed every time he looked at her.

⊕N THE FIELD

Practice time had arrived. Once Mike arrived at the field
house, he was in no hurry to put on the stinky gear. Mike loved
the game, but even he dreaded practice most of the time. The
early preseason drills on the football field were repetitive,
boring and usually exhausting. He could recite what the
coaches would say, line by line: "You must get ready to play!
You must prepare to win!" Coach Carter in particular had said
this over and over.

Mike thought, We're only preparing to run, crawl, duck-
walk and roll in the grass. Just a few days earlier, he had told
his mother, "I feel more like a chigger than a football player."

Nobody enjoyed this part of the season. But Mike knew
someday it would end and the season would begin. And
something else was beginning: the black players had not been
allowed to participate in practice before school had started—
someone had said that it had to do with "official enrollment"—
but on this first day of school the black students would be
allowed to try out.

After running numerous drills, rolling in the grass,
sprints, and killing the sled dummies, Coach Carter called
everyone together. The first thing he did was line up the
offense based on last year's returning starters. Bobby Willet
was at tailback. Coach Carter, with his authoritative, ex-
Marine officer voice, laid out the ground rules. Coach Carter

had been a star at Florida State and a Marine Corps captain in Korea.

"This is my first offense, for now," he said. "But every position is to be earned and not given.

"All—and I mean all—will be given a chance to earn a spot. But you have to be in class, making your grades, staying out of trouble, and you absolutely must be at practice. If you mess up once, you and I will talk. Mess up twice, and you are gone!"

Everybody was looking straight at Coach Carter as he gazed at his players' eyes, just looking for some poor soul not paying attention.

"Any questions?"

No one was foolish enough to speak out.

"Okay, let's run a few base plays and see what it looks like."

The offense huddled. Coach Carter leaned over his quarterback and said, "Strong I right, thirty-six wham on one."

This was basically student body right, an off-tackle isolation power play. It allowed the tailback to go for daylight. Bobby Willet did so, although this was an execution and timing drill, against air.

The reserve players watched and listened. There was some cheering after the play. Running scrimmage plays was much more fun that blocking and tackling drills. Most of the black players were huddled together, watching, hoping they would get a chance. Arthur Sanderson was in front of this group, waiting for his shot. He had been a great player at Bozeman High, one of the very best.

"Same play, go left," Coach Carter instructed.

They did so, gracefully defeating the atmosphere.

"Huddle up!" Ray cried.

Coach Carter called for substitutes: "Mike Thomas, fullback; Arthur Sanderson, tailback."

Ray winked at Mike as he joined the huddle. Arthur

seemed surprised his own name had been called. Lee patted him on the back as Arthur pulled on his helmet. Lee leaned in close and quietly said, "Show 'em, brother!"

"Boys, you look scared to death," Coach Carter said. "You know this play. Arthur, do you know what to do?"

"Yes, sir, Coach!"

"Okay, run it, then! Quit standin' around like a bunch of old ladies."

Even though this play was against air, "Gone" Sanderson was gone. He accelerated through the handoff, made one cut, then ran forty yards as fast as anyone ever had on this field. It was all Coach Carter could do to not say "Wow!" out loud. Even so, he dropped his whistle.

As the players jogged back to the huddle, Ray looked at Mike, laughed, and exclaimed, "Holy shit!"

That brought Coach Carter firmly back to earth. "Shut up, Cary; he almost ran over your slow butt. Redshirts in here!"

This was Coach Carter's cry to end practice.

It was time for every player's least favorite part of practice, wind sprints. But Gone Sanderson had lit a spark of excitement in his teammates. Though in Bobby Willet, that excitement was full on anger and jealousy.

Coach Carter felt optimistic about this team. He was concerned about the new chemistry, with the addition of the black players. But already he could see that they added an element of enthusiasm and talent to the team. He really wasn't worried about the black players—but he was worried about the attitudes of some of the white players. This team could be really good if it could avoid destroying itself.

As Bobby ran the sprints, he worried about his place on the team. If he were beaten out of his starting position, he would lose face in front of the entire town. That would be humiliating enough. But his father, Big Bob, would dole out the real punishment. Losing the tailback spot to a colored boy was just not acceptable.

Bobby was angry and scared. As always, it seemed he could not please Sheriff Big Bob, his father.

WALKING HOME

After practice, Mike walked his morning route in reverse. As he started through the shortcut in the woods, he felt a cool breeze in his face and heard pine needles rustle. He felt as if something or someone was there, and for a brief moment he thought he heard laughter. He stopped and looked behind him, but saw nothing. For the span of a few heartbeats he felt anxious, but the feeling passed. This had happened before. It felt like someone was close by, and the laughter sounded like that of a child. It was often startling, but he never felt threatened. He couldn't explain it, but he knew there was nothing to fear. Mike began to hum "Proud Mary." Songs always helped.

As he neared home, he saw his mother in the driveway, getting out of the car. "Mike, please get the groceries out of the trunk," she said. "Larry is coming over for supper."

Mike liked Larry, but he had many stories to tell her about school and football. Tonight, he wanted her full attention.

DINNER

Mike, Larry and Ruth Anne did have a good talk at dinner. He told them about Bobby Willet's lunchtime anger and how fast both Gone and Lee were on the football field.

Ruth Anne was very grateful there had been no ugly scenes with the Negro students, or at least nothing violent.

But Mike was speechless when his mother asked if he met the new girl in town, Rebecca Patterson.

Mike recovered and answered, "Well I saw her, I think, but I really didn't talk to her."

"You should introduce yourself and welcome her to town!"

The thought of that just terrified Mike. The embarrassment he'd suffered in science class returned full force. A real knot formed in his belly. The only response he could manage was, "Okay, Mom."

Mike helped his mom clean up the kitchen, grabbed a handful of Oreos and headed upstairs to his room to do some homework, listen to the radio—and dream about Rebecca Patterson (soon to be just Becky). He hoped he wouldn't have a complete heart attack or cerebral stroke the next time he saw her.

TELEPHONES

Many of the town's schoolgirls spent lots of time talking to their friends on the phone, trying to find ways to hide away for secret conversations, away from the listening ears of snooping parents or annoying brothers and sisters.

Rebecca Patterson, or Becky, as she preferred, and Suzy Carter, daughter of Coach Carter and a longtime acquaintance of the three, now four, musketeers, had decided to talk. Suzy and Becky were becoming quick friends. They'd had a chance to talk between classes and at lunch. Becky's family had moved to town only a few days before school began, so the first day of school was her first real chance to meet anyone. Becky and Suzy had hit it off quickly. Becky had told her mother about Suzy, and her mom made sure busy Becky had a chance to talk.

Becky was hiding on the floor of the coat closet by the telephone table, phone in hand and with the door pulled almost completely shut. Suzy was all alone in the basement. It didn't take long for the conversation to turn to Mike. Suzy laughed, retelling the roll call debacle in science class. She said, "Mike is very cute, but very shy."

"Do you think he'll ever talk to me now?"

"Absolutely. Ray and I will work on him. But it might take a while to get him up to complete sentences."

Suzy explained how she and Ray were just good friends. She also explained that she was sort of an unofficial member

31

of the gang of three.

Becky asked, "You mean Ray, Mike and the short boy with the funny grin?"

"Yeah, that's A.J.," Suzy said. "Sometimes I call him the mad professor. But he's harmless. He and Mike have been good friends for a very long time. Mike has always been good about making sure A.J. is included in things. A.J. had a birthday party once a few years ago and Mike made sure everyone came. But I think in some way that A.J. is really good for Mike. And Ray is their guardian bear."

"That seems odd, the cute jock, the gentle giant and the professor. A.J. limps and seems very awkward. Is he okay?"

"Yeah, he's fine," Suzy said. "He's no athlete; he moves like a fish out of water. Mike has always been A.J.'s buddy. They both like science and weird stuff, and they can bore you to death. Even when we were much younger, Mike and A.J. were buddies. They would sit together, fish together and often get in trouble at school together."

Becky was beginning to get a clear picture of the three friends. Maybe she had stumbled onto some good friend candidates. She replied, "That's funny, but kind of sweet."

Suzy giggled and continued, "Mike has a big heart and A.J. is just a mischievous little boy. Ray is nice, but dumb as a rock sometimes."

"We'll have to work on that big heart and build up his confidence."

"We will."

Becky was already thinking of things to say to Mike. "I hope it doesn't take too long."

"Mike is really good at science and math. Maybe we can use that."

"Maybe he'll help little ol' me!" Becky said in a very Scarlett O'Hara-like voice.

Both girls laughed. They now had a plan.

The conversation soon turned to Becky's run-in with

Bobby Willet. Suzy and Becky agreed that Bobby was trouble looking for a chance to happen. Suzy advised Becky, "Stay away from him every chance you get. You pinned the tail on that donkey. He's an ass!"

"I'll stay as far away as I can."

Becky was soon chased off the phone.

"You get off that phone. Somebody important might call!"

BOBBY'S EVENING

Bobby spent the evening with his posse, hanging out, drinking beer. The profane talk was about girls and the new black students. Bobby said very little; he mostly just listened in silence, brooding. All he could think about was the new challenge that Gone Sanderson represented. Bobby was no longer the best tailback. How would he face his father, Big Bob Willet? Bobby had no idea about the long and sad history of the struggles between the Willets and the Sandersons. But, ready or not, the struggle was about to pull him in.

Part 2
The More Things Change, the More
They Stay the Same

THE SANDERSONS

The Ivy Sanderson home was located down a narrow dirt road leading west from Lilac Road. The road turned off Lilac near the church. It had been known as the Low Road for many years because it passed through some swampy ground on the way to the Sanderson home. At one time the road served as the back door to the old Thomas farm. For a period of time after the Civil War, Miss Ellie and Susannah Thomas, Mike's great-great-grandmother, had served as local midwives for the community. Many people had used the Low Road in the dark of night seeking their assistance for a woman, or young girl, in labor. This part of Fair Creek had seen hard and too often heartbreaking times for too many years.

Miss Ellie was Ivy's grandmother. Ivy and her young husband had built a new house just after her husband's return from World War I. The young Sandersons had many children through the 1920s and '30s. But all of them had turned away from the small farm and had either moved to Atlanta, Detroit or Florida. But the youngest son did stay around for a while as a young man.

Arthur Sanderson Sr. was not one to look for trouble, but trouble came looking for him all too often. As a soldier around the time of the Korean conflict, he developed a taste for the nightlife that he found that the nightclubs and bars around military bases. After the war, he returned to Fair Creek to live with his mother and father. Arthur was a lady killer and soon had two sons, Arthur Jr. and Lee. The mothers of these children were waitresses and dancers at Good Times, an all-black club on the north end of Lilac Road. The girls were only sixteen years old, but lived together in a small shanty near Good Times. Arthur Sr. spent most evenings at the club, while Ivy watched over the boys. On Sundays she would pray at the church for something good to work out. It would, but not exactly as she hoped or expected.

At times, Arthur would take work on the docks, where the river barges would stop on the way to the Atlantic. It was hard labor, but it paid cash. In 1957, Arthur's father collapsed while picking peaches, and he died only two days later. This put more pressure on Arthur to provide, and cut into his party time. So, during the days he worked longer hours on the docks and in the early mornings he helped his mother farm.

Soon there was a new and forbidden temptation at the docks: the secretary and office manager was the young and pretty daughter of the dock owner and shop boss. This girl and Arthur began a secret, lusty affair behind the cotton bales in the warehouse. In a few months, just after Thanksgiving, she discovered she was pregnant. Out of fear, she told her father and a young deputy, Big Bob Willet, that Arthur Sanderson had raped her. Her father feared that this was not the whole story, but he said nothing.

Just a few days later, Deputy Bob Willet, Sheriff Foss and others lay in wait in the wee hours of the morning along the Low Road—all dressed in their white Knights of the Klan apparel. There had been a Christmas party at Good Times that night. As a drunken, stumbling Arthur approached them, they lit their torches. Too shocked and drunk to run, Arthur was clubbed down by Big Bob. He was tied and placed on the tailgate of a pickup truck; noose fitted, tree selected.

Deputy Willet's voice boomed a dark sentence of death: "Arthur Sanderson, you are guilty of fornication and the rape of a white woman, and you will pay for this sin in the eyes of God and the decent white people of this community!"

Deputy Willet signaled the driver of the pickup truck, and it lurched forward, dropping Arthur like a rock. The lynching of Arthur Sanderson was complete. Sheriff Foss poured gasoline on the body, still hanging from the tree, and set it on fire with a lit cigarette. The Klan party placed a cross in the road and set it, too, ablaze. The Klansmen then drove off in the pickup truck, laughing and opening cold beers.

One old spirit, wearing the butternut uniform of the Confederate infantry, laughed in the shadows as the body burned. Another cried silently and spoke words no one heard: "Are we not better than this?"

The next morning, a young Reverend Amos Ross saw smoke and investigated. Through tears of rage and sadness, he cut down the body and kneeled and prayed, fighting the anger. "Oh God," he asked, "what have we done to deserve this? Will hearts ever change?"

Another shadow, an old man, watched from deep in the trees. His smile had faded some, but he whispered, "Not today, not today, but a good day, a better day, is coming."

On Christmas Eve, the two mothers of Arthur Jr. and Lee brought the boys to Ivy Sanderson's house with small bags containing the few clothes they owned. The girls left the boys, two and four years old, on her back porch and headed to Atlanta to become prostitutes. Neither would be alive in five years; Ivy never knew their fate.

So, by Christmas of 1957, Ivy Sanderson had two boys to raise and no man to help. On Christmas morning she made a big breakfast for the boys and then picked out their best clothes. Together they walked to the church for the Christmas morning service. Reverend Ross greeted her warmly. He escorted them to the second pew, up front and right up under the pulpit. The boys, especially Lee, were mesmerized by the strong voice of the young preacher and the happy songs of the choir.

After the service, many gathered around Ivy as she talked about how she would now have to raise these boys. Reverend Ross spoke for everyone: "Miss Ivy, we will always be here for you and these young men. God will grant you strength to do this."

"Lord, I sure hope so," she said. "But I didn't even have a Christmas present for them yet. I have them some new clothes, but you know little boys like toys."

While the church folk talked, Reverend Ross quickly ran to his house and placed an old football and a couple of old toy trucks in a burlap bag. He gave the bag to Ivy and told her, "When you get home, give this to the boys."

"God bless you, Reverend Ross," she said.

That was a good Christmas Day. And before it was over, several people brought cookies, candy and other treats.

Ivy always did her best and in the end would be just fine. But good spirits sometimes gave a little help. It wasn't long before Ivy was known to all as "Momma," or "Sweet Momma."

Years later, the boys would learn how Sheriff Willet had murdered their father. They knew all they needed to know about this man.

FISHING

On the Saturday after his first week in an integrated school system, Lee wanted to get a line in the water. But first he had to help Momma Sanderson cut kindling, hang the laundry, change sheets and mop the kitchen.

"Can I go?" Lee pleaded.

"Okay, but be home by noon. Reverend Ross is coming by for dinner."

"Will Mandy come?"

Mandy was Reverend Ross's daughter, a longtime friend of Lee's. They had been since that Christmas of 1957.

Momma suppressed a laugh. "Don't know. Maybe."

Lee grabbed his gear and headed to Fair Creek. His route was very secluded, through the woods and over ground that had been the Thomas farm long ago. As he approached the creek, ready to work his favorite holes, he noticed a tall, smiling old man who was also fishing. Lee had seen the old man at the creek before, but he didn't know him. The old man just seemed to show up. He also seemed to know everyone.

"Hello, young man," he said to Lee. "I been getting a few bites."

Lee tied on a doll fly, and the old man laughed.

"I don't have any idea why fish would bite that ugly thing! If I' ze a fish, I wouldn't take a sniff of it."

Lee felt like the old man was making fun of him, but the

old man's smile dispelled any anger. "Well, sometimes it'll work."

"Maybe for a blind fish. But you need a grasshoppa!"

Lee retied on a short shank hook as the old man handed over a modest-size grasshopper. When he cast the twitching grasshopper in the creek by a rock he got an immediate hit and pulled in a good largemouth bass.

"I never thought to try that!" Lee said.

"Well, don't be too dumb to try something new!"

Lee spent the next few hours pulling good fish out of every little hole. He wanted to never leave the creek, but he also didn't want to make Momma mad.

"Well, I gotta get home," he said. "But I'll be back."

"Uh-huh," said the old man. "You don't want to make Ivy mad!"

How does he know that? Lee wondered. He turmed and started to ask, but the old man was gone.

"That's just weird," Lee said aloud, and he headed home. He thought he heard laughter following along behind, but when he looked, he didn't see anything.

MOM AND MOMMA—
LUNCHES

As Lee walked into the house, the smells were amazing and overwhelming. He heard Reverend Ross and Momma laughing about their children. Lee entered the dining room and Reverend Ross jumped up and shook Lee's hand. "How are you, young brother?"

"Fine, I guess. Hungry for sure!"

"Well that's a good sign. Sister Momma has prepared us a feast."

This modest feast included fried chicken, gravy and mashed potatoes, green beans and corn muffins just oozing with butter. Both lemonade and sweet tea were in abundance. Everybody was too busy eating to talk about anything much until after the cherry cobbler was served with coffee.

"Lee, Momma and I were talking," Reverend Ross said. "We want you to know that we want you to do well in school. It'll be hard because many people do not want you to succeed. But you cannot go looking for trouble. There is talk about a certain boy who smarted off to a teacher in school this week."

"Yes, sir... but he asked for it!"

"Maybe so, but you cannot react the way you did. If you have questions or if you need help, I want you to promise to go to Mr. Penner."

Lee ran the science class scene through his head again.

Sweet Momma, Coach Carter and others had told him to be careful. But he really didn't feel like it had been his fault. He was minding his own business and doing the schoolwork. Mr. Foss had tried to embarrass him, in front of the whole class, no less. He thought, Now Sweet Momma has brought Reverend Ross down on my butt.

Reverend Ross and Momma were talking about the next day's sermon while Lee sat quietly. Reverend Ross turned to Lee again and asked, "How well do you know Mike Thomas?"

"We've fished together, he's on the football team, and we have some classes together. No big deal."

"Well, be careful. Protect yourself! It could be a big deal. The Thomases are fine people, but others may resent your friendship. Just be careful."

Lee didn't understand that these situations could turn violent, quickly. He didn't know the risks. Lee was aware of much of his family's history, but he didn't know as much as Momma and Reverend Ross did. They remembered Lee's father all too well.

Lee asked to be excused, already thinking about how to catch grasshoppers. As he headed for the door, Reverend Ross called out, "Mandy hopes to see you in church tomorrow!"

That would just maybe be enough to get Lee in the pew the next morning.

That same Saturday morning, Mike had been doing chores around the house while his mother worked. She came home at noon and the two sat in the small kitchen over a simple lunch, oven-baked chicken pies. Mike was very proud of his culinary skills, limited as they were. If the goal was scrambled eggs or peanut butter sandwiches, or maybe baking frozen pies, he was a champion. Ruth Anne bragged about Mike. She really did appreciate his willingness to help out around the house.

"Mike, I had an interesting visit with a patient at the clinic this morning," she said.

"Oh yeah? Who?"

"Coach Carter's wife, Darlene, and her daughter, Suzy, were in. We had a good talk!"

"Hopefully not about me!"

"Well... you were part of it."

"Oh, dear Lord, Mom."

"Well, Suzy said her dad was proud that you helped make some of the black boys feel welcome."

"Sure, but don't call them boys!"

"That's silly—you are boys."

Mike shook his head. There was no way he could really explain this to his mother. Mike learned about it in the locker room, and there was no way Ruth Anne was going to be in the football locker room. So he explained, "Yes, but that word is disrespectful. Maybe Lee can explain it to me so that I understand, but I know the black players don't like to be called "boy".

"Well, I'll tell you again: be careful, but be respectful."

"Could Lee come by here someday?"

After some silence, his mother answered with a very soft smile. "Maybe, we'll see. I have no problem. He seems to be a very nice boy. But it would be best if I and maybe Larry were here when he visits."

Mike wasn't sure if he needed to respond. It seemed odd to him that he could've brought Bobby Willet and his hoodlum gang by and nobody would say anything, but if Lee, a person everyone liked and trusted, came by, it would be a big deal indeed.

Thinking of Lee made Mike think of the creek. Changing the subject, he asked if he could go fishing.

"Sure, if your chores are done."

Mike began taking the dishes to the sink. This made his mother smile.

"Oh, Mike, one more thing," she said. "Suzy said the

blonde girl that you like's name is Rebecca Patterson. She's the daughter of the new elementary school principal. They'll be in church tomorrow morning."

Mike immediately tuned back in.

"Suzy says Rebecca is very nice, and that she really wants to meet you." Ruth Anne couldn't resist saying what came next: "Rebecca thought you were really cute when you were blushing!"

"Oh, for heaven's sake, Mother."

Ruth Anne was only "Mother" when Mike was annoyed or in very deep trouble.

"I just thought you would want to know!"

Mike's face registered annoyance, but his heart was singing the hallelujah chorus.

"Mike, Larry and I may go shopping in Macon this afternoon and we'll probably have dinner there. So, can you take care of yourself, and not stay out too late?"

"No problem, Mom." Mike's mind turned back to important matters: "Mom can I have a couple bucks to buy fishhooks?"

Bait shop

Often on the way to Fair Creek Mike would get supplies and a snack at Froggy's, the small bait-and-tackle shop on Lilac Road. Today he wanted to see if Froggy had any new doll flies or poppin' bugs. As Mike approached the counter to pay for his treasures, Froggy smiled. Froggy had run this little bait-and-tackle shop for years. Mike had seen many people pass through the shop, but not a single one had been black. Lee would sometimes give money to Mike to buy things, and Mike would always share with Lee.

"Mike, son, you look more like your daddy every day!" Froggy said.

"You've been talking to my mom."

"No, not lately, but tell Ms. Ruth Anne hello for me."

Froggy was a sponsor of the high school teams and loved keeping up with them. "How's the football coming along?"

"Okay, I think. I hope we can win some games!"

"Me, too!"

"The new players really will help. Gone Sanderson is amazing, so incredibly fast. Just like a bat out of hell!"

"Coach Carter should not allow the colored boys to play," Froggy said. "It will destroy the game."

Froggy's response shocked Mike. Mike had always liked Froggy and knew that Froggy was a longtime family friend. Froggy was always willing to help repair a fishing rod or reel, and he was a great source of local fishing knowledge. He was almost an uncle to Mike. Mike didn't understand why Froggy suddenly seemed so angry. Mike's response was pure innocence. "It will not destroy the offense," he said. "We can be amazing!"

"You just don't understand, do you, son?"

"I guess not."

Mike felt like he had done something wrong, but didn't know exactly what it was. Whatever was sitting in Froggy's heart and soul wasn't present in Mike's. He headed towards the creek with a half dozen new doll flies. Fishing always made things better.

Black people were not welcome at Froggy's—the sign on the front door said so. But there were things Mike didn't know about Froggy, including the fact that Froggy was a distinguished Knight of the Klan, and had driven the pickup truck the night Deputy Willet and Sheriff Foss killed Arthur Sanderson.

Froggy just could not tolerate the idea of black boys wearing Hawkinsville Hawks uniforms.

The spirits were busy.

FISHING AGAIN—
SOMETHING BETTER

As Mike approached Lee along the pool where so many of their ancestors had fished, he could see the smile on Lee's face.

"Mike, this is unbelievable!"

"What is?"

"I caught some green grasshoppers and I'm catchin' fish like crazy. Watch!"

Mike watched: as soon as the grasshopper hit the water and twitched twice, a bigmouth bass sucked it in. Lee showed Mike a stringer with several fish.

In just a minute Mike had his own 'hopper in the water, and quickly a fish on the bank. This continued until it was almost too dark to see. The boys packed up and headed out. As they got near the point where they often split, Lee said, "Come on over to my house and Momma will fix us a feast."

Mike agreed immediately, and then had a funny thought: I bet Froggy would just love this!

Sweet Momma, Jesus and Cornbread

The first thing Mike and Lee did was clean fish in a big galvanized washtub with a garden hose. Momma came out with a flashlight to inspect. She leaned on the clothesline pole and watched the boys, shining the light on them and the washtub.

"Lee, what have you drug home? It don't look like a puppy!"

"It's just Mike Thomas," Lee said. "And he looks awful hungry and skinny. If we don't feed him he's going to waste away to nothin'!" Lee laughed through every word.

"Can you stay for supper, Mike?" Momma asked.

"Yes, ma'am!"

"Well, I guess we'll feed him. Boy, do you like fried fish, hush puppies, onion rings, cornbread, green beans and roasted 'taters? I got some leftover cherry cobbler too."

"Yes, ma'am. That would be great!" Then Mike remembered his manners and quickly added, "Thank you very much!"

"Ain't fed you yet; wait until we set down and say grace. We thank God first, then you can thank me. Besides that, you caught some of these fish, didn't you?"

Mike was very hungry and asked if he could help Momma in the kitchen.

Momma laughed and said, "I doubt it. But get that mud and fish guts off of you before you come in my house. And both of you wash your faces and your hands."

Before too long, both boys sat down to an incredible feast, ready to dig in. But Momma called from the kitchen, "Don't touch nothin' yet. I'm bringing the cornbread."

Mike was almost slobbering, and his belly growled. Momma brought in an iron skillet with cornbread cakes. Mike didn't know where to start. It was fabulous. The cornbread was the best he'd ever had.

After a bit, Gone came in and joined the banquet. As Gone sat down, Momma cried out, "Oh my Lord, I forgot something."

Mike could not imagine what could be missing.

"We forgot to say grace!"

Gone laughed and said with a chuckle, "Thank you, Lord! Now, gimme some cornbread before these pigs eat it all."

Momma reached across the table, pinched Gone's ear like he was a little boy and said, "Hang on, boy—we going to say grace proper!" Momma began, "Lord, thank you for all you give us. We are your unworthy children and we thank you for your blessings. Lord, keep these sweet boys safe. Forgive us of our transgressions and keep us in your love. Amen."

Gone echoed, "Amen. Mike, you had any transgressions today?"

Mike wasn't completely sure what a transgression was, but it sounded bad. He said, "Well, I did let one good bass get off the hook."

"I'm not sure the Lord will forgive that," Gone said. "I heard he likes fishin'."

Momma just shook her head. "Gone, the Lord will punish you for your impertinence!"

"Well, that sounds worse than a transgression. Anyway, I sure am glad you are feeding this skinny boy. He's gonna be blocking for me and he needs some meat on his bones so he can knock somebody down. He's so skinny, sometimes I think he's just gonna bounce off."

Mike had finished off one big helping of cobbler, but in response to Gone's comments he asked Momma, "I guess it's okay then if I have another helping of cobbler?"

"Mercy sakes, sure, boy!"

As supper closed out, there wasn't much left but smiles and big bellies. Mike helped carry the dishes to the sink and thanked Momma at least four times. As he left the Sanderson home, Momma walked him to the front porch, where she gave him a hug and surprised him with her farewell statement: "Mike, you are always welcome here. Lee and Arthur Jr. like you very much. You represent a new start—and you will learn that in time. Please watch my boys. Tell your mother hello for me. I knowd' that she'd raise you right. Bless you, boy."

Mike watched Momma as she sat down in her rocker on the porch. She had huge tears on her cheeks. Mike was touched, although he didn't entirely understand what she'd meant. Mike, like all the young people of the community, was aware of the difficulties created by the many racial tensions. He was certainly aware that desegregation of the schools was historical and represented something new for the local people. But he hadn't lived through the old days like Sweet Momma had. Still, he sensed the peace in her heart. He reached back and patted her hand, again said, "Thank you!" and turned to leave.

Momma laughed and called out, "Oh, I almost forgot. That sweet blonde-haired girl likes you!"

Just maybe Mike would work up enough courage to talk to Rebecca at church tomorrow. Maybe. How in the world did Momma know that Rebecca liked him? How did Momma even know who she was? Then again, Momma didn't seem to miss much.

Sunday—
TWO CHURCHES

- **Lilac Road Baptist Tabernacle**

The next morning there were two separate but similar events that happened in the Fair Creek-Hawkinsville community, both taking place in the centers of the local culture. In the South, churches molded and gradually changed the culture, hindered only by human weaknesses. But on this day, both churches hosted simple "boy tries to meet girl" events.

Lee Sanderson chose to go to church with his grandmother, Momma Sanderson, but he really wasn't looking for a dose of religion. No, he was looking for Mandy. Momma knew this, but she thought it wouldn't hurt for Lee to get a dose of religion anyway. Momma usually sat in the middle of the second pew, right up front, so she wouldn't miss a word from Reverend Ross. And listen she did. At Sunday dinner she would usually recite the whole sermon, though she didn't spit as much as Reverend Ross.

Lee didn't think it necessary to sit in the second pew. You could probably hear every word all the way up Lilac Road, or even beyond. Reverend Ross was not shy about preaching the gospel and the choir was not shy about singing. But Lee didn't mind sitting up front today. Mandy Ross and her mother, Angelica, were in the choir chamber. Lee and Mandy continually exchanged glances, especially during the songs, when the congregation's attention was drawn to the singing.

The singing in the Lilac Road Baptist Tabernacle and Holy House of Prayer and Praise was absolutely amazing. Not many people knew the whole name of the church, which wouldn't fit on one sign and so became Lilac Road Baptist Tabernacle. The rhythm, harmony and simple joy expressed in the songs were truly soulful. Every Sunday offered one of the best concerts around. And, although no one called it dancing, there was much movement. Even Lee enjoyed songs like "I'm a Soldier in the Army of the Lord" and "I'm Going Home." He also enjoyed watching Mandy sing. Every person in the Lilac Road Baptist Tabernacle brought their best on Sunday—their best clothes, voices, smiles and open hearts.

After about ninety minutes, the service drew to a close. Many of the congregation shook Lee's hand and patted him on the back.

"Lee, it is so good seeing you."

"Boy, you sing so fine."

"Please keep coming!"

He heard this over and over as people pressed in on him. He was so busy greeting all of his neighbors and cousins that he didn't notice Mandy in her dark maroon choir robe come up from behind.

After she called his name for the third time, he turned. The devil or a cat or just dumb excitement seized his tongue. He just meekly nodded and managed to squeak out a hello.

Even Angelica thought it funny, and she and Momma smiled real big.

Mandy was also smiling as she said, "Lee, can you come over for lunch? We would be pleased to have you visit."

Angelica, standing just behind Mandy, said, "Momma, you can come to!"

Lee said, "Sure, if it's okay with Momma."

Momma laughed and said, "Of course boy! Don't be stupid. You go on over to the Rosses'!"

Angelica put her arm on Momma's shoulder and urged her to come too.

"No," Momma said, "I got me a roast in the oven and some yeast rolls risin'. Lee, you just get home in time to get your lessons for tomorrow!"

No one suspected what was really keeping Sweet Momma from coming along—her vision was beginning to fail and she felt anxious in unfamiliar places.

Lee had one of the best afternoons of his life at the Rosses'. He finally relaxed a bit and did an okay job when Reverend Ross asked him to say grace. As Reverend Ross made this request, Lee looked down the table at Reverend Ross, seated at the head; above him on the wall was a large painting of a black Jesus. This image intimidated Lee and he thought about running out the door. But, just as Momma had taught him, he said a very good, and short, prayer: "Heavenly Father, thank you for all you have provided. We are grateful for this fine dinner. Please continue to bless this family. Help us be good servants and take care of those around us. Forgive us of our sins, and... oh, and bless Momma and keep her strong. In Jesus's name, amen."

When he finished, Reverend Ross delivered a thundering "Amen!"

Mandy smiled at him in a very warm way that said, Well done—Daddy liked it!

Lee would remember that smile for a long time. None of the Rosses knew that as Lee began the prayer, he had silently asked the Lord to help him not to mess up. And he had not messed up. That evening, when he was answering Momma's 103 questions, Momma was beaming proud. Lee didn't know that Angelica Ross had called Momma on the party line and delivered a full report. How mothers do plot!

- **Main Street Methodist Church**

The worship service at the Main Street Methodist Church

was a very different experience. The difference had nothing to do with neither religious zeal nor depth of devotion: the white Protestant churches just wanted to be sure that no one got too excited. There were and still are exceptions to this, but someone not familiar with the variations among expressions of faith would question whether the Lilac Road Baptist Tabernacle and Main Street Methodist Church were of the same Christian religion.

Mike and Ruth Anne Thomas were of course dressed in their Sunday best. Mike hated ties, but he managed it for a few hours on Sundays. As he sat through the dignified and very reverent service, he noticed Coach Carter, a few seats over, looking just as uncomfortable as Mike felt. That is, until Coach fell asleep. To keep from laughing, Mike looked back towards his mother. Mike was always proud to sit with his mother because she was always the prettiest lady in the church. Nevertheless, Mike played the game of "hating to go to church" very well. Sitting behind Coach Carter, whose head now dangled backwards at an odd angle—and Mike was pretty sure he could hear snoring—sat Suzy Carter and Rebecca Patterson. But there was no way Mike could turn to look at them without being noticed.

Towards the very end of the service, as the organ began to play the prelude to "God of Our Fathers," Mike excused himself to the rear to get a drink of water. As he entered the aisle, Mike snuck a peek at the girls. As he looked, Rebecca's eyes were already on him and Mike damn near fainted and almost stopped in his tracks. Rebecca was smiling, and Mike managed a quick one in return. As the service ended, he stood in the back and waited, hoping for a chance to say hello, or something smart. Soon the congregation began to file out.

"Mike, how is school?"

"Mike, is the team ready for Macon High?"

"Boy you get taller every day!"

The friendly greetings seemed to just go on and on. Even

Coach Carter shook his hand and said, "Good to see you here, Mike. Be ready tomorrow—I'm going to give you a big chance."

Mike fought off a brief surge of fear and excitement, then spotted Suzy and Rebecca coming out of the sanctuary, both smiling and laughing. Mike forgot about football and returned to being terrified of the girls. After the girls greeted the minister, Mike stepped up to them. "Hi!" he said. This took almost as much bravery as storming the beaches at Normandy.

That was it. That was all that came out. The "Good morning, how are you?" speech he had practiced and practiced was forgotten. Suzy shook her head and smiled. She had known Mike since before they were even in school, but she had never seen him so moonstruck.

"Mike, have you met Becky, formally?" she asked.

Mike stammered a no, then said, "I've seen her in school, but we haven't really had a chance to talk."

Because you're an idiot, Suzy thought. She said, "Well, Mike, this is Becky Patterson!"

Smiling, Becky quickly spoke first: "Hello, Mike. It is nice to meet you!"

All Mike heard was the smile. In fact, Suzy would have to remind him the next day that he agreed to study with Becky.

"Hello... Becky..." he mumbled. "Welcome to Hawkinsville. Do you like the school?" Dumb, dumb, dumb and stupid, Mike thought.

No matter—the stone was rolling downhill. Mike would eventually recover, and they did briefly discuss school and geometry. Becky reinforced the suggestion that they study together sometime. As their parents approached and everyone was introduced, Mike was still foggy and deep in the stupid zone.

When Mike and his mother got in the car to leave, she asked, "I saw you talking to Rebecca. Isn't she very sweet?"

Mike nodded and answered, "Yep... I have a couple classes

with her.

"That's nice. Mike, I noticed you were very nice and respectful to the people that greeted you. I'm proud of you!"

This generated a huge blush, and Mike felt embarrassed. He was almost always a good boy, but his mother still liked to say this stuff. Mike had a funny thought: Maybe I should be a bad boy, just once. Next Sunday I'll tell Mrs. Johnson that her blue dress is not as ugly as the green one. Wouldn't that be different?

But Ruth Anne Thomas's Mike would never do such a thing. As time passed, Mike would learn to express his feelings to his mother, but this ability came slowly. He didn't know it at the time, but Becky would help.

Mike did respond enthusiastically to his mother's next suggestion: "Let's go out for lunch at the Town Diner!"

Mike replied as if he were attacking a linebacker: "That is a good idea!"

White Fields—
AN APPRECIATION OF TALENT

Sunday always becomes Monday: it's every schoolboy's dread. But Mike had a strong motivation to get to geometry class. He walked to school at a brisk pace, again singing about having sunshine on a cloudy day.

Even his mother noticed the well-combed hair and eagerness to get to school. It reminded her of Mike's father, which made her sad. Ruth Anne had been widowed when Mike was very young. Her husband, a respected and well-liked state police officer, had been killed on duty the same Christmas Eve that Gone and Lee were delivered to Sweet Momma.

Becky was already in class when Mike arrived. Big Ray was talking to her and Mike thought, This can't be good. What is that big clown saying to her?

What he said next, with a big grin, was, "Have you two started speaking yet, or are you just going to blush and smile forever?"

Both Becky and Mike smiled... and blushed. Ray laughed and said, "Mike, my boy, you are hopeless!"

Mike replied very quickly, "Ray, my boy, you are worthless!"

Miss Majors called the class to order. Mike and Becky did speak a little, then said goodbye in the hall as they blended into the mass of students going to their next class. Mike went only about two steps before someone thumped him on the arm with a fist, hard enough to hurt a little.

Mike spun around, assuming it was Ray, but instead he saw Suzy, wearing a very frustrated, angry look. "Remember, idiot friend," she said, "you promised to help her study geometry, even though she's probably ten times smarter than you."

Her reminder made him happy, though he sure wasn't going to admit it.

The rest of the day was uneventful. After school, the ballplayers migrated to the locker room and field.

It wasn't long into practice that the coaches organized a full-speed scrimmage. Mike and Lee started out on second defense, but they easily stopped the first-string offense. It was clear that several of the black players had quickness and ability. Lee took down Bobby Willet hard on a clean open-field tackle.

Coach Carter screamed at Bobby, "The idea is to not get tackled! That was a piss-poor effort. Arthur Sanderson, get in there at tailback!"

Bobby jogged back towards the offensive huddle. He ripped off his helmet, glared at Gone and took a step towards him, but an assistant coach stepped between them and said to Bobby, "Back off, Willet—you'll get your chance!"

Arthur stepped into the huddle. Ray looked at him and said, "Smoke 'em, Gone!"

Gone winked. Coach Carter called the play. Gone was handed the ball and took off. Mike had a chance to tackle him, but he had never seen such speed, and such an incredible limp-leg move. Mike caught nothing but air and a face full of dirt. There was absolutely no doubt that Gone Sanderson was going to be the number-one tailback.

Coach Carter smiled as he yelled at Mike, "Great tackle, Thomas, but you missed the ball carrier!"

Throughout practice, Gone continued to impress. At one

point, Coach Carter put Mike in at fullback. It was apparent to Coach Carter that Mike was quick enough to match Gone as a lead blocker, and Mike proved him right.

After practice, Gone walked by Mike and quietly said to him, "Good job, son! We gonna have to keep feeding you good cornbread!"

This made Mike feel very good, but he was also happy that Lee was getting playing time with the number-one offense. Lee was just as fast as Gone.

In the locker room, Ray came up to Mike and said, "Don't forget to call Becky, your precious little sweetheart!"

Ray said this loud enough so that everyone, including the coaches, heard. This brought out a loud chorus of cheers, jeers and laughter. Ray winked at him. Mike was completely humiliated. There would be payback.

One person was not cheering nor smiling. Bobby Willet was angry—at Coach Carter, Gone, Mike and the entire team. Ray didn't help things when he asked Bobby if he might consider playing on the line. This was beneath the former starting tailback.

Angry spirits were not far away.

Hate and anger at Bert's Oil

At the same time football practice was winding down, Sheriff Robert Willet—Big Bob, Bobby's father—was holding court at Bert's Oil. Bert's Oil was a small gasoline station just a few blocks from the high school, towards downtown. It was just a few blocks from the Pulaski County Courthouse and the sheriff's office. Bob Willet had been sheriff for several years now. The Willets, as so-called keepers of the peace, had long been involved with much of the local dirt as so-called keepers of the peace. Very few people liked Big Bob, but he did generally enforce the law.

It was also widely known that Big Bob could make it hard on a black man. He was disliked and feared by many, for good reason. Bert Andrews Jr. owned the small gas station that his father had started. Besides gas, it sold a few bottles of pop, candy and chips, and every once in a great while they might fix a flat or change the oil in someone's car.

Bert Andrews III was a senior on the football team, but he seldom played. He was slow and clumsy, and when he ran he looked like a hog dancing on ice. But he was a member of Bobby Willet's gang. Sam Elkins and Ray Allen, both part-time deputies and full-time idiots in the eye of the sheriff. Even Big Bob considered them Barney Fifes. He rarely let them carry a gun or take on a dangerous task. Both Sam and Ray worshiped Big Bob and never questioned him, although that was partly because it had been a while since either one of them had thought up a question other than "What's for supper?"

Ray's younger brother, Shorty Allen, often worked for Bert Andrews at the gas station. Paul Foss, the science teacher, was sometimes part of the gang, and he was present on this Monday afternoon, huddled with the others in the office of the gas station. The AC Spark Plug clock said it was 5:00 p.m. Like in most Southern small towns, the status of the local football team was a frequent topic of conversation. A mixture of parents, longtime fans and ex-players made up an unofficial football clan, a pigskin mafia. Big Bob and his posse were only members, but in their minds, they were the bosses.

Bert had just filled up a big Chrysler when an old pickup truck pulled in, Froggy Allen behind the wheel. Froggy saw the posse in the back, grabbed a cold Coke out of the cooler and pulled up a chair.

The talk was of Gone Sanderson's talent and performance on the practice field, and Froggy leaped right into the conversation: "I'm afraid the ol' world is just bustin' apart at the seams."

All of the posse just sat there shaking their empty heads. They looked to Big Bob to see what he would say.

"I was hopin' Coach Carter would have the sense to keep the colored boys on the sidelines," he said, "but I'm not sure what that old fool's gonna do. I'm not worried, though—the Sanderson kid will mess up and I'll get his ass. All in good time."

Paul Foss added, "All them colored boys need to learn some respect and learn their place."

This was met with typical silly responses such as "I heard that" and "You can say that again" and "Oh, yeah!"

After a moment of what passed for silent contemplation, Big Bob said, "I'm gonna start turning up the heat and get this all straightened out, you just mark my word."

None of the gang doubted Big Bob, but Big Bob was

65

worried, very worried. That sorry son of his was letting a black boy beat him out of a starting spot. Maybe Coach Carter needed a visit.

Bert's Oil had additional visitors late that night, after closing time. Bobby Willet and Bert Andrews III occasionally snuck in the gas station after hours using a stolen key. After a few Cokes and snacks, they would take any money in the elder Bert's not-so-secret hiding place. Bert suspected his son but was afraid to ask him about it. Like everyone else, he was afraid of the Willet gang.

Bobby and Bert took their stolen goodies and shared a big laugh in Bobby's red Charger. Spirits watched the boys... just waiting for the right time. Little trouble grows into big trouble with a little help from an angry spirit.

Big Bob delivers a message

That same evening, after practice, and after the meeting of the football mafia, Mike was walking home via the usual route. As he reached Lilac Road, he saw the sheriff driving slowly down the street towards him. Most of the black people were wary, if not outright scared, of the sheriff; Mike just didn't like him. Big Bob pulled up alongside Mike, the big blue Ford Galaxy cutting him off from walking on. Mike saw that Ray Allen was riding shotgun and grinning like a young possum in a persimmon tree.

"Mike, son," Big Bob said. "How are you doing?"

"Okay, Sheriff Willet. Just going home."

"I hear you're doing good in practice, but I gotta ask you something."

"Yes, sir?"

"Mike, why are you working so hard to help those Sanderson boys? Bobby sure could use your help."

"I block for Bobby, too."

"That's not what I'm saying, son. I'm telling you to be careful who you pick as friends."

Mike felt uncomfortable and didn't reply.

Sheriff Willet let Mike sit in silence for a moment, with Mike unsure about where this was going. He was trying to think of a response when the sheriff spat pieces of cigar towards Mike and said, pointing his finger right at Mike, "You better listen to good advice, boy, or you just might get yourself in very hot water. People might just get hurt." He paused, not taking his eyes off Mike. Then he put the Galaxy back in gear, and said, "Tell your mom hello."

Mike was beginning to shake a little as he realized that this man could really hurt people. The sheriff pulled away, his tires slinging gravel at Mike. It slowly sunk in that he, Lee and Gone had just been threatened.

A few seconds later, he felt a cool breeze in his face, and the honeysuckle in the ditch rustled softly for no obvious reason. Though he saw or heard nothing else, Mike again felt like someone was there.

It made him feel less alone.

REVEREND AMOS ROSS GIVES ADVICE

From a distance, without being seen, Reverend Ross watched the conversation between Mike and the sheriff. Although he couldn't hear it, he sensed the gist. After the sheriff drove off, Amos stepped out into the parking lot and called to Mike. "Mike, are you okay? I can give you a ride home."

"No, sir, thank you anyway. I'm okay. I just don't like that man!"

"I don't believe even his own momma likes him very much!"

Both Amos and Mike smiled and then shared a good laugh.

"Mike," Reverend Amos continued. "You be careful. That man is dumb as a loaf of bread but he's mean as a cold copperhead snake. He can hurt you and he ain't afraid to do it."

"Yes, sir, I believe you."

"You get on home. Straight home! I know your mother; she is one of God's saints. So you get home to her."

Surprising himself, Mike said, "I would like to visit your church sometime."

Reverend Ross smiled and responded, "Now that would be different, but you would always be welcome. I know you like to sing."

"Yes, I do," Mike answered.

"We'll see," the reverend said. "We'll see."

Mike waved and headed on home. He needed to get home if he was going to call Becky by 7:00 p.m., her phone curfew on school nights.

Neither Amos nor Mike saw the faint shadow of smilin' Zeke in the trees. The old-man spirit had been watching for a long time. He smiled and whispered to the breeze, "We will see, sho' 'nuff, Reverend, yes indeed, we will see!"

He turned to his companions and said, "Let's go, young'uns, enough for today. More work tomorrow."

PART 3
THE NEXT SCHOOL DAY—CHANGES
CONTINUE AS SPIRITS ENGAGE

Rocks from the Charger

As it usually happens in a small town, word had spread among the Willet gang about Big Bob's encounter with Mike along Lilac Road. As the story had spread, it had grown to include a part where Mike was handcuffed and another part where, as the sheriff drove away, the flying gravel gave Mike a cut on the cheek and a black eye.

None of the imaginary parts were true, but when did the truth ever have anything to do with a good story? The only real hurt to Mike was the embarrassment of knowing he'd let Big Bob scare him. Mike felt it again as he walked to school the next morning, especially as he neared the church. But he just walked on. A few people out that morning noticed that Mike was not humming or singing. Mike had taken notice of the worry on his mother's face over the last few days, and it seemed everyone was telling him to be careful. He was beginning to understand this concern.

Nearing the baseball field fence, he didn't notice the red Dodge Charger coming up from behind. Much like the sheriff's approach the evening before, the car slipped just past Mike and cut him off. Bert Andrews the younger was riding shotgun. He stepped out of the car, laughing loudly. Behind him, Bobby Willet sat in the driver's seat with an angry smirk. Bert's hands were full of something Mike couldn't identify.

"We hear you like rocks in the face!" Bert said.

"Not really," Mike replied, lifting his geometry book to block what he expected to come. Bert unloaded both handfuls of gravel right at Mike at a distance of about six feet. Mike blocked most from his face, but the pebbles stung his hands and arms as he covered his face.

Mike stepped towards Bert, but Bert dove into the car as Bobby put it in reverse. As they drove off, Bert leaned out of the window and threw a beer bottle at Mike. Because Bert was twisted and off balance, the throw didn't have much on it. The bottle landed softly at Mike's feet.

Mike's surprise was now replaced with a need to return fire. He grabbed the bottle by the neck and threw it at the retreating Charger. It was a perfect shot, crushing the Charger's right rear taillight, the sound of smashed glass coinciding with the sound of Mike yelling "Cowards!"

As the Charger burned rubber down the street, Mike felt as if he had chased away the dragon. Then he realized his shirt was wet and smelled like beer. As he had thrown the bottle, some of its old, stale beer had spilled. Mike thought out loud: "No one will believe me about this."

Mike walked on to school but then hung around outside, waiting as long as he could before going into geometry.

He entered class just as the bell rang and quickly moved to his seat. He wasn't there long before some of the guys around him began to snicker. Notes and whispers got around to Becky and Suzy. After class they headed out, noses in the air, without even glancing at Mike. He was crushed.

In the hall, Ray put his arm around Mike and laughed. "Mike, you are the last kid in this school that I thought would be drinking before class in the mornings."

"I still am," he said.

He proceeded to tell the story to Ray and Lee, with gravel cuts on his hands to prove it. Ray slipped out to the parking lot just to see the cracked taillight.

Later, at lunch, Ray sat with Becky and Suzy and told the

story, loud enough for others to hear. His version was indeed a comical one, Mike vs. the red Charger dragon. Mike didn't feel like a knight in shining armor, he just felt like an idiot with a dirty shirt. But at least Becky smiled at him afterwards.

Becky was again thinking that Bobby was nothing but trouble. She feared that this might get ugly. She would be right, very right. But she had no idea how very ugly and violent it would become.

Hard things to hear

When Lee told the Mike vs. the dragon story to Mandy Ross just before English class, Mandy responded with a frown. "Boys are so dumb," she said.

Lee smiled and said, "And girls are smarter?"

Mandy gave a two-fingered point at Lee and said, "You so dumb—wait, this isn't a joke. Do you believe that all these white boys like you? You think Mike or Ray would risk theyselves for you? Playing a game is one thing; they like you because you're good. It's cool to have a black buddy! But sooner or later they'll turn away from you because they won't be willing to pay the price that friendship requires!"

Lee was taken aback by the sudden outburst.

"Mike and Ray seem to be just fine," Mandy continued, "but some of their kind have a history of hurting people, especially black people—even your own family! If Ray or Mike have to make choices, you may just get left out, or even worse, hurt."

Mandy and Lee were aware of much of the past history involving their families. The memories were never very far away. But Mike and Ray and most of their other new white classmates didn't know these stories, and so they didn't comprehend the risk for Mandy and Lee. Not yet.

Lee stood in silence; these thoughts were serious and made him angry - at nothing in particular, just angry.

Lee said, "Mike's been my friend for years."

Mandy raised one eyebrow and asked, with sarcasm, "Friend or fishing buddy?"

"Both!" Lee countered quickly as they entered class.

Mandy came one step closer to Lee and fired off one last shot: "You are going to be the loser in this white-boy fight."

Lee flinched. Lee had thought of Mike only as a friend, and now a teammate. He had never thought of Mike as belonging to a part of the world that still longed for the darkness of segregation and bigotry. This troubled Lee, and also hurt him, as he felt guilty for doubting Mike.

Lee couldn't manage to pay attention to the teacher in his next class. He couldn't get over Mandy's words, and he thought, Man, she can be hard—and her eyes are fierce when she's mad!

Softer Brown Eyes

English class couldn't end soon enough for Lee. He was very troubled by Mandy's anger and he wondered if she was right. He feared she might be right, and that was hard to accept. Lee also knew he didn't do well on the vocabulary quiz, not because he was distracted but because he hadn't studied. The distractions didn't help.

As Lee tried to slip out of class, Mandy caught him from behind and reached out to touch his arm. "Lee."

"Yeah?"

"I'm sorry I said those things. It wasn't my place to say that stuff. But I worry about you."

"It's okay; I feel uneasy sometimes. It seems like something ain't right."

"Can you come by my house after practice? We can talk some more there."

"Okay, that's cool! Anyway, somebody is going to have to teach me to spell. I hate spelling."

"You just gotta try harder."

As they parted, Lee thought, maybe I need to struggle a little on the spelling so that I can get a more help on the homework!

More time with Mandy would be a good thing. But the exposed doubts and worries about his relationship with Mike were lingering, like a case of mild heartburn.

4. The new number-one backfield

The day progressed like any other school day. By now, integration was accepted, if not liked, by most. It was obvious to Coach Carter that the students, teachers and other coaches generally accepted the future before the rest of the community. It amazed Coach Carter that so many people questioned him about who would play on the coming Friday nights. He was asked so many times, "Will the colored boys play?"

His answer was always consistent: "If they earn a spot, they will play!"

It really didn't surprise Coach Carter that people left unsigned notes on his car, usually saying things like "This team should be pure!" This was crazy; most schools and colleges had already passed this stage, even in the South. But Coach Carter was determined that the best players would play. It did bother Coach Carter that people would sometimes drop hints to his wife at places like church or in the grocery store. This made him angry, and he worried for his family and his team.

At today's practice, he was ready to name the starters. He called the team into a huddle and named his starters, with great authority. "Okay, men, listen up," he began. "As I call your name, line up over here. These will be my starters on offense.

"But don't get too big-headed—you'd better keep working hard or I'll set your butt down."

Coach Carter started with the backfield.

"Quarterback: Stevens. Fullback: Mike Thomas."

Mike could hardly believe his own ears.

"Thomas, close your mouth and line up next to Stevens." Then he continued reading the names. "Tailback: Arthur Sanderson. Wing: Lee Sanderson."

When Lee moved to the lineup, he and Mike exchanged

smiles and a high five. Mike saw Bobby Willet out of the corner of his eye, and he could see the rage forming. Sometimes you can tell a big storm is coming.

Other black players were named to the starting eleven, including Sammy "Stretch" Kyle, who was named the starting tight end. The Hawkinsville Hawks were indeed integrated, and all the better for it.

Coach Carter felt good. He believed this to be the best mix of players. But he also knew that many challenges would follow. He just didn't know how soon.

As the starters huddled, Coach Carter watched as three white boys walked off the field. The rest of the players soon were watching this little protest. Marching away in rebellion were Bert Andrews, Jimmy Kletus and Bobby Willet.

Bobby Quits

Bobby Willet, Bert Andrews and Jimmy Kletus ... all members of the little Willet gang... indeed walked off the field. The boys were soon followed by Coach Alan, but not immediately. Coach Alan looked back at Coach Carter and both men knew exactly what needed to be done. Both men nodded their heads in acknowledgment and Coach Alan hurried to catch up with the quitters.

Once the three boys entered the old field house, Coach Alan got in their faces. "If you walk off like this," he shouted, "you are done with football—for good!"

Bobby spoke first, getting right in Coach Alan's face. "I'm not going to ride the bench and watch no colored boy take my spot. That was my position."

Bobby's anger was coming out. He was right in Coach Alan's face and yelling and shaking. Spit was flying and Coach Alan noticed a trace of a tear on Bobby's face.

Bobby was furious. For weeks he could see this moment coming, and now it had arrived. All of the hate he had learned from his father now had a focal point, a real flesh-and-blood target. These stupid coaches were destroying his world because of one colored boy. Bobby was afraid, afraid of how his father would take this news and afraid of what he might do. Bobby had lost his standing among his friends, coaches and his father.

Coach Alan would not back down. "Bobby, you could be a better man and you could play," he said. "You could help this team be better. But you are not man enough to compete honestly. Gone Sanderson is the best tailback I've ever seen. He's stronger, faster and just plain better than you are! He beat you out. He was the best tailback in practice!"

"But he's just a no-account colored boy."

"And you're a big crybaby! Get out of here, now! Drop your gear, get dressed and gone. You have two minutes."

The boys stripped and slammed their equipment at Coach Alan's feet while he watched silently.

As they finished cleaning out their lockers, Bobby growled at Coach Alan and spoke through clenched teeth, "I will make you pay for this. This is not right."

"Yeah!" said Bert, so scared he was shaking.

Coach Alan turned on Bert. Shaking his head, he asked, "Do you have to ask Willet when to take a piss? Andrews, you ought to rethink who your friends are."

Bobby yelled, "You leave my friends alone!"

Coach Alan turned back to Bobby. He said nothing; he just stared him down, then finally said, "Do not speak to me again and get the eternal hell out of here. You disgrace this place."

The three boys finally left. But as they walked away from the field house, Bobby shouted, "I'm gonna tell my daddy about this!"

Bert and Jimmy found this pathetic, like a little baby whimpering. But neither had the strength to say so, not yet.

Bert would come to regret not stepping away from Bobby.

CRUISING AFTER PRACTICE

When practice ended, Mike was so pumped that he showered and dressed faster than ever. In fact, he had even blazed through wind sprints. Coach Carter had told him he should do that every day.

Mike headed out of the locker room and towards home. He couldn't wait to tell his mom that he was a starter, and as a sophomore no less. But as he came out of the locker room, Ray called him over.

"Let me give you a ride home, number-one fullback!"

"Okay, number-one center!"

Ray had gotten a car on his sixteenth birthday, a very nice blue Chevelle Super Sport. Everyone in town assumed his father had bought it for him, but actually Ray had worked at several part-time and summer jobs and had purchased the car from his own hard-earned money. Ray had mowed lawns, hauled hay, loaded cotton bales and even been a babysitter for his young cousin.

"Let's go by the Burger Circle and grab a snack!" he suggested.

Mike smiled. Ray and food—never far apart.

Becky now worked part time at the Circle some afternoons after school. Mike didn't know if she would be there, but there was always hope.

The Burger Circle was a small, locally owned drive-through/drive-up burger shack. It was also the unofficial social spot for the high school kids. The Circle marked one end of the "cruise" circuit. The other end was the big parking lot at the Piggly Wiggly grocery store on the south side of town. There were always cars circling the circle and crowds of kids standing around, usually segregated into groups of boys and groups of girls. Every once in a while the groups would intermingle. Almost all activities of social consequence started or ended at the Circle.

Ray pulled out and headed toward the Piggly Wiggly. After one round on the cruise, Ray and Mike pulled into the Circle, where Norman Greenbaum's "Spirit in the Sky" played on the speakers. Mike tried to not be too obvious in looking for Becky, but he spotted her in her Burger Circle apron, taking a tray of food to a car. The apron was very large, pink with red trim. It bore the image of a Hawkinsville Hawk with a burger in one hand and a milkshake in the other. Becky's hair was pulled into a ponytail, and she wore the same smile that Mike looked for.

Ray pulled into a slot and ordered two Cokes and two fries. Becky had seen Mike, but she was able to hide it a little better because she was very busy. When the order was ready, she delivered it to Ray's car.

"Here you go, guys; I made one substitution."

"And what was that?" Ray asked with a big grin. "How dare you?"

"I know Mike likes Dr Pepper, so I swapped it."

Ray laughed out loud, pounded Mike's shoulder and said, "Aw... wasn't that sweet?"

"Thanks," Mike said, blushing as usual. Once again, his brain disconnected.

"Becky, you better leave so Mike can breathe again!"

"Okay," she said. "But I have a break coming, so I'll come over before you leave."

Ray was simultaneously laughing and stuffing French fries

in his mouth.

"Mike, you are one hopeless, lovesick fool! You have got to get over this blushing."

Mike said nothing—he couldn't think straight yet.

Several friends came by, and Ray told them all that Mike was going to get to start in the first game. Mike was proud, but he mostly tried to think of something to say to Becky, about something besides football. A few minutes later Becky came over and leaned in the car window on the passenger side. She smiled at Mike and said softly, "Can we go over to the picnic table and talk?"

"Sure," Mike said while opening the door.

He would never forget the freckles on her cute little nose, nor her smile. As they walked to the table, Mike did remember to say, "How was band practice?"

"Okay. Boring. The national anthem gets boring to play over and over again."

"You play clarinet, right?"

"How did you know?"

"I saw you at the pep band last week."

"Cool. Are you a musician?"

Mike thought of his singing, but that sure didn't qualify.

"No," he said. "I'm afraid football and being in the band don't mix. Instead I get to be pounded by big ugly tackles. It would be nice to be closer to a pretty musician."

That was the first almost-smart thing Mike had ever said to her. But his brain kept saying, Dumb... just dumb!

But Becky laughed. She seemed to think it was a cute comment—even if also dumb.

"Listen, Mike, Bobby Willet and his band of idiots was by here earlier. He was bragging about how he quit the team. I'm very afraid he could do something really stupid. Please, please be careful."

What Mike didn't know was that Bobby had continued to ask Becky out. Pestered her, more like it. Becky didn't know how much Mike was aware of Bobby's attentions, but she did know that Bobby thought of Mike as just a big momma's boy. Becky had no interest in Bobby; in fact, she loathed him. But Becky feared that Bobby would strike back at Mike.

"I gotta get back to work, but I'm glad you came by. Come back again. Service with a smile!"

Mike finally engaged the cerebral cortex. "I'll be okay," he said. But he was worried for Becky, because any association with Bobby Willet couldn't be good. So he asked, "What about you? How are you getting home?"

"Daddy will come get me. I'll be okay, too!"

"See you tomorrow!"

"Okay," she said. "Oh, and congratulations—number-one fullback!"

"Thanks. How did you know?"

"Coach Carter told me a few days ago, when I was visiting Suzy. But he made me promise not to tell!"

"Okay, see you later," Mike said, then added, with a big grin, "number-one princess!"

Boy, that was a special kind of dumb, he thought, but Becky laughed and smiled. Dumb it was, but she liked it.

Neither Becky nor Mike knew that Ray had saved the day with his offer of a ride. The Willet gang had set an ambush for Mike beyond the baseball field. By the time Mike would have arrived, a couple of six-packs of beer had been consumed. It would have been real trouble.

Becky was right; Bobby would have done something stupid.

LARRY AND MOM COME TO THE RESCUE

After Mike failed to show up along his usual route home, Reverend Ross grew worried and called Mrs. Thomas. Earlier, Lee had been at the Ross home and had told the Rosses the story of the black starters and the white quitters, including Bobby Willet. This was why Reverend Ross kept a special lookout for Mike, and why he didn't wait long before calling Ruth Anne.

Just as Mike was climbing back into Ray's car at the Circle, he spotted a state trooper cruiser pull into the lot, with Larry Wayne at the wheel and Ruth Anne riding shotgun. "We're going to grab something to eat," his mom said, "and then head home. Want to ride with us?"

Mike said goodbye to his friends and teammates. Ray followed him a few steps toward the cruiser and said, "I hope you never take me away in your cruiser, Officer Wayne!"

"One of these days, Ray, one of these days!" Larry replied.

Ruth Anne was relieved to find Mike safe and sound. She and Larry had smelled trouble when Reverend Ross called. They'd been right too.

As the cruiser pulled away, Mike waved to Becky. As she waved back, she thought, It's not every day you're happy the state trooper hauled off your boyfriend—or hope-to-be boyfriend!

Sweet Momma—
No Cornbread Tonight

After practice, Lee headed straight to the Rosses' home. As soon as he entered the house, the smells of dinner cooking, not to mention Mandy's soft brown eyes, convinced him to stay. Before supper, he told the Rosses all about football practice and the new starting lineup. Mrs. Ross called Sweet Momma to let her know Lee was there and safe.

Gone, with his friends, usually would hang out at bars like Good Times, like his father had done. Gone had been going to these clubs since he was fifteen; he looked older and he could take care of himself. Sweet Momma worried about Gone, but she worried more for young Lee.

Once again Lee looked down the table at Reverend Ross and the black Jesus portrait, and once again he delivered a good prayer. While Lee was praying, a red Dodge Charger cruised by the Lilac Road church, looking for trouble. In a mighty act of false bravery, the Willet gang threw empty beer bottles at the church's front door. The breaking glass interrupted supper. Lee and the Rosses watched in stunned silence through the living room window.

After dinner, Lee and Reverend Ross cleaned up the mess. When they finished, Reverend Ross told Lee, "Get on home, Lee. Make sure Sweet Momma is okay! Call us as soon as you get there."

Lee went straight home.

When he arrived, he found Sweet Momma on the porch in her rocker. She had started supper for herself, but she had little appetite these days. Her vision was growing fuzzy and she often had headaches. Tonight she was sitting alone, crying. Lee didn't expect to see her sitting on the porch. He especially didn't expect to see her sitting on the porch and crying.

"Momma, what's wrong?"

"Lee, I'm feeling weakly, and dizzy. Everything is going in circles."

"Let's go inside and I'll get something for you."

They went in the house, Lee leading Momma by the arm. Once inside, she leaned on Lee's shoulder. "Lee, I am afraid. I feel so bad."

Lee helped her into her favorite chair. It was then he noticed she had on two sweaters. Lee called the Rosses and expressed his concern. Reverend Ross hung up and immediately called Ruth Anne.

By this time Larry, Ruth Anne and Mike were home. This was Reverend Ross's second call to the Thomas home that day: both calls were lifesavers. The trio jumped back into the state cruiser, picked up the Rosses and headed to the Sanderson home.

Ruth Anne quickly looked over Sweet Momma, taking her vitals. "Your blood pressure is very high," Ruth Anne said. "We need to get you to the hospital!"

"Oh Lord, can't we go tomorrow?"

"No, ma'am. now!"

Reverend Ross chimed in, "Mike and I will go get my car and we'll come on to the hospital. Everybody else, go with Trooper Wayne to the hospital."

Reverend Ross carried Sweet Momma to the car like a little baby. With tears in his eyes, he prayed, "Dear Lord, take care of this good woman. We need her here with us."

Mrs. Ross said, "Amen, please God, please!"

Trooper Wayne turned on the emergency lights and with Sweet Momma in the middle and Ruth Anne shotgun they tore out, with Mrs. Ross, Lee and Mandy in the back seat. Lee was shaking and crying softly. Mandy gently took his hand and Lee squeezed hers hard.

It would be a little while before Lee had a chance to call the Good Times club and tell Gone that Sweet Momma was now in the hospital.

DISAGREEMENTS AMONG SPIRITS

Before this makeshift rescue squad left the Sanderson home, Ruth Anne instructed Mike to call Dr. Roberts. Dr. Roberts was waiting in the emergency room when they arrived. With a wild flurry of activity, the full force of modern medicine went to work on Sweet Momma in the emergency room. One thing Mike would never forget was the looks of disgust on the faces of some of the white nurses and staff. It made Mike very angry, even though no one else seemed to notice. Black patients had been allowed at the hospital for some time now, but there was still an unspoken reluctance to provide care.

While this great medical struggle raged, there was a greater, and perhaps more important, struggle outside. It was a battle of spirits.

In the park across the street from the hospital, at the sight of an old pecan grove where the Pulaski Volunteers, local soldiers in the Confederate Army, had once trained and had waited to march to war, an old black man stood alone. It was the shadow spirit Zeke, but he was not smiling right now. There were other spirits moving in the trees, all unseen. The sound of the groaning wind drowned out all other sounds of the night.

Zeke spoke strongly, but only the spirits heard: "You cannot take this woman! She is a good woman and I need her here. We have work to do. This is not finished!"

The other spirits seemed to close in on Zeke. There was a soft yellow glow in the trees. The sounds of the groaning wind increased and seemed to become angrier.

"You cannot take this woman, not now!" As the movement picked up in the trees, Zeke pleaded, "Please give us more time, please! You can change your mind, you can change fate, we must win this battle."

For a few moments, the winds continued to howl. It was as if the breeze was having a discussion and making a grand decision. But finally, the wind settled, the glow faded and the sounds of night returned. The spirits had moved away.

Zeke hung his head and said, "Thank you, Lord. Please let us rest soon."

Some old shadow spirits shed real tears.

Across the park, another spirit had watched this event: a young Confederate sergeant in dirty butternut. His eyes glowed red with anger. "Oh no," he said. "We certainly are not finished."

These two old spirits had known one another for many years. They had once been as close as family. But the old soldier had lost touch with hope and all good things. He had completely surrendered to anger. In life he had suffered much, perhaps too much. He existed now only to sow hate and violence.

The doctors determined that Ms. Ivy Sanderson was losing her vision, but that she would live. The next morning, she held Lee's hand and said, "There's something I have to do. I don't know what it is, but the Lord is calling me."

Lee had been there all night; he was tired, but was happy Sweet Momma was okay. "You got to get better so I can take you home," he said. "That's all you gotta do."

Lee thought about Gone, asleep in the lobby, drunk. Lee was disgusted with his brother. He said softly, so that Momma wouldn't hear him, "The Lord is calling me, too," he said. "To kick Gone's ass. If I can catch him."

It wouldn't be long before these spirits would get working again. One spirit would look for resolution and peace; another wished to sow hate and foster anger. Hate and anger had been a vicious cycle for such a long time. There seemed to be no escape from it. Was there any hope? Could there ever be a new beginning? Even those with good hearts have to overcome the temptations offered by very old demons. These old spirits had been fighting these battles for a long time; they were good at it.

PART 4
PLAYERS IN A VERY OLD STRUGGLE

The spirits of Zeke and the Confederate soldier had been around Fair Creek for some time. The struggle was not new to them, and both were very experienced in the ways of mankind. Anger and hatred had a firm hold on the old sergeant, and gentle Zeke hadn't been able to loosen evil's grip. In fact, their time along Fair Creek had begun well over one hundred years earlier, in the time of Mike's great-great-grandfather. It began in Fair Creek and continued through a great war on battlefields far to the north.

1863

Andrew Jefferson Thomas sat in the shade on a very warm July morning in 1863, just outside of Gettysburg, Pennsylvania. It was still early, but the day already promised to be a real scorcher. Like everyone else in Company G of the 8th Regiment of the Confederate States Army, he was tired, hungry and needed a new pair of shoes. These shoes had covered a great deal of ground. They would cover more yet. Andy knew there would be a big fight on this day. He could almost hear what was coming: the pop of the muskets, the screaming, the fear. The anguish, pain and death. Even so, in this early-morning peace and quiet his mind drifted back to Fair Creek.

On an otherwise promising spring day a little over two years earlier, Andy Thomas had heard the cannon. He had joined the Pulaski Volunteers in Hawkinsville early in the spring as secession fever spread through Georgia. Their training camp had been a beautiful pecan grove by the Methodist church in Hawkinsville. The young soldiers had been allowed to return home to attend to spring farming, but with the understanding that the firing of the cannon was the call to muster. So, Andy gathered his kit and said goodbye to Betsy on the morning of her twentieth birthday. He bent over and kissed his young son, Bobby Jeff. Then he turned away from the log home he and his father had built, and followed

Fair Creek in to Hawkinsville.

As Andy sat in the shade two years later at Gettysburg, he could still taste Betsy's tears. The Pulaski Volunteers had formed at the old courthouse square that day in early May to begin their journey into history and fate. After a brief time in camp in Hawkinsville, the company of volunteers was ordered to Virginia to join the battles to come.

The boys travelled to Richmond by train through Buzzard Roost and Macon to Wilmington, North Carolina, then on to Petersburg, Virginia, finally arriving in Richmond in late May 1861. In Richmond, the 8th Regiment was organized into companies of soldiers from Georgia: the Pulaski Volunteers became Company G, with Dr. Thomas Ryan as captain. After only two weeks, the regiment was ordered to Harpers Ferry and then to Winchester. The regiment's first casualties fell in Winchester at the hands of the oldest enemy to any army, disease. Three of the Volunteers died from the measles. One was a young farm neighbor of the Thomases', Roy Willet. He was only seventeen and had helped Andy build his small barn. Roy was good with mules and made good corn cakes—he would be missed.

In July, the boys of the 8th Regiment moved towards Manassas Junction. On the morning of the 20th of July, the Pulaski Volunteers heard the cannon again. The boys moved to fight on the double quick, passed Bull Run Creek and joined the fighting on Beauregard's left flank. On that first day of battle, the boys held, allowing Beauregard and Johnston time to reorganize and win the day at the stone bridge. But this victory was costly. The Pulaski Volunteers became experienced soldiers that day—experienced in digging trenches, living in filth and burying their friends.

After spending the fall and winter of 1861 and into 1862 in northern Virginia near Manassas Junction, Company G and the 8th Georgia fought in the Peninsula campaign near Yorktown. All through that summer the boys played a bloody role in the Seven Days Battles, Malvern Hill and the never-ending fight against mud. The balance of 1862 saw more destruction, at the second battle of Manassas and at Sharpsburg.

As the second Christmas away from home approached, the veterans of Company G were camped near Fredericksburg. Even though they were not in the thick of that fight, death, destruction, freezing rain, hunger and wet shoes were all around. Homesick men and boys sang Christmas carols at night: Billy Yank and Johnny Reb sang together across the pickets and trenches. It may have been some comfort for the wounded and dying soldiers, but it made Andy Thomas homesick—he missed Betsy's soft voice singing "Silent Night," with a little tremor as she held "night." Andy couldn't join the singing; he just wept silently, all alone and cold. There was another first at Fredericksburg: Company G's first desertions. Another winter passed.

The spring of 1863 began with great promise for the Confederate Army. Longstreet's Corps, including the 8th Georgia, was sent south to Petersburg to check a Union advance. The corps then returned to the Rappahannock, just after Lee's victory at Chancellorsville. But the promise of a bright spring began to turn dark on hearing of the loss of the great Stonewall. It was only a few days later when the 8th Georgia Regiment and all of Longstreet's Corps marched in to Pennsylvania.

While Andy sat in the cool shade near Gettysburg on that hot, sticky morning, General Lee gave his orders to his corps commanders. The great tragedy of Gettysburg was beginning. No one knew it at that moment, but the Confederate States Army was just beginning to die. General Lee was not himself. The first signs of heart disease were beginning to show. He, too, was beginning to die.

The first thing Longstreet's Corps had to do was march from the unfinished railroad cut above Chambersburg Pike across Hagerstown Pike down Willoughby Run to positions almost parallel with the Emmitsburg Road. Andy left his shady spot and walked three miles in the hot July sun with no water. In front of him lay the Round Tops, the Devil's Den, the wheat field, the peach orchard and Cemetery Ridge. It took from just after dawn until three thirty in the hot afternoon for the troops to get into position. General Longstreet had no scouting information on the best way to advance his corps.

Andy Thomas and the Pulaski Volunteers were on the far Confederate right, under the command of Brigadier George Anderson. The Georgia Regiment was part of General Hood's division. The frustrated soldiers of Hood's division faced east and attacked at about 4:00 p.m. A very angry, frustrated Andy Thomas was part of this attack. As they crossed Emmitsburg Road under fire, he wondered, Will we ever do anything right?

The Volunteers battled slowly through the peach orchard and on into the wheat field. Mistakes would rule the day. The soldiers under Longstreet moved late, with incorrect information, or no information, on Union positions and strength. A Union general ordered a retreat, creating a brief opening in the Union lines. Just when it looked as if the Confederates would take Little Round Top and Cemetery Ridge, Union reinforcements arrived and halted the advance of Hood's boys. But General Hood had been removed from the field, severely wounded. By 8:00 p.m., sunlight and hope faded for the Confederates. As the last brave attacks faltered near Cemetery Ridge, the Confederate lines crumbled. Between four and eight o'clock, there were over fifteen thousand casualties on this hallowed ground. There were no horses left alive to remove the guns or the wounded.

As the sun set on July 2, an angry, hungry, thirsty Andy Thomas collapsed by a creek bank and fell asleep. He was so tired that he didn't realize his aching right arm was broken just above the elbow. He had blocked a swinging rifle blow delivered by a homesick boy from Minnesota.

On July 3, the badly damaged 8th Regiment assembled and held their ground, anticipating a Federal counterattack that never came, although the Federal cavalry did feign an advance. Mostly Andy listened to the sounds of the destruction of Pickett's division as they attacked the Angle. More hallowed ground was created to be consecrated. Andy Thomas's sadness turned to intense anger and pain.

Andy had spent most of the day of July 3 with other wounded soldiers, sitting in the shade behind the defensive lines on the west side of Emmitsburg Road. When the day began, there were dozens of wounded soldiers gathered in the shade. More arrived through the day, some limping, some crawling and some carried. One of the Pulaski Volunteers—Tom Roberts, Betsy's older brother—brought Andy a green apple and some water. Using the torn colors of a Federal unit, he helped Andy form a makeshift sling.

As he helped Andy find a place to rest, he said, "I hope Betsy knows we made it."

"Me too. I haven't heard from home in a while."

"I reckon none of us have. Maybe you'll get a trip back there."

"I'm scared to hope," Andy said. "Or maybe just too tired."

"Rest easy, Andy. I hear we're going back south soon. Does it hurt?"

"Everything hurts."

Both Tom and Andy were blinking away tears.

The next day, as Andy was assisted into a wagon, he noted that many of the recently wounded were now among the dead.

A few days later, when the casualty lists were published in Hawkinsville, the Young, Budd, Gordon, Lynch, Walker, Bohannon, Hudson, Bridges, McCall and Scarborough families had reason to weep. Betsy was at home, sick with consumption, but her younger sister ran to tell her that Andy and Tom weren't listed as casualties.

The girls held each other and cried while Bobby Jeff

watched. He had a new puppy, Shady. Shady was a terrier mix that stayed by Bobby Jeff's side. To Bobby Jeff, it seemed the puppy was the only creature in the whole world happy to play with him.

The Trip South with Pete— HOME

After a short time in Virginia, all sections of Longstreet's Corps were transferred to the Army of Tennessee. The 8th Georgia Regiment arrived at Chickamauga just after the battle was over. The regiment would participate in Longstreet's Tennessee campaign, but that wasn't Andy's fate. As the regiment travelled by rail car through South Carolina, they stopped for several days near Charleston and Fort James.

Soon after arriving in Charleston, Lt. Bohannon approached Andy with a small shoulder bag. Andy's arm was still in the makeshift flag sling, but he did not want to go to a hospital. He had developed a real dislike for hospitals, seeing them just as places people went to die.

The lieutenant said, "Andy, I have orders for you to travel to Atlanta and on to Macon and then find your way to Hawkinsville. You've been granted leave for thirty days. I have letters for you to carry from our boys to those at home."

For the first time in over two years, Andy felt a small amount of hope and sensed something to look forward to.

"Private Thomas, you are to leave immediately!"

"Yes, sir, I am on my way."

Andy grabbed the bag and headed for the trains. He had nothing else to pack, as the tattered uniform, torn hat and bad shoes were all he owned. He gave his rifle and bayonet to a fellow soldier who had no rifle.

On the train from Charlestown to Atlanta, Andy was treated with a respect that was almost reverence by a group of old men, some veterans of the Mexican War who remembered Thomas Jackson and Bobby Lee. They nodded, and ladies wiped their eyes, as Andy told of losing companions and friends. As Andy told the story of the second and third days of battle at Gettysburg, he could not hold back the tears.

A little later, as Andy tried to fall asleep, a handsome young woman wearing a black dress with a pretty little girl, also in black, approached Andy's seat. "Sir, may I set with you for a moment?" she asked.

"Yes, ma'am, please do."

As Andy looked at the shy little girl, she blushed. Andy said, "I am Private Andy Thomas of Company G of the 8th Georgia Infantry Regiment. What is your name?"

The little girl buried her head in her mother's bosom without making a sound.

Her mother laughed softly. "This is Sarah. My name is Mary Forsyth. My husband was Major Samuel Forsyth. I am so sad to say he lost his life as a member of General Stuart's cavalry near Chancellorsville. I am so very proud of him, but I miss him so much. Sarah and I are travelling to be near family in Atlanta."

"I am sorry for your loss, ma'am. We've lost so many husbands, sons and fathers. I pray this will end soon."

"Private Thomas, I noticed that your sling is in miserable condition. And, frankly, sir, it smells... well, it smells very strongly. I have an extra shawl that will serve you much better, if you will allow me."

Andy's clothes and the sling were indeed dirty and smelly; Andy was already embarrassed enough to be so dirty around all these good people, without it being directly mentioned. He hung his head and said, "It would be an honor, ma'am."

Mrs. Forsyth proceeded to remove the old flag rag, wasting

no time.

A portly gentleman watching from close by laughed at the sight and announced, "We have all been praying the smell would go away soon!"

Mrs. Forsyth stood and looked the man straight in the eye. She stated in loud, clipped voice, "The only thing fouling the air is your disrespectful comment. This young man deserves better."

Andy felt very uneasy and humiliated. He softly apologized to those around him for the odor, then sat staring at the floor, feeling very lonely.

The conductor stepped up and gently touched Andy's good shoulder. "Come with me, young man."

They walked together to the last car, which had a few sleeper births. "Wait here; I'll be back." In moments he returned with a clean pair of pants and a pullover work shirt. "Put these on, please. And chuck that old stuff out the window."

Andy looked at the conductor and said, "I can't pay you, sir."

"No need. These came from a valise left on the train. I wish I had better shoes for you."

Andy returned to his seat quietly. He had indeed chucked the worn-out butternut uniform out the window, with its stains of dirt and blood from the Northern battlefields. If only he could throw all of the pain in his heart out the window, too.

But he had rolled up the tattered flag-sling and put it in his shoulder bag for a keepsake. The pants were too large and the shirt swallowed him, but he had never felt so good in new clothing.

Mrs. Mary Forsyth and Sarah approached again. "May we trouble you again, sir?"

"No trouble," Andy replied and winked at Sarah. Sarah extended her arm and offered Andy something in a linen napkin. It was warm, and Andy detected an aroma he had missed for some time.

Sarah stated very proudly, "It's a ham biscuit with butter. Momma and I thought you might be hungry."

"Yes, ma'am, Miss Sarah, I am hungry and it smells just heavenly. Thank you!"

Andy unwrapped the biscuit with care, as if it were the greatest present ever. By the second bite, tears of gratitude rolled down his cheeks.

Sarah was startled at Andy's tears. She couldn't imagine that anyone would cry about a ham biscuit. She leaned to her mother and whispered, "The biscuits must be just awful, Momma."

Andy chuckled and said, "No, child. It's the best biscuit in all of Georgia."

Mrs. Forsyth handed Andy a small jar of buttermilk to finish the feast. He had never been served a finer meal. As more tears rolled down Andy's cheeks, Sarah said, "Buttermilk makes me cry, too!"

A series of trains finally got Private Andy Thomas to Macon, and then wagons, mules and boats got him to Hawkinsville. The sad and tired soldier had returned home.

Andy knew he still had a chance for some happiness in this life, but only if he could avoid more heartbreak and forced cruelty. In this land of rage and war, that might prove difficult.

Andy quickly dropped off the mailbag and headed on foot to Fair Creek, but he kept the old tattered flag rag. As he passed the Methodist church where the Volunteers had trained, he briefly felt a strong tug at his heart. Dozens of those young volunteers were now buried in unmarked mass graves. Andy wondered if they would be remembered.

He sat in the shade for a short spell, but doing so only brought back memories of Gettysburg. Still tired, Andy set out along Fair Creek, heading home. He hadn't yet seen anyone he knew, but that was okay—he really didn't want to stop and talk to anyone anyway.

He was almost sick from a combination of worry and anxiousness over seeing Betsy and Bobby Jeff. As he climbed a small rise, nearly close enough to home to yell a hello, he almost ran right into a man who was walking in the opposite direction, pulling a handcart with a few small baskets of okra and potatoes. He recognized the familiar, kindly old face of Ezekiel "Zeke" James.

Andy was startled and said, "Mr. James, I'm sorry. I almost ran you over."

"Land o' Goshen, boy, you sho did!" Zeke's jaw dropped when he got a closer look at Andy. With the summer katydids singing in the background like a Southern woodlands choir, Zeke put his hand on Andy's good shoulder and said, "Well I'll be, Andy. Goodness gracious, boy. Have you eaten anything since you left?"

"Not much, Zeke," Andy said. "Can I have a tater?"

"Have 'em all, son. Oh Lord, you look poorly."

"I feel poorly, so I reckon I ought to look it! But I gotta be a-gittin' on. I need to get home and see Betsy."

Zeke's smile and shoulders immediately sagged. "Oh, Andy. Oh Lord, Andy. I hate to tell you this. Let's set down by the creek and talk a spell. You gonna need to be a-settin'."

Andy could scarcely breathe. "What's wrong, Zeke?"

"Andy, I have some real bad news about Betsy. Oh my sweet Lord, Betsy, sweet Betsy."

Zeke James had been born a slave in Old Carolina sometime around 1790. He didn't remember his mother or any brothers or sisters. He did remember farming cotton and tobacco, and being sold from plantation to plantation. Andy's father had inherited Zeke and his wife soon after the Thomas family moved from Carolina to Georgia. Mr. Thomas had not liked the idea of slavery; he'd allowed Zeke James to earn his freedom, paying him as a farmhand. He had provided a small cabin for Zeke and his wife, who had passed on a few years before the war.

"Andy, your sweet Betsy came down sick this past spring," Zeke said. "She wasn't able to work and take care of Bobby Jeff. Your mother and father took in Betsy and her sister and the boy. Your momma and daddy were so brave, and they have sacrificed so much. We've all been workin' hard just to make do. But just about three weeks ago, Betsy got much worse, and was unable to rise from bed. Betsy was always thinking about you and praying for you. Betsy passed in her sleep just about two weeks ago. She knowed you were probably still alive."

Andy leaned forward and buried his face in his hands. It seemed the last of his heart had just been ripped away. He was dizzy with grief.

Zeke put his hand back on Andy's shoulder and softly said, "Take a deep breath, son. Let's just set here a minute."

Andy quietly sobbed into his hands, with Zeke sitting by his side. After a few minutes, Andy stood and asked Zeke, "Can you take me to her grave?"

"Sure, son, but I think we need to get to your momma's house first. They'll be a-wantin' to see you. Bobby Jeff is sprouting up like a cornstalk in June."

"Mr. James? May God damn this war!"

As Andy approached his family home, Zeke called out, "Hey in the house, we have a stranger come to call!"

Andy's mother stepped out onto the porch wiping her hands on her apron. Her face quickly registered shock and happiness. She ran to Andy as quickly as she could, smothering him with hugs, kisses and tears. A shy little boy with a growing puppy behind him peered from around the corner of the house. Who was this dirty, skinny stranger, hugging his mammaw?

Mrs. Thomas turned to him and said, "Robert Jefferson, come and hug your daddy."

Bobby Jeff shyly approached the man. Andy smiled and said to the boy, "I know that I probably look like a bearded scarecrow, but I'm your daddy!" Andy lifted Bobby Jeff with his good arm, trying to find joy in the moment despite the heartbreak of losing his sweet Betsy.

Just after a very good but modest supper, Andy and his father walked to the family cemetery. The soil over Betsy's grave was still bare. Andy's father placed his hand on Andy's shoulder and said, "Andy, Betsy was a brave and good woman. She loved you and your boy fiercely. The doc said it was consumption, but I fear it was a lonely, broken heart."

Soon, Andy had no more tears left to cry. His heart was completely broken. He was angry, angry at life, death and everything in between. On the long train ride he had looked forward to seeing Betsy, and all he got to see was her grave. So many dead, so many lost. For what? Andy had lost sight of any cause for the war. His world was out of control and he could do nothing to stop the death. His deep grief was turning to a very hot, smoldering rage.

Early the next morning, Andy woke to find his mother in the kitchen with Susannah Roberts, Betsy's younger sister. Zeke had told her that Andy was home, so she had woken early and brought some flour to Mrs. Thomas for biscuits.

Soon Bobby Jeff woke and came into the kitchen where all of the grownups were sitting. He climbed onto Susannah's lap. Mr. Thomas began to explain how things were on the farm. "Conscriptors have taken all of our horses and mules," he said.

Andy shook his head and told his father, "The poor horses don't last long in battle. And the marches are hard and long."

"We have little money," his father continued, "so we trade a few vegetables or cured pork for salt and flour. But our hogs are gone now. And the tax collectors will take half of our cotton, as poor as it is. I think that we are fighting ourselves as much as we fight the Yanks."

Andy was struggling with the consequences of all of these destructive actions, even at home. He said, "I haven't seen any sign of a good decision for some time."

Susannah didn't want Bobby Jeff to hear this talk, so she

took her nephew outside until breakfast was ready.

Andy's mother, putting the biscuits in the oven, begged Andy to stay at the house. "Susannah is a sweet girl," she said, "and she would be proud to be your wife. She's like a momma to Bobby Jeff."

"Momma, you're a good matchmaker, and that's a tempting offer," Andy said. "But I must go back. I just pray this ends soon. Besides, Susannah might think me too bony. I would be a poor risk for her to put her hopes in."

"Andrew Jefferson, it would just break my heart to see you give in to this war. We need to find hope in something."

Later that same morning, Andy taught Bobby Jeff to catch crawdads for fishing. They also found about two dozen night crawlers. Andy was having good fun, back to being barefoot in the creek.

Susannah walked along the bank watching the boys. Andy watched her, too, and they would smile at each other. For a few minutes in the warm morning sun, Andy forgot the war and some of his grief. He noticed that Susannah was slightly taller than Betsy, and that she had a few very cute freckles on her nose. She seemed to enjoy watching the boys have fun in the creek. The little trio moved upstream to some deeper, cooler pools. It was very warm for late September of 1863.

Susannah called to the boys, "Let's set in the shade and see if we can catch something for dinner."

But Andy preferred to sit in the sun, even though it was getting a bit uncomfortable in the late-morning heat. When Andy sat in the shade, it reminded him of the morning of July the second, when he watched thousands of good men die. Soldiers suffer internal wounds that can never heal, not completely. But for a few moments, sitting in the sun, Andy forgot about line-abreast formation, screaming canister shot, the sounds of torn flesh and bones, and forcing roll call to see how many were no longer present.

After a while, Zeke came along with a pole and a bucket

and took a spot close to Andy and Susannah. "This has always been a fine spot," he said. "I showed it to you when you were just a boy about the size of Bobby Jeff. He's a good boy, Andy! I want you to know I will always help watch him."

"Mr. James, I'm sure you will."

Bobby Jeff began chucking rocks in the water. "Here now!" Zeke said. "You gonna scare the fish!"

"What fish? We ain't catchin' nothin'!"

"Boy, it takes patience! You got to get a line in the water if you want to catch any fish!"

After a while, Zeke did catch one small catfish. Soon Susannah got to her feet and placed her hand on Andy's shoulder. She said, "We better get back before Ms. Thomas gets worried about us."

As they headed home, with Bobby Jeff carrying their catch, Andy felt very tired again, like he always did when a big battle was approaching. When they arrived at the house, there were two horses tied at the post by the front porch. Two men waited, wearing the butternut of the Confederate States Army. Their uniforms were pristine, clearly having never seen battle. And these fat, sloppy conscriptors inside their showboat uniforms had obviously never faced shell and shot.

Andy's parents were on the porch, tears heavy in their eyes. Andy knew what they were going to say before they said it. His heart sank.

"You are to come with us immediately," one of the men said. "Your leave is cancelled. We have orders for you."

His mother held him tightly and cried loudly. His father stood with his head down, one hand on his wife's shoulder. Bobby Jeff dropped the catfish as Susannah picked him up and walked him over to Andy. After a quick round of tearful hugs, Andrew Jefferson Thomas marched to war again, still nursing a broken arm. He muttered, "God damn this war!"

God already has damned this war, Zeke James thought to himself as he watched Andy walk away. He already has.

The lazy conscriptors made Andy walk. If he resisted or ran, the men would strike him down.

Anger was gaining a firm grip on Andy Thomas's heart. And poor Zeke had no comfort to offer. He could see Andy slipping away and it broke his heart. Zeke, like most black folk, was aware that the root of this war was slavery and the struggle for real freedom for his race. But he also felt a great sadness that it was forcing the loss of so many and creating great sorrow across the land.

Sorrow that would last a long time. A very long time.

Part 5
Girls in 1970—Oh Lord Have Mercy

THE WEEK PASSES

As the cuts on Mike's arm and face healed from the incident with the Charger and gravel, the word of the integrated starters on the varsity team spread. It was bad news for the backward-thinkers and welcome, happy news for others. The week passed into history.

There were three general reactions to this new form of integration. A very few people were very angry and also very afraid. They were vocal among their friends about the "great tragedy" of desegregation.

There were many other people who were simply afraid to express or demonstrate any outward acceptance of the changes. They, too, were scared of change and unwilling to invest in it. Their reluctance to speak out had at times empowered the extreme actions and words of the first group.

The third faction was accepting of the changes, based on a quiet, calm realization that it was the right thing to do – a good first step.

The football team itself—at least most of the team—was part of the third group. The majority of the players and coaches had moved on. One reason for this was the very simple truth that this team, if it had its best players on the field, could be special.

All through the week the players and coaches hit the field with enthusiasm, vocal and aggressive with each other. A shaky trust was developing. Coach Carter felt this trust growing and was beginning to feel some confidence in these young men. The first game was less than two weeks away and the excitement was palpable.

One of the players most enthusiastic and proud of his team was Mike Thomas. He was very excited about the coming week and the first game, to the point where Ruth Anne noticed that Mike had been eager to get out the door each morning. Each day as he walked towards school, the songs just poured out: "Ride Captain Ride," "Love Grows (Where My Rosemary Goes)," "Bridge Over Troubled Water."

On Friday, the classes just seemed to drag by. But finally, science class with the wizard ended and the school week was over.

Mike and Becky spoke just after class. Becky smiled and said, "Get Big Ray to bring you to the Circle. I'm working this evening."

"A cheeseburger should be a good enough bribe for Ray."

There was no practice that afternoon, but Coach Carter did have a short meeting with his team in an empty classroom. He gave the boys the schedule for the next week and explained exactly what he wanted.

"Men, next week is what we all have been waiting for and looking forward to," he began. "Every one of you has earned the right to be here. I'm proud of you. But you have to be smart now. In everything you do you represent yourself, your family, your school and this team! Make good decisions, be responsible people and always help each other. We have to count on each other. If you ever have problems or get in trouble, you can always come to me. And I hope I can come to you.

"You are among the leaders in this town. We will show them how the best people work together. We have a chance to be very special, on and off the field. Be careful, be smart and be the best you can be."

Do teenage boys ever listen? Well, some do, sometimes. The enormity of the coach's challenge would someday hit home.

After the meeting broke up and the players started filtering out, Lee stepped over to Mike and Ray and said, "Let's meet at the creek tomorrow morning! I feel the need to drown some grasshoppers and get a line in the water!"

Ray chuckled and said, "You guys are crazy. I'd rather sleep."

But Mike told Lee he'd meet him at the creek.

Lee nodded, and as he walked away he was already thinking about finding Mandy to walk her home.

Mike and Ray were heading to the Circle. The cheeseburger bribe had worked.

FRIDAY NIGHT ON THE CIRCUIT

In 1970, the American car culture was in high gear. Teenagers in most every town in the United States were participating in an activity fueled by relatively inexpensive cars, affordable insurance and cheap gasoline. The cars were magical: Chargers, Road Runners, Mustangs, Firebirds, Camaros, Chevelles, Barracudas. Cruising was a social event where most of the local kids would chat about not just the cars, but life—love, hate and everything in between.

As Mike and Ray drove towards the Piggly Wiggly (the "Pig"), they were laughing and joking, excited to see their friends and to talk about the other kids. Who was out cruisin' tonight? Who were they with, or who were they not with? These were the important topics. Cliques had been formed long ago: the bad boys like Bobby Willet and his posse; the older jocks. Ray and Mike were only junior apprentices in this latter gang, but everyone, no matter their status, was just trying to fit in, to be cool - to belong to something.

Since both Mike and Ray were among the younger kids on the circuit, they were often the targets of jokes and friendly ribbing. It was just part of the rite of passage. However, being varsity starters was beginning to lift their social status in the warped world of Southern high school football.

But because of that, these two young boys were also feeling a pressure to be somebody. Sure, there was plenty of external pressure on these kids to excel, but most of this social pressure was self-applied.

Windows down, radios blaring, cars moved in a herky-jerky fashion, with the shotgun co-pilots leaning out the windows. It made for a colorful and loud parade, scented with exhaust fumes from leaded gasoline.

After one round of the Piggly Wiggly parking lot, Ray said, "Off to the Circle. I'm hungry!"

"You're always hungry, Ray," countered Mike.

"You owe me a cheeseburger!" Ray said. "Never forget to feed your lineman friend that blocks for you."

It took a few minutes, but eventually they pulled into a prime spot for the Chevelle at the Circle.

As Ray was about to order and Mike was waving to Becky, Bobby Willet and his posse surrounded the Chevelle. Bobby put his hands on the driver door. He looked at Ray for a moment, and then looked back at his gang. Grinning wide, he said, "Well, I'll be. You sure don't look black enough to pal around with this guy. Are you his driver?"

Ray smiled and leaned out the window just a little. Bobby looked cocky and confident, but Ray shattered that confidence in a heartbeat. Bobby hadn't expected a response from Ray; he was used to being able to deliver sarcastic comments to anyone he chose with no consequences. After all, he was Big Bob.

He underestimated Ray by a country mile.

As Bobby realized he'd just poked a dangerous bear with enormous arms and shoulders, he began to lean back. Ray reached out with lightning speed and grabbed the collar of Bobby's shirt. "Gotcha!"

Bobby yelled, sort of a primal, trapped-rabbit scream. He pulled back as hard as he could. His eyes were as big as Kennedy half dollars and glowed with real fear. His shirt ripped and buttons popped. Everyone, even his posse, laughed at him.

Becky, who had been walking towards the Chevelle, stood with her hand over her mouth, trying not to laugh. She was standing right by the front fender on the driver's side—right in Bobby's path of retreat. But, try as she might to suppress it, a giggle popped out. Bobby saw her laugh as he stumbled away from the Chevelle. He knew he had to defend himself, to save face in at least some small way. The only opportunity was to insult Becky. "You will regret that, bitch!" he spat.

Immediately Mike was out the door, but Bobby turned and ran as fast as he could back to his Charger, his posse trailing, also trying to stifle laughs.

Becky watched Bobby retreat. Mike placed his right hand on Becky's shoulder; his hand trembled slightly, but the touch was firm. He asked if she was okay, and she said she was.

Mike had seen the shock register on Becky's face as Bobby passed by. He didn't hear what Bobby said, but it was clear that it had upset Becky. "What did he say?" he asked her.

"Nothing," she said. "He's just dumb!"

"Yes, but dumb can be dangerous. Please tell me what that idiot said!"

It was clear to Becky that Mike was eager to take action against Bobby. She suddenly wanted to protect him and end this face-off.

Becky moved a little closer to Mike and smiled. Worried eyes turned to soft, happy eyes, and Becky could feel the tension drain from Mike. His grip on her shoulder softened. "Not tonight," she said. "But I do think my knight in shining armor deserves a Dr. Pepper."

"Okay," he said. "But this a Beatles T-shirt, not shiny armor."

"I'll get the usual for you guys," Becky said. "Let's lighten things up around here."

After a while, the evening began to wind down and all of the flirting, car talk, school talk and plain talk came to an end. Mike and Becky agreed to meet at one o'clock Saturday afternoon at the Circle. Becky had it all planned out: "I'm working from ten to one here at the Circle. If you can get here about one o'clock, you can walk me home and we can study geometry." Then she said something that strikes terror in any young man's heart: "Mom and Dad want to meet you!"

Maybe, just maybe, Mike thought, this girl likes me.

"Okay, I'll be here," he said. "But speaking of getting home, how about tonight? You're not walking home, are you?"

"No. Suzy and I are going to her house. I'm going to spend the night there."

"Cool. Do you want a ride? Ray and I can take you."

"Sure. I'll tell Suzy."

A little later, Mike climbed in the back seat with Becky, and Suzy grabbed front shotgun. Ray asked, "Where are we going?"

Mike replied, "Suzy's house."

Suzy quickly added, "But we have to cruise the Pig first!"

Ray answered, with a nervous gulp, "Okay, but you think it'll be all right with your... with Coach... with your dad... Coach Carter?"

Mike thought this was priceless: Ray was suddenly nervous to see Coach Carter! Big Ray, the man-boy who whips triple teams with one arm tied behind his back, terrified of facing the coach in the presence of his daughter. Mike laughed out loud.

Suzy winked at Mike and Becky and said to Ray, "You're going to tell my father that Bobby threatened Becky, and you and Mike are escorting us home."

The story of Bobby's threat to Becky was already circulating, and had grown to include Bobby threatening to murder her family or burn down her house.

"That's a good idea," Ray responded with a slowly spreading grin. "But why are we cruising the pig?"

Suzy laughed and said, "We don't have to tell him that part. I already called Dad and said you were bringing us home.

Let's go!"

As they pulled out of the Circle, Ray worked the clutch to get a little rocking going and give Mike and Becky a chance to slide closer together. Becky seized Mike's hand so fast that it startled him, but he did not let go. Becky leaned on Mike's shoulder, and they both enjoyed the ride around the Pig a couple of times. And then it was off to Suzy's.

When they arrived at Suzy's house, Ray and Mike walked the girls to the front door. The porch light was on and Coach Carter was sitting in the rocking chair on the porch holding a fly swatter.

"Boys, thank you for bringing the girls home. I appreciate it. Now, say goodbye and get home, straight home! You done good."

Coach Carter stood up and looked up at Ray. His eyes conveyed the message that he meant what he said. Coach turned and went in the house. Before the screen door closed, Mrs. Carter came out and said, "Children, come in. I have some fresh-baked cookies."

"Yes, ma'am," Ray said, and then he just simply followed his nose. The promise of a freshly baked cookie made him forget what Coach had said. Coach laughed and said, "Not too many Ray—your butt's big enough!"

"Daddy!" "Jimmy!" Suzy and Mrs. Carter said at the same time.

"It's okay," Ray responded. "He'll run it off of me on Monday."

"Damn straight, you ugly hog!" Coach Carter laughed and Ray smiled while inhaling four cookies.

Mike and Becky were still standing back by the front door, still holding hands. Mike heard Ray coming back out and quickly said, "See you tomorrow; I'll be at the Circle at one."

"You better be," she said. "We're gonna have fun tomorrow."

"With geometry?" Mike asked, with a crinkled brow and a

half smile.

"If we're together, yeah." Becky seized the moment and quickly kissed Mike. Poor Mike was shocked and amazed, so blissed-out that he forgot about getting a cookie.

Ray burst out the door with Coach Carter on his tail. "Raymond Cary, how many cookies can you eat?"

"Well, I could stay a little while and we'll count 'em!"

"Get home, both of you!" the coach said. "Lord save us, my two tough starters: one is going to founder himself on chocolate chip cookies and the other is going to die of love sickness over a pretty little girl!"

Everyone parted, waving and laughing. Coach had to act tough, but God he was proud of these boys. Mike and Ray went straight home, Ray munching on a handful of cookies without offering Mike a single one. What a night!

Coach Daddy Explains

After the boys left, Mrs. Carter and the girls sat together in the kitchen, sharing whatever cookies Ray had not inhaled or walked off with.

Suzy said, "Did Mike get a cookie?"

Becky shook her head and replied, "I don't think so."

The girls all giggled.

Suzy said as she laughed, "Mike has always been shy. He might faint if his mother hugged him."

"But he is so cute," added a winking Mrs. Carter.

The girls were sitting at a small table tucked against the wall near the door leading to the dining room. The table formed a sort of breakfast nook in the kitchen. Mrs. Carter had decorated the room very well, making a homey Southern kitchen. Pastel paintings of flower gardens hung on the walls. Over the table was a small bulletin board showing pictures of Suzy and her older brother, Adam. Adam was a Marine Corps officer, like his father. Adam had played football at Hawkinsville and then at the Naval Academy. He was now deployed with the First Marine Battalion in the Que Son Valley in Vietnam. Mrs. Carter was always nervous, almost terrified, for her firstborn son, and she lived for every letter from him.

Mrs. Carter said, "Mike reminds me of Adam. He was so shy at that age." But Mrs. Carter didn't want to dwell on this thought, so she asked the girls to tell her about their evening.

Becky and Suzy shared a quick glance. When Suzy had called her mother, she hadn't said anything about the Bobby incident, though she sensed her mom knew something had happened.

"It really wasn't a big deal," Suzy began.

Becky nodded in agreement as she poured milk from an antique crystal pitcher into a Tupperware tumbler. She was curious to know how Suzy would describe the night.

"Boys are idiots," Suzy said.

"Suzy, that's not nice!" Mrs. Carter frowned.

"But it's true!" Suzy said, and all three laughed again. Then Suzy told her mother about the incident at the Circle.

"So that's when you called me?" Mrs. Carter asked.

"Yes, though I asked Ray to make a trip to the Pig first. That was my idea, I confess. But I wanted Becky to have some time to teach Mike how to hold hands. Boys are idiots. Even the nice ones. You have to help them sometimes."

Mrs. Carter and Suzy looked at Becky, and Becky blushed.

Coach Carter had overheard the story and now entered the kitchen. He was after a cookie, in theory, but more so the opportunity to coach. He was still dressed in the day's athletic apparel, complete with the whistle around his neck on a bright orange lanyard, but he now had on his in-the-house flip flops, and had removed his cover (hat—it was bad manners to wear a hat inside).

Coach Carter was smiling and placed his hand on his daughter's shoulder.

Suzy looked up at her father and asked, using one of her father's favorite phrases, "Daddy, why is Bobby a special kind of stupid?"

"Jimmy," Mrs. Carter pleaded, "set with us girls for a minute and talk to us."

Mrs. Carter was the only person other than Coach's mother who called him Jimmy. Coach Daddy sat by his wife and took a bite of a cookie. After he swallowed and took a big

125

swig of milk, he began to explain: "I've seen trouble ahead for Bobby for a long time. I wish I were able go back and deal with him differently. He could have contributed to our team and avoided so much useless anger." He reached for another cookie and continued. "I've spent a lot of time thinking about this. Bobby feels like he always has to be in charge, be the big man, be number one. The problem is, in many situations, he never had to earn that. It was given to him, the money, the cars, on and on."

Coach put his cookie down and took in a few deep breaths. He looked up at the girls and kept on with his message. "You know," he said, "he was good at football, but the arrival of Gone Sanderson really shook him up. Gone is the best running back I've ever seen. Bobby didn't have a chance. He just assumed that I would make him the number-one tailback because he's white; and because he's Bobby Willet, the son of Big Bob."

Mrs. Carter laughed and said, "'Bobby Willet, the son of Big Bob.' Sounds like a registered bird-dog!"

It was obvious to the girls that this was a tough topic for Coach Carter. Coaches are supposed to help young adults grow up and evolve into good people, but they can never fix all of them. It's hard to live with the memories of the ones who slip through the cracks.

Coach leaned back in his chair to continue. "Bobby was not man enough to face the truth," he said. "After Bobby's mother passed away a few years ago, it was just him and his father. So when Bobby lost his starting spot at tailback, he really lost face with his father, the only family he has. I'm sure that Big Bob ridiculed him for this, like he does about many other things. It's sad that Bobby doesn't have support at home. But it's easier for Big Bob and Bobby to blame me and my assistants. I can assure you that Sheriff Willet and his pigskin mafia blame me for integrating the team. But I don't care; I did the right thing. It is way past time to desegregate our schools and teams. The best players will play."

"But Daddy, why does he make a fool of himself?"

"Suzy, Bobby is afraid, and angry. This is all a really big thing to him. His status has been reduced and he's powerless to change it. He wants revenge and he wants to embarrass others. It's very ugly, because he uses his bigotry as an excuse to blame and attack blacks, or those who do not outwardly practice his type of racism.

"Bobby is like a dog that bites out of fear. If you don't crowd him, he'll just run away. But he'll make a lot of noise while he does it. If you girls just keep your distance, he'll keep his." Coach Carter paused, and then looked at Becky. "Becky, do all you can to keep Mike and Bobby apart."

"Yes, sir," Becky said. "But I don't think Mike would start a fight."

"Becky, I'm not worried about Mike starting a fight. But that boy is a tiger. He's a good kid, but he will not back down if threatened. He may be just a shy little boy, as you girls say, but he will defend himself—and those he cares about."

Suzy laughed. "You should have seen him bust out of the car tonight to get to Becky."

"I can imagine," Coach Carter said. "Girls, you must always know who your friends are. Who you can count on."

Coach stood up to leave the girls and kissed his wife as he stepped way.

Suzy stood and hugged her father. "Thank you, Coach Daddy."

Coach Carter waved goodbye to Becky and said, "Becky, I'm glad you're here tonight."

"Thank you for having me over, sir."

"Just call me Coach. We're not in the Corps here."

"Okay, Coach!" She laughed and then made her own request: "And, Coach, can you please tell Mike he doesn't need to be scared of me?"

"Yes, I can tell him, but I doubt it will do any good."

All laughed as Coach left the room.

"Becky," Mrs. Carter said, "Mike will be just fine, but believe you me, it is good to have a boyfriend that respects you."

"I know. That's what Suzy says and my mother says. But I wish he would loosen up some."

Mrs. Carter responded, "He will, he will."

Suzy said, "Oh, he's just a sweet little idiot boy!"

The girls cleaned up and headed up to Suzy's room. There was so much to talk about!

As the evening faded and the lights went out, a red Charger slowly slipped down the street outside the Carter home. Bobby had been told where Mike and Ray had taken the girls. Maybe a brick thrown through the front window would send a message? Bobby was very angry and hurt, but he knew he didn't have enough courage to throw a brick. At least, not yet. He might be seen or get caught. Bobby just silently cruised by and did nothing but let his rage build inside.

A shadow of a long-ago soldier stood in the azaleas by the front porch of the Carters' home. This spirit realized that Bobby Willet couldn't make things happen; his fear and lack of confidence outweighed his hate and anger. The soldier would have to work his evil through others; there were plenty of other people with a large supply of hatred and the courage to use it. It had always been easy to create pain and hopelessness, and it always would be.

The old soldier whispered, "I'll come back around to this boy, before he destroys himself."

Only the soft summer wind heard the words. But inside, Becky felt a sudden chill, a sense of dread she did not understand. She curled up and pulled the covers over her head. Sleep came slowly and she had a terrible nightmare. She soon forgot the details, but knew it had something to do with Bobby's red Charger.

Mike Forgets—
DOES THE GEOMETRY

As Saturday morning dawned, Mike was up unusually early. Ruth Anne was working that morning, so Mike volunteered to do the dishes. His mother also assigned some additional tasks; Mike was so focused on getting to the Circle that nothing else mattered. He was going to get the chores done, and then work on the geometry so he could help Becky, or at least not look like a complete idiot. Mike had totally forgotten his promise to go fishing with Lee. The excitement about the Circle and his time with Becky captivated Mike's planning.

Ruth Anne noticed her son's enthusiasm to get after the chores. She had a pretty good idea why he was hustling, but she wanted to get a little more information... and maybe have a little fun with him, too. So she asked, "Mike, what do you plan to do today?"

This was a bit of a test. She was curious what Mike would say. Mrs. Patterson had told Ruth Anne the kids' plans yesterday in the drugstore.

"Well," he said, "I'll finish these chores and then study geometry a bit."

"That's good. Why the sudden love of geometry?"

"Well, if it's okay, I was hoping to go to Becky's house so we can study together?"

"Sure. Let me know when to expect you home."

"Okay, Mom."

"The Pattersons may ask you to stay for supper."

"Is it okay with you if I stay for supper?"

"Sure, if they ask. Be very respectful, grateful and mindful of your manners."

"Yes, Mother."

"And don't forget your lonely mother. I'll always be here."

Ruth Anne was smiling as she left for town. Mike was also smiling, and attacked the chores as if they were an opposing linebacker. In his joy and enthusiasm, he forgot about Lee and Fair Creek. This was a first—only plans with Becky could make him forget Lee and fishing.

LEE FISHES... ALONE

This Saturday morning was clear and sunny. The summer days were growing shorter and there was a bit of a chill as real fall approached. Lee walked through the woods to Fair Creek along the same old paths that Zeke and Andy and Bobby Jeff and Susannah had walked so many years before. It was about the same time of the year as Andy's recall to duty in 1863.

The sun filtered softly through the tree leaves, creating bright, sunlit spots on the ground and on the leaves along the path. Spider webs, wet with the dew, sparkled like crystal where the sunbeams struck them. There was no wind and the trees were silent. Lee could hear squirrels barking a warning and the soft ripples of the creek as he approached.

Lee's heart rate picked up as he neared the creek. The water temperatures were still warm and he knew that using a top water popping bug or a grasshopper would be magic. Fishing on top water is the most fun, especially when the water is calm. You can see the fish come up under the lure and simply explode into a thrashing fight as they take a hook. The water in the still pools was like a sheet of glass, absolutely perfect.

As he prepared to cast in the old, good pool, he wondered where Mike was.

Mike was usually the first to arrive, but not today. Lee quickly reeled in a good bass. As he progressed through the well-rehearsed process of fishing, he began to talk to himself: "Why should I worry where Mike is? He can do as he pleases. The weather and the water are perfect, so I have fishin' to get done!"

Logical, yes, but Lee missed his friend. Their fishing trips were almost always joint expeditions. Once, when Mike had the flu, Lee decided not to fish until his friend could join him. Mike was a bit of a klutz, and Lee enjoyed helping him and teasing him.

"Damnation, Mike, where are you? We just don't get many days this good."

It was still very quiet, so quiet that Lee could hear every little noise he made as if it were magnified. The wiggling, splashing fish were very loud. His poppin' bug landed with his cast like a big flat rock hitting the water. The mosquitoes around his head were like airplane motors. But he did not hear the very soft steps of the old man approaching from behind.

ZEKE AND LEE

"What a glorious morning! How is Miss Ivy?"

Lee nearly jumped out of his shoes. "Jesus Christ, old man," he said. "Did you sneak up just to scare the piss out of me?"

At first Lee was a little angry, but it quickly faded into more of an embarrassed funny feeling.

The old man answered, "No, but it was sort of funny!" The old man wore a big smile as usual.

"I've seen you before," Lee said. "I know you know Momma. Please tell me yo' name."

"Ezekiel James. But Zeke is good 'nuff."

"Okay. I'm Lee."

"I know. I been watchin' since you was a little scrapper."

"Well, that's good I guess."

"Where is yo' buddy, Michael?"

"You know Mike?"

"Of course I know him. I've watched him too."

"Well, I don't know where he is, but he should be here."

"How's that?"

"Well, after school yesterday we agreed to meet here this morning. It's not like Mike to forget. Unless he's sick or something, he always comes."

"I don't think he's sick. I believe it's the something."

"Well, he's not here."

"Sometimes things happen that you don't count on," Zeke said. "I bet Mike is smitten. He'll come around to his senses eventually."

"Yeah, I guess so."

"So, how is Miss Ivy?"

Zeke had moved up alongside Lee. He had a very old cane jigging pole with a cotton string line. His old hands softly tied on a hook. Out of his top overall pocket he pulled out a small brass box and plucked out a "grasshoppa."

"Young man, let me show you how to fish!"

"I'm doin' okay."

"Yeah, but you need to relax," Zeke said. "Watch me, and tell me how Miss Ivy is doin', now."

"Oh yeah, sorry. She's doing better now. She can't see, so she can't do many things. Mrs. Ross has been helping her. She's a great lady, Mrs. Ross."

"Yep. She got a pretty little daughter too!"

This made Lee feel awkward, but Zeke laughed and put him at ease. To hide his embarrassment, Lee replied, "They're a great family. Little heavy on the religion."

"That won't hurt you none."

"I hope not."

"If Miss Mandy had asked you to come over you would've forgotten about fishin' too—just like Mike did!"

Lee realized that the old man was right; he remembered how he'd hustled to catch up with Mandy so they could walk home yesterday afternoon. He nodded and said, "I bet that's where Mike is. With Becky."

"Yep. Mike is your friend, but, like I said, he's a smitten boy right now. Give him some time."

As Zeke chuckled, he pulled out a very nice bass on the end of his cane pole and flipped it right at Lee's feet. Lee laughed and jumped, tripping and falling, sitting down right in the water with a mighty splash.

Zeke and Lee both laughed, although Lee was glad no one

else had seen him fall.

"Young Lee—Mike is your friend," Zeke said. "Others may doubt that and may try to sever your friendship. But you must hang onto it. You'll have to give each other some space. You two are friends, so don't be too hard on each other. Even good friends may disappoint you sometimes. Don't let it mess you up."

Lee let this sink in for a few minutes. The silence returned: only the mosquitoes, the stream and the cicadas made any sound.

Zeke went on. "There will be more days on the creek with Mike. In time, you will teach your children to fish here." These last words came in a faint, fading voice—almost a whisper, a suggestion. Lee turned to reply, but Zeke was gone.

Lee said, "That old man comes and goes like a durn ghost."

For a brief moment, Lee thought he heard a laugh—and a very distant bark.

MIKE WALKS TO THE CIRCLE

As Mike headed towards the Circle, he was in a great mood and stepped quickly, almost bouncing. His route would usually be direct up Scenic Drive, bypassing downtown to turn right onto Broad Street, and then up a few blocks to the Circle. But he chose to turn from Scenic right through the center of downtown towards the hospital parking lot by the old Methodist church and the pecan grove. It was a nice day and he had a little time to kill before Becky got off work. He enjoyed seeing the many historical sites in the old town. It was only a few blocks up to the Pig from the hospital parking lot. It was early on Saturday, but Mike thought he might get lucky and get a ride from the Pig to the Circle.

Walking through downtown Hawkinsville was a history lesson. Most of the banks and mercantile stores had been built between 1840 and 1890. Old Church Street cut through the center of town. At the site of one of the old, long-since-gone churches was the city cemetery. The cemetery was very old, and there had been no burials there for almost fifty years. Many of the graves were marked with service stars of the Confederate States Army. There were half a dozen grave markers, laid by the Daughters of the American Revolution, denoting Revolutionary War veterans. Ruth Anne Thomas was a D.A.R. member and loved the quaint little tea parties. Mike had many memories of tagging along with his mom as a small boy, dressed in his freshly starched shirt and tie. But the promised trip to the Circle afterwards was usually his reason for attending.

The D.A.R. and other social groups kept the cemetery in good shape. Mike always felt the presence of the history around him and took some strength from that. Since Mike had come to learn the sad history of how the War Between the States affected the local citizenry, he'd also begun to feel sad when considering the suffering of the people of that time. It seemed like such a waste that so many southerners had suffered and died for such a terrible and flawed cause. He respected the bravery of the Confederate soldiers, but he couldn't help but wonder why they couldn't see the futility of their cause.

Today the cemetery was freshly mowed, and new flowers adorned many of the graves the markers. Mike could smell them, with the temperature and humidity on the rise this late-summer/early-fall day. The Methodist church came next, where Mike and Ruth Anne attended services every Sunday. The old church was a monument in and of itself. But as Mike walked by, he stepped up on the wide steps, sentimentally recalling his introduction to Becky by Suzy. As Mike headed away from the church he turned and looked back at Pecan Grove Park. He could see the historical markers denoting the muster site for the Pulaski Volunteers. He could imagine the groups of young men, boys, really, forming squads in drill. Mike had been in "the Grove" many times and always felt he was not alone there. This old town provided an anchor and an identity to the many children of the community, and had done so for generations. Hawkinsville and Fair Creek would always be home for Mike.

But, on to the new. Going up towards Sixth Street, Mike transected the hospital parking lot; not too many cars there today. He thought of Sweet Momma and then felt a crush of guilt that became a huge punch in the gut as he remembered

Lee and their plans to fish.

For a moment he wanted to rush to Lee's and tell him they'd have to postpone their fishing. But it was too late: apologies would have to come when Mike would next see Lee, maybe at school Monday. Mike was very excited to see Becky and he pushed on. It was just a few blocks to the Circle from the Pig.

Mike didn't recognize any cars in the lot, so he just walked on. A familiar face in a state trooper cruiser came up from behind him in the parking lot. "Hey, boy," Larry Wayne said. "You want to cruise with a trooper?"

"Am I under arrest?"

"Not if you just get in." Mike climbed into the car. "Headin' to the Circle?"

"Yeah. I need to get there soon."

"Why are you carrying school books?"

"Becky and I are going to study."

"At the Circle?" Larry said. "Good Lord, boy!"

"No, we're going to Becky's house."

"That sounds much better. Let me escort the fine couple."

As Mike got out at the Circle, Larry said, "I'll be back in a few minutes. Wait for me."

Mike got out and sat at the picnic table. He was a few minutes early. Becky spotted him, waved from across the lot, and shouted, "I'll be there in a minute."

Larry headed back down Broad Street. There had been complaints of a red Charger hot-rodding on Broad. He knew Big Bob and his deputy posse would do absolutely nothing. That Willet kid's gonna hurt somebody one of these days, Larry thought. Experience had taught him to smell trouble.

Bobby had a lot of things going for him, Larry knew—but common sense was not one of them. It would help if his daddy would teach him right from wrong. But that would assume Big Bob even knows right from wrong himself, Larry thought. Or cares.

If there was one thing Larry knew, it was that somebody was going to get hurt.

CHEAP-SHOT QUEEN

Mike enjoyed watching Becky interact with customers; she was friendly, always smiling. She managed people very well, always relaxed and able to engage anyone in conversation. She was smart, too, damn smart. She delivered orders with the grace of a princess—or that's how Mike saw it.

Becky was sharing this shift with another carhop, Lisa Rose. Lisa was a pretty girl, but not always pleasant to be around: she certainly didn't have Becky's way with people. But she did have a way with Bobby Willet: she'd been his on-again, off-again girlfriend for some time now.

Bobby was planning to pick up Lisa at one o'clock. Neither Becky nor Mike knew this.

As Becky finished her shift, she brought Mike a Dr. Pepper and handed him a small bag. "Here you go," she said. "Two of Mrs. Carter's cookies!"

Mike split a cookie in two, gave half to Becky and stuffed the other into his mouth. Through a mouthful of cookie, Mike muttered, "Th-th-th.. anks!"

"Don't talk with your mouth full!" Becky said, her mouth full. Both fell to laughing.

Mike told her that he'd arranged a ride with Larry.

"Daddy will love that!" Becky said.

"What?"

"Delivered home by a state trooper!"

"Oh. Well, it's just Larry."

"Officer Larry Wayne, sir!"

"No, just Larry."

"Officer Wayne, sir."

"No, just Larry."

Becky and Mike were having so much fun going back and forth that they didn't notice Lisa walk up.

Lisa rarely truly smiled, but she often wore a grinning smirk, along with a stare that could freeze a lake of fire in hell, with eyes to match. Her dark black hair was pulled back in a ponytail. As Becky turned, Lisa flashed her dark eyes towards Mike. Mike was sitting on the tabletop with his feet on the bench, facing Becky. Mike braced himself: he couldn't remember ever hearing Lisa say anything good.

With a quick smile, Becky conveyed to Mike her desire that he keep his cool.

"Oh, look," Lisa shot. "It's Romeo and Juliet."

Mike wanted to, but didn't, say, "And Lisa, the new wicked witch of the west!"

"Hi, Lisa," Becky jumped in. "Are you working tomorrow?"

Lisa ignored her and kept glaring at Mike. "I hear you like the black players more than the white players," she said. "Won't be long until you find yourself a black girlfriend, huh?"

She turned to Becky. "What're you gonna do when sweet little Mikey starts running around with the colored girls?"

Mike started to stand and engage, he was going to tell Lisa to shut up, or something clever like that, but Becky froze him by squeezing his hand, hard.

As Larry turned into the parking lot, Lisa turned up her nose and walked away.

Mike's mouth was hanging open. He stammered and stuttered, then finally said, "Becky, everything she says is wrong!"

"Mike, I know. She's just one black-hearted bitch!"

Mike's jaw dropped again. Becky smiled and winked. "Close your mouth, sweetheart, you might catch a fly!"

This little princess had the heart of a spitfire in her. Mike liked it.

The Afternoon at Becky's

The rest of the afternoon really went well. Becky's calm control had the effect of relaxing Mike. For the most part, the young couple sat in the dining room and went over the geometry problems. Becky let Mike "teach," and gently corrected where needed. When they finished, Becky gave him a brief tour of the house, with her two younger sisters trailing.

The house was an older two-story in the Southern River Heights neighborhood. The front yard shrubs and flower gardens were right out of Southern Living. The lawn was trimmed perfectly. The wide front porch held a swing and rocking chairs with scattered potted flowers. Mike was a little jealous because he knew his mother would love to have such a flower garden, but didn't have room or time.

The backyard was deep with mature pecan and willow oak trees, good shade trees. There was a large back deck, fringed by roses and azaleas. Becky and Mike had just sat on the deck lounge chairs when Mrs. Patterson came out on the deck. She asked, "Mike, can you stay for supper?"

"Yes, ma'am, I would be pleased to. Thank you!"

"That is great! We're having Mr. Patterson's favorite, liver and onions."

Mike tried hard not to make a face, but Becky noticed and had to stifle a laugh. She took his hand and said, "Don't worry, Mom always makes something edible to go with it."

"I will do my best to try to like it."

"That will impress Daddy."

"And it'll just about kill me. You can put 'Daddy liked him' on my tombstone."

"It's not that bad."

"Do you like it?"

"No, I hate it."

"Nuff' said!"

Mrs. Patterson soon called from the kitchen, "Can you kids help set the table?"

Liver and Onions
with Redemption by Ice Cream

As the family sat at the table for supper, Mike was placed across the table from Becky, and beside Mr. Patterson. After a quick blessing, Mr. Patterson slapped Mike's shoulder and said, "Mike, it's nice to have another man at the table."

"Well, thank you for having me stay. This table looks great."

Mrs. Patterson smiled and the little girls giggled.

This dining room was decorated and organized classically and beautifully. The large oak table had a perfect linen tablecloth with matching napkins. The table legs were carved with very elegant curves, and lions' paws for feet. Mike was impressed by the fine home, but he worried that he didn't fit into this elegant setting. He was a little bit nervous as he sat with the family. Mike could not imagine using the pressed linen napkins to wipe greasy food from his face. The silverware was placed perfectly. Becky had given Mike a lesson on setting the silverware properly, as fine folks would expect. Mike was confused a bit: which fork, what knife, when to use the spoon?

"Remember," Becky had told him. "When you stir the lemon and sugar in your tea, do not clink the spoon on the side of the glass!"

But the elegance of the room didn't stop with the table. It

was a large room. The table could seat eight, and the matching, padded linen chairs were stately. Along the wall were a matched pie safe and china hutch. Mike wondered if they ate every meal this way.

There was a large painting over the pie safe of Jesus at the Last Supper. Upper-class homes in the South usually had paintings of religious significance. But Mike hadn't seen any pictures of Stonewall Jackson or Elvis, though, at least it seemed to him, all Southern homes had them somewhere. But this was not a typical home. Mike would soon learn that the Pattersons were good people, with no pretense of belonging to a false upper crust. He would fit in fine—but not without some comedy along the way.

As he looked down at his food, Becky smiled and said, "Mother, I believe Mike likes liver and onions."

Mr. Patterson responded, "Mike, it is one of my favorites and my sweet wife prepares them perfectly."

Mike was almost speechless, but he squeaked out, "I can't wait!"

Becky smiled. The sisters giggled. Mrs. Patterson passed the bowl of liver and onions. Mr. Patterson provided instruction, "Here's how you do it: first you take a good helping of mashed potatoes, and then you just smother it with the liver and onions." Then he demonstrated.

The sisters, with wrinkled noses, said, "Ewww."

Mike swallowed a gag.

Mrs. Patterson scowled at the sisters and said, "Girls, that is not polite! You were not raised in a barn."

Mike followed direction, but he noticed Becky was not doing so. The girls didn't like liver and onions, and their mother spared them the agony of trying to eat it. This was a treat for Mr. Patterson only.

Becky was smiling and trying not to laugh.

At this point, Mike was determined that, in this room of great elegance, he would be a champion of social grace and eat the damn liver, onions and all! He looked at Becky and gave her a determined nod.

Becky was ready to have fun with this. The moment Mike took a bite, she tried to get her father to address him by saying, "Mike is the number-one fullback, Daddy!"

"Is that right, Mike? Do you only play offense?"

This forced Mike to swallow quickly and answer. Throughout the rest of the meal, Becky timed her statements and questions perfectly. Poor Mike barely had a chance to chew. Well, he thought, if I have to eat the damn liver and onions, may as well do it quickly.

"Daddy, Mike fishes a lot. Maybe he can show you some good spots."

"Is that right, Mike? That's great. Do you fish on the river?"

Mike dug in with grim determination. Over and over, Becky would say something to her father about Mike, Mr. Patterson would responded by asking Mike a question, Mike would swallow hard and answer, and the sisters would giggle. Between the swallowing and the speaking, Mike barely had time to breathe.

Finally, Mike's plate was nearly clean. Mike straightened up, lifted his shoulders, looked at Becky and said, "Mrs. Patterson, that was absolutely the best liver and onions I have ever had!" What he didn't add was, and the only liver and onions I have ever had and will ever have!

The sisters giggled, looked at each other, wrinkled their freckled noses and said "Ewwww" one last time.

Becky laughed out loud, covering her mouth with both hands. Mr. and Mrs. Patterson both beamed with pride, until Mrs. Patterson provided rescue and deliverance: "If you boys will go to the grocery and get a pint of fresh cream," she said, "we can make homemade ice cream on the back porch for dessert."

"Sounds great," said Mr. Patterson. "Mike, maybe you can

also show me a good fishing spot?"

"You bet!"

"Becky, do you want to come along?"

"No, Daddy, I'll help Mother clean up!" To Mike, Becky said, "Can you help me carry some of the dishes to the kitchen?"

"Sure, my pleasure!"

The sisters, Annie and Angie, giggled as Becky headed towards the kitchen. They surrounded Mike as he stood. Annie said, "Becky says you're cute!"

Mike laughed as Angie followed, "But she says that sometimes you are so dumb!"

The girls ran from the dining room, giggling.

Mike found this pretty cute, and he thought he would use this new information. Becky had heard her little sisters talking to Mike. As Mike carried a couple of larger bowls to the sink where Becky was working, Becky planted a quick kiss on his cheek and said, "I am sorry, I couldn't resist. You are an angel!"

"And you are a devil, at least a little bit."

"I cannot believe you ate that whole plate."

"Me either. But the bite, chew, swallow, talk cycle made it go quickly."

"The expression on your face was priceless."

"Just promise me one thing."

"What?"

"If I'm ever asked for supper again, please, no liver and onions!"

"That might be hard," Becky said. "They think you love liver and onions now and that's your own fault."

"Then promise to give me time to breathe and maybe chew?"

"No, you said to promise one thing. But I'll let you enjoy the ice cream." Becky kissed him again on the cheek and whispered, "You are a cute little dumbass."

THE INTRODUCTION
AND A BRIEF MOMENT OF DOUBT

As Mr. Patterson and Mike pulled out of the driveway, the sisters waved from the front porch.

"The girls were very excited to have you over," Mr. Patterson said. "They've been having fun planning this for several days."

Mike was surprised, but, even considering the liver and onions, it had been a good day. Mike was also realizing that Becky was a bit of a practical joker; maybe there would be a chance to get her back.

Mike had told Mr. Patterson that he would show him some good places to fish. "Just go on Scenic Drive towards Fair Creek and we'll go in the back entrance to the park," he said. "That's a close walk to the better fishing spots."

In just a few minutes they arrived at the park. They parked the big Galaxy 500 and started walking down towards the creek, then across a bridge to the east side of the stream.

"If you take these paths along the creek bank," Mike said, "you'll come to some slower pools. They've always been good for me."

"This looks great," said an obviously excited Mr. Patterson. "I may come tomorrow afternoon."

As Mike and Mr. Patterson walked along the creek, they talked about types of lures and approaches to working the stream, both heavily focused on the discussion. As they reached the lower creek, they walked up on Lee, who was just leaving. He had been at the stream all day, except for lunch at home.

Mike was surprised but immediately happy to see Lee, though he also had a strange and uncomfortable feeling. Mike wasn't sure how Mr. Patterson would feel about his friend— his black friend. Mike's recent run-ins with people who had no respect for the black folks of the community had made him wary, and he didn't know where Mr. Patterson fell in this spectrum of beliefs. This could be ugly, and turn quickly. Mike's guts were turning, too. He stood to retain the respect and friendship of Mr. Patterson or lose it, very quickly.

For a moment, Mike was tempted to just say a brief hello and not acknowledge Lee as a close friend, but that wouldn't be right or honest. If Mike acknowledged Lee as a very close friend, would it jeopardize his relationship with Becky's family? Mike knew that Becky had no problem with Lee, but he wasn't sure about her parents.

He did not know how Mr. Patterson would react. Mike made his choice.

Stepping up toward Lee, he said, "Mr. Patterson, this is my good friend, fishing buddy and teammate, Lee Sanderson. Lee, this is Mr. Patterson, Becky's father. He likes to fish."

Mike held his breath and watched Mr. Patterson's eyes very closely.

For a few brief seconds, Lee wanted to withdraw. He was very tempted to hold back and not open up to this new person. It was a response he knew how to deliver when faced with a white man's arrogance.

The introduction surprised Mr. Patterson, but clearly didn't shock him. After just a brief hesitation, he extended his hand to Lee. This very simple gesture allowed Lee to choose to open up as a new friend and equal, though he was a little hesitant to take his hand. He glanced at Mike and saw that

Mike was reacting with his usual stupid, big-toothed grin.

"Hello, Mr. Patterson," Lee said. "Mike knows the good spots—but first I had to teach him how to fish."

"Pleased to meet you, Lee," Mr. Patterson said. "Maybe I'll see you at the creek?"

"I hope so!"

Mike exhaled quietly, feeling tremendous relief. It was going to be okay.

He apologized to Lee for forgetting their fishing plans; Lee shrugged and said, "It's cool, there'll be other days. But you missed a fabulous day to fish!"

Both boys had been more than a little apprehensive about the introduction. The future of their relationship had been on the line. Mike could have been forced to choose between the Pattersons or Lee; Lee could have been humiliated and lost a longtime friend. Both recognized the tension and traps created by the expectations and bigotry of others. And both had simultaneously chosen friendship. Mike had chosen not to worry about what other people thought about Lee, and Lee had chosen to forgive his friend.

But this had been just a little test. Larger tests were coming.

When the men arrived back at the Patterson home, everyone was ready to make ice cream. Mrs. Patterson had called Ruth Anne and invited her to come and have ice cream. Mrs. Patterson was giving her a tour of the many flower gardens and the beautiful landscaping when Mr. Patterson and Mike arrived.

Mike told Mrs. Patterson that it was the best ice cream he had ever had, and this time he really meant it.

LEE WALKS HOME

As the daylight faded, and as Lee approached home, he felt good and confident, though he wasn't sure why. He didn't completely understand the anger that Gone, Arthur and many others sometimes let overwhelm their judgment. Lee certainly recognized both the subtle and overt racism around him. Sweet Momma had often admonished him to avoid hate and anger. They served no good. She would say, "Don't let anyone change your behavior. You take the high road, and do what is right."

Today, Lee had chosen the high road. It felt good; he had trusted his friend Mike instead of reacting from fear or anger. But there was always a nagging fear, and a recurring question: Can I do it right the next time, too?

There was risk for Lee—if he opened up to the wrong person, he could be hurt.

As he got near the house he walked around to the front porch because he knew Momma would be there. Since she had come home from the hospital, she spent a lot of time on the porch. As he stepped onto the porch, Sweet Momma, from her rocking chair, said, "Take those nasty shoes off! Don't track in my house!"

"Momma, you can't even see my shoes."

"Don't have to; I can smell 'em."

That night, as Mike and Lee fell asleep in different houses

in different parts of town in different worlds, both felt good about their friendship. It had always been strong, but both young men had a fear deep in their hearts. Neither one of them could really articulate this fear; but it was there, always present. Both Mike and Lee were becoming more aware of the real world around them, and how it was often a cauldron of hate, fear and anger. Both of these young men were afraid that events beyond their control might divide them. And that would be a tragic loss, like losing a brother.

A cool breeze was blowing in the trees that night. It shared the same worries as Mike and Lee.

In the wee hours of the morning, the town was hit by a very strong thunderstorm. The thunder woke Mike, and he was startled by the rapid-fire lightning that created very strange shadows in his familiar bedroom. Mike usually felt very comfortable in his bedroom—it was his sanctuary—but these strange shadows made the familiar and comfortable seem different, and he felt almost unwelcome. As he rose to close his bedroom window, he had a strange feeling that the thunderstorm was the opening bell of a big fight. He was right.

Part 6
A Path of Destruction

⊕LD AND DIRTY, STILL DIRTY, SECRETS

The big storm seemed to clean the air. The late-summer grass and leaves all took on a fresher look and smell. The air was clean and the ever-present stifling Georgia humidity wasn't too heavy this morning. Mike noticed these things as he walked to school on Monday morning, the first day of the big week of his first varsity game as the number-one fullback. It was a Creedence Clearwater Revival song that Mike was singing today: "And I wonder, still I wonder... who'll stop the rain."

As Mike passed the Lilac Road Church, Reverend Ross waved from the parking lot, nodding and stepping in rhythm with Mike's singing. "Boy, you have got to come sing with us sometime!" he said.

Mike enjoyed his walk to school that morning—he felt this would be a great week. He had completely forgotten the dread he'd felt during Saturday night's thunderstorm.

But the air and crisp green grass were clean and pure only on the surface. There was still dirt in this town. It had been swept under the rug and hidden from most people, but that old rug would soon be pulled up, exposing the old filth.

Janet Allen, wife of Froggy Allen, was Big Bob Willet's secretary and keeper of the sheriff's office. Froggy and Janet had no children and lived in a modest home near Ruth Anne and Mike.

Froggy was part of Big Bob's posse, although not a first-stringer. Froggy was generally simple-minded and rarely suspected anything bad about anyone. That was, of course, excepting black folk—extreme racism was a prerequisite to being part of Bob's gang. Froggy would've been better off spending time with a more open minded gang.

Janet Allen and Bert Andrews had carried an on-again, off-again tryst for several years. Bert's wife had died in an automobile accident about 1960. The affair began soon after. Both would sneak to Macon and meet at the Sundown Motel. Janet's sister managed the motel, and she helped Janet keep things quiet. Though the affair had lasted over ten years, the only person in Hawkinsville who suspected anything was Sheriff Willet. Just by coincidence, while Big Bob was in Macon, he saw Janet's and Bert's cars parked near the motel. It took some time, but he managed to get proof of this clandestine affair: he'd hired a private investigator from Atlanta to snap pictures at the motel.

One afternoon, Sheriff Willet confronted Janet in the office, showed her the pictures and started a series of blackmails. He used Janet to mysteriously "misplace" evidence, steal evidence money and other such activities. Janet was well-liked and trusted, and she was very good at being discreet. The sheriff complicated things by also giving her some of the cash, further involving her in the crime and sealing her silence.

Bert Andrews didn't know that the sheriff was aware of the affair. Janet had wanted to end the relationship with Bert, but the good sheriff had insisted it continue. Big Bob didn't need more dirt—he just enjoyed keeping people in misery. By this late summer of 1970, Janet, so torn with guilt and shame, was nearly ready to end this and confess all. But it wouldn't happen that way.

Janet was also concerned about how Froggy would take the news. It troubled her very deeply to think about how much

Froggy would be hurt. He knew nothing and suspected nothing, but if he did learn about the affair, he could easily turn into a different person.

There was only one other who knew about this mess. And the angry old spirit soldier knew just how to use such information.

THE CALL ON THE RADIO

On Monday afternoon, the sheriff sat in his cruiser in the lot of an abandoned gas station on Scenic Drive. It looked like he was watching traffic, looking for speeders. But he could care less about traffic. Big Bob was consumed with anger and frustration. Bobby would not start on Friday night; wouldn't even be on the team. He was mad at Bobby, Coach Carter, integrated schools and snotty kids like Mike Thomas, a good-for-nothing little momma's boy. He wanted to hurt them all in the worst way. But he couldn't decide how. He knew he couldn't intimidate Coach Carter. Big Bob sat with his beefy left arm hanging out of the window and chomping the stub of his nasty cigar. For once he was out of ideas.

The radio crackled and startled him. "What the hell do you want now, Janet?" he barked. A strong static crackle came through the speakers, followed by silence. The puzzled sheriff bent forward and tapped the radio. A stronger but still low voice came through: "Sheriff Willet?"

Silence. Sheriff Willet didn't recognize the voice.

"Sheriff Willet," it came again. "I know you hear me."

Silence. The voice was hoarse and low, not human, nothing like Big Bob had ever heard.

"Sheriff Willet," the voice came back, this time stronger. "I can help you restore your place and make things as they were."

Sheriff Willet reached for the microphone. "Do not use the device," the voice said. "I can hear you."

Big Bob looked around but didn't see a soul. For a moment he was tempted to flee the car. He reached for the keys in the ignition, but the strange, firm voice stopped him again: "Sheriff, you had better listen to me."

"What do you want?"

"Come to Pecan Grove Park. I'll be under the trees on the west side. We'll speak there."

"Why should I do that? I don't know who you are!"

"We want the same things."

"And what things do we want?"

"Revenge," the voice said. "To take them down! Watch them cry."

For a moment, Big Bob considered just going home. It was late enough in the day. This was just too weird.

"Sheriff."

"What?"

"I know about every time you stole money from your grandmother's purse, starting when you were twelve years old."

This took Big Bob's breath.

"It's best you come to the park," the voice said. "I can hurt you in many ways."

Sheriff Willet wasn't used to being threatened. It was usually he who was hurting other people and living on threats. He had a lot of things to hide. The big, bad sheriff, trembling, said, "Okay, I'll be there!"

BIG BOB AND THE HAINT

It took only a few minutes for Big Bob to get to the park. The west parking lot was deserted. He saw no one under the trees, and it was incredibly quiet. Big Bob got out of the car as the radio crackled one more time: "Good—you did listen to me."

The puzzled sheriff looked around again but still saw no one. Although he felt no breeze, the leaves began to move, with a barely perceptible green glow among them. The air was heavy and dirty, with a slight hint of death and corruption.

Big Bob turned towards the hospital but saw no one there, either. He turned back to the car and nearly came out of his shoes: there was a man, clad in the strange-looking clothes of a dirty Confederate infantry sergeant.

The soldier was just two feet from the sheriff, but the sheriff hadn't heard or seen him approach. "Sheriff Willet," the solider said, "you need to do only one thing for now. You are aware of the pictures of your secretary in your safe?"

"Yes. Why?"

"I will tell you what you need to know, and no more."

These two stood staring at each other as if they were in a contest.

"Go to your office," the solider said. "No one is there right now. Take out the pictures and leave them on your desk."

"How will that do anything?"

The old—very old—soldier just smiled a very evil, chilling smile.

"You will see in time... soon. For now, just do as I say. You'll see."

"Where can I find you?"

"You'll not need to find me. I'll use the device to speak to you."

"When?"

"Soon. Just go do as I say."

The old soldier turned to walk away, towards a thick clump of honeysuckle. The trees began to settle. The air seemed clean again.

Big Bob walked slowly to his car. He was trembling and sweating. As he opened the car door, he said to himself, "This is a load of bullshit! I'm going home."

The "device" crackled and the hoarse voice said, "Sheriff, if you go home and do not do what I said, you will not leave your home ever again. You must do what I demand or you will suffer."

Big Bob felt a vice grip on his throat, but no hand or person was present. "Okay, okay," he squeaked out. "I'll do it!"

The pressure lifted, and a strange, low laugh came from the speakers, along with the foul, sulfuric smell of death. The smell scared Bob more than the voice.

This spirit had power, a power it used to manipulate emotions based on hate, fear and anger. But that had always been just enough power to precipitate terrible things.

The old spirit had considered just choking the life out of the sheriff. But that time might come soon enough.

Every Picture Tells a Story

Late that same night, a shadow figure slipped into the sheriff's office. This figure was very powerful, but there were some limitations to the abilities and reach of these spirits. They could take action only if a person chose to interact with them. Once Sheriff Willet allowed the old soldier to influence him, once he answered the radio call, his fate was cast. Once an angry spirit was allowed in, it would be all but impossible to turn back.

On Wednesday night, the spirit took the pictures and placed the envelope in the mailbox at Froggy's bait shop. That would be enough. Thursday, when Froggy picked up the mail, he took note of the old crumpled envelope.

Most weekdays, especially after school started, business was very slow. Froggy was alone in the shop. He sat at his desk behind the cash register. This was an old roll-top desk that had several small shelves, drawers and cabinets. It was heavy oak, finished with a light stain, making the many chips and cuts obvious. There was a thick clutter of many years of fishing magazines and fading photos of customers and friends showing off trophy fish. There were also pictures of Janet, including, on the top shelf, front and center, a photo from their wedding.

The next moment, the unsuspecting, trusting Froggy felt a crush on his heart unlike anything he had ever felt before. The pictures were clear and there was no mistaking who was involved and what they were doing.

Froggy locked the door of the shop and left. It would take only a couple of days for the hurt and rejection to turn to anger, and for the anger to generate a plan.

Froggy drove home and left a note for Janet. It read, "I am going to visit my brother in Florida. I know."

But he did not go to Florida. Not yet.

When Janet got home, she found the note on the kitchen table, on top of a picture. It would be many, many nights before Janet would sleep well.

WIZARD'S FIRE

That same Thursday evening, about the time Janet found the note, Big Bob was cruising around town looking busy. Big Bob was good at that. Soon he was summoned on the radio. It was that evil, deep voice of the old spirit he had met in the Grove.

"Come to the parking lot of the Good Times club."

Big Bob didn't answer; he just changed directions and drove straight to the club on the north end of Lilac Road.

The place appeared to be empty; the crowd usually didn't arrive until well after dark. The shadow figure of Sergeant Andy Thomas, the old soldier spirit, walked from the trees. He provided instruction to Big Bob to complete two acts of hatred.

Both of these actions would involve another person under the sheriff's influence: Mr. Foss, the teacher and Klan wizard, who had a long history of very dirty work. Paul Foss had liked to tinker with fireworks as a young boy. He gained a well-earned reputation for setting fires and making fireworks. Many of his friends called him "Pyro" as a teenager. Burning crosses came way too easy to this Klansman. In college, he perfected the art of making firebombs. He used these toys mostly in the line of duty for the Klan. Very few people outside the posse knew of the source of the fireworks. But the sheriff had even more dirt on Paul Foss. There had been a few times where Foss had been contracted, through Big Bob, by various criminals to plant firebombs. These actions served one of two purposes. One, either somebody wanted to burn down a building, or two, someone wanted to hurt or scare somebody. These actions had resulted in deaths and serious injuries. Paul Foss was a murderer. These hits were usually far away— Miami, Nashville, Memphis - not close to home. But Big Bob knew about each and every one of them, and he did have evidence. He would use this information to force Paul to carry out two tasks. One required a firebomb. The second did not require a bomb, but it would inflict a terrible hurt, just like a bad burn. These tasks were both to take place close to home, not in some far-off place.

PART 7:
CHILI CHEESEBURGER DAY

$5

Friday morning at breakfast was a lot like the first day of the school year had been: an excitement about something new, in this case the first game of the season. Almost everything had been building to this day for Mike. This morning's song of choice was "Raindrops Keep Falling on My Head." Once again Ruth Anne tuned off the radio.

"Mom!"

Ruth Anne smiled at Mike and answered, "I have something for you."

"Oh well. I guess you have to give it to me in total silence; clearly the radio causes some kind of mom-son interference," he said as he grabbed his third piece of cinnamon toast.

It was indeed a special day.

"I don't want to yell at you over the radio," she explained. "Today you should have fun."

"I am planning on it!"

"You should tell Coach Carter thank you!"

"Mom, you don't thank the coach. I've never heard of anyone thanking the coach. What would I thank him for?"

"For giving you a chance. For believing in you."

"Oh," Mike said. "Well, I never thought about it that way."

"Well, think about it!"

"Okay."

"He'll act rough and tough, but he would appreciate it. Ask

about his son, Adam.”

“I'll try, Mom, but I don't get too many chances to talk to him just one on one.”

“Make one,” she said, and with a wink added, “I know you can do it!” Ruth Anne turned to pick up her purse, and said, “And here.”

She held out a five-dollar bill.

“Get something to eat after school, before the game,” she said. “Good luck, sweetheart. I'll be there!”

“Thanks, Mom. I'll do my best.”

Soon both were out the door. Mike was wearing his football jersey and Ruth Anne was in her nurse's uniform. This five-dollar handout would become a Ruth Anne-and-Mike game-day tradition.

Much would happen before Mike and Ruth Anne would speak again.

Pep rally

Just after the lunch period, all students, staff and faculty assembled, enthusiastically, in the gymnasium. Although some groups of blacks and whites maintained their own segregated groups, a few groups were beginning to mix. One of these mixers was Mike and Lee and their friends.

As the pep rally began, Becky got up to join the band at one end of the gym. As she left, Mr. Penner walked over and sat with Mike, Lee, A.J. and Ray.

"Gentlemen, how did you do on the geometry quiz this morning?"

All three boys smiled and laughed. Mike answered, "Okay... but I'm sure Becky aced it."

"Lee, how about you?"

"Man, I tore it up!"

"Does that mean you did well or that you destroyed the paper because you did poorly?"

"No, I did good!"

"No, you did well."

"Sure did!"

Mr. Penner laughed as he walked away. The band started the school fight song, "Mighty Hawks." Everyone stood and cheered, jumped and yelled or made noise any way possible. The folding wooden bleachers shook and made their own noise. If you looked closely enough, you could see dust coming up from the gym floor. The band played, cheerleaders cheered and led the students, and the players were introduced by Coach Carter. It was thirty minutes of loud chaos, music and fun.

Once the pep rally got going, no one noticed the science teacher slip off behind the school. He walked to the football field house. When he saw that no one was looking, he walked in through the players' entrance. The entryway passed by an ice machine that was very noisy. Past the ice machine there was a second door on which hung a Georgia Bulldog poster featuring Vince Dooley. Through this door were the lockers. Each locker had the name of a player written on athletic tape across the top. Mr. Foss saw that the lockers of the black players were mostly clustered together. He found the locker he wanted, reached in and lifted out the helmet. Inside he placed a folded piece of paper.

One task complete, one more to go. For now.

PIGSKIN MAFIA

As the pep rally wound down, Big Bob and his posse were gathering at the Downtown Cafe, just across from the courthouse. The cafe was a frequent lunch spot for many of the people that worked downtown, especially those from the courthouse and county offices. The lunch crowd was beginning to dwindle. There was a short line at the cash register. Sally Mae, the cashier and owner of the Downtown Cafe, was working quickly. On her white apron, she sported a big "Go Hawks" fight button. Tonight's game was a frequent point of discussion among the customers. That was also the topic of the conversation in the back corner table, frequent home of the Big Bob posse at lunchtime. The back corner had framed copies of old local newspapers on the wall. These were mingled with older Hawks team photos, pendants and posters. Sally's son Eddie Joe Mae had been a star a decade ago: his photo was on the wall. Also on the wall, behind the cash register, were photos of seven former Hawks who had been killed or lost in action in Vietnam, the Republic of.

For years, there had been an unofficial tradition that football players would eat supper at the cafe before heading to the locker room. Sally had known these seven boys who had died in Vietnam; she had known all the Hawks over the last twenty or so years.

But, for now, she thought only of the posse, minus Froggy,

at the table, and was hoping they would just get out. The posse, and especially the sheriff, made Sally feel very uncomfortable. The members of the posse often took turns making crude jokes at her expense. Bert Andrews had tried to slap her behind once, but she had smacked his glasses off his face. At least they now kept their hands to themselves. Today they had been served and they were done; best if they would just go. As Sally caught up, she picked up a fresh pot of coffee and headed to their table. While she was filling cups for the posse, Big Bob looked up at her and asked, "Are you gonna serve the colored boys this evening?"

"If they come, yes," she said. "No reason not to."

"If you do, I'll never be back."

The posse members were all nodding.

Sally's heart was happy. A smile crept onto her face. Very deliberately she said, "Well, I am just so sorry. Too bad."

Sally sat the hot pot on the table and walked away. She had never liked the big jerk anyway. Roy Allen, Froggy's brother, addressed Big Bob, "Do you really think that stupid Coach Carter will start those colored boys?"

"He said he would; I think he will."

Bert Andrews spoke up and said, "Worse yet, he's run off the good white boys."

The entire pathetic group was staring at Big Bob, waiting on his words of wisdom. They came, finally, like an eternal judgment: "James Carter will regret his choices. You wait and see."

Sam Elkins, deputy sheriff, was beginning to feel that Big Bob was not as firmly in control as he usually was. Big Bob hadn't been able to exert any influence on the football situation. Was he losing control? Was his little world falling apart? It seemed that Big Bob was angrier and more nervous than usual. In fact, he wanted out of this place. So without saying a word, he got up and left.

COACH CARTER—
DOING THE RIGHT THING

Soon after the pep rally, Coach Carter walked from the school to the field house by the stadium. Coach loved game-day Fridays, every aspect of the experience. As long as the Hawks won, he enjoyed everything. When the Hawks lost, he wasn't very happy.

He would meet with his assistants in the afternoon to review game plans, injuries and to encourage the young assistants to be leaders. He would then meet with team managers to let them know what he expected. As he was slowly walking and thinking, he passed through a small faculty parking lot. One of the vehicles was his 1958 Chevy pickup. It was light blue with a white cab. He opened the passenger door to get his game shirt and tie. Coach did not see Sheriff Bob Willet walk up from behind.

After the sheriff left the café he had driven to the school, wanting one last chance to take a shot at the coach. He figured he had no hope of changing things at this point; he just wanted to make a subtle point and hopefully make the coach even more uneasy.

Big Bob had little concern for Bobby; he was a helpless, spoiled little idiot. Neither did Big Bob have any concern for the other student-athletes or their families. He had no concern for what was right.

The sheriff did feel a little sadness as he realized that football was over for Bobby, but he tried to force it down. Coach Carter did care for his team, Big Bob must admit. Every single player.

As Coach Carter turned to face the sheriff, he saw the sheriff's car parked behind his truck, the engine running. This wouldn't last long.

"So, Coach, are you really going to start and play those colored boys?" Big Bob said.

Coach was neither intimidated nor afraid, but he was annoyed. He replied firmly, crisply: "They earned it; they'll play."

"Well, I'm sorry you have decided to be this stupid."

"Just go and leave me alone."

Big Bob grinned like a mule eating saw briars, then laughed mockingly with his nasty cigar bobbing up and down. The sheriff was sweating heavily. Coach Carter thought it would be funny to smack the grin and cigar off his face, but it would probably not be the right thing to do.

"Have you thought about what this night is gonna cost, Coach? What it will cost other people around you?"

"Everything has a price, Bob. I'll do what I know is right. Do not threaten me."

"Coach, whatever happens, happens."

The sheriff shuffled away, fell into the cruiser, slammed the door and left.

A little later in the afternoon, Coach Carter gathered his assistant coaches in his office. They were dressed as a team, gray pants, black shoes and maroon shirts. They looked sharp, ready. Coach Cater was also sharp and ready, except he had on a white, short-sleeved dress shirt and maroon tie. The first part of their discussion was a typical coaches' meeting. The game strategy was sound. The Hawks were expected to dominate the team from South Macon Consolidated High.

"Strategy," Coach Carter said: "Give Gone the ball and

block like hell!"

The coaches ran through the starters; all seemed ready. But there was a big, unspoken thing hanging in the air. Until Coach Carter popped that bubble: "Okay," he said. "We all know that some folks are not happy with this group of starters. Now is your chance to tell me if you have a problem with this. Things might go roughly if we don't win. Things might go roughly if we do."

The assistants sat quietly. No one said a word. The silence lasted for at least half a minute.

Finally Coach Alan smiled and said, "We're with you, and the kids are with you. I think that has been obvious all week. It's as plain as the nose on your face."

Coach Harris, the spirited linebacker coach, nodded in agreement. "Let's just play the game. To hell with 'em!"

The coaches and team were going to do the right thing. There was no doubt. But Coach Carter knew that sometimes doing the right thing had a price. And not knowing what the price might be, well, that bothered him.

⊕THER FRIENDS

After final bell, Becky, Suzy and Mandy met behind the school. Mandy had walked up to the other girls, carrying her books and purse. "Suzy, are you sure this is okay?"

"Sure. It's perfectly fine."

"It" was an invitation from Becky and Suzy to join them at the Downtown Cafe. Mrs. Carter was offering a ride for all three. Ray, Mike and Lee were going in Ray's car. Mandy was still a bit nervous about this rather sudden form of integration.

Mrs. Carter insisted that Mandy sit in the front seat. Between the four girls, there were more giggles than a baby-tickling contest.

Suzy drove the conversation. "What are you wearing to the game?"

Becky answered, with a little sarcasm, "The hot, sticky band uniform."

Giggles.

"Who will we set with?"

Mandy answered, "Well, Mr. Penner asked my father to say the benediction prayer before the game, so I have to set with my parents."

"That's nice!" said Mrs. Carter.

"Mom, Mandy wants to be with us!"

Becky laughed and said, "Us? I'll be with the band."

"Mandy, maybe after the game starts you can find me and

set with me?"

"I will try."

Becky asked a very important question: "Did you see that trashy skirt that Lisa was wearing?"

Giggles.

Becky also said, partly to herself but out loud, "Mike is so cute in that jersey!"

Giggles.

The Downtown Cafe was full of kids and Sally was happy. She lived for these Friday afternoons, with her and her staff trying to fill drink and food orders as fast as they could. The place was loud and there were many noisy, happy voices blending into one joyous, excited buzz.

Ray, Mike and Lee sat together in the back corner in a large booth close to the wall. There was something on the jukebox, but who could hear it? The girls came in and Mike stood. They all crowded into this corner booth, sliding easy over the vinyl seat covers. The tables were wooden and old, many sets of initials and dates carved into them, like "Sam and Emma, 1948."

Suzy gave Ray a mock slug on the arm. "Are you ready to play?"

"Sure, if I can eat first."

"I'm not going to stop you."

"Good!"

Mike had the old, crinkled menu in his hands and Becky was trying to take it, a friendly tug of war. They were playing just a little rough and laughing, but when neither would give up, the old menu ripped right down the middle.

"Becky!" Mike said as if she had done something totally shocking.

"It was your fault, Mike."

"You were trying to keep a hungry boy from eating!"

"Can't be done!" Ray added with a laugh.

Lee smiled and joined in. "Becky, you're usually so sweet. What brought out this anger?"

Becky ignored Lee and turned to Mike with her nose just a little bit up in the air. "Mike, you don't need the menu. I know exactly what you will order."

"And what is that?"

"Double cheeseburger, add chili, lettuce, mustard with large fries and a Dr Pepper."

Becky had nailed it. Mike already smelled the frying burgers. He was ready, Becky was right.

The chili cheeseburger became Mike's pregame tradition. Ray ate two of them himself, and everyone's leftover fries.

The boys soon left, heading for the field house. They thought they were indeed men. But life needed to jerk them around a bit more before they would earn that title.

The girls also left, but made plans to get together after the game. Usually the players, family members, good friends and coaches would meet in the school cafeteria for a big meal after the game.

Mrs. Carter gave Becky a ride home. Her father was planning to take her back to the school soon.

The band usually assembled in the music rooms to march onto the field. They would form lines through which the football team would enter the field just before the national anthem. The kickoff would soon follow.

But Becky was at home now and changing to more comfortable clothes. She would put her uniform on at the school. While she changed, the window was braced open to provide some cool air. She heard a soft rustle in the shrubs outside. It seemed unusual, because the weather was fine; it sounded like someone had just run by the window. She looked outside but saw nothing. She did feel a cool breeze on her face. It was odd, for sure, but in a comforting way.

"Strange," she said, turning away from the window.

But she froze when she heard laughter. It was very faint,

as if it came from far away.

Papers

When Mike and his friends arrived to the locker room, Mike began to feel the nerves. He wondered if the heavy chili cheeseburger had been a good idea. The players came in one by one, and thus began the suiting up, ankle taping, knee taping, eye blacking, "remember-to-go-to-the-bathroom-before-you-put-all-that-stuff-on" routine. As Mike and Lee helped each other pull jerseys over shoulder pads, it began to feel very real. Cleats were next to last. Mike had taken his home to clean and polish. For a few minutes, they were clean and crisp and did not seem like football cleats. However, no amount of polish could remove the smell.

To release some tension, Mike chewed on his mouthpiece while sitting on the floor in front of his locker, his knees pulled up. Lee was beside him in the exact same position. Mike was tense, Lee was not. In fact, Lee was paging through a fishing magazine, checking out different types of reels. He had the magazine hidden behind his helmet so no one could see what he was looking at.

Coach Carter had been walking among the players, patting shoulders, looking players in the eye, getting them ready. Mike heard Coach Alan call out "Two minutes." The team was about to go out for warmups. Taking his time, Mike stood and took a deep breath. The last piece of equipment was the helmet. He turned to reach for the brain bucket.

As Mike turned, he felt a cool blast of air on the back of his neck. He turned back to look but saw nothing. No one else seemed to notice. Mike grabbed his helmet. What he didn't see was that the breeze pushed a folded piece of paper out of the helmet and in to the back of the locker. Mike didn't see the paper—not tonight, anyway.

Warmups flew by. Mike was still nervous but it helped to get a little loose, hit a little, work up a sweat and loosen the stiff pads. Mike and his teammates couldn't help but sneak looks down the field to watch their opponents. Any opposing team always looked like giants, like an NFL team. But the excitement and eagerness grew as the warmups progressed. Coach Carter decided to get the boys back in the locker room so they wouldn't peak too early.

The players sat on the floor quietly, hearing the sounds of the stadium crowd and drumming band as it marched into the stadium and onto the field. As the band marched closer to the Stadium, they entered through the traditional entrance that also passed right by the field house. As the drums and the whistles became louder, the crowd made even more noise. This was an orchestrated pageant and parade designed to drive excitement. The rhythm of the drums certainly drove up the excitement level in the players. This grand performance had been repeated on Friday nights for many years.

Coach Carter slowly walked to the center of the locker room, clinching his fists and pumping his aims. "Are you ready? Let me hear it!"

Seventy-five young men jumped to their feet, pounding seventy-five sets of shoulder pads and seventy-five helmets. At the same time, seventy-five voices yelled and growled like seventy-five angry bears. Even the crowd heard the noise coming from the locker room.

Becky was in her spot in the line, marching in place to the rhythm of the snare drums and the booming bass drum, ready to play "Mighty Hawks."

Suzy was on her feet in the stands with good friends. Mandy and her mother and father were standing. This was very, very special. Today, young black men were invited in to the Downtown Café—to eat, not to bus tables. Tonight, young black men would take the field with young white men.

In the locker room, Coach Carter settled the boys and drew them shoulder to shoulder very close together, circling him. He led a simple prayer. "Lord, keep us safe, keep us strong and keep us together."

"Amen."

"Men," he said. "Let's go out there and show them how we do it!"

Then the team, senior captains first, was out the door and smashed through the paper banner. The band played with spirit. Mike knew where Becky stood and he ran by her side of the line. He was so nervous he couldn't talk, but he managed a jerky wink.

GONE, GONE AND GONE AGAIN

The Hawks started the game kicking off to the team from Macon. Mike was on kickoff coverage. Sprinting full speed, shedding a block and hitting the ball carrier took all of his nervousness away. Now Mike was ready to play ball, and so was everyone else.

As the very late-summer evening cooled, the grass became slick and wet with dew. The cool sod was very comfortable and familiar for the players. The game field was much cleaner and smoother than the practice field. There were no rocks and big dirt clods to tear up your hands and elbows.

By now these young men had reached their second wind. The plays came easy. The band and crowd noises became a distant background. The sounds of signal calling and cracking pads were close. The pace of the game was quick. The scoreless first quarter was over in a flash.

As the second quarter began, the Hawks had the ball and called an off-tackle smash. Mike's job was to kick out the defensive end and Gone would run through the gap. Mike knocked the end flat on his back with a crushing block. Gone cut right behind the block and was in the end zone in less than three seconds. The Hawks were ahead. Just before halftime and then again early in the third quarter, Gone was gone again. Mike was delivering crushing blocks on the linebackers and defensive ends. Later, as the Macon team crowded the box expecting another run, Lee slipped behind the safety and caught a pass for a long touchdown. The rout was definitely on. So far it was the Sanderson Show. Early in the fourth quarter, Mike faked a block on the linebacker and turned in the flats. The pass was perfect and Mike outran everyone to the end zone. Wow! It felt good. The final score was 34-0. When the final whistle blew, it seemed to Mike that the game had only just begun.

There was great excitement as the team left the field. This team had weapons and they looked good. The local fans were standing and cheering, the band played "Mighty Hawks" for the hundredth time, or so it seemed to Becky. As the players burst into the locker room after the game, Coach Carter was there to meet them.

Screaming, jumping players and coaches were all around. Even the managers were dancing. It was loud and joyous. Dirty jerseys, socks, pads and other things like chunks of mud from cleats were flying. All of the players enjoyed this part of the game. It was a great night.

The game ball went to Gone Sanderson.

AIRWAVES

Sweet Momma wasn't able to go to the game, although Reverend Ross had done his best to talk her into it. Momma was comfortable in her house, with her things, where she didn't have to see. She was even learning to do some things in the house. She did enjoy going to church, but that was about the only reason she'd leave home. She was even making progress teaching Lee to cook. Lee and Momma enjoyed the successes and laughed over the failures.

On this Friday, Lee had set up the radio on the porch by the rocking chair so Momma could listen to the game. Lee and Gone had received permission to leave school at lunchtime; Mr. Penner had come with them to get the porch set up for Momma.

At game time, Momma moved to the rocker and turned on the radio. She had loved the boys' games and did miss going, but she wasn't yet comfortable in public.

When Gone scored his first touchdown, this is what she heard: "It is third and four for the Hawks offense. Coach Carter has signaled in the play. The Hawks need to convert this first down to have a chance at a sustained drive. We've seen glimpses of good ball movement, but no consistency. The Hawks break the huddle and line up slot left. Lee Sanderson comes in motion to the right. The snap. Sammy spins and gives the ball to the tailback. Big hole. Gone cuts inside the safety. Oh my, sweet Lord! Gone is gone!"

The crowd noise poured through the radio; she almost wondered if she was hearing it all the way from the stadium.

"Oh my," the announcer said. "The Hawks have their first touchdown. Folks, I have never seen such power and speed."

The color commentator added, "Yes, and Mike Thomas, one of the amazing sophomores, absolutely crushed the defensive end of the Macon team, and he is still down."

Sweet Momma laughed. "I guess some cornbread helped that boy!"

With the band and the celebration still raucous, Momma wiped a single tear and said, "Oh Lord, watch these boys. Keep them safe."

As she said this she sensed an old spirit approach. She looked out towards the roses by the old well pump, as if she could see. She could almost sense a shadow there. Momma just smiled and called out, "Come on up to the porch and set with me. I know who you is."

Sweet Momma had seen this old man around for a long time. She first learned of Zeke from her grandmother. She had always thought of him as absolutely harmless. She really couldn't explain what Zeke was, but her grandmother had always responded to her questions about him by saying, "Don't question gifts from God."

So a young Ivy just learned to not worry about Zeke. She knew he was a force for good. Zeke had intervened for people in trouble at times. But since Momma had lost her sight, she now sensed there was something much more to this old man. He was more than just an old man in the community. But only a very few had actually ever seen him close, let alone spoken to him. She didn't understand it, not yet. But she felt in her heart that she had nothing to fear from this old man. It was not natural—she could not explain his presence—but it must be the Lord's will.

Smilin' Zeke came up and sat lightly in the swing. He

smiled and shook his head. "I don't understand these contraptions."

"I've got to listen to my boys, Arthur and Lee."

"They in that box?"

"No, they at the school on the ball field."

"Well, how can you hear them in that box?"

"I ain't able to explain it. But they say it on the airwaves and it comes out in this box. It's called a radio."

Zeke just smiled. "The only thing on the airwaves that I can detect is that it smells like somebody ate sweet taters for supper."

"Oh hush, you ole' fool."

Both laughed.

He didn't understand most of the words he heard from the box, but he could tell Momma was happy about them. As the game wound down, Zeke stood and walked directly in front of Miss Ivy.

"Don't ever lose hope and don't give up on 'em. We have a real good chance, better than ever."

"I know... but I'm afraid."

Momma wasn't exactly sure what they were talking about, but she did sense strongly that trouble was coming and that her boys would be threatened. She still felt like there were things she needed to do, but she didn't know what they were yet. But she felt very strongly that one of the keys would be the strength of Mike and Lee's friendship.

"Me too. We gonna see some rough days comin' soon. Very soon."

"Probably so," she said. "Probably so."

"It'll start soon; maybe already has."

"I'll be fine, ol' man, but Lee and Mike have to stay tight!"

"Yep."

"It will be hard. But I think they'll hang on."

"Hope so."

"I wish I felt as good for Arthur."

"Hard to see for Arthur, because it's hard to see what Arthur will do."

"I know," Momma said. "That boy has one eye for trouble."

As Zeke faded away, he said one last thing: "Be strong, and don't doubt them!"

Momma couldn't have seen that Zeke's eyes were glowing a faint blue. As he faded to nothing, the eyes were the last to go.

Momma was soon in bed, praying. She did not sleep well.

AFTER THE GAME

After these games on Friday night, the players, close friends, family members and coaches would meet in the cafeteria. The mothers and fathers would prepare a big postgame dinner for all. It was most fun after a win. These hungry kids would eat fried chicken with all the fixins at an absolutely amazing rate. Mike had invited Becky, and she sat with Mike, Larry and Ruth Anne. It was a good day and a good night.

Reverend Ross placed his hand on Mike's shoulder and congratulated him. Gone, Lee and Mandy sat just to Mike's left. Gone and Ray were trying to see who could eat the most. It looked like Ray was winning.

Gone shook his head and said, "You one ugly hog, but I love you!"

Ray just smiled. In fact, everyone smiled. Ruth Anne noticed that the kids were all very tired; eventually the jokes and the laughs began to slow down. Mike wore a soft smile and expression that reminded her of when he was much younger. She patted Larry's hand and said, "Time to go home, boys and girls!"

They all began to leave the cafeteria. Suzy said her goodbyes and went to find her mother. Lee looked at Mike and asked, "Tomorrow?"

"Tomorrow, yes!" answered Mike.

Both knew this meant fishing, lines in the water.

The Sanderson brothers left with Reverend Ross and his family. Mandy hugged Becky and softly whispered, "Thank you for today."

Mandy seemed much more relaxed now. She trusted Becky.

Ruth Anne drove home, with Larry in the passenger seat and Mike and Becky in back. They left Larry by his cruiser, which was parked by the stadium. As they started the drive towards Southern Heights, Becky nuzzled into Mike's shoulder and he put his arm around her. She said, very softly, "I am proud of you!"

"I am a lucky guy!"

"Not just everyone gets to be a football hero!"

"Nope," he said. "that's not it... not everyone gets to hold the prettiest, sweetest, smartest girl in school."

"I'm proud of you, sweetheart."

It had been a good day. The goodnight kiss was the best part. Saturday held promise too, fishing with Lee and meeting the girls at the movies.

Could it get any better?

Probably not, but it could get worse.

PART 8
VERY HIGH CRIMES AND VERY LOW THOUGHTS

Fishing Again

Mike and Lee, and for that matter almost all of the football team, slept in a bit on Saturday. Mike was surprised at how sore his neck and shoulders were. He wondered how the other guys felt, and, remembering the opposing player he knocked down, he hoped he was okay this morning.

Mike loved the game but sometimes the thoughts that came afterwards were a little uncomfortable. It would always bother Mike to see serious injuries. He would suffer a few serious injuries himself along the way: everyone who ever played the game eventually ran into somebody bigger and stronger.

His mom had left a note: "Clean up the kitchen and don't forget Lee!"

Mike did not forget Lee. He finished in the kitchen and headed for Fair Creek.

The conditions for fishing were not as perfect as they'd been the week before, but the day was still good. There was a little breeze from the northwest that helped keep the humidity down. Mike's shoulders and legs loosened up a bit as he walked. Before long he was singing.

The breeze rustled the leaves in the trees along the old familiar path. Many of the black folk still referred to this path as the Old Thomas Road; this was the old path from town to the Thomas farm. Since summer was coming slowly to a close, the leaves were now drier and the rustle from the breeze was crisper. A few leaves had snapped off and were floating on the breeze in front of Mike as he walked.

Mike was going at a moderate pace, not in a big rush. He felt a sudden cool breeze blast on his face, and it stopped him in his tracks.

The air was quieter now and he looked around. He saw and heard nothing. But just as he started to walk again, a fat cottonmouth dropped from a tree branch onto the trail right in front of him. It slithered in slow motion towards the creek.

"That was close," he said aloud. Mike was not afraid of snakes, but those big cottonmouths had a nasty temper as the days cooled.

It wasn't far to where Lee was waiting, at the spot that Mike and Lee referred to as Number One. Lee was relaxed as usual, but today he had stretched out on the grass in the sun.

"Hey, Mike," he said. "Are your neck, shoulders and butt sore?"

"I hurt all over," Mike said, "but walking here helped some."

"Does singing help? I been hearing you sing for the last ten minutes. You couldn't sneak up on anybody if your life depended on it. Time to fish!"

"Yes, sirree."

Lee added, with a note of caution, "Be careful; Momma says full-moon days in the late summer get the snakes moving. She said it was a snake moon last night."

"Well, she's right. One dropped out of a sweet gum sapling right on the trail in front of me. Almost peed my pants."

"That would have been funny, little Mikey peeing his pants."

"Real funny, Lee, real funny! We'll see how funny it is if one of those black demons drops on you."

"Better a black one than a white one."

Mike turned to look a Lee, who was getting up and dusting

his britches. They looked each other in the eye, then both of them grinned and then laughed. Today, it seemed right to work at a slow, easy pace. No need to rush.

Mike was just glad to be here. He admired the smooth grace of Lee's cast. He had a firm, delicate touch on the rod as he made the plastic night crawler seem alive. In no time, Lee landed a good four-pound bass.

"Amazing!" said Mike.

"Just quit gawkin' at me and get a line in the water."

"Yes, sir!"

Mike cast his line, but he wasn't concentrating on the fishing. Mike realized that he enjoyed watching Lee fish as much as he enjoyed fishing itself. These times on the creek seemed almost magical, the most perfect place on the earth.

"Lee, do you remember the first day we met here?"

"I remember. Why?"

"I don't know. I just remember the big bluegill you caught and that you taught me how to use doll flies and tie better knots."

"Mike, my boy, I taught you everything you know about fishing, and you've done gone and forgot half of it."

"Are you sayin' I ain't smart?"

"No, man, you're smarter than most people—you're just real good at forgettin' stuff!"

"Well, I do have an idea about the movies tonight."

"Do you? You'd better be tellin' me, before you forget!"

"When I get all grown up and leave Hawkinsville, how am I gonna get along without you?"

"You won't."

"How do you know?"

"Because you love me too much. I'm like your second mother; me and Ms. Thomas have to tell you everything."

"I did okay last night," Mike said. "Even Becky said so!"

Mike was getting a little chippy and defensive. Lee knew exactly how to get him on edge. He also knew how to back him off the edge. Lee smiled and laughed.

"Whoa, ease up, buddy," he said. "Hey... did you give her a goodnight kiss?"

Mike blushed so red his ears glowed. "Yes, doggone it.'"

"I bet it was more like Becky had to grab you and take the lead!"

"She did not!"

"I'll ask her!"

"You will not. Good grief, Lee!"

Lee was chuckling; he knew he had Mike's goat. "Ease up, buddy, I'm just giving you a hard time," Lee said. "It's just too easy to get your head messed up. Now, what's this idea of yours?"

Mike took a deep breath and dropped the rock he was about to throw at Lee. He explained his idea, and Lee actually thought it was a good one, and might be fun. This plan of Mike's had never been done before, not at the movie theater in Hawkinsville. It was going to be great.

But it was a snake moon, and snakes would crawl.

The Starlight—Triple Date

The feature on Saturday night was a John Wayne movie, Chisum. Mike loved Westerns and John Wayne, especially when Forrest Tucker was the sidekick. Mike was the only one of Ray, Lee, Suzy, Mandy and Becky who thought it would be a good movie. But it was 1970, and in 1970 you went to see the one movie that was showing; you didn't pick one of ten options in a big multiplex theater.

This group of moviegoers met at the theater, but it took some effort to get them all sitting together.

The schools may have integrated but the Starlight had not. Black folk had to come in the side entrance; they couldn't go through the main lobby. They had to walk along a roped-off path to the stairs to the balcony.

So, the black folks of Hawkinsville had the balcony all to themselves. The irony in this was that the balcony had the best seats.

The theater was magnificent. The tile in the front lobby had very ornate swirls and lines of scarlet and purple on a cream-colored background. The snack counter and popcorn machines were lit in a way that the shelves seemed to glow. The place was magical, very warm and homey. After many years of attending movies here, Mike still got excited every time he stepped into the lobby. The red carpet started at the two large swinging doors that led to the auditorium. In the auditorium, soft lights along the aisles lit the footpaths. The old, stained carpet seemed like a sheet of velvet on the floor. The walls had large circular swirl designs, with shade-covered lights in the center that provided a soft glow. A few very small and well-spaced lights on the ceiling did give the feel of starlight, like sitting outside on a comfortable summer evening.

Mike, Becky, Ray and Suzy sat near the back, close to the aisle on the right side. The crowd was light tonight, especially for a Saturday. Mike's plan was simple: when the cartoon and previews started, the gang would get up, quietly walk to the balcony stairs and proceed quickly and quietly to the balcony seats. No one saw them. Lee had scouted the balcony to be sure everything looked okay. He met them on the stairs and escorted them up.

No one saw them except Mr. Lane, working in the projection booth. He really didn't care where these young rebels sat, as long as they were quiet.

They were quiet, and they all enjoyed the movie. The same kids who had desegregated the school, the Downtown Cafe, the football team, the band and everyday life today desegregated the Starlight. But it was a secret for now.

At other places in town, snakes were moving with very evil intentions.

THE OLDEST SNAKE STRIKES

The old spirit snake waited in the shadows for the frog to arrive. It would be the frog that would strike for him. But there was no doubt that the old spirit had set this play in motion and was directing the players towards an ugly final scene. This old spirit had once been a good man with a good life, but anger and hatred had now eliminated any goodness. This darkness had begun over one hundred years before this night. The old spirit had little memory of better times, happier times. There had been happy times, but the events of a great and tragic war had set in motion everything that led to this night of murder.

From the time Froggy saw the revealing photos of Janet and Bert and then left home, he was alone and confused. On Thursday and Friday night, he had slept in his truck, hiding in old spots around Fair Creek Park. During the day, with his truck well hidden, he walked in the woods around the park and around old fishing spots. The quiet woods allowed him to grieve and think. He was torn. One side of him wanted to just leave town and be done forever. Another side wanted to strike back. Bert had been a friend since childhood, but now an overwhelming and consuming hatred and anger were blazing in Froggy's soul. When Froggy thought of Janet he felt an overwhelming and crushing pain in his chest. He felt betrayed and rejected; it hurt terribly. When he thought of Bert, anger overwhelmed him. Froggy was simply overflowing with a desire to inflict pain and revenge. But there was still a part of him that just wanted to get away from the pain and the anger.

Late Saturday afternoon, he was walking through the park and heard Mike and Lee talking, heading home to get ready for their big night at the movies. He cared little for their specific plans; he didn't even take notice of the fact that Mike was fishing with this black boy. But it did irritate him that anyone seemed to be having a good time. Soon after, Froggy went to his truck and made a choice. The old sergeant made some suggestions, too.

Froggy drove straight to Bert's Esso.

He knew Bert's general routines and what time he closed on Saturdays. Froggy drove down the back alley off Scenic Drive so as not to be seen. He quietly parked beside Bert's old Plymouth and waited.

Froggy wasn't nervous or scared; he was very focused, and barely able to contain his rage. He sat in his truck taking deep breaths and slowly releasing them. He was actually beginning to have a little doubt about his plan, but his mind kept returning to the photographs. Froggy leaned forward and placed both hands on the dash. He closed his eyes and made one last decision.

Froggy grabbed the crowbar from his floorboard. He walked from the truck and stood beside the back door so that he wouldn't be seen as Bert left the building. He knew that Bert would pass through the back door. He waited, as a snake would wait, coiled, ready.

About the same time as Mike and Lee and the gang were settling in at the Starlight, Froggy saw the lights go out in the gas station. For a very brief second, Froggy considered dropping the tool and running, but a voice floated to him: "Finish!"

The door opened, and Bert stepped out, keys in hand. As Bert was turning to lock the door, he saw a very odd sight. There appeared to be two floating, yellow eyes staring at him.

This got his attention—it was very odd, to say the least. He turned towards the floating eyes and cocked his head, as if he were trying to sort out a puzzle. This distraction turned him away from Froggy and made sure that he didn't see Froggy step towards him. Froggy struck—a hard blow across the back of Bert's head. Bert never saw it coming. He was instantly unconscious. He fell against the door and slid down awkwardly. Froggy pulled him back by the pants leg and delivered a second strike, using both hands.

Froggy walked backwards away from Bert, wiping blood from his hands and face. He threw the crowbar into the truck bed, got in and slowly drove away.

After a matter of seconds, Bert's legs gave a few final twitches and his last breath escaped slowly. The massive blunt trauma and cranial bleeding quickly claimed his life.

THE SNAKE CRAWLS AWAY

Froggy drove away, back down the same alley, not caring if anyone saw him. He was heading south. For good. As he reached the south side of town, he stopped at the Trailways bus station. He had no intentions of taking a bus; he just wanted to use the phone at the outside phone booth. He called Janet.

Janet had been home all day, crying. Her sister had come to stay with her.

"Froggy, Froggy," she begged. "Please come home!"

"No, it is not a home for me now."

"Froggy, I am so sorry," she said, her hoarse, dry voice muffled by sobs.

"I'm leaving for good."

More sobs. "Froggy, please, please come home."

"I killed Bert. It's all over."

At this, Janet dropped the phone and collapsed into her sister's arms.

Froggy made a second call, to the police, to report a murder. The night dispatcher, an overweight retired deputy named Fred Dobbs, had never taken such a strange call. Mostly he spent his shifts eating cookies, reading magazines—if they had good pictures—and taking naps. Not much happened most nights.

This night, he was working through a bag of chocolate chip

cookies with his feet on the desk, looking through an old Field & Stream. When the phone rang, he dropped his cookie and almost turned the chair over backwards. "Well, shit fire and save matches!" He grabbed the phone and, spitting wet crumbs on the receiver, said, "Pulaski County Sheriff's Office."

"Send someone to Bert's Esso. There has been a crime. Look behind the building."

"Who is this?"

"A citizen of the community."

"What's your name?"

"Send someone to Bert's Esso. There has been a crime. Look behind the building."

With a click, the phone went dead.

"Big Bob will love this," Fred said, reaching for the microphone of his desktop radio.

BIG BOB INVESTIGATES WITH
SPIRITUAL ADVICE

For much of this Snake Moon Saturday, Big Bob had been sitting in his cruiser near Good Times. On Saturday nights he would often hide near the club and pull over patrons, almost all young black men, as they would leave. Over the years the sheriff had worked out a profitable deal. Word was out that if you would just palm the sheriff a couple of twenties, he would let you go. If you didn't slip him the cash, you stood a good chance of getting a nightstick whooping for resisting arrest. Occasionally Big Bob would just beat the crap out of somebody anyway. Beating the crap out of young black men relieved his tension headaches far better than aspirin ever could.

The radio crackled and the voice of the dispatcher followed: "Sheriff Willet, you got your ears on?"

This was about as formal as it got for Big Bob and his crew. "Yeah, Fred," he said. "What you got?" Big Bob was relieved that it wasn't the voice of his haint.

"Someone said there was a crime behind Bert's Esso."

"Who said?"

"He did not ID hisself."

"Figures. Ten-four, I'm on my way. I'll let you know if I need help."

"Ten-four."

"Oh ten-four my ass. Just eat a damn cookie and don't say

208

anything to anyone unless I tell you to!"

Big Bob drove to the gas station and as he did his guts began to tighten up. Ever since he had set out the pictures for the spirit, he'd been very worried that Froggy would learn about Janet's affair and perhaps cause trouble. But he had only expected a drunken Froggy to start a fight or something like that.

As Big Bob pulled in the front of the old gas station, he saw absolutely nothing. The lights were out and everything looked fine. The radio buzzed again. This time it was the deep voice of the old demon: "Drive to the backside," it said. "I will be there."

This command, delivered in that low, guttural voice, filled Big Bob with fear and dread. He felt a wave of nausea as he smelled the old demon soldier. But he drove around to the back like he was told.

In the weird light and shadows of the cruiser's headlights, Big Bob could see a crumpled body. He knew the jacket and clothes well enough to know it was Bert without getting closer. He could also see the blood spatter on the door and wall. This had been a vicious hit.

As Big Bob got out of the cruiser, he saw the glowing eyes of Andy Thomas off to the right.

He walked quietly to the body, shaking his big head. Andy approached him quietly and his dirty smile was obvious.

Big Bob felt like he had to take charge. "I'll start the deputies looking for Froggy," he said.

"You are an idiot. We care nothing for Froggy. Let him go."

"Isn't this what you wanted?"

"Yes... but I'll tell you what to do from here. I'm not sure if you're lazy or stupid, or a special combination of both."

Big Bob followed instructions. He opened the back door and left it open. Bert had dropped the keys, attached by a small chain to the cash bag, by the door when he was hit. Andy's eyes glowed a bright yellow as he pointed at the body. "Take his watch and his wallet."

The sheriff did so. Next, he was instructed to ransack the inside of the gas station, like a thief in a hurry. "Open the vending machines and take the coins," Andy said. "Take a few pop bottles and bags of potato chips and some of the candy. Take these things to your car and hide them."

The sheriff did so, his every move deepening his involvement in this conspiracy. He didn't consider resisting, but he did realize that he was entering into dangerous territory. The thought briefly occurred to him that there was no way out of this, but he continued anyway—he wanted to get his revenge, no matter the consequences.

"I'll give you more instructions tomorrow," Andy told him. "Now call this in on the device and get other lawmen here! Remember, they do not know of the link to Froggy or to Janet. Play dumb, Sheriff. You're good at it. Act naturally."

This finally angered Big Bob. He reached for his gun, vowing he was going to end this strange man. As he reached his pistol, it became glowing red-hot. It burned his hand and he instantly let go, screaming, "Damn you!"

"Yes, and you too, Sheriff!"

The stench and the old soldier faded.

Within the half hour, deputies, state police and agents from the Georgia Bureau of Investigation were on the site. Things like this just didn't happen in Hawkinsville. Members of Big Bob's posse were very much shaken. It would be easy to play on their prejudice and bigotry.

Trooper Larry Wayne represented the state police. As Larry walked around the scene with his flashlight, he took in the detail. He and the GBI officer shared subtle glances. The GBI man had a camera and took some photos.

It was obvious there had been two blows and that the body was dragged after the first strike. There were clearly two splatter patterns, one for each strike. There were no signs of a fight or struggle, and Bert's hands were clean, showing no sign

210

of defensive injuries.

Larry had been to the scene of many break-ins and robberies. It was rare for a common thief to murder like this. Bert hadn't surprised the thief—he had been ambushed. Why? The sheriff had laid out the suspected sequence of events, but the timeline didn't seem right to Larry. He made a mental note to check the radio logbooks later.

He started to ask Big Bob some questions but decided not to. He knew he wouldn't get a straight answer anyway, and he didn't want to make Big Bob suspicious. Larry's intuition told him something was wrong; this was far more than the reactions of a scared robber. So, why not let Big Bob keep thinking he's smarter than the average bear.

He looked at Big Bob. The sheriff was sitting on the tailgate of an old Ford truck, nursing his burned hand. Larry decided not to ask about the burn. The many headlights, flashing police lights and flashlights created a strange effect of bleached faces and moving and fading shadows. Big Bob was sweating profusely, drops beading on his face, his shirt soaked.

Larry thought, Well, now I have seen a hog sweat.

He shined his flashlight right into the sheriff's face and said, after a few seconds' pause, "Bob, let me know if you need help. I'll be in touch."

Big Bob didn't even acknowledge Larry.

Larry soon left and let the local guys clean up. He wondered about Bert Jr., and knew by instinct that none of the local police had thought to contact him. Probably for the best: Larry didn't enjoy this part of the job, but he did want to be sure it was done properly.

Deputy Elkins helped Larry get it done. To Larry, the deputy seemed very shocked and very quiet. Too quiet maybe. Deputy Elkins had always been a very quiet and efficient officer. He tried to do a good job, which was out of character for one of Big Bob's posse. But Larry had taken notice of

Deputy Elkins.

Maybe Larry wasn't the only lawman who doubted Big Bob?

SWEET MOMMA AND ANDY

At about the same time the kids were enjoying the movie and Larry was leaving Bert's Esso, Sweet Momma was rocking on the porch, accompanied only by the sounds of crickets chirping and frogs croaking. She knew where Lee was, but she didn't know where Arthur was and that was always troubling.

Momma became aware that all sound had stopped. It was a very cold feeling. And, for the first time, she smelled death.

She was filled with fear. Something—not someone, but something—was standing in her yard. "You should leave my house," she said. "I serve the Lord."

"Not for much longer, old lady," Andy Thomas said.

"Leave me."

The old spirit laughed. "You will be gone soon and I'm here to tell you that you and your boys will suffer. I will destroy them. Before you leave this old world, you will hurt."

"You should leave all these boys alone. You've already caused too many good boys to suffer."

Just a low dirty laugh was Andy's response. Andy's heart had long ago turned dark. He was good at bringing pain and suffering. And now he had a chance to hurt many people at once.

Sweet Momma quickly continued. "I have helpers, too!"

"That old man is nothing," Andy said. "He has no power."

"There are others, both the living and the long dead."

"It has begun, old lady, and you will pay!"

"You have made us all pay—too much, too long—and you need to leave."

The noises of the Southern night returned. It was clear to Momma what she must do, but she just couldn't see how to do it. Who could she trust? Who would help her? She thought about the trust Ruth Anne Thomas clearly put in Larry Wayne, and wondered if she should do the same.

But why would Larry, or anyone else, believe her and not think she was just a crazy old woman? Yet she felt a trickle of hope, a little light shining. "Oh Lord, help me with this," she said. "Make that man listen to me!"

It was so hard for even the good Sweet Momma to trust a white man with a badge.

THE NEWS SPREADS—
SUNDAY IN HAWKINSVILLE

Sundays in these small Southern towns in the early autumn usually were quiet days centered around family, church services and maybe a football game on television. Even the cruise circuit was quiet. But on this Sunday, there was a big local story. Word spread by telephone and through the churches. There were very few businesses open, but by noon the majority of the townspeople knew about the murder of Bert Andrews.

Larry had stopped by late Saturday evening and told Ruth Anne and Mike what had happened. Neither Mike nor his mom slept very well. Mike remembered how he had felt after the huge storm just a week earlier. He was afraid some fight would begin, a struggle that would draw in many of the people he knew and loved. He didn't understand how, but this killing seemed connected to that struggle.

Mike broke the news to Becky and Suzy just before Sunday school. There were no text messages, email, Facebook, Twitter, or even cellphones then; only direct word of mouth. Archaic. But somehow the news spread. It was on the local radio and even the TV news by Sunday evening.

Big Bob was hiding away in his patrol car by the river. He had not slept at all and tried to catch a few winks. He felt like he was trapped in a very bad place. But he had more work to do. One thing he couldn't hide from was the demon Andy Thomas. There was no escape.

The sheriff, on instructions from the old sergeant, had gone to see Paul Foss.

"Tomorrow during school," Big Bob said, "I want you to place this wallet in Arthur Sanderson's locker and these candy bars and rolls of quarters in Lee Sanderson's locker. Get this done well before lunch."

The wizard nodded. Snakes were on the move again.

"Plant this bank bag and keys in the weeds along the Low Road behind the Lilac Road Church."

Again the wizard nodded, no questions asked.

"Is your big firecracker ready?"

The sheriff later drove up Lilac Road towards Good Times to hire an "eyewitness." This was all too easy, with just a little bit of money.

Smokey Wright was a longtime customer and sometimes assistant of the Good Times club. He was dirt poor, and so Big Bob could get almost any story or deed from him for no more than five bucks. Today he showed Smokey a ten-dollar bill. Oh my! Smokey was sitting in the shade on an old oak chair in front of the little shack he called home. The little shack was near Good Times, in a small grove of peach trees, a long-lost orchard.

Big Bob waved the bill and said, "Tomorrow morning, you call the office and say that you saw Gone Sanderson walking on the Low Road carrying a bag. And, you say that he was flashing a lot of cash Saturday night at the club."

"Okay," Smokey said.

"Do this and I'll get you much more than just ten dollars. Do you understand what to do?"

Smokey nodded. If he had any worries about what he was getting into, he didn't show it. Big Bob had always taken care of him. There was no need to worry.

Being a dirty cop was hard work. Bob needed to get home

and drink himself to sleep.

A STRANGE PLACE FOR A WIZARD

On that same Sunday evening, Mike was riding his bike down Lilac Road. He had been to Becky's to study and visit, though not exactly in that order of importance. It had been a sad, quiet day. Mike wasn't sure why he felt so down. Even Becky's smile and soft hands didn't lift his spirits. Of course, the murder was upsetting, but there seemed to be a dark cloud hanging over the town that he couldn't describe or understand.

Mike was gliding along Lilac Road, nearing the church, eyes down. He was not singing.

Suddenly, he felt the familiar burst of cool air on his face, and he heard a voice, the very familiar voice of an old man, say, "Look behind the church!"

Mike came to a quick stop, startled by the voice. He looked past the church but all he saw was a truck. It took him a few minutes to recognize the truck. This recognition overcame his apprehension. This was strange; it made no sense. The truck belonged to Mr. Foss.

"Why is he here?" he muttered to himself.

Mike started to head towards the truck, but the voice on the breeze stopped him: "Go home, now!" it demanded.

Mike did so. The voice was familiar, but he still wasn't sure who it belonged to. He looked around again but didn't see anyone. He would make a note to remember Mr. Foss's truck:

maybe it would prove important.

Mike didn't see the wizard himself because he was hiding in the woods, waiting—for dark, when he could sneak up and place the firecracker under Sweet Momma's porch.

PART 9
ARRESTS—MONDAY

PHONE CALLS—WEAVING THE WEB

On Monday morning, just about the same time that first period geometry class was beginning, a very sleepy, still hungover Smokey Wright walked, very slowly, from his shack to the back door of the Good Times club. The place was deserted on weekdays, especially early in the mornings, when Smokey would take out trash, sweep and clean. Smokey's cleaning job was his only source of income. He lived on food scraps from the club and spent the money on beer. It would be difficult to say that Smokey really cleaned, but the clientele of Good Times didn't complain. And if someone did, Eddie Joe Tate, the owner of the club and chief bartender, would point to the janitor's closet and say, "Help yourself, partner!"

Smokey would often refer to himself as the assistant manager. The dancers, mostly teenage runaways from Atlanta, called him "Boss Daddy." Smokey liked this nickname, and would return the favor by doing little things like bringing food or drinks to the girls. Smokey knew what it was like to be young and on your own; he had been living by himself since he was twelve. Smokey didn't have any enemies, but he was about to place himself in a bad situation, and he knew that the local law enforcement would just as soon see him disappear.

Smokey grabbed a cold Blue Ribbon and sat at the bar, which was solid oak with a dark finish, showing the wear and tear of decades in service. But it was still very strong and sturdy. Smokey had pulled up over the old rotary dial phone. Although Smokey couldn't read, he did know numbers; up to about a hundred, anyway. He could read the phone number of the police station, printed on the calendar hanging on the wall by the bar. The sheriff always gave calendars to good voters, especially those that paid him to look the other way. Smokey dialed the number and waited for an answer.

Because Janet Allen had not returned to work, nor ever would, Big Bob and the deputies were answering calls themselves. The office was a noisy, chaotic mess, with reporters, worried citizens and other law enforcement groups milling around and asking lots of questions. All this commotion annoyed Big Bob. His temper was shorter than usual, and he hadn't slept much. He was waiting on the call from Smokey, growing nervous about his plan and wanting to get on with things. Right now, everything depended on the phone call from Smokey. But the reporters and others in his office were asking him question after question, and he knew that repeating "No comments on an ongoing investigation!" wasn't going to work for long.

The sheriff knew who had killed Bert and he knew what was going to happen, so he wasn't investigating very much of anything. After all, he had set the whole thing in motion himself. Big Bob picked up the phone when Smokey called. "Sheriff's Office, Pulaski County."

After a few seconds of silence, Smokey cleared his throat. He was tempted to just hang up and not have to deal with this trouble. But he needed the cash. He was a sick man and needed his medicine. He didn't have the energy to change his ways, not now. Finally, he spoke. "Sheriff Willet, this is Smokey Wright, assistant manager of Good Times."

"What is it, Smokey? I'm busy as hell."

"I heard Bert Andrews was robbed and murdered Saturday night."

"And?"

"Well, I see'd two things that you might want to hear about."

"Go on, hurry up!"

"When I's walkin' home from Fair Creek, I'd been thinkin' about goin' fishin'," he said. "Then I seen Gone Sanderson on early Saturday evening, carryin' a tote sack, running along the Low Road. Gone sure was hurryin'. He was headed toward his house."

"Okay. Anything else?"

"He sure is fast!"

"Anything else, Smoky?"

Smokey hesitated, feeling a hint of caution. Maybe this was all wrong. He liked Gone Sanderson. But the need for the cash ruled his conscience.

Big Bob was growing aggravated and his patience was wearing thin.

"Anything else about what?" Smokey said. "When do I get the rest of the money?"

"Smokey, damn it, did you see Gone at the club later on Saturday night?"

"Oh yeah," Smokey said. "He sure did have a big wad of cash. Girls was all over him."

"Okay. I'll see you later."

The sheriff hung up the phone. He had heard everything he needed—and expected—to hear. He proceeded to complete the warrants that he had already started – knowing that Smokey would call.

Smokey was telling the truth about the girls and Gone, but that was always the case, he didn't need a big wad of cash.

The wizard had placed the evidence in the Sanderson brothers' lockers, before school started on Monday, just as he had been instructed. He had slipped into the cafeteria carrying a small satchel. Isaiah James had seen him and thought it very odd. But he said nothing for now.

Larry and Sweet Momma

That same Monday morning, Momma'd had a bad feeling at the breakfast table. Lee had made coffee, fried ham and eggs and half-decent biscuits. Sometimes he would get them a little too done, but not today. Momma never complained anyway, but Gone sure would have.

The talk at the table was about nothing much, except that Gone liked to kid his younger brother about Mandy Ross. In truth, he was a little jealous of Lee because Mandy wouldn't give Gone the time of day. Lee could give as good as he got. But Lee and Gone were very close, although they had different personalities and were just different people. It wouldn't be long before Lee would have to assume the role of mother.

As Lee and Gone prepared to leave for school, both wrapped ham biscuits to take along, and Lee took an extra one for Mike. Both young men hugged their grandmother and left out the front door. The noisy banter and banging was gone, and all was quiet as Momma settled into her rocker, sipping coffee and worrying. She was getting all too good at worrying. She was very afraid that the fight was beginning, and she wanted desperately to talk to someone. Her first thought this morning had been of Reverend Ross. But she wasn't sure if even he could do anything. She didn't need a sermon. A prayer would be good, but not just yet.

"Let's not trouble the good Lord until we know what we

are asking for!" she said to herself. But maybe that's it! she thought. "Oh Lord in heaven, help me figure it out!" she said. "I seem to be forgettin' a lot of stuff."

Shortly thereafter a thought came as clear as a church bell on Easter Sunday. She remembered her thoughts about a helper after her run-in with the soldier spirit on Saturday night. Momma needed to make a phone call.

Momma's world had drawn down to very simple since she'd lost her vision. She could still sense sunlight and enjoyed her good south-facing window on these days, sitting in the rocker her grandmother had padded long ago. She was wearing a pink sweater and had covered herself with an old embroidered afghan decorated with pink dogwood flowers surrounded by small redbud flowers on white wool. Her grandmother had spun the wool to make the cover. It was old, soft and warm and was truly a comforter in every sense of the word. She could no longer see the detail, but she knew it and she felt it. She remembered sitting on her grandmother's lap, snuggled in this very same comforter. Miss Ellie had been a very special person.

Lee had fixed a table on her right for her coffee cup, her Bible and a picture of her husband and children. She remembered every tiny detail of that picture. On her left was the telephone table, on which she would usually lean her cane. Even though she couldn't see, she usually had the television on, or the radio.

Momma picked up the phone and very carefully dialed the number, counting each finger hole to get it right. After two misdials, she got the right number.

"Dr. Roberts's office, how may I help you?"

"May I speak to Mrs. Thomas?"

After a moment, Ruth Anne picked up.

"Ruth Anne, this is Ivy Sanderson."

"Momma, are you okay?" Ruth Anne asked. "Do you need help?"

227

"No, No, child, I'm fine. Unless you have a miracle pill to get back my sight?"

Both women laughed.

"I wish I did," Ruth Anne said. "I would run it over to you myself. But Momma, what do you need?"

"I need to be about forty-five years younger."

Again, they both laughed.

"Ruth Anne, how can I get in touch with your friend Larry Wayne? I need to speak to him, but I need to keep it quiet."

"Well, you can call the state police office in Macon."

"No, I don't want any official reports. Can I trust him?"

"Of course, absolutely, by all means! Larry's a saint."

"Can you get him to come see me?"

"I'll try. I can call his dispatch office and tell him I need to see him."

"Please do. He can come anytime, but he must come alone!"

"Can I come, too?"

"Sweetie, you can come see me any other time, but I need to see your trooper alone. I promise I won't steal him!"

After they hung up, Ruth Anne followed through, asking Larry if he could stop by the office and saying nothing about Sweet Momma. Larry showed up half an hour later, and Ruth Anne quickly ushered him back to an exam room.

After she stole a quick kiss, she told him about the call from Sweet Momma, urging him to get straight to her house. He agreed,

"Ok, I'll go on and go now."

The trooper stole another kiss, winked and left.

Trooper Wayne had been cruising the Pulaski County highways all morning and it was getting on towards noon. He had been mostly thinking of ways to dig deeper into this murder. He believed the robbery was a decoy and that someone had wanted only to kill Bert. But he knew of no motive. Everyone liked Bert; he was your typical small-town

Southern boy, no more, no less. His flaws were largely a byproduct of the time and culture.

Larry had very little respect for the sheriff; he didn't trust Big Bob and had every reason to doubt his police work. It seemed possible to Larry that the sheriff might even have had a hand in this. But what was his angle? Why? Larry couldn't figure out a connection: he had lots of suspicions but no evidence and no good ideas.

Larry planned that afternoon to meet with state investigators. The murder was all over the news. He really wanted to get the call logs from the sheriff's office, but he had to be subtle about it. Big Bob was good at hiding things and keeping information close to the vest. Larry also knew that Bert had been part of the sheriff's informal posse. This was just too much of a puzzle, and it all could easily turn into a legal jurisdiction fight, with Larry being shut out.

But there had been a terribly violent, gruesome murder, and these kinds of crimes needed to be solved. A killer was free somewhere in the community.

Larry pulled up in front of the Sanderson home. He had considered taking Reverend Amos Ross with him, but Ruth Anne had said to go alone.

It was quiet as he got out of the car, not much wind. The grass was a bit long, and the azaleas and the other flowers were fading and dying, just like the summer. As Trooper Wayne walked up onto the porch he was singing a Merle Haggard tune: "I turned twenty-one in prison..."

Larry was curious but relaxed. He had no idea what Sweet Momma needed to see him about, but he figured it was hard for her to invite a state patrol officer into her home—he knew interactions between her family and lawmen had not gone well over the years.

Sweet Momma had every reason to be scared, but she chose to just trust the good Lord. Things needed changing.

"... doin' life without parole," Larry sang. He knocked on

the door, firmly. "Hello in the house!"

"Come on in!" Momma called. "But stop singin'. I hate that song!"

The command surprised Larry and got his attention. He walked in and crossed over to the rocking chair. Momma sat up to greet Larry.

"Hello, Mrs. Sanderson. Do you remember me. I'm Lar—"

"Nobody this side of heaven calls me Mrs. Sanderson!" Momma cut in. "Just call me Momma!"

"Yes, ma'am. I'm Trooper Larry Wayne."

Larry was uncomfortable being in a house with a blind person. He had addressed Sweet Momma as Mrs. Sanderson simply out of respect.

"Is that what your momma called you?" she asked.

"No," he said. "Just Larry most of the time. I knew I was in trouble if she called me Larry Edgar Wayne."

"I'll call you Larry. I want to be like a good mother and give you some advice."

"Well, that's good. My mother always looked after me."

"Have you had dinner?"

"No, ma' am, but I'm okay. I'll get something to eat later."

"There is some biscuits and ham on the stove. Cornbread too. You help yourself."

"Thank you, but no thanks."

"Larry, I can hear your stomach talking!"

"Okay, okay," he said.

Larry walked back to the kitchen through the long dining room. He noted the family pictures that must have gone back nearly one hundred years. He also saw the framed Bible verses. The dining room table was oak, simple but elegant, covered with a plain white tablecloth. As Larry walked into the kitchen he spotted an old wood stove, very well-kept. It was no longer in use; the sterile white electric stove was against the far wall. But the old stove had character and strength. It said that although time may move on, it would never go anywhere.

Larry spotted the cornbread in an iron skillet on the old stove. Just as his mind formed the question, Momma called out, "There's good, cold buttermilk in the icebox."

Larry pounced on it: this was going to be the best lunch he'd had in a long time. Momma directed him to a quart-sized mason jar. He crumbled the day-old cornbread into the jar, then drowned it with cold buttermilk. He grabbed a big spoon and returned to the living room, then sat in a chair beside Momma and engaged in the feast.

"Cornbread and buttermilk sho' is good, ain't it?" Momma said.

"Yes, ma'am!" Between bites, Larry said, "Ruth Anne said you wanted to see—I mean, uh, talk to me?"

Larry blushed over his slip but Momma just cackled. "Well, she's right. I wish I could see you! Ruth Anne said you're a fine-lookin' man!"

Larry's mild red went to deep scarlet.

"Larry, I can hear you blushin'." Sweet Momma laughed again and then settled back in her chair. "I do want to talk to you. I'm very afraid, and I need to know someone will look for the truth."

"I'll do my best, but—"

Momma held up her hand and kept going. "Some folk, like our wonderful sheriff, bless his black little heart, will use a little truth to cover a big lie. Others like him have done the same through the years, usually to hurt people. Especially young black men."

"Yes, ma'am, you're right about that. But do you know something I should know?"

"I know that, in some way, this murder and all of this ugliness will be used to hurt my boys."

"How so?"

"I dunno."

"Then what can I do?"

231

"Don't know yet."

"Yet?"

"Not yet."

"Well... when will you know?"

"Don't know."

"How will you find out?"

"Don't know."

"Who will tell you?"

"Don't know."

Larry was quiet for a good minute. Where was this going? Momma rocked. Larry stared at the jar, clinking his spoon and thinking. Then he exhaled, communicating his frustration to the sightless woman.

Momma cleared her throat and said, "Bad manners to clink your spoon!"

"You know that?"

"Yes, I do know that."

"Okay, so, we've established the fact that I have bad manners while eating buttermilk and cornbread. What else can we establish? If we can't establish anything else, I can't help you."

"I can establish that you're getting huffy with me."

Larry sat back, took a deep breath and smiled. "You're right, and I apologize. Let's start over. Please?"

"That's better."

"I'm ready to listen."

"Very good, son," she said. "You are a fine young man, I can tell. If that were not true, Ruth Anne wouldn't waste her time on you. But it's hard for me to trust any lawman. My family has had some hard history with your kind. Arthur and Lee lost their father to the murderous Klan and that sheriff, Big Bob. They know who killed their father. Can you imagine how much that hurts them, and how hard it is to not be angry all the time?"

This stunned Larry, and he didn't know how to respond.

Momma rocked quietly and placed her finger on her cheek, deep in thought. Finally, she spoke, and her great wisdom and experience poured out. "I know that a demon of hatred will lie, and use those lies to destroy lives. The lies will seem so believable. Too many people want to believe the lie. I need to know that you will continue to look for the truth."

"I will," he said. "But I wish I knew more. I'm confused, Momma."

"Yes, the demon confuses as well as lies. Confusion and lies are one and the same. Just keep looking. Please help me protect my boys."

"I will."

"The demon will strike very soon, but if we can find the lie and show the truth, then we will win."

"Do you know of any reason either Arthur or Lee could be involved in this?"

"No, God in heaven, no! And don't you ask me that ever again! "

"Is there anything you can tell me?"

"Ruth Anne is a wonderful, beautiful woman. She will make a wonderful wife."

Larry blushed again.

"You blush easy, boy."

"Is there anything else you can tell me?"

"I can tell you that old top hog Big Bob will make a move soon. We are under a snake moon. Just promise me you won't believe his lies and that you'll keep looking."

"That I will promise to you. I'll do my best."

"And I meant what I said about Ruth Anne."

"I know you're right," he said. "But nobody knows we're going to get married except Ruth Anne and me. Did she tell you?"

"No, she ain't told me nothin'. I was just having some fun with you. But I thought you might slip something out. I promise I won't say anything to Ruth Anne! Is there anything else you want to ask me?"

"Can you teach me to make cornbread?"

Momma laughed again, raising both hands over her head. "Laws of mercy, yes!" she said. "You come back anytime and I'll show you."

As Larry drove away, he thought about how this had been the strangest conversation he'd ever had. Larry, like almost everyone else, liked Sweet Momma. She was always fun to talk to. But Larry wondered if she still had control of all her mental faculties. Larry's only conclusion was that Sweet Momma was very worried about Gone and Lee. Just maybe she knew something about this crime?

Larry was mostly worried about how he didn't yet know what to worry about - or how he could help Momma's boys.

But even stranger conversations were in his future. "Strange" would soon take on a whole new meaning.

ARRESTS

Not long after leaving the Sanderson home, as Larry drove by the Lilac Road church, he received a call to proceed to the sheriff's office. Warrants for arrest had been issued and an arrest operation was to begin soon. Larry had planned to visit Ruth Anne again, but instead he turned to go downtown. At the sheriff's office, Big Bob, three deputies, two state police officers and Larry were crowded into a room with the county prosecutor. Big Bob stepped up and laid out the plan. "Based on information received by my office and evidence recovered in a field investigation," he said, "we have obtained warrants for the arrest of two suspects.

"One, Arthur Sanderson, will be arrested for second-degree murder and armed robbery.

"Two, Lee Sanderson, will be arrested as a suspected accomplice and for concealing evidence. Further, we have warrants to search their school lockers and proceed with questioning based on any evidence found.

"We will enter the school by the library side door. The principal will meet us there. We will proceed first to Arthur Sanderson's class and make the arrest. Trooper Wayne, will you cooperate with us?"

Larry's heart was in his throat. Could this be right? "Of course. How can I help?"

"When we reach the school, go with Mr. Penner to the

science class and be sure Lee Sanderson stays put. Once the older Sanderson brother is secured and cuffed, we will do the same with Lee Sanderson. Once these arrests are complete, we will search their lockers. The principal and assistant principal will assist and escort us through the school. Any questions?"

Only Larry spoke up. "Can you share the evidence with us? I would like to know why and for what reasons I'm about to destroy these young men's lives."

"No, not now," Big Bob said. "I'll brief you later with the prosecutors present, after the arrests are made. But, believe me, the evidence is solid."

Big Bob and Sam Elkins had located Bert's bank bag and keychain in the brush along the Low Road in an amazingly quick and productive search—though it had helped to know exactly where Paul Foss had placed this "evidence." Sam had found it strange that Big Bob waltzed into the bushes and found the bag in less than a minute. But he'd said nothing.

Larry also said nothing. For now, it was pointless to do anything but serve the warrants and make the arrests. Questions could come later. Larry was almost sick to his stomach; he felt he had already dropped his promise to Momma.

But Larry had a second thought that worried him even more: Big Bob had a history of hurting suspects during the arrest process. Larry vowed to himself to intervene to protect the boys, if need be.

The chain of four squad cars went to the high school quietly so as not to draw too much attention. They parked by the library. Larry and Mr. Penner walked together to the science class, with Mr. Penner carrying a look of great sadness and apprehension. They did not talk as they walked. The few people they passed in the halls were surprised to see the state troopers. It wouldn't take long for stories to spread.

Gone Sanderson was stunned and surprised, and until the warrant was presented to him, he had no earthly idea why he was being cuffed. He was too surprised to resist. As he was led away, Coach Carter ran up the hall. "What in the holy hell is going on?" he shouted.

"Coach, I don't know," Gone said. "I haven't done anything!"

The officers ignored him and shoved past. Big Bob looked at Coach Carter and said, "Your star running back is a no-account, stupid, thieving, murdering colored boy. You really know how to pick 'em. I hope you are proud of yourself."

Coach Carter yelled to Gone, "Keep your head up, and be smart. I'll send help."

"Coach, please see to Momma and Lee," Gone said.

"I will, I promise!"

But Coach Carter felt terrible. He couldn't help but wonder if his decision to play Gone and the other black players had led to this. None of it made sense, but still he felt responsible. He stepped up and got in the sheriff's face. "Don't you hurt this boy," he said. "He's twice the man you are!"

Sheriff Willet snorted. "You're the big loser today, Coach."

The sheriff and a deputy then proceeded to the science class for the second arrest.

The Runner

When Mr. Foss saw the trooper outside his classroom door, he had a pretty good idea what was happening, but he feigned surprise and bewilderment. "You're here to arrest someone?"

Now how could he know that? Larry thought. I could be here for any number of reasons. He made a note to remember this moment.

His thoughts continued, constructing a puzzle, "We could be here to notify someone of an emergency or just to get information or even address a school discipline issue."

Larry did not act surprised at all, he was cool as could be. Inwardly he felt like he had found the key to the door. But he did not know what would be inside the door, not yet.

Soon Big Bob came down the hall with Deputy Elkins. Mr. Penner stood in the doorway as the lawmen moved into the class. The students sat with mouths dropped open, eyes wide. Big Bob pointed to Lee and said, "Lee Sanderson, stand and place your arms behind your back."

There were far less conspicuous ways to make an arrest, but Big Bob wanted to humiliate not just Lee, but Lee's friends—especially Mike Thomas.

The silence in the classroom was deafening. Then Becky spoke up: "Why in the world would you arrest Lee?"

Sherriff Willet snapped back, "Shut up, young lady, and

mind your own business!"

Mike jumped to his feet and stepped towards the sheriff, but Larry stepped between them. "Sit down, Mike!" he bellowed. "Now!"

Mike sat. He looked at Becky. She lifted her hand signaling him to keep his cool.

Big Bob just smirked, looking at Mike. "I'll take care of you later," he said. "Lee Sanderson, stand up now, boy."

Lee hesitated, but then stood slowly, his hands shaking. He was every bit as confused and surprised as Gone had been. Mandy began to cry softly and Becky moved to put her arm around her. Big Bob scowled at her. "Stay in your seat!" he commanded.

Defiantly, Becky stepped over and squeezed into Mandy's seat.

Larry wanted to get Lee out of the classroom as soon as he could, before things escalated further. He walked to Lee and said, "Hands behind your back, son. Let's go easy. Nobody needs to get hurt here."

Big Bob laughed. The wizard, Paul Foss, watched with a smirk. Meanwhile, Sam Elkins felt that something didn't add up here.

As Larry reached to cuff Lee, Lee turned to Mike, Mandy and Becky and very softly said, "Check on Momma."

Then Lee actually smiled and winked at Mike, who sat in stunned silence. Becky and Mandy saw the message. Becky nodded.

Mike was confused and hurt; he felt very threatened by this giant bully, Big Bob. Looking at Lee, he asked, "Lee, what on earth did you do?"

Lee deflated, and Mike felt instantly ashamed.

Big Bob hitched his pants up and laughed aloud. He stuck his nightstick in Mike's face, daring him to say more. "I told you to be careful about who you choose as friends," he said. "You don't listen very good, do you?"

Larry was torn: protect Mike or hold Lee? His hesitation lasted only seconds, but that was enough. Lee ripped his hands from Larry and exploded past Mr. Penner. Larry started to chase but tripped on a desk. He fell hard, cutting his eye on the corner of a desk.

Big Bob and Deputy Elkins followed Lee in a hurry, but those two hogs weren't going to chase anything very far. Larry got up slowly.

Mr. Foss also started to give chase, but Mr. Penner grabbed him and said, "Mr. Foss, kindly stay with your class."

Lee didn't slow down until he made it into the woods south of the school. The lawmen would assume he would head west, towards home, so instead he went south.

Mr. Penner followed a bleeding Larry out into the hallway. Larry smiled and quietly said, "I'm fine."

"I don't understand what's happening."

"Neither do I, yet. But I will. I can't help but feel glad that Lee got away."

"Me too," Mr. Penner said. "I'm worried for that boy."

"Me too - I'll find him later. Big Bob will be busy with his prisoner and he will put on a show for the press."

Larry had worries, too. He was concerned for Gone, but he'd do his best to make sure Gone was unharmed while in custody. But he was really worried for Lee. As a fugitive on the run, he could get hurt. He would need to find Lee to protect him. But why did he run?

Larry didn't realize how easy of a decision it had been for Lee. He wasn't about to let the man who murdered his father take him into custody. He saw a chance to run and he took it. But the only other people in that classroom that knew that story were Big Bob, and the Wizard.

But as he continued to make his way south through the woods, Lee wondered how he was going to get out of this mess. And hearing Mike assume he'd done something wrong was a crushing blow. Maybe Mandy had been right after all.

MIKE'S SHAME

Word spread quickly, and the rumors spun out of control: Gone Sanderson had killed Bert Andrews, some said; Lee had helped; Gone was locked up for good; Lee had punched a cop and was on the run, therefore he must be guilty as sin.

Mr. Penner had taken Mandy Ross to his office, where she waited for her father to come pick her up. Mike drifted slowly towards football practice, but he was listless and in shock, and felt both an incredible anger and sadness. He didn't yet realize the full severity of the charges and the situation. The magnitude of what had just happened was sinking in slowly. Mike was torn between going to practice and heading out to help Lee. But what could he do? What had Lee done to deserve arrest?

Several students passed Mike and either laughed out loud or shook their heads, just to be sure to let Mike know they thought him an idiot. Mike paid little attention. He was far more worried about what would happen to his fishing buddy and best friend. The look on Mike's face revealed a real sense of shame, but he wasn't ashamed of his friend, like people assumed: instead Mike felt ashamed and embarrassed for doubting Lee. He couldn't have done this, Mike thought. Mike was coming out of the shock and thinking more clearly.

Becky and Suzy pursued him down the hall. Becky walked up from behind Mike and took his arm, turning him towards her. "Mike, Lee will be okay," she said. "We know where he was on Saturday night. This will be okay."

"Probably so, but I'm very worried. This is tearing me up."

"It'll be okay, sweetheart. Please smile for me."

"I don't think I can manage a smile right now."

"Oh, please," she said. "This is breaking my heart too."

"Becky, I failed Lee," Mike said. "He will hate me now. I should've kept my big mouth shut."

"Mike, there was nothing you could have done."

"I should've kept my mouth shut. I should've let him know that I believe in him."

Suzy put her hand on her forehead and shook her head. "Mike, you can be so stupid. There was nothing you could have done to change what happened in that classroom."

"Maybe not, but..." he trailed off.

Becky squeezed Mike's hand and said, "Mike, this will absolutely not help Lee. We have to think clearly; there's no room for blame. Besides, this isn't our fault."

"Becky, I feel so bad. I... I should've spoken up, I should've said something to Lee to let him know I won't abandon him. I should've let him know that I'm his friend. I sat there like a rock and then asked a stupid question. Now I know how Saint Peter felt when Jesus was arrested."

"Oh, good Lord!" Suzy said.

Becky reached up and pinched Mike's ear, hard. Mike was startled and pulled back, but Becky would not let go. She stepped in closer and said, "Mike, if Lee thought you had abandoned him and weren't his friend, why did he ask you to check on Mrs. Sanderson?"

Mike had forgotten that request. While it didn't take away his worry for his friend, it did provide a little relief. Mike lowered his head and smiled, just a little. "I didn't think about that."

Becky released his ear and laid her hand on his cheek. "I know, sugar. That's why I'm here. Thank God!"

Suzy laughed and said, "Mike the Apostle, you better get to practice before my daddy crucifies us all."

A VERY MISERABLE PRACTICE

As the football team took the practice field, every coach and player felt the loss and sensed the great change. The players, to a man, felt like they had lost brothers in Gone and Lee. A few weeks earlier, many of the white players had never spoken directly to a black person, and many of the black players had never spoken to a white person. Now they were becoming a family of sorts. And Coach Carter needed to be the father today. Today was not about good footwork, good blocking techniques or snap-count discipline. Today was about coping with the loss so that life could continue.

These young men proceeded quietly through warmups and agility drills. There was no passion, no competitive fire. There was no laughter, no yelling or joking around. The coaches tried to bring this out, but their efforts also lacked zeal. Monday practices were usually very low key and relaxed anyway; the team wore shorts and T-shirts, and no pads, only helmets. There was no contact. It was just a day to loosen up, run drills and receive specific instruction. Sometimes the team reviewed game films. But today Coach Carter sensed that these young men needed something different. He aborted practice and told his players to follow him into the locker room. The team jogged together into the field house; the coaches followed.

Inside, the team was quiet as Coach Carter drew them into

a circle. "Boys," he began, "I wish I could say something to make you feel better and help us all understand some of this. I am hurting as much, maybe more, than you are. Also, I don't know how this will turn out. Gone and Lee are still our teammates. I still have faith in them. I also have faith in you.

"This will be hard, but we will fight on together."

Coach Carter paused and took a deep breath; this reminded him so much of addressing his Marines whenever they lost good buddies in Korea. It tugged at his heart as he thought of his son, Adam, in Vietnam.

"I want you to go home and tell your mother and father you love them. I usually don't give football players much homework, but I want you to write down five things you are thankful for; five things that are good in your life. One of my five is the chance—no, the blessing—to be your coach. We've made great progress already this year. No one can take that away. We are a good team. Tomorrow we will practice like a good team. My expectations of you and for you have not changed. They will never change."

Coach Carter paused and looked around at all of his players. Every eye was on him.

"Does anyone have anything to say?"

Ray stood and faced Coach Carter. "I do!"

"Go ahead, Ray. Turn and face your team."

Ray turned and looked around at his teammates. He wore a look of anger and determination. "If anyone says anything bad about Gone or Lee or anyone else, I will personally kick your ass."

Everyone was shocked, eyes wide open and with dropped jaws.

"What Ray is saying," Coach Carter cut in, "is that outside of this team, just don't talk to anyone about this. Keep it in the team. And Ray? If anybody kicks anybody else's ass, it'll be me. Do you understand?"

Ray gulped, with a tear in his eye, and said, "Yes, sir."

Coach Carter pulled his team into a tight huddle. "Let's have a silent moment, as a team." He closed his eyes and asked for a guardian angel to look after his boys, Gone and Lee, and also Adam, so far away.

As Mike was putting away his gear, hurrying to leave, he noticed a folded piece of paper in the back of his locker. He picked it up and unfolded it. There was a short message, addressed to him. The handwriting was scratchy but it was readable:

Mike, Stay out of this. I will hurt people close to you. You're not going to beat me. Last warning. Choose better friends next time.

As Mike thought about this message, he began to burn slowly. This burned in one thought, "I have chosen my friends and I will stick with them."

But Mike felt empty, not knowing what to do.

Bobby and Becky Again

After music class, Becky was making her way to the buses to go home. Her worries for Gone, Mike and Lee were like rocks in her stomach. She wanted very much to get home. As she was walking, almost running, to the exit door at the end of the long hallway, a familiar and unfriendly face stepped out to block her path.

Bobby!

Startled, she recovered quickly, stepped back and tried to go around him. He was alone this time; no posse.

"Bobby, you're in my way. I do not have time for your silliness right now!"

She almost made it past him, but he grabbed her arm and violently spun her around. He laughed, a very snotty, bully laugh. He tried to pull her towards him, but she held her books up and blocked him.

She could smell his foul breath and a faint trace of nasty cologne. Bobby forced her back against the wall by the door, squeezing her arm very hard. His eyes were wide open and raging. He reached for her face with his free hand.

Just as Becky was about to scream for help, he quickly pulled back his hand and pointed at her, his fingers just inches from her face. "Where is your hero now?" He sneered. "He can't do a thing to stop me if I decide to have you. I will smash that little pissant!"

Bobby pushed back and gave Becky one last smash against the wall. And just like that, he let her go. She dashed out the door.

Becky barely made it to the bus before the doors closed. She sat in the first empty seat. Scared and angry, she sat alone shaking and crying softly, hoping no one would notice. This had not been a good day.

ZEKE AND MISS IVY—
THE BACK DOOR

When Reverend Ross reached home after picking up Mandy at the school, he was almost overcome with rage. Mandy and her mother were angry too, as well as afraid and sad. Ms. Ross knew that Amos had been the one to cut down Arthur Sanderson's burned body; she knew that today's arrests made him remember that horrible event. Mandy wasn't aware of this history.

Their thoughts turned to Sweet Momma, and they immediately set out for the Sanderson home. Momma was in her rocking chair. She had heard nothing. Amos was very glad to get to the house before Sheriff Willet or his deputies arrived, looking for Lee.

But the Rosses hadn't been there for long before the posse did arrive and told Momma of Gone's arrest on suspicion of murder and robbery. Momma and the Rosses sat quietly while Deputy Elkins asked questions and looked around.

"I'll be back," Deputy Elkins warned as he left.

Momma was glad Lee was not in a jail cell, but she worried that one of Big Bob's gang would hurt him if they found him.

Next to come by were Ruth Anne and Mike. It was near supper and Ruth Anne brought chicken and other finger foods for all. Tears and hugs were abundant. After a bit, everyone migrated to the big dining room table, nibbling on small bites.

No one had much of an appetite except Mike. He loaded a plate, walked into the living room and sat on the rug in front of Sweet Momma. She smiled, sniffling and wiping a tear, and said, "Lee would set there and read when he was little. He loved the Hardy Boys books."

Mike thought, I hope Lee isn't going hungry, wherever he is.

"Go on and eat, boy. I know you's starvin'."

"Can I get you something?"

"No, child, bless you."

As Mike ate, there came a soft knock on the front door. Mike started to get up to answer, but Momma shouted out, "Come on in, Zeke, we're all friends."

Zeke walked in, slowly opening the screen door and then closing it softly. As he came in from the dark, Mike thought he saw a faint glow in the old man's eyes, but just for a second. Zeke looked at Mike, nodded and smiled softly. "You sho' do remind me of someone I knew ages ago. He was a good boy; loved fishin'."

Momma laughed and said, "Zeke so old it might have been George Washington!"

"No, Miss Ivy," Zeke said. "But I do remember one time hearing—"

"Be quiet, you old fool," Momma cut in. "Ain't nobody gonna believe your ol' stories."

Zeke was going to tell about hearing about President Washington's death. It was true, he did remember it, but it would've been taken as a silly joke anyway. "Miss Ivy, I sure am sorry about the boys," he said.

"I know, Zeke. It just makes me sad to think about sad times gone on before. I am sho' 'nuff afraid."

"Me too, but maybe Arthur is better off in that jail for now."

"He is better off at home!" Momma thundered.

As he crossed the room to sit by Momma, Zeke rubbed

Mike's hair, like he was a little dog. Mike and Lee had seen and spoken to the old man many times on the creek. He never caused any fear or uneasiness with the boys, even when they were much younger. His smile was gentle and immediately reassuring.

"Miss Ivy," Zeke began, "we gotta watch these demons."

Demons? Mike thought.

"I ain't gonna be watchin' much of nothin' these days," Momma replied.

Even Mike laughed.

"Miss Ivy, you know what I's meanin'."

"I sho' do, I sho' 'nuff do."

"These old demons just want to hurt as many as they can. The big old fat snake has struck, and he will strike again."

"He just might," said Momma.

"But remember, they's little snakes crawlin' around too."

"I know."

"Them little crawlin' varmints will sneak in the back door."

Mike had no idea what snakes had to do with anything, or what the hell Zeke and Momma were talking about to begin with. He was about to ask, but then Zeke got up to take his leave and said, "Andy—I mean Mike. Remember what you saw yesterday at the church? Tell Trooper Wayne. You can trust him."

"What did I see?"

Momma wondered the same: "What did you see, boy?"

"I don't know, Momma."

Zeke walked towards the door and said, "You must, and you will, remember. Tell Larry." Zeke faced Momma, said, "Watch the back door," and then he was gone.

Mike said to Sweet Momma, "He seems friendly enough, but he's friendly in a strange way. And he knows everything!"

"You'll understand more with time. Thank God he is still with us."

"Where does he live, anyway?"

"Don't know. Maybe under a rock."

"That's just weird."

"More than you know, child."

As the evening wore on, several more friends and neighbors dropped by. This arrest did not sit well among the Lilac Road community. All feared for Lee. But, for reasons Mike could not explain, he felt Lee was safe. He had begun to feel this way during Zeke's visit, even though they didn't speak of it.

It wasn't too long after Zeke left that Ruth Anne and Mike took their own leave. As they drove out Low Road and approached the Lilac Road church, Mike suddenly remembered what he was supposed to remember—he had seen Mr. Foss's truck on Sunday parked near the church. He wasn't sure what it meant, but somehow he knew it was important.

"When we get home, I need to see Larry," he told his mother. "There's something I need to tell him. I believe I remember now. I don't understand what it means, but I know I need to tell him." He paused. "And I need to call Becky, too."

MIKE LEANS ON HIS FRIENDS

When they arrived back at the Thomas home, Ruth Anne invited Larry over for a cup of coffee. Whatever Mike had to say seemed important, but Ruth Anne was worried at Mike's need to be involved.

Larry hadn't gone back to the Sanderson home because he didn't think it was a good idea. He also was very worried that somehow Gone and Lee had some role in this murder. But he didn't trust the sheriff, and he doubted that Big Bob would truly investigate it. Larry was very concerned for all of his friends. His lawman instincts made him feel that something wasn't right—he just wasn't sure what it was. He also felt bad that he had some doubt regarding Gone and Lee. But that doubt was not grounded in fact. Larry was very conflicted by his emotions and concerns for the boys. What he needed were some hard pieces of evidence. Some facts.

Mike called Becky as soon as he got home. It was after seven o'clock, and Mike apologized for calling so late when Mrs. Patterson answered.

"It's okay, Mike," she said. "I know Becky needs to talk to you."

Becky came to the phone and Mike immediately sensed her voice was softer, weaker than usual. "Mike, I was hoping you'd call; I wanted to talk to you."

"I'm sorry it's so late. I should've called earlier. Are you okay?"

"I'm okay now. But I was worried about you. Are you okay?"

"I'm fine. Just worried about Gone and Lee. This makes no sense."

"Me too. Mike, you be careful. Bobby scared me this afternoon."

Becky proceeded to tell Mike what had happened with Bobby that afternoon, but she didn't share quite how angry and violent Bobby had seemed to be. She made it seem as if Bobby had just passed by in the hallway and said something off color.

But Mike saw through it. He was getting very angry as she spoke. He recalled the note in his locker, and wondered if Bobby had been its author. "This guy is asking for big trouble," he said. "I'm going to tell him to stay away from you, and I'll make sure he does."

Becky was very afraid of what might happen during such a discussion. She remembered Coach Carter's warning. "Mike, you have to promise me to stay away from him. Let's both stay away from him. He's not worth the trouble."

Mike eventually promised, but he was still very angry. Bobby was using Becky to get to him.

"Mike, be careful tomorrow. I can't wait to see you at school. I don't like this."

"I don't like it either. You be careful also; make sure you're with someone at all times."

"I hope it'll be you."

"Me too," he said. "Goodnight, pretty girl. Love you."

"Love you, too!"

Becky tried not to cry—she didn't want Mike to hear that, not now. But as she hung up the phone, she sat down on the floor with her mother and sobbed.

Larry arrived in just a few minutes, dressed casually in jeans and a red Bulldog sweatshirt. Larry was far more interested in being a friend for Mike now, rather than a law enforcement officer. It had been a long day. Longer days were coming.

Ruth Anne poured coffee, and for the first time ever she fixed a cup for Mike, who sipped it slowly. He thought it tasted like something dredged up from a mud puddle. He added three teaspoons of sugar and pretended to like it. Mike got a little bit of it down, but Ruth Anne got up and poured him a glass of sweet tea instead. Much better.

Larry was about to ask Mike what he knew, but Mike asked a question first. "Larry, why do they think Gone and Lee did this? I don't believe it, not for a minute. I know where Lee was Saturday evening. He was with me."

Larry had to be careful here. Much of the information wasn't public yet. Arthur Sanderson had not yet been arraigned, and Larry didn't know the entire case against Gone and Lee.

"'Mike, I can't tell you very much now," he said. "But there were tips regarding evidence, cash, property and merchandise. These tips and evidence implicated Gone and Lee. I can tell you the evidence is very strong, but it needs to be checked out."

"Do you really think Gone killed Mr. Andrews?"

"Honestly, it's hard to believe. But I have to remain open-minded." Larry remembered Sweet Momma's plea and his promise to keep looking. "What do you want to tell me, Mike?"

"I really don't know if this is important."

"Let me be the judge of that."

Ruth Anne was setting beside Larry, but reached across the table and took Mike's hand. "I hate that something like this has fallen on you boys. I'm afraid for all of you."

Larry nodded and again prompted Mike to talk.

"Okay," Mike began. "When I was riding my bike home from Becky's on Sunday evening, I saw Mr. Foss's truck parked behind the church. It was just before dark, but I could see it plainly."

"You mean the Lilac Road Church?"

"Yes, where Reverend Ross is the pastor."

Larry made a very quick connection between Mike's revelation and Mr. Foss's reaction when he and Mr. Penner had come to the classroom to arrest Lee. Mr. Foss had seemed to know too much. Was he involved? But Larry was calm, cool, and collected, and continued with his questions. "Did you see Mr. Foss?'

"No."

"Are you sure it was his truck?"

"Absolutely sure. Everyone knows that jerk's—I mean, that guy's truck."

"I'm going to ask again, because this is important: did you see Mr. Foss?"

"No."

"Tell me again what time it was."

Larry went through the story about three times, until he was sure Mike was telling exactly what he had seen.

"Well," Larry said, "I don't know how this ties in, but it could be important."

Larry was sure as death and taxes that it was important, but he was going to hold this close to the vest for now and see if the wizard would slip again. Big Bob's web of lies had just lost another strand.

"Larry, will Lee be okay?" Mike asked. "Can we do something? I feel as if I have just abandoned him."

"Mike, we need to find him. We can protect him best if we get him in custody soon."

"How did he get away?"

Larry said, "I was distracted by the actions in the classroom, and I tripped and stumbled. Lee pulled away and took off. Lord, he is fast. We need to get him in custody. That's where I can best protect him. Do you understand, Mike?"

"I understand."

"If you know where he is, you have to tell me."

"I know. But it would make me feel like a traitor to Lee. I already did that once today."

"Mike, I understand how you feel. But hiding Lee is not a good way to go. That could place Lee in real danger."

"Larry, I don't know where he is."

Larry was beginning to form a plan, but he kept it to himself for now. He needed to find Lee. Larry was very worried that he wouldn't be able to protect all these boys.

Mike also told Larry about Bobby's threats to Becky, and about the note in his locker. As he was telling Larry the story, he had a strong feeling that something bad was going to happen.

Larry told Mike that he would speak to the school staff and make sure there were eyes on Becky at all times. Larry also thought that he might have to have a talk with Bobby, but he didn't tell Mike that part. "If I have to," he said, "I'll arrest him and get him off of the street."

"I don't know what to do," Mike said. "I'm afraid for everyone. And Becky shouldn't be drawn into this because of me. Bobby will make her miserable and it'll be my fault."

"Mike, you and Becky need to be under watchful eyes at all times. I'll see that it's done."

After a few minutes of silence, Mike began laughing softly.

"What on earth is so funny about this?"

"Watching Big Bob and Deputy Elkins chase Lee was one of the funniest things I have ever seen. Two hogs chasing a racehorse."

Both laughed.

Later, much later, Mike would often kid Lee: "You better hustle—there's hogs on your ass!"

LEE—YOU CAN ALWAYS COME TO ME

With Lee in a full sprint, there was only one person in the county who could've caught him, and that person was in police custody. Lee worked his way south then east, wondering if Gone was okay. He used ditches, shrubs and any cover available to move. Not a single soul saw him. Before the sheriff could put together an organized search, Lee had already reached his objective.

He found an unlocked side door on a garage and entered. The garage had a storage loft and he quietly climbed the ladder. In a corner behind two old trunks, there was a stack of old moving quilts. Lee made a bed on the floor and then stretched out on the quilts to relax and keep quiet. Lee, the cool fugitive, was asleep in ten minutes. Later that evening, around ten o'clock, he quietly went back down the ladder and crept to the back door of the house. A few lights were still on. He took a deep breath and knocked on the back door.

A voice from inside, very strong, very masculine, said, "Who's there?"

"Coach, it's Lee Sanderson."

Coach opened the door, pulled Lee into the kitchen and hugged him.

Mrs. Carter and Suzy prepared a late-night breakfast of French toast, scrambled eggs and sausage. Lee ate ravenously. Suzy let Lee know how upset—and how dumb—Mike had been.

Even Lee had a laugh about it. "Poor Mike, he takes everything so seriously."

Mrs. Carter added, "Well, I understand. This is damn serious. You don't see your best friend arrested just every day!"

"They didn't arrest me."

After the meal, Lee and Coach went to the basement den. The den was very warm and homey. There were bookshelves by the fireplace, and the walls were covered with numerous family photos. Coach proudly described them to Lee. He spoke for a long time about Adam and his days as a football player. Soon Mrs. Carter brought some blankets for the couch. "Lee, sleep well. We'll figure out what to do in the morning."

"Coach, thank you for taking me in tonight. I was afraid."

Lee knew he was putting the coach and his family in some danger. It was risky for them to take him in, but they'd done it without hesitation.

"Lee, I'm glad to help," Coach Carter said. "I don't believe the charges. Suzy told us about where you were Saturday night, at the movies. I am proud you had enough faith in me to come here."

Coach left Lee alone in the basement. He paced for a long time upstairs and could not sleep. He was so tempted at times to pick up the phone and call the sheriff's office, but he never made the call, his loyalty to his player and to doing the right thing prevented it—at least for tonight. He would find a way to work this out and protect Lee.

But these things often don't go as you plan them. Things can sometimes turn very bad very quickly.

PART 10
ARRESTS—LONG AGO

Down through the years there had been many other arrests with terrible consequences. These arrests were not about enforcing the law, but instead were intended to break the human spirit. It had happened in Fair Creek plenty of times. Both Zeke and Andy had suffered this same injustice long ago.

DEFENSE OF ATLANTA AND RETURN HOME

By October of 1863, the 8th Georgia Infantry was involved in Longstreet's East Tennessee Campaign. Soon, they would be engaged in the battles of the Southern Heights in Knoxville and the failed attack on Fort Sanders in November 1863.

Many University of Tennessee students in later years would walk to class on "The Hill" along paths that were once artillery parapets overlooking the Tennessee River. But none of this would involve young Andy Thomas. The 8th would eventually be transferred back to Virginia and would fight at Spotsylvania, the Wilderness, Petersburg, Cold Harbor, and the final Richmond campaigns, and would be with Lee at Appomattox. The Pulaski Volunteers were the bravest of soldiers and they cared deeply for one another, but they were in a fight for a doomed and poor cause.

The excitement and eagerness of the young soldiers in the early part of the war had disappeared and been replaced with fear, hate, anger and loss. This hopelessness and anger were exactly what Andy had felt when he first joined his new unit, as a complete stranger. He felt no hope and no confidence, and constantly feared for his family. But at least he was now fighting to defend Georgia. As a funny twist of fate and quirk of military history, there was another 8th. The 8th Georgia Battalion was mustered in the spring of 1862 near Savannah.

The infantry unit had seen service in Mississippi, Alabama and Florida. The 8th Battalion was part of the evacuation of Jackson, Mississippi, soon after the fall of Vicksburg. After moving to Chattanooga by early September 1863, the unit was part of the Confederate victory at Chickamauga. The 8th Battalion also had been engaged in the sieges of Chattanooga and Missionary Ridge.

Now a sergeant, Andy Thomas joined the 8th Battalion at Chattanooga. As 1863 came to a close, the Confederate hold of the lower Tennessee Valley was precarious. As part of the Army of Tennessee under General Joe Johnston, the 8th Battalion was part of this fight.

In a series of battles through the spring of 1864, the Union Army under William Tecumseh Sherman consistently outmaneuvered, outfought and outthought the Confederates. At the Rocky Faced Bridge, Mill Creek, Cassville, Pumpkin Vine Creek, Dallas, New Hope, Marietta and Kennesaw Mountain, Johnston's Corps fought and then retreated, and were eventually forced to defend Atlanta, pushed back to the city in the early days of July 1864.

As part of the battles for Atlanta, General Johnston's Corps held a few bridge heads on the Chattahoochee River just north of Atlanta. But Sherman's forces were masters at flanking. They moved around and behind the Confederates' fixed positions. On the night of July 9, Johnston pulled his forces back to positions on a ridge overlooking Peachtree Creek. Within a week, Sherman had his entire army marching on Atlanta, pushing hard to surround the city and destroy the railroads.

Sergeant Thomas was trying to help his boys settle into some cover along the creek, but it was hard to rest with an artillery battery just to their left. Most of the young boys were recent conscripts. All they knew of this war was fight and retreat. But they had learned what real fear was like.

One soldier was a heavyset blond-haired boy from the

Atlanta area. The fear in his eyes was very clear.

"Sergeant Thomas, do you think they will come?"

"They always do, son!"

"Can we hold?"

Another young boy piped up, "We ain't yet! What's keepin' 'em from coming on?"

Another young trooper said, "They gonna let us set up here and starve and cook in the sun. They'll come when we're good and roasted."

Andy couldn't find any words to argue or encourage. "Just shut up and get some rest."

But the nervous banter of the teenage boys continued. "I heard the Yankees were all swimmin' in the Chattahoochee."

"General Hood will make 'em pay for that, I reckon!"

Andy just shook his head and said, "There will be a price to pay for all of us."

Sure enough, as General Hood had taken command for Johnston on the 17th of July, the Confederates attacked the XX Corps of Joseph Hooker, an advance force moving on Atlanta from the north. Because the Union divisions were slow coming across Peachtree Creek, Hood's attack had to be delayed until four in the afternoon. This delay reminded Andy of the second day at Gettysburg—it was all too familiar; July 1864 was feeling a lot like July 1863. As the 8th Battalion moved forward, Andy had a sick feeling in his gut. The men moved hard on the Union left flank going across the Marietta Road. Andy remembered all too well the feeling crossing the Emmitsburg Road into the hell of the Gettysburg peach orchard and the wheat field.

The fighting was intense and the Union positions were well supported by artillery. Even so, the Confederate attack was beginning to turn the Union left. General Hardee sensed the battle was turning and was about to commit another Confederate division to the attack when Hood countermanded the order and sent the division east to check a rapidly advancing Union threat. Union brigades were advancing in counterattacks and Andy sensed the day was lost. It was just exactly like the second day of Gettysburg. As the Union reinforcements came downhill from the east, it reminded Andy of the Union reinforcements coming across Cemetery Ridge at Gettysburg.

Andy and a small group of his boys had advanced well into the flanks of the counterattacking Yankees. They were down to six soldiers, two of whom were wounded. As darkness fell, Andy got them into a ditch by a small road cut behind a copse of trees. "Get down and stay quiet," he ordered.

One of the very young soldiers had a low gut wound and was suffering terribly. The other had a broken ankle and most of his other foot was missing. Although it was now getting dark, Andy knew all of these hungry, tired, thirsty and scared boys were looking to him for a way out.

"Sergeant Thomas, what do we do?"

Andy buried his face in the dirt. He had no answer. His own fear and frustration were almost overwhelming. There was no hope left.

The answer that came to Andy would have been inconceivable just a few weeks earlier. Several desperate options came to Andy all at once, and he had to choose the best of the bad bunch.

Lying flat on his stomach, Andy gave his last set of orders as a soldier to his boys. "We leave the wounded here," he said. "The boy with the gut shot will be dead soon. The Yankees will find the other. They have doctors and medicine, we don't. The rest of us should split up and travel by ourselves to our lines. There will be pickets and skirmishers just past the road. They'll shoot your ass if you do not be careful. I'll go last. I'll speak to the wounded. Move out, now!"

Andy waited a few minutes after watching the boys scatter, one by one. He had to help each one find courage to flee. Then he crawled to the boy with the belly wound. Andy

266

reached and touched his face to see if he was breathing, but he was not; Andy felt no emotion or sympathy. For a brief moment, he just felt rage. The boy with the foot wound was leaning against a tree and smiled at Andy as he crawled near. Andy could see his teeth through the smile, even though it was dark, because of the grime and blood smeared on the boy's face.

"I hope there ain't no poison vine here, it makes me itch worse'n chiggers."

"Maybe it'll take your mind off that foot!"

"What are we going to do?"

"You are going to stay put. The Yanks will find you. I hear they have good docs."

"I'd bet they're good with a saw. They'll cut my foot off, won't they?"

"Probably so, but you'll be alive."

"Do you have any water?"

"No."

"What are you going to do, Sergeant Thomas?"

"I'm going to work back toward our lines." It was only a partial lie. "I wish I had more to give you," Andy said as he shook the boy's hand and headed east.

For Andy Thomas, the American Civil War was finished. His bravery and his willingness to sacrifice weren't the issue, and they weren't in question. This war was simply a lost cause, and Andy'd had enough of it.

On this day, July 20, over five thousand men died. Many more would die in the next few days. Atlanta would burn, Sherman would march to the sea and the South would be broken. But Andy Thomas was already broken. His heart was so heavy that he no longer felt the sharp pains of loss. As he worked his way first east then south, sneaking around and living off the land, his one thought was to get to Bobby Jeff. The shy boy with a big smile, his mother's smile, was the last good thing he had to look forward to. It took many days, but

Andy arrived home in early September. Once again, he shocked his mother. Once again, she smothered him in a tight bear hug.

In the following days of the fall, Andy stayed at the farm, hiding from the outside world. Fishing trips to the creek with Zeke, Bobby Jeff and Susannah were frequent. What started as blushing smiles and hand-holding ended up as a very simple, but elegant, private, family-only wedding in the home kitchen. By late November, Susannah knew she was to be a mother.

THE FINAL CRUELTY

As the early winter of 1864 began, Andy and his father considered their future prospects. Andy would always be a deserter in the opinion of the people of Pulaski County. The farm was not doing well, nor could it. Mr. Thomas had decided to secretly sell the farm, and with Andy and Zeke he had discussed heading west, maybe to Kansas—a good free state. They often discussed this in the early evenings after supper.

Mr. Thomas would usually begin the discussion with, "There is nothing left for us here."

Andy was afraid to travel with his young pregnant wife. But he knew that it was only a matter of time before the sheriff or the conscriptors would find him.

"We should travel light and quick," Andy said. "West first, then up to Tennessee and Ohio by river." Andy had thought this out. "We need one wagon, one horse, and horses are very scarce. If we had the horse, we could go soon."

Andy's father replied, "It'll be dangerous. There are many gangs of roaming thieves, mostly deserters."

This made Andy shudder. "No more dangerous than stayin' put!"

The morning after one of these talks, their answer was found near the barn. A stray horse, with Union Army brands, was nibbling at frost-covered grass. Andy got a rope from the barn and quickly haltered the horse, then hid him in a barn stall. This horse was like an answered prayer, and did give Andy hope. But Andy also knew that he must be very careful with this animal. Sherman's cavalry and scouts were roaming all over the countryside.

This was a dangerous horse for Andy. Being a deserter was bad enough, but a deserter and horse thief was worse. One could be shot and hung all at once. But Andy and Zeke also saw this horse as their big chance, like manna from heaven. This tall bay gelding might be just the ticket. Once again, a small, tiny trickle of hope fought its way into Andy's heart. But this time cruelty and bad luck would crush it, more so than any canister shot or bullet could.

After dinner, Zeke headed to town to get flour and salt, hoping the store had some to sell. Andy decided to hitch Buck, as Bobby Jeff had named the horse, to their wagon.

"Let's see how this big boy does pulling wagons," he said.

It was obvious this horse was used to a harness and being hitched. He was calm and took to the leads very well. Andy led the small parade of horse, wagon, Bobby Jeff and the dog, Shady, around the pasture. For someone not understanding what was happening, this would have looked comical.

As the wagon moved up the hill, Andy observed, "This is a sure-footed horse; he moves easy."

"Can I ride, can I ride?" Bobby Jeff pleaded while pulling on Andy's britches.

"Okay, I reckon."

Andy planted Bobby Jeff on the horse's back. Buck lifted his head and seemed to like it. Andy climbed up on the wagon.

"That's a good sign. These artillery horses are used to soldiers riding as they pull the guns and caissons."

As they moved up the hill, Bobby Jeff laughed with pure delight. The entire parade was happy. Even Shady wagged his approval.

The little happy parade was unaware that other events were unfolding close by. A Union Army mounted patrol was observing from the trees at the top of the hill. They were scouting south of the lines of Union Army occupation. These patrols had been burning bridges, scavenging fodder for the horses, taking livestock and anything else they could take with them. They would burn the rest. There were eight soldiers in this patrol. They were led by a very tough, no-nonsense sergeant.

Zeke was standing among them. The cavalry scouts had taken Zeke captive as he was returning to the farm, snatching him from behind on the Low Road.

"Hold on there, old timer!" The sergeant had brought everyone to a stop. "We are here to free you. You have now been emancipated!"

As the soldiers closed around Zeke, he felt uneasy. He knew how destructive these patrols could be, and he didn't want to see the Thomas family hurt. Maybe he could convince this patrol to move along.

"I appreciate your offer," he said, "but I'm already a free man. You can move along."

"Is that right? Where are you taking this scrappy little load?"

"None of yo' business."

"Home to yo' masta'?"

This short exchange frustrated Zeke. His liberators had no real respect for him. They may have been President Lincoln's army of freedom, but that didn't make a black man fully human in their eyes.

Zeke repeated his answer, looking the sergeant square in the eyes: "I said, none of yo' business!"

"Private Frazier, take this man prisoner. I am going to make it my business."

One of the troopers quickly dismounted and placed a pistol at Zeke's back. He pushed him to the front of the sergeant's horse.

"Now we'll go on down this road and you will lead us," the

sergeant said. "If you run, I will shoot you. Let's see what you're hiding."

They moved slowly towards the Thomas farm and crested a hill where they could see the wagon parade approaching. They stayed in the cover of the trees and watched for a few minutes. The sergeant barked his orders, "When they circle up to the top of the hill, we'll move. We'll go right in the front and stop the wagon."

He instructed his soldiers how to move around the wagon. He also noticed that Andy carried a pistol at his side.

As they topped the crest of the hill, the soldiers made their play. When they moved out, Andy immediately stopped the wagon. The first thing Andy saw was Zeke leading the mounted squad, but he didn't see that the soldier was holding a pistol at Zeke's back. Andy also noticed that these cavalry troops were well armed and well mounted. He was trapped.

Zeke continued walking in front of the mounted sergeant, coming up slowly to join the assembly. Andy felt betrayed—it seemed as if Zeke had volunteered to lead the soldiers here. But that made no sense.

The sergeant brought his horse up on the right side of the wagon. He pointed his pistol at Andy and said, "Drop that hand cannon to the ground and get off the wagon. It belongs to the U.S. Army now."

One of the soldiers moved up on Buck and saw the Union artillery brands. "Sarge, it looks like Johnny Reb stole this horse."

"Well, I'm glad I brought a rope," the sergeant said. "We are going to have to string up this horse thief."

Zeke started to speak, but was cut off. "Shut up, old man. You are not his slave anymore. You'll come with us. You have just been emancipated! You are not Johnny Reb's property anymore."

Andy had stepped off the wagon. He snapped a response. "Zeke can always do as he wishes. He never has been my slave.

Zeke, why did you lead these Yankees here?"

Andy was in a difficult place. He was a man with no country. The Confederacy had betrayed him and destroyed his homeland. But the blue-clad Yankees were still a bitter and invading enemy.

Before Zeke could answer, the sergeant asked, "Old man, what do you wish to do? You want to go with us or be strung up with yo' masta'?"

The soldiers laughed at this. But Smilin' Zeke was not laughing; he was becoming angry and afraid for Andy. "Andy is not a thief," Zeke said. "This horse was a stray. He found us."

The soldiers and the sergeant laughed harder. "Sounds like a technicality to me. I say he is a thief!"

One of the soldiers dismounted and stepped forward to lift Bobby Jeff from the horse. Shady had been setting quietly under the wagon, growling softly. When the soldier reached for the boy, Shady exploded, barking and charging at the soldier. The soldier backed up, startled by the dog. One of the other soldiers pulled his pistol and shot Shady, killing him instantly. All of the soldiers laughed.

The dog barking, the commotion and loud laughter had spooked the horses; Buck reared and Bobby Jeff fell.

Andy screamed: "Noooo!"

He watched the boy land awkwardly on his head and shoulder, instantly breaking his neck. Andy ran to charge the still-mounted sergeant, but he was quickly overpowered by the others. They tied his hands behind his back.

The sergeant turned to Zeke again. "Make your choice, old man. I'm getting tired of this mess. Come with us or die here as a horse thief."

Zeke stumbled backwards.

Andy watched Zeke stumble backwards and assumed that Zeke had chosen to abandon him. He cried out, "Why Zeke, why? Why did you lead them here?"

But Zeke was suffering as much as Andy; the pain and fear

had triggered a massive heart attack. He couldn't answer. Zeke simply stumbled and fell down backwards in the field. His last words were whispered: "I am so sorry. Listen to me. Andy is a good man."

No one heard.

Andy tried to speak. He was no thief, he wanted to explain. But as he began to speak, the soldiers clubbed him down. They pushed and beat him and placed him on a horse for the hanging. Soon the act was finished and the patrol rode away with the Thomas wagon and Buck. It was not a clean hanging—Andy slowly strangled, a spirit of rage and hate consuming him. Andy faded away. The new, ugly spirit that was born then took over and focused the anger on the many people who had destroyed him and his family. And he thought of his former friend and stand-in grandfather, Zeke—Zeke, who had betrayed him. His heart burned for revenge and only revenge. This old soldier's spirit would hang onto that hate for a long, long time, striking everywhere he could—but especially at black people. Zeke and his race became the target of his hatred. The Sanderson brothers would one day become his victims.

Andy's father found Andy, Bobby Jeff, Shady and Zeke that afternoon, just as the shadows were growing long. He buried them as the sun set in the small family cemetery where Betsy had been buried. There was no real funeral, no real grave marker. Mr. Thomas was devastated. No man should have to bury his son, grandson and old friend all at once. He buried Shady just beside Bobby Jeff.

In less than a year, Mr. and Mrs. Thomas would also be in the cemetery. Susannah Thomas would have to raise her child the best way she could. She would do just fine, but it was going to be hard. The helpers that would come into her life would set off a chain of events that would eventually change many things and allow the good spirits a chance to win, for once, finally.

Part 11
Guests for Supper—Tuesday

SMOKEY FOUND

The Ocmulgee River winds its way through Georgia, heading south and taking a big turn around the eastern edge of Hawkinsville. The current is steady as the big river heads to the Atlantic Ocean. On this Tuesday morning, about the time students were starting their first-period classes, a body floated past a large, slow cotton barge on the river just south of the highway bridge on the east side of town. The barge crew used a rope and a treble hook to pull in the body. The gunshot to the back of the head and the hands tied behind the back told the tale: someone had wanted somebody to be very, very dead and very quiet. A dead man cannot testify.

But coincidence can be a very funny thing. The odds of this body being found in the big river were very low, almost nonexistent. But it didn't work out that way. The only time Smokey had the long shot work in his favor was after he was dead and gone.

It looked like the murderer was very lazy in this case, perhaps so overconfident that he or she didn't work very hard to cover their tracks. Smokey had been easy to trick with a promise of a payoff, right up to the end. The killer hadn't even bothered to clean up very well. The killer's plan was already coming apart at the seams.

The barge crew helped transfer Smokey's body to the barge and a tugboat came up alongside. The tug and all of the crew headed to the docks just below town. The crew had laid Smokey on the deck and covered him with an old canvas tarp. At the dock a crowd gathered. One older black person knew Smokey and identified him. "I been seein' bodies out of this water for a many a year. This'n ain't been in the water long."

The barge pilot asked, "Do you know him?"

"Yep, that's Smokey Wright. Can't figure anyone hurtin' him. He ain't never hurt a soul. Killed many a beer though."

The barge pilot shook his head. "Somebody wanted him dead."

A call was placed to the rescue squad.

Larry heard the radio call go out. He was east of town a ways but headed back as quickly as he could. It seemed like big trouble was coming in spades; it was getting hard to keep up.

He had stopped by the high school earlier in the day and asked the staff to watch after Becky and let him know if there were any problems. They knew not to call the sheriff to deal with any problem related to Bobby Willet. Mr. Penner told Larry that Mr. Patterson, Becky's father, had also called.

There had been no name on the radio call, but Larry had a feeling he needed to see this. He drove to the docks as quickly as he could, bubblegum light flashing, siren blowing.

When Larry got to the docks a pretty large crowd had gathered. The boat crew, dockworkers and millworkers all now seemed to be arriving. Larry left his bubblegum light flashing and pushed through. Most stepped back and let him pass. Larry hadn't known Smokey well, but he had seen him around the Good Times club. Larry knelt beside the body and felt a wake of regret and sadness. The gunshot had been delivered at very close range. There was an entry wound above the bridge of the nose and a large exit wound out the back of the skull. Smokey's hands were tied behind his back with an old leather belt. Larry'd have bet it was Smokey's own belt. The body couldn't have been in the water longer than a few hours. Smokey had been alive on Monday morning, on the phone with Big Bob. But now, nobody could ask Smokey any questions. Dead men tell no tales.

There was nothing Larry or anyone could do except see that a thorough autopsy was completed. How long had Smokey been dead and how long had he been in the water? Those details would be important. So Larry stayed at the docks long enough to see that the body was transported to the morgue at the hospital, where the county coroner, Dr. Roberts, could perform the autopsy.

Sheriff Willet arrived, but he just hung out at the docks until the crowd began to break up. He did nothing, said nothing; he simply let Larry handle it.

As soon as Smokey's body was heading to the morgue, Larry made his way to the courthouse and the sheriff's office.

LARRY AND THE COOKIE MONSTER

Larry hurried to the sheriff's office in the hopes that he could get some information before the sheriff returned. Larry got lucky in two ways: one, Big Bob headed to get a cup of coffee with his posse; two, Fred Dobbs, the part-time dispatcher, was filling in this morning. Larry wasted no time.

"Fred, who took the call on Saturday night about the murder?"

Fred was sitting at Janet's desk, which held multiple telephones, heavy rotary dial sets with push buttons for multiple lines that would light up if busy. The radio set was on the left and microphone on the desk in front of Fred.

"I did."

"What time?"

Fred reached for the logbook on his right. Larry stepped around the desk so he could see over Fred's shoulder.

"Sometimes I don't write down anything, and sometimes Big Bob will tell me not to enter things. It has been a little messy since Janet left."

Fred wasn't sharp enough to hide anything; he just blurted out facts. It sure seemed odd to Larry that an experienced and good office manager would be out at a time like this, but no matter for now. He said, "I did enter the call this time. Nine o'clock, Saturday night."

"Who made the call?"

"He never identified himself, just said he was a local citizen or something like that."

"What did he say, exactly?"

"Well, not much, just that there had been a crime at... no, behind the gas station."

"That's all?"

"That was all."

"So you called the sheriff on the radio?"

"Yes, I called Big Bob, who was out on patrol."

Larry cleared his throat, thinking. Big Bob hadn't done any real patrolling in twenty years. Crooked is bad; crooked and lazy is pathetic. Larry began reading the log.

"So, you called Big Bob immediately?"

"Sure did!"

"What did he say?"

"Well, he was grumpy, for sure. He told me to eat a cookie and not say or do anything until he told me to."

"And that is what you did?"

"Yup. I think it was chocolate chip."

Even Larry had to smile at that one. He continued scanning the log. "So, Sheriff Willet had the call by nine fifteen, but he didn't call you back until about ten fifteen?"

"That's right. I guess he was investigating."

Larry was taking mental notes. "Okay Fred, thanks for your help!"

"Trooper Wayne, if it's okay with you, don't tell Big Bob we talked. He might get mad, and I need this job."

"Don't worry, Fred. I'll keep quiet if you will."

Larry suspected that the sheriff was cooking the books and the investigation, but he didn't know how or why just yet. He could tell that Fred was also nervous about this and that he felt like he was in a precarious spot.

Fred replied, "Fine by me."

"We have a deal. Make sure that log doesn't disappear."

"Trooper Wayne, something fishy goin' on here, or am I

281

just crazy as a June bug?"

"No, Fred, it does seem odd. Keep quiet and we'll figure it out."

Larry was glad to realize that Fred didn't trust the sheriff and seemed not to have any misplaced loyalty.

The sheriff's office was in a very old section of the courthouse. In the front receiving room, visitors had to pass through a swinging gate attached to a counter. The dispatcher's desk was behind the counter. An open door led to a hall. The hall led to the sheriff's office, meeting rooms, a map room, the deputies' offices and two simple interrogation rooms. Larry was trying to figure out what to do next, but events forced his hand.

As Fred and Larry finished the discussion they heard a clamor outside. They could hear Big Bob's laugh. When Big Bob came in the front door, the laugh turned to an angry scowl.

"What are you doing here, Trooper Wayne?"

"Waiting on you, Sheriff," Larry said. "Waiting on you."

CHARMING A SNAKE

By now, Larry held a few of the little pieces of the puzzle. It was still a puzzle, but some of it was coming clear. Larry didn't want the sheriff to know about his uncertainty of the timeline, or his suspicion of Paul Foss. And he sure didn't want Big Bob to know what Mike had seen on Sunday evening. Larry decided to make this a discussion about Smokey's death.

"Bob, what did Smokey say to you?" he asked. "I think you said that he called you yesterday morning?"

"Yes, he called from Good Times, I think."

"And what was the tip?"

"He said he saw Gone Sanderson running along the Low Road, toward his house, near the church, on Saturday evening just after dark."

"And you said that he saw Gone at the club with lots of cash?"

"Yup, that's what Smokey said."

"Who would kill Smokey? That makes less sense to me than Bert's murder."

"I don't know. Maybe revenge." The sheriff folded his arms and looked at the floor. Larry let the silence build and enjoyed watching Big Bob squirm.

"Not many people know that Smokey was the source of the tip," Larry said. "That information hasn't been released."

Big Bob was clearly uncomfortable and almost openly

angry. "Trooper Wayne, you should mind your own business," he said. "I will handle this."

"Has someone been to his shack to look around?"

"We'll investigate the murder scene very soon."

Larry stood as cool as could be, his little trap delivered perfectly. Again, he let the sheriff stand in silence. Larry knew that his next question would ramp up the pressure.

"Sheriff, how do you know that Smokey's shack is the murder scene? Smokey was found about a mile downstream of town."

The scowl on Big Bob's face just screwed his face tighter. His voice was a little shaky now. He was beginning to sweat; his forehead was visibly wet.

"I don't know anything for sure, I'm just guessin', but—"

"Sheriff, I'm going to get some additional help from the state police," Larry said. "You are in over your head."

"It's just a simple case of lowlife, no-account colored folks taking revenge. Maybe Smokey cheated somebody playin' Rook."

In Larry's mind, the sheriff was either really incompetent or very much involved. But all Larry had for now was suspicion and instinct. "Your star informant dies less than twenty-four hours after giving you a case-breaking tip and you don't seem worried about it?"

"Do not interfere with my case—I'm warning you now!"

The sheriff was very angry and shaken. The thought of more state police and the GBI was worrying him. No one had spent much time looking over his shoulder before. "Trooper Wayne, my son tells me that Mike Thomas and some of the other kids were with Lee Sanderson on Saturday evening. Do you know if this is correct, and do you know where he is?"

"Yes, I believe they went to see the movie on Saturday evening. But I do not know where he is now. How would I know that?"

"I plan to question all of the kids, especially Mike. Do not interfere with me."

Larry said not a word. The sheriff had just made a very clear threat to get Larry to back off. He had been leaning on the back wall, facing the sheriff. In response, Larry just straightened up and walked out. He now had something to work with; the timeline as recorded had some real holes, and the sheriff was likely directly involved in Smokey's murder as well. This was enough to get the state involved on suspicion of conspiracy.

Larry left the sheriff's office and drove straight to Dr. Roberts's office. Once there, he asked Dr. Roberts if he could make some phone calls. Minutes later, state police investigators and GBI agents were on the way. Larry also called Reverend Ross and arranged to use the church as a meeting place.

Next, Larry asked Ruth Anne to get Mike out of school and bring him to the church. It was going to be necessary to protect Mike and the other kids—especially Lee, assuming they could find him. Larry had a very serious look on his face and was speaking in his command-and-control voice. "Ruth Anne, sugar, we need to find Lee," he said. "Maybe Reverend Ross can help."

"Larry, you're scaring me!"

"We're headed into snake country. But Sweet Momma told me that if I can find the lie, we can get the truth out."

"I need to check on her."

"Yes, get Mike to the church and then go see her."

"Larry, please tell me everything will be okay!"

"Ruth Anne, we are going to cut the head off this snake. I am sure of it. I'll do everything possible to protect you, you know that."

"And Mike?"

"Yes, for sure. You know I love that boy, and his momma."

Ruth Anne put her head on Larry's shoulder and could not stifle a good cry. Larry held her tightly. "Larry, as always, thank you!"

Shortly after Larry left the doctor's office, Ruth Anne called the school and requested that Mike be summoned to the front office. She also called the Burger Circle and placed an order to go. Ruth Anne then went directly to the school to pick up Mike.

Mr. Penner found Mike in the cafeteria and escorted him to the office. Mike quickly said goodbye to Ray, Suzy and Becky and waved to Mandy across the room.

Bobby Willet passed by in the hall and made a very public joke in a very loud voice: "Here comes the white boy hero from the jailbird backfield! They gonna lock you up too?"

Most of those who heard laughed.

Mike turned and began to step towards Bobby. Bobby began to back up. He hadn't anticipated that Mike would answer the call.

Mr. Penner moved between them quickly and spoke softly to Mike: "Don't listen to that fool. He's not worth the effort. Ignore him."

Mike stopped and looked at Mr. Penner. He took a deep breath and released the tension. Not now, he thought. Just watch out for Becky.

Ruth Anne was waiting in the office. She and Mike left quickly. As they left, Mr. Penner handed Ruth Anne a folded note. "This is from Coach Carter. Read it later, please."

Ruth Anne nodded and left.

Becky spent the rest of the day at school very worried, but Suzy and Mandy stuck to her all day, like Elmer's glue.

Mr. Penner and Coach Carter had met early in the morning in Mr. Penner's office. Coach had told Mr. Penner about Lee coming to his house. Both men were very worried about this situation, and they wanted to get Lee to a safer place. They wanted to get word to Larry Wayne, but they didn't want to risk another police visit to the school. When Mr. Penner learned that Ruth Anne was coming to the school for

Mike, he and Coach Carter quickly decided to give her the note. It would be a while before she would remember to read it.

LARRY'S TEAM KICKS OFF

Larry left Dr. Roberts's office and drove straight to the Lilac Road Church. Reverend Ross was the only person there. Amos invited Larry into his office, a small room with simple furniture including a small desk. Most of the wall space was made up of bookshelves, and they held a very impressive collection of books on religion, history and sociology. On the left side of the desk there was a stack of books that were from the reverend's seminary studies. On top of the stack was a large King James Bible. In front of the books was a photograph of Mrs. Ross and Mandy.

Larry sat in the only visitor's chair. Both the desk chair and visitor's chair were a simple but sturdy oak. Amos started the conversation. "Trooper Wayne, what can I do for you? What happens next?"

"Just Larry, please. Thank you for letting us use your church as a meeting place."

"Well, it's not fancy and it's not mine; it belongs to God."

"I will be sure to thank the good Lord. We just need a good table and a few chairs. This will do very well."

"Glad to help, but what's going on?"

"Well, I was hoping you'd know where Lee is."

"I wish I did. I'm worried for him. Mandy is literally sick with worry. She hasn't been able to eat."

"I'm worried, too."

"You know what can happen to young black men that are labeled as suspects by a bunch of redneck good ol' boys with guns and badges?"

"That is why I want to find him."

"A little bird told me you promised to protect Lee and Gone."

"And was that little bird named Ivy Sanderson?"

"I ain't in the business of namin' birds."

"I promised to find the truth." Larry realized that it must not have seemed to the reverend like he had protected Gone or Lee. Why would Amos Ross trust his promises?

"Larry, do you think Gone murdered that man?"

"Well, unofficially, no. But the evidence is strong, or was strong. I need to destroy that evidence and expose the lies."

"How can I help?"

"I may need help finding Lee and perhaps some other information. You may be able to ask some questions to some people that won't trust me because I'm a white lawman."

"I see."

"Did you know Smokey Wright?"

"I know him. But you said that in past tense, as If Smokey is gone. Is something wrong?"

"He is dead. He was murdered."

Larry proceeded to tell Amos about finding Smokey's body. Amos sat back in his chair and his shoulders slumped.

"Smokey was harmless, but trapped in a bad life," he said. "No one knew but me and Doc Roberts, but Smokey was dying of lung cancer, too many non-filter Camels.

"He came to me about a month ago and asked if I could get him to the doctor. Nothing they could do. They gave him some pain pills. I paid for the medicine. Dr. Roberts and Ms. Ruth Anne are saints."

"We agree on that for sure."

"You need to marry her before someone else does, else you're plumb crazy."

"You're not the first person to say that."

"Well, you best listen!"

"Well," Larry said, "I didn't come for marriage counseling. Let's set up a table and get ready."

Amos and Larry moved to the kitchen and set up a sturdy dining table and chairs. There was a telephone on the wall, beside a large farmers' almanac calendar. Beside the calendar was a chalkboard and a large painting of the church. Larry and Amos talked about the weather, football and families. None of that had any consequence, except that these two men became fast friends. The longer they talked, the more relaxed they became.

This was a unique friendship, it would never have happened except for the strange circumstances of a violent murder and many acts of anger.

When Ruth Anne and Mike arrived at the church, they saw several state cruisers parked at the church along with a couple of unmarked cars. The burgers were welcomed as Larry made introductions. The officers were polite, respectful and serious. It was also very obvious that Larry was respected by his fellow officers and agents.

Amos smiled and said to Ruth Anne, "Ain't never been this many white folks in this church. I think we need a special blessing over these hamburgers." He stood and prayed out loud, "Lord, for all you give us, thank you. I ask your mighty blessing on these men that we find the truth. Help us heal the innocent, free the ones in unrighteous bondage and calm our neighbors. We ask your forgiveness and mercy for all. May your mighty spirit be on us so that we find and deliver peace and respect for all. In the name of Jesus Christ, Amen."

Mike was awestruck. He had never heard a prayer delivered with such grace and power; Reverend Ross made the words flow like a smooth waterfall, with a strong Southern flavor. It sounded like the Gettysburg Address, The Sermon on the Mount and all rolled into one prayer.

After a few moments, Ruth Anne and Amos left to go check on Sweet Momma. For the moment, Ruth Anne had forgotten about Mr. Penner's note. But she would remember soon enough.

The first part of Larry's plan was to have one of the officers take Mike to his home and stay with him, with the cruiser parked in the front of the house.

Before Mike left, he asked Reverend Ross to pray that someone watch over Becky and Mandy.

"Amen," said Reverend Ross.

Soon the lawmen were working the case. Larry explained to the investigators, his team, "At first the evidence as described by Sheriff Willet seemed very strong. But when you look at the whole body of evidence, it just doesn't make much sense. A common thief, even a really dumb thief, would not ambush the person when they could easily wait a few minutes and not be seen. Also, the principle witness has been murdered.

"We know that the bank bag and service keys were found near here, along Low Road. They were found in a quick search—maybe too quick. We know that a truck belonging to a high school teacher, a known Klansman, was seen on Sunday evening here at this church. On the basis of tips from Smokey Wright, and the location of the bank bag, Gone Sanderson was named a key suspect. A sealed arrest warrant was issued for Gone and his brother, Lee. Honestly, at that point, I wasn't sure exactly why Lee was included. But cash and merchandise with Bert's wallet were found in their school lockers. Gone was arrested, Lee is at large.

"There are problems with the evidence. I think Smoky's tips were made up, planted. I believe evidence was planted. We need to find out two things, obviously. One, who killed Bert and why—this troubles me; I have a hard time understanding the why. And two, who planted the evidence and why? Who would have a motive?"

Larry went on to explain why he thought the sheriff was involved, at least in the cover-up and the frame job.

"We need to catch a break," he went on. "We should bring in the owner of the truck and put some heat on him. We need to get with the people at Good Times and see if any of Smokey's report of Gone with cash is true. We need to look at Smokey's shack and see if we find anything."

One of the agents asked, "Do we want to speak to the sheriff?"

Larry took a breath before he answered. It was never easy to investigate other law enforcement agencies. And it could be dangerous. "Sure, but not just yet. I think we need more evidence first."

Dale Katz, the senior GBI officer, spoke up. "I like your plan," he said, "and I certainly see that your suspicions are well grounded. This looks like it could be a grand-scale conspiracy. I will take official tactical command for the state and let the sheriff know we're investigating multiple murders and conspiracy. If we put some pressure on, something will break loose. Somebody out there knows something. Let's ask lots of questions around town: the school, the club, just anywhere. Word will get around. Trooper Wayne, you find Lee and protect the boys. Who saw the truck?"

"Mike Thomas, the boy just here," Larry said. "All I told you before was that he was Lee's friend and had received threats. But only the people in this room know that he was the one who saw the truck. The sheriff plans to question many of the kids. That's why I want to protect Mike."

"Well done," Katz said. "Let's get to work."

THE NOTE

Amos and Ruth Anne found Sweet Momma asleep in her rocking chair. The warm September sun had helped her doze off. But she hadn't slept well. The anxiety was exhausting her. She heard footsteps on the porch and startled. "My goodness gracious, you tryin' to give me a heart attack!"

Everyone laughed, and Ruth Anne bent and hugged Sweet Momma. Amos put his hand on her shoulder and said, "No, we just seein' if you still just bein' lazy!"

More laughs. Sweet Momma reached for her cane and started to get up. Ruth Anne stopped her. "Where are you going?"

"I thought I would put on a pot of coffee."

"No, I'll do it. Just set still."

"Okay, sweetheart."

Sweet Momma did not look well, and it worried Ruth Anne. She walked to the kitchen and in just a minute had a pot on the stove. While she waited on the percolator, she sat at the small kitchen counter and put her hand in her sweater pocket. The note from Mr. Penner was there. She had forgotten about it. She opened the folded paper. It was written on a notepad with the company logo of Atlanta Sports Supply at the top. It read:

I can give your friend a second chance to tackle an elusive back that escaped.

Coach C

Ruth Anne smiled. She hurried to finish and just a few minutes later she took a tray with a few cookies and the coffee to the porch. "I have some very good news," she said. "I'm now sure that Lee is safe and in very good hands."

Sweet Momma was lifting the coffee to take a sip but she stopped. She began to shake, and Ruth Anne quickly took the coffee cup. Both women held each other, crying. Reverend Ross asked, "When and how did you come by this?"

"Very recently, but I cannot say more now."

"Okay, but that is a good surprise," he said. "A very good surprise."

Sweet Momma was drying her eyes and said, "That is such good news. You are my special angel."

"I'm no angel, but I think things will be fine."

Amos smiled and said, "The Lord answers prayers!"

Ruth Anne made some calls. Those calls were answered too.

Guests for Supper

Tuesday afternoon and evening turned out to be an eventful time. As the state police and investigators began to make their presence known, talk spread though the town. Sergeant Katz visited the sheriff and told him they were beginning a conspiracy investigation regarding the murders and the circumstances surrounding them. For a moment, Big Bob considered running, but his own arrogance was his own doom.

Besides, the voice of the spirit had warned him not to run.

Larry and another trooper went to Smokey's shack near Good Times. The owner helped them look around for any sign of something not right. The only thing Larry saw was some evidence of a scuffle in the front room of Smokey's shack, but they found nothing of value. Larry's fellow officer walked with the owner over to the club to look there. Larry walked behind the shack and was startled to find Zeke standing in the shade of an old peach tree. "This used to be a fine orchard," Zeke said.

"My Lord, old man, you scared the crap out of me."

"Sorry, didn't mean to."

"It's okay. Why are you here?"

"I thought you might need some help finding something."

"Well, do you know anything?"

"I think I do. Look over there. See all them yeller' jackets swarming on the ground?"

Larry nodded and walked carefully to where Zeke was pointing. There were a few apples on the ground and flies and bees were all over them. But there was one spot where they were even thicker, almost entirely covering the ground. Larry looked closely, but very carefully—he was afraid of bees. He could see, on the thin grass and leaves, blood smears and splatters, along with bits of brain and bone.

Larry backed up and bent over. He was faint, but the feeling passed. He took his handkerchief and wiped his face. It was warm out, and the smell was terrible. He finally said to Zeke, "Whoever did this thought no one would bother to look."

"It would be easy to miss," Zeke added.

Larry took a deep breath and stepped back. He began walking to the car to radio in, but Zeke stepped between Larry and the car and said, "Larry, for now, I want you to keep this to yourself. This will become important later."

"Why did you show me this if I can't use it in the investigation?"

"You can use it, but for now, just for now, keep it quiet. That fat ass sheriff will just frame someone else if he thinks you know."

This troubled Larry, but he agreed to keep quiet. Larry thought this was a real hammer, very solid evidence to link the sheriff after his slip about the murder site. He took a deep breath, thought for a brief moment and answered, "Just for now, but I will have to report it soon."

Larry and his officer friend soon left. Zeke watched from the trees. "Living folk are just too much in a big hurry."

Later that afternoon the state police team gathered at the Thomas home. It was going to be burgers again, but this time Mike and Larry set up the grill on the small back patio.

Ruth Anne was glad to see the officers relax a bit and just talk about everything and nothing at all, but she was troubled to see Larry so reserved, and not smiling much. While everyone was sitting out back on folding chairs borrowed from the Lilac Road Church, Ruth Anne and Larry sat in the dining room alone for a moment. Larry was staring into his coffee cup. Ruth Anne walked up behind him and rubbed his shoulders. She asked, "What's wrong, sugar?"

"The violence and evil underneath all of this is just very troublesome."

"I'm sorry you have to see all of this horror. Can I help?"

These events had forced Ruth Anne to think about the nature of Larry's work. This time it involved friends and family. Her worry and fear were growing stronger. Larry finally answered. "No, not really. But thanks for inviting us here. It really helps."

"Why don't you go out there with your buddies while I go back to the Piggly Wiggly. I ordered a cake and I'll get some ice cream."

"Do you need company?" Larry stood from the table and hugged Ruth Anne. She saw a trace of a tear in his eye.

She kissed him and answered, "No. I have it taken care of."

Indeed she did. Ruth Anne had made some phone calls that afternoon. She was expecting more guests for dessert.

GUESTS FOR DESSERT

In just a short time, Ruth Anne returned. Mike heard the car pull up in the drive. He walked around the house and was surprised to see Becky carrying a large sheet cake.

Ruth Anne laughed at Mike's big smile and said, "Look who I found at the Pig'!"

Mike replied, "Mom doesn't bring home many stray girls."

Becky smiled and said, "I'm not a stray girl, am I?"

"Well, welcome to our home, stray girl," he said. "Maybe we'll let you stay a while!"

Ruth Anne said, "Son, quit being lazy and take these bags!"

Becky reinforced the command. "Do what your mother says, sweetheart! Else I might just take my cake and go home."

As they were setting up the dessert on the table, Becky said, "I got my mom to get me out of school early so I could make the cake!"

"You did this all by yourself?" Mike asked.

"Sure did, doubting Thomas!"

"You skipped band?"

"I'd do anything not to miss all this fun!"

"Do I have to eat liver and onions this time?"

"Nope!"

"Mom," Mike said, "looks like you planned this out very well."

"I did."

"Are there more surprises in store?"

"Of course. Coach Carter will be here soon."

"Oh, good Lord, he'll make me run wind sprints for missing practice!"

"He did mention that."

"Thanks, Mother!"

She smiled. "I just try to do the very best for my little Mikey!"

Mike just smiled and shook his head. "I have to admit, this cake looks wonderful. Can we hurry up and cut the doggone thing?"

Becky walked around the table, smiling, and she took Mike's hand. For a few minutes, the two of them were alone in the kitchen. Mike asked, "Any more trouble from our good friend Bobby?"

"No, not today. I wonder if someone had a talk with him."

"Well, this scares me. I'm worried for you and the others. Maybe we should get Larry to find a way to keep us as far away from this as we can."

"So long as I'm with you."

It wasn't long before Coach Carter arrived with Suzy—and Lee. Ruth Anne had told them to park and come straight in. Lee had made the trip hiding in the rear floorboard. "Don't knock, don't linger; just come in quickly," Ruth Anne had told them.

Mike was so surprised to see Lee, he dropped Becky's hand. Mike and Lee just stared at each other as large smiles began to appear on all faces. Mike felt the embarrassment of his performance during the arrest the day before. Once again he was paralyzed by indecision. He wanted to apologize to Lee, but he didn't know where to start.

Becky broke the silence and said, "This is what you two idiots should do." She walked Mike by the arm to Lee, then placed each of their arms on each other's shoulders. Then she put her own arms around Ruth Anne, very warmly, very sincerely. "This is called a hug," she said.

Mike and Lee sort of did the same thing, but both felt awkward and quickly let go.

"Absolutely pathetic!" Becky said as she laughed.

Larry and the officers walked in from the back patio to greet the newcomers. When they saw Lee, there was a moment of awkward silence. Larry wasn't sure what to do, but Ruth Anne came to the rescue. "Larry, we have cake and ice cream."

"Well, Lee," Larry said, "I think I'm supposed to arrest you. If you won't run this time, we'll figure out what to do after we eat. But consider yourself arrested."

Lee's face registered confusion and concern. He had no desire to join Gone in the Pulaski County jail.

Coach Carter said, with all of his coaching-voice authority, "He will not run, until the next time he's running sprints for me."

"Good," Larry said. "Then let's eat!"

These words were hardly out of Larry's mouth when the doorbell rang. It was Amos Ross, Mrs. Ross, Mandy and Sweet Momma. As Ruth Anne welcomed them inside, she took Sweet Momma by the hand and led her to Lee.

Lee softly cried, "Momma," and took her in his arms.

There were few dry eyes.

It was Ruth Anne who got things going again. "We have a really good cake here," she said. "Reverend Ross, we have never had this many black folk in this house. Will you please ask for the good Lord's blessing?"

"Amen!" said Coach Carter.

Reverend Amos cleared his throat. His wife handed him a tissue to dry his eyes. He reached in his coat pocket, took out a small Bible and held it in his right hand. He reached that hand up and said, like Moses with his staff standing in front of Pharaoh, "Y'all pray with me, please.

300

"Lord in heaven above. We see your love and mighty power. This boy has been delivered. We ask for your blessings on these your good and honest servants. Forgive us all of our faults and weaknesses and make us strong in your righteous grace. In the mighty name of Jesus Christ, we ask this. Amen."

Once again, Mike was in awe, amazed by Reverend Ross's voice.

Becky punched him in the ribs and softly said, "Do I have to tell you everything? Get your shy butt over there and hug Sweet Momma!"

Ruth Anne added, "Do as she says, Mike!"

Becky and Mike walked over and hugged Sweet Mamma.

Dale Katz stepped up to Larry and asked, "Do good and honest servants make more money than state troopers? Do I get a raise soon?"

"He wasn't talking about you."

Both officers laughed.

BACKYARD CONCERT

This small army of good and honest servants gathered on the patio as the evening faded. They were to a person very happy, but also very tired. The extreme swings of worry and happiness definitely had taken a toll. Larry was the unofficial but very real worrier-in-chief. He was very concerned that more violence could erupt. In his discussions with Amos, he had become acutely aware of the growing frustration among the black community over this all-too-obvious frame job.

The officers left first, except for Larry and an officer named Steve Anderson. They would stay the night, with their two state police cruisers parked out front. Lee was staying also. The plan for now was to meet at the church first thing on Wednesday morning, with Mike and Lee under their watchful eye. The two boys would remain in the custody of a trooper at all times. Mrs. Ross promised biscuits and sausage gravy with apple-cinnamon muffins to chase. Mike felt hungry already.

Soon, Becky's father, with her younger sisters, arrived to take Becky home. He stayed long enough to eat one of the last pieces of cake. When he finished up, he placed his hand on Becky's shoulder and said, "Time to go home, little girl."

Becky's sisters had come along and they were swooning all over Mike.

Becky said, "Okay, but Mike and Lee promised us a show, a little concert!"

The sisters, almost in perfect unison, said, "Please Daddy, please, can we watch?"

"Sure, this just might be good!" Mr. Patterson settled back in his chair.

Mike and Lee, on fishing trips at Fair Creek, had been rehearsing their own version of the Jackson 5's "ABC," with Mike as Michael Jackson and Lee singing backup. This would be the first time they'd done this with an audience. They stood on the patio and began a less-than-impressive but still entertaining concert.

With a very simple one-two step, they began. They cycled through the first verse and the chorus, because that was all they really remembered well enough to sing. It was silly and goofy, but everyone had fun. Years later, Mike and Lee would repeat this for their football team, as young coaches, but that's a story for another day.

After the performance, Mike walked Becky to her father's car. Before she got in, Mike stole a quick kiss and said, "You did not have to tell me to kiss you!"

"Will wonders ever cease?" Becky kissed him back and hugged him very tightly. "We cannot abandon Lee," she reminded him. "Be strong, tiger."

Mike knew she was right; he had almost abandoned his friend once—he would not do it again. He wanted to never again hurt anyone close to him.

Ruth Anne had to tell Mike and Lee to shut up and go to sleep several times, but they talked deep into the night just like a couple of little kids on their very first sleepover. Which it was.

PART 12
FINALLY IN THE LILAC ROAD CHURCH CHOIR—WEDNESDAY

BREAKFAST

Early Wednesday morning, Larry, Mike and Lee left the Thomas home and headed for the Lilac Road Church in the trooper cruiser. Larry didn't want them to be spotted, not yet, so he took back roads. Still, it was only a matter of time until most of the town would know what was going on. That wouldn't be all bad.

All three were hungry and looking forward to Angelica Ross's big breakfast. When they pulled in to the parking lot, they could already smell the food. Lee led the charge, like he was wide open on a deep post route. "That smells fine. Holy cow!"

"I think it's holy pig," Mike said. "Sausage in a church."

Angelica and Mandy Ross were finishing the setup when the boys entered. A huge bowl of sausage gravy and a monstrous pile of cat-head biscuits, butter, apple butter and dewberry jam were on the table, spread in a glorious array fit for any king. A huge platter of muffins, just out of the oven, smelled amazing. All of the officers were lining up.

When the party all settled into their chairs, Revered Ross stood up, looked at Lee and said, "Lee, will you turn grace for us?"

Mike turned his head, laughing softly. The thought of Lee leading a prayer!

Larry elbowed Mike in the ribs and whispered, "Show

some respect, boy!"

This took the grin right off Mike's face. Lee cleared his throat, then he noticed that Mandy had walked up behind him. This made him even more nervous. He cleared his throat again. "Dear Jesus," he began.

Mike was biting his tongue and looking at the floor to keep from laughing. When he looked up, he saw that Reverend Ross was giving him a very serious, almost evil, look.

"Thank you for all you give us," Lee continued. "Thank you for this good food and the good people that prepared it. Forgive our trespasses. Thy will be done. Amen." And then he added, "Oh, and bless my grandmother and Gone. Please protect them."

Suddenly Mike felt bad for laughing.

As everyone began to work through the food line, Amos Ross and Mandy approached Mike and Lee. "We're heading to school now," Mandy said. "You remember school? Some of us still have to go."

Mike laughed and said, "We're really digging this fugitive thing!"

"Well, do you want me to pick up your homework assignments?"

Larry spoke up at this suggestion, although Mandy had offered it as a joke. "You shouldn't do that. I really don't think we can keep this going for very long. We may have to put Lee and Mike in protective custody as material witnesses."

"In Macon," he added. "Big Bob threatened Lee and Mike, but I can only swing this 'fugitive thing' for a few days at most."

Everyone went silent; no one liked this idea.

Larry continued, "We'll see where we are at the end of the day. I have a hunch that things will break loose soon. I hope so."

Mike said, "I don't miss the homework, but I miss school."

Mandy smirked and said, "Message received—I'll tell Becky

you miss her already!"

Mike blushed as Lee and Larry laughed. As Amos and Mandy were leaving, Amos turned to Mike with a big grin and sang, "I got sunshine - on a cloudy day."

THE SQUEEZE

Dale Katz was a senior officer and investigator for the Georgia State Police. After years as a state trooper, he became a tough and successful investigator. He was feared by any criminal suspect who came under his attention. He even intimidated other law officials.

Word had spread quickly among Big Bob's posse that Dale Katz was looking into the particulars of the murder cases. Like Larry, Dale questioned the official report on these murder cases. The direct evidence and weak conclusions as presented by the sheriff did not pass the smell test. That was enough to get Dale digging.

Word of this investigation was getting around to the sheriff's deputies. This was particularly worrisome for Sam Elkins, who was growing more suspicious of Big Bob and who didn't want to ride down the tubes with the lazy, arrogant sheriff.

The plan for Wednesday morning was for Dale and Steve Anderson to visit the sheriff's office and ask some questions. They also wanted to see if Gone was okay. Larry and another trooper would visit the school and just fly the flag, to see if anyone would volunteer any new information. Larry wanted to be sure Paul Foss saw him there at the school.

Dale and Steve arrived to find the sheriff and his posse in the front office. All of them had their feet on desks, bellies in the air, coffee in mugs and about one half of a giant box of donuts finished. None of them moved or even flinched when Dale and Steve entered. They knew Dale was trying to look into their business and they clearly resented his presence. Sam Elkins was very nervous, but he stayed quiet.

"Sheriff, I need to ask you some questions," Dale said. "Your office?"

"Nope, right here," Big Bob said. "I have no secrets from these boys."

"Like hell you don't, but okay, right here."

"Well, at least I have a real office, by the courthouse, and not at colored church house."

Dale's first question for the sheriff was intended to stir the pot, and it did. "Is this breakfast," he said, "or you just sloppin' hogs?"

Big Bob jumped up, sloshing coffee all over the desk. "Now just a damn minute, you—"

Dale cut off the sheriff with a look that had melted many a hardened criminal. "Set your big ass down and answer my questions!"

Fred Dobbs spoke up: "It's breakfast."

Big Bob thundered, "Fred, just shut up!"

Everyone was quiet, but then Big Bob did slowly take his seat. Dale was thinking this situation through. He didn't know if he would get any new information, but maybe he could create some doubt among the deputies. Dale let Big Bob cook for a minute before he finally asked, "Why did it take so long for you to call for assistance after you found Bert Andrews dead?"

"It took a while to look around," Big Bob said. "I don't remember exactly how long. Why do you care?"

"Didn't the informant tell you exactly where to look? Fred, am I right?"

The sheriff didn't answer; he just glared at Fred. Dale let the question sink in, then asked again, "Fred, am I right, or not?"

Fred took a deep breath and answered in a meek but honest voice, "Yes, sir, the caller said to look behind the building."

Big Bob, teeth gritted, said, "Fred, I told you to shut up. How do you even remember all of this?"

"Well, Trooper Wayne asked me the same question Monday."

Bob rose to his feet again. "Katz, you need to leave. You are not welcome here."

"That's okay," Dale said. "I wasn't expecting a fuzzy, warm hug from you. Why did you fail to interview Smokey Wright and fail to have his statement recorded properly? You're the only person that heard his statement."

"I didn't have time. You need to leave now."

But Dale wasn't going anywhere. "You had all day Monday."

"You best leave now!"

"I want to see Gone Sanderson."

"Ain't gonna happen!"

Dale just laughed and told the sheriff, "Go wash the donut sugar off your face while I check on your suspect."

Dale Katz and Steve Anderson walked right through the posse. Dale took Fred Hobbs by the arm and said, "Lead the way, Fred. Bring the donuts."

Fred led them to the small jail cell, inside of which Gone was sleeping on his side. Dale spoke out, "Arthur, are you okay in there?"

Gone startled and sat up. "Yes, sir! Who are you?"

Dale introduced himself and Steve Anderson.

"I didn't do anything," Gone said. "When can I get out of here?"

"Are they feeding you okay?"

"Not much. Fred brings me a little."

"Is that right, Fred?"

Fred looked around nervously to see if anyone was listening before answering, "Yes. I have to sneak it in. But I try."

"I'll fix that. Fred, give Arthur the donuts. Have they asked you any questions, son?"

"No, just where I thought Lee might hide."

"Don't you tell them anything. I'll get you an attorney. Keep quiet. Believe me, Mr. Sanderson, I will help you. Lee and Mrs. Sanderson are fine. I'll let them know you are too!"

As Dale, Steve and Fred left the holding area, Dale said to Fred, "You come with us. I need a good assistant. You can be in charge of taking care of Gone."

"Yes, sir."

As they went back through the front office, Dale pointed at Big Bob and said, "Don't leave town. I'll have more questions for you."

Dale Katz could scare a confession out of Satan.

Later that evening, Dale and Fred went by the Burger Circle, got two cheeseburgers, a big box of fries, a milkshake and a peach fried pie. Back at the station, Dale walked right by the deputy on duty and delivered the food to Gone.

"Remember, Arthur, keep quiet!"

"Yes, sir. I will. Is your name Jesus?"

Dale smiled. "Most people think I work for the other side."

Not long after Dale left, Big Bob walked back to the cell and glared at Gone through the bars, sipping coffee from a paper cup. Gone turned to the wall to ignore the sheriff.

This made Big Bob very angry. He threw the coffee at Gone through the bars, burning the back of his neck and ears. "There's some coffee to go with your donuts."

Gone jumped and screamed, grabbing the bars.

Big Bob laughed the laugh he usually reserved for beating black men with his nightstick. "Gone, your ass is grass, I have you! Be careful what you say; there's no telling what might happen if you try to cross me."

Gone was about to explode, but there was nothing he could do. Not now.

Big Bob's offer

Big Bob set to work on a backup plan. He needed it. He was getting more worried by the minute. He had a good idea who had killed Bert Andrews, and of course he knew exactly who'd killed Smokey. He also knew a lot about stolen and false evidence. He had an idea to force a false confession, but he wasn't sure it would work.

Big Bob left the office alone and drove to the parking lot of the Fair Creek Park. He pulled into a remote area behind a large patch of dewberry brambles and honeysuckle, where it was unlikely anyone would see him. He wove his way through the woods along the same path that Lee used to go fishing. By the time he reached the Sanderson home, he was sweaty, out of breath and had his shirttail out. He walked to the front of the house, where Sweet Momma was sitting in her rocker. She asked who was there.

"It's Sheriff Willet. I want to talk to you."

"What if'n I don't want to talk to you?"

"Just hear me out. Won't take long."

"Say it and get out of here."

Big Bob walked up onto the porch, still huffing and puffing.

"You all right? Sounds like a top hog sucking wind."

"You listen to me," he said. "I have an offer for you. A trade."

"What could you possibly have to offer me?"

"Well, if you'll say that Gone killed Bert Andrews, I'll drop all charges against Lee."

The sheriff was still working from his old assumption that most people, including Sweet Momma, feared him. Both Big Bob and Sweet Momma knew that the sheriff had lynched her son many years earlier. But her paralyzing fear of him was crumbling. For once, Sweet Momma thought she could stand strong.

"You and I both know Gone didn't kill nobody," she said. "So why would I say he did?"

"This is your only chance to save Lee. All you have to do is say that Gone did it."

"Sheriff Willet, if you are my only chance to save Lee, I'm in a bad place."

"This is your last chance."

"No, I don't think so."

Big Bob wasn't used to being turned away—his threats always worked. "Then both your boys are doomed!" he said.

"Don't think so," Sweet Momma shot back. "You don't know where Lee is."

"Where is he?"

Momma just laughed.

The sheriff reached to grab Momma's arm in an effort to scare her. His big feet pounded the front porch boards. But as he stepped towards the chair, a very old black man appeared behind Momma. The visage wasn't solid, instead appearing as a thin gray image. But the eyes were bright green and stared deep into the sheriff's soul. Big Bob stepped backwards off the porch, missing a step and stumbling. Old Zeke pointed at Big Bob and said, in a voice only Bob could hear, "Leave this place."

Big Bob yelled back, "Who—who are you? What..."

Sweet Momma laughed. "Who you talkin' to, Sheriff? You know who I am!"

Big Bob couldn't get out an answer. As he backed away, a mighty breeze began to flow right at him. The grass rushed, and old dead leaves whipped around. This little dust devil was directed right towards him, from nowhere. Rocks began to strike him on the cheek, on the belly and on the butt as he turned to run. But the rock-chucking whirlwind stayed on him.

As the noise settled, Sweet Momma and Zeke shared a laugh. "Old man, that was awful. You scared him half to death."

"I'd say more than half, but he won't be back."

"Reckon not."

"I got to move on. That was fun. Ain't scared nobody like that in many a year."

"I heard about the last time you did it."

"Long time ago."

"Yes, it was. But I remember the story well. That old white man was abusing little girls and you made him stop."

"Yep. He wet his britches too!"

Zeke left soon after, Sweet Momma had been shaken by this exchange.

Neither Zeke nor Ivie were aware of the Wizard's bomb under the porch.

At the High School

Around lunchtime there was usually a lot of traffic in the hallways. Larry and Steve made their presence obvious. They really had no specific plan except to be seen, turn up the heat on those keeping dark secrets.

Larry made sure that Paul Foss was one of the people to see him in the hallways.

Both troopers wandered over to the cafeteria just before lunch. Larry was walking through the kitchen when he was approached by a tall, smiling man, Isaiah James. Isaiah asked, "Do you know how Gone is doing?"

"Well, okay, I think."

"I sure was surprised when he was arrested."

Larry was a reluctant to say much, but the old man seemed genuinely concerned for Gone. Larry answered, "Well, I probably shouldn't say much, but me too."

As they were talking, they saw Paul Foss enter the cafeteria.

"Mr. James, do you know him?"

"Everybody knows him. Big reptile snake. Fire-breathing dragon in the Klan."

On a gut feeling, Larry asked, "Are you around early in the mornings?"

"We start work in the cafeteria about six thirty."

"Seen anything unusual lately?"

"I saw the wizard come in early on Monday."

Larry stood up straight. "You did!?"

"Yep."

"Why did you not tell anyone?"

Larry finally had a good idea how the evidence had made it into the boys' lockers.

Isaiah shrugged and replied, "Well, it was odd, but I really didn't think much about it."

"Tell me exactly what you saw."

"I saw Mr. Foss come in the back door. It was early, not long after I started workin'."

"So you don't usually see him at that time?"

"That was the first time ever. He was totin' one of them sports bags, pretty good-size bag."

"And you're sure it was Paul Foss?"

"If 'n I'm lyin', I'm dyin'! I was loadin' sacks of flour on a cart on the dock. I don't think he noticed me."

Larry had a very confident smile and he was nodding his head. This was an "aha" moment. "Isaiah, I'm glad we talked," Larry said.

Later, I may need to take a statement from you, I will be in touch."

Larry bounced out of the school on a cloud, chanting a line from a TV show: "Here come the judge, here come the judge... I am going to get a warrant."

ADVICE FROM SWEET MOMMA

Larry left the school and headed towards the Lilac Road Church. The state police team had agreed to meet about two o'clock. Larry had plenty of time, so he decided to go on to the Sanderson home. He wanted to see if Sweet Momma was doing okay, and maybe provide some encouragement. As he drove up to the front of the house, he saw Reverend Ross sitting on the porch with Momma. Larry parked his cruiser under a large mimosa tree and walked over. Reverend Ross called out, "Hello Larry, come on up!"

"Howdy," Larry said. "How is everyone today?"

Sweet Momma was the first to answer: "I be just fine; how 'bout you?"

"I'll be doing better if you have some cornbread."

"Not today, sweetie, but I'll make you some soon."

"You know I might starve without your good 'pone bread."

Sweet Momma laughed loudly and said, "I know how to take care of my boys."

Amos chimed in, "Momma been tellin' me all about how Big Bob came by a bit ago."

Momma added, "Sho' did. Made me an offer!"

"What was that?" Larry asked.

Momma told the story, though she left out the part about Zeke.

Larry had settled into an old ladder-back chair in the

shade. He shook his head and said, "Bob Willet is as dumb as he is big!"

Reverend Ross laughed. "Dumb as a loaf of bread."

"Well, Momma," Larry said, "I can't say much, but I think we've caught the snake. There are still many things I don't know, though. But the real story's coming out—I feel it. I think we'll find many lies. We'll have Gone out soon."

At this, Momma just sat back and rocked. A tear trickled down her cheek. "Amos, I knew Ruth Anne's Larry was a good man, a very good man."

"He's all right, I reckon."

No one spoke for a couple of minutes. Larry was growing very comfortable with the gentle sound of the breeze and cicadas. He noticed Amos, in the swing, had his eyes closed and was softly smiling. Everyone seemed content.

Momma broke the silence with a softly placed question, but it was a stunner: "Larry, are you ready to be a father?"

"What?" Larry sat up at full attention, now wide awake. "Well, someday I hope to—"

Momma cut him off. "Don't worry, son, everything is okay. But you might have to take on Mike and Lee soon. Those boys gonna need you."

Larry let this sink in, but it was hard to grasp. He didn't want to lose Sweet Momma. He couldn't think of much to say. All he got out was, "Well, I'll always try to help them as best I can."

Momma jumped back in, "You must always be honest and show them what is right. Don't tell them—show them!"

"I will try."

"Amos and I think you are up to the job."

Larry stood and acknowledged this passing of the baton. "That's good, I reckon."

When Momma began to fall asleep, Amos pushed himself out of the swing, grabbed Larry's arm and said, "Let's get out of here, back to the church. I think we got work to do."

"Good. Maybe then you can explain what I've just been asked to do. I don't understand."

"Momma says we will understand by and by."

"That gives me great comfort, but I'm still not sure what we're talking about. Is she going to a nursing home? I hope she is really not about to pass away."

"Me neither, Trooper Wayne, me neither."

Momma had drifted off to sleep and didn't hear this part of the conversation. She would have just laughed at them anyway. It just did not matter what they understood, it would all happen anyway, ready or not.

THE WIZARD FOLDS— OFF TO MACON

Right after lunchtime, the team assembled at the church. Carefully, Larry related his conversation with Isaiah James. When he finished, there was silence around the table, until Dale Katz broke it. "I cannot wait to question this dragon!"

Trooper Anderson spoke up, "The kids at school often call Foss Mr. Wizard."

Larry asked, "So how do we go about pickin' him up?"

Dale already had a plan worked out. "Let's go pick him up for questioning," he said. "I think we have enough evidence to arrest him as a conspiracy suspect. Let's arrest him the same way Gone was arrested—right in the middle of school hours. I'll get the warrant."

All heads were nodding and a few faces had big smiles.

"I'll go to the principal's office and tell them what's going to happen," Dale continued. "Trooper Wayne and Trooper Anderson, you will go straight to the science class and arrest Mr. Wizard - but I will get his real name on the warrant, what the hell is it?"

"Paul Foss." Larry answered as he wrote it out for Dale.

"Okay, I will arrange the warrant. As soon as I have the judge's authorization, we go."

Steve asked, "Are we going to take him to Macon?"

"Absolutely. Steve, you and I will take him."

Larry added, "What about Mike and Lee tonight?"

Reverend Ross spoke up, "They are at my house while we're working here. I'll take them with me to prayer meeting. Coach Carter wants them at his house tonight."

Dale Katz nodded. "Sounds like a plan. Stand by. I'll call the judge and we'll go get that son of a bitch."

Amos frowned and pointed at the painting of Calvary on the wall. "Do not speak that way in the Lord's house!" he said.

"I'm sorry, Reverend Ross," Dale said. "Will you say a prayer asking for forgiveness for me and His blessing on arresting that slimy bastard—oh, I mean—oh, shit."

"Dale, just stop talking," Larry said as he stifled a laugh.

Reverend Ross prayed; he was just a little fired up.

The plan went as it was supposed to. Dale Katz went in the front door, straight to the principal's office, and told them what was happening. Mr. Penner said, "I'll come with you and take charge of the class."

As Dale Katz and Mr. Penner walked down the hall, Larry and Steve burst into the classroom. They quickly closed the cuffs on Paul Foss and escorted him out the door as Mr. Penner took control in the classroom.

Bang - bang, it was done.

Larry addressed the trembling wizard: "You, sir, are under arrest for conspiracy. We're taking you to the Macon state police headquarters for questioning and confinement. Your legal options will be explained and you will have the right to an attorney."

"I'm willing to deal," Foss said. "I know things."

It actually surprised Larry that the fire dragon would fold so quickly. It often surprised Larry when criminals turned out to be cowards, especially some of the violent ones. "You need to know when to keep your big mouth shut," Larry said. "So, I'm going to give you some free legal advice: shut your damn mouth."

Larry and Steve escorted their prisoner down the hall towards their cruiser. Dale Katz met them and fell in. He couldn't resist singing as they walked, in a bad monotone, not at all like Judy Garland: "We're off to see the wizard."

Back in class, Mr. Penner calmed the students. Suzy Carter turned to Becky and Mandy and said, "This is the best class ever!"

They laughed together. Suzy followed by saying,

"My house, 8:30 tonight!"

IN THE CHOIR

Wednesday evenings at the Lilac Road Church usually involved an informal choir practice and some songs for the whole congregation. Isaiah James was the choir director. Of course he had no formal training or music education, but that didn't matter; no one else in the choir did either. But the heartfelt worship in their songs was obvious. The will to sing praises from the heart and a little experience doing so was a sufficient music education.

Mandy and Ms. Ross were in the choir, too. Reverend Ross started the simple service with a prayer, of course calling on the Lord to remember Sweet Momma. After the prayer, a young boy in the church read the beatitudes from the Gospel of Matthew. After this, Reverend Ross introduced his two guests:

"Tonight, we are so happy to have some of our good friends and neighbors with us. Y'all know Lee Sanderson. He is one of our own, but he lays out so much that he just seems like a guest."

That brought a response of nodding and verbal calls:

"Uh huh!"

"That's right, Brother Amos, Amen."

"Praise God!"

"But young Lee is here tonight!" Reverend Ross went on.

"Hallelujah, praise Jehovah!" came the responses. "Thank

you, Lord, have mercy, Lord!"

"Now tonight we also have Mike Thomas," said the reverend, "our very good friend and neighbor. Many of you know Singin' Mike!"

This introduction brought big smiles and much laughter and more praises. Mike blushed.

"'Bout time!"

"Thank God."

"Welcome, Mike."

Reverend Ross said, "I think it is perfectly fitting that Mike and Lee join the choir!"

A big cheer and a round of applause broke loose. Both boys moved into the choir box, Lee on one side of Mandy and Mike beside Mrs. Ross. There was risk in this visit. Mike and Lee were now not directly in the custody of a trooper. There were some concerned that this might bring the Klan or the sheriff down on the church and its congregation. But it also seemed right.

Isaiah skillfully led the choir through several songs, including "One of These Days," "Climbing Jacob's Ladder," "This Little Light of Mine" and "To Canaan's Land." Mike really liked "When I Can Read My Title Clear."

Mike was having a really good time. Lee was not; church bored him most of the time. Lee would have rather been almost anywhere else.

In a few minutes, that would become really obvious—and very prophetic.

ANOTHER MEETING

At Big Bob's office, all was quiet. The sheriff was alone at his desk, sipping bourbon. With the arrest of Paul Foss, Big Bob had some real concerns now. He was seriously considering slipping out of town. Everything was falling apart.

Big Bob smelled the old soldier before he saw him.

"Lee Sanderson is at the colored church," the spirit of Andy Thomas said. "If you get there now, you can arrest him. As long as the Sanderson boys are in custody, you can get other witnesses."

Big Bob saw this as a last chance and a possible bargaining chip. He ran out to his cruiser without calling for backup.

IDEAS

As the singing continued, Amos Ross walked around the auditorium, listening, and making note of who was present and who was not.

He was standing in the back when suddenly Zeke was beside him. The old spirit said, "Hide the boys. The sheriff is coming."

Reverend Ross walked quickly to the front and interrupted the choir as they sang "In the Army of the Lord."

"We have to get Lee and Mike out," he said quietly but firmly. "The sheriff is on his way."

There was an eruption of talk and commotion as the message spread into the congregation. "Come with me, boys," the reverend said. "To the basement."

As they began to move, the flashing lights from the sheriff's cruiser came in through the stained-glass windows. As the trio hustled down the middle aisle, Zeke appeared again. "He's here—time's up!"

All could see the flashing lights from the Sheriff's cruiser coming through the stained-glass windows.

Mrs. Ross cried out, "What can we do?"

Karen Walker, a young woman in the choir, a young woman with a strong voice, answered, "I have an idea!"

THE SEARCH

Karen and Sharron Walker were twin sisters who had been in the choir for years. Both had strong voices and were well-known for their abilities. They sang at funerals, weddings and almost any other cause for celebration or mourning. Also, both of them were big girls, tall and broad in every direction. Neither men nor cherry pies stood a chance against these sisters.

"Lee, Mike, come here!" Karen waved for them to come back into the choir chamber. "Mike, you get under my choir robe and Lee you get under Sharron's."

Lee stopped in his tracks: "Say what?"

"You heard me! Hide under our robes. Now!"

Both Karen and Sharron lifted their robes and pushed the boys down. Just as Lee dropped to the floor, Sharron grabbed his ear and said, "Don't you be peekin' at nothin'!"

But Lee had already determined to keep his eyes clenched close. He didn't want to do any peekin', none at all!

Just as the choir robes dropped over the boys, the drunk, wobbly sheriff came through the front door. He leaned for a moment on the back pew, to gain his balance.

All was graveyard quiet as he slowly walked to the front of the church. He wobbled to a stop at the front and turned to face the congregation. There were few people in the church whom he hadn't wronged in some way.

"I'm looking for Lee Sanderson and Mike Thomas," he announced. "I have it on good authority that they're here."

Isaiah answered, "Sheriff Willet, I don't see no white boy."

"I'm going to look around. Nobody move."

Big Bob looked around—around and under and over people, pews and chairs. As he slowly walked around, the congregation remained quiet and still. Finally, Reverend Ross spoke up, "Sheriff, you are not going to find them here."

"Let's look in your office. Everyone stay here!"

Reverend Ross escorted the sheriff through classrooms, restrooms, the kitchen, the office. Again, Amos tried to bring this to a close. Big Bob was liable to hurt someone. He had before, many times.

"You need to leave and cease this evil."

"I know they're here somewhere," Big Bob said.

"You know very little. Please leave this church."

The sheriff did finally leave, not sure what his next move would be, confused at the spirit's mistake. He was running out of options.

Amos returned to the auditorium after watching the frustrated sheriff leave and drive off down Lilac Road.

As he walked back into the auditorium, a huge smile broke across his face. "He's gone—praise Jesus!" A wild, loud frenzy of laughter, dance, hallelujahs and smiles came forth. "Just like baby Moses, the Lord has delivered!"

Isaiah added, "The Lord delivered his children - under the robes!"

Mike and Lee came out of hiding, very relieved. This would be a story oft retold, with both Mike and Lee accusing one another of peekin'.

Isaiah started the choir in "Victory Is Mine!"

Everybody clapped and sang:

"Victory is mine, hallelujah!

Victory today is mine!

I told ol' Satan, get thee behind! Victory today is mine!"

331

DESSERT FOR THE FUGITIVES

Just as the celebration song was winding down, Larry and Ruth Anne drove up to the church. They then escorted Mandy, Mike and Lee to the cruiser and headed to Coach Carter's house.

As they rode, Mandy told the story of the search, laughing so hard that she cried and almost wet herself. She would never forget the look of shock on Lee's face as he went under the robe, and the look of complete embarrassment as the story was retold. For once, the always quick-witted, outspoken Lee was silent.

"Under the robe" was a new phrase in their lexicon and it would always have a very special meaning.

Larry drove and listened silently as Mandy told the story. He secretly resolved to get Big Bob off the streets as soon as possible. This was potentially explosive, and more people could be hurt. He had taken too great of a risk this evening, and he vowed not to do it again.

The group arrived at the Carter house, where Becky, Suzy and Ray were waiting on the porch to greet them.

Everyone was happy to see the group together, but it was a quiet and subdued celebration – even with dewberry cobbler.

Becky and Mike sat on the front porch swing, alone, for some time. Becky put her head on Mike's shoulder and Mike hugged her.

"I liked it much better when you were just a shy fullback," she said. "This hiding stuff scares me. Besides, I think word is getting around that the troopers are holding you. Whose robe will you hide under next time?"

Both of them laughed, and Mike answered, "You never know! You're such a petite little thing that I don't think I can hide under your robe!"

"I don't think I would let you under my robe. I'll just let Big Bob have you."

You never do know. Stranger things would happen very soon. You just never know.

Coach Carter ended the party early. "Got to get to bed, everybody," he said. "Mike and Lee, we're going to be up early. You owe me several sprints! We gonna have PT fun!"

PART 13
THE STORY COMES OUT—THURSDAY

CARTER'S BASEMENT AND BACKYARD PT

Coach Carter woke Lee and Mike at sunrise, just as the troopers outside the house swapped shifts. There had been no activity during the night, nothing to worry about. Coach Carter had the boys up, dressed and in the back yard in just a few minutes. As they descended from the back porch, Lee saw that Coach had set cones in strategic places. Lee and Mike glanced at each other, both knowing what was coming next: a series of stretching warmups and then twenty-yard forward and backward sprints, about twenty of each, then ten sets of touch-and-goes, four cone drills and a few more sprints.

"Just to stay loose!" Coach explained.

By the time Coach was satisfied, Mike and Lee were gasping, hands on knees.

"Let's go inside," the coach said. "I want to talk to you. After fifty more crunches and pushups apiece."

Back in the house, Coach Carter said, "I want you two to stay here today. Mr. Penner has arranged to have some of your schoolwork delivered. You can catch up a bit. The troopers will be here off and on. Remember, you are in official custody. My custody."

Before this morning, Mike and Lee had thought of the Carter home as a warm, friendly place. Now it was a football-drill torture chamber.

Lee answered, "Don't worry, Coach. Even if we wanted to leave, we couldn't. Neither of us can walk."

ISAIAH WATCHES OVER THINGS

Shortly after geometry class, Becky and Suzy were walking to their next class, with A.J. and Ray not far behind. As they rounded a corner, Bobby and his brave companions stepped in front to cut the girls off.

"Well hello, girls! So nice to see you!" Bobby said.

The girls were instantly afraid. Ray came around the corner and spotted this face-off. He rushed right to Bobby.

Bobby went from fox to rabbit very quickly. He was beginning to back off, but Ray kept coming. Out of nowhere, Isaiah James stepped in between Ray and Bobby. He grabbed Ray's arm and said, "Ray, son, hold on a minute."

Ray did, but he was still ready to go after Bobby. He was fired up.

Isaiah turned to Bobby and his gang. "Git on, now. I just saved yo' rear ends. He would have whupped you like a bad dog. All of you-ens. Now, git!"

The posse left quickly.

"Next time I won't stop him!" Isaiah called out as they scurried away. But he was smiling. "Now, let me walk you children to class."

Isaiah James became the girls' unofficial, but very effective, guardian angel.

An Invitation to Lunch

Thursday turned out to be a busy day in Dr. Roberts's office. It was busy enough for Ruth Anne even without everyone wanting to chat about Mike and the million rumors they had heard. Ruth Anne would smile and say that she really couldn't talk about it. That didn't stop people from trying anyway. Ruth Anne was working between patients, juggling several cases, when she was told she had a phone call.

The other side was quiet for a moment and then a very soft and shaky voice answered, "Ruth Anne, this is Janet Allen."

Ruth Anne was surprised and sharply inhaled. "Oh, Janet, it's good to hear from you. How can I help you?"

Ruth Anne knew that Janet had been gone; Larry had mentioned it. But she didn't know why.

"Ruth Anne, I have information about those murders. I'm in Macon with my sister, but I don't want Sheriff Willet to know that. I need to speak to someone. Could I meet with you and Larry?"

Ruth Anne's instincts told her that Janet's information would prove important. She stalled a moment, then said, "When? I'm really busy today."

"I know it's terrible of me to ask, but how about lunchtime? We can meet at Tom's Grill on Macon Highway. They have a quiet side room."

"Well, I don't know about Larry."

"Please ask him. If he knows I have information, maybe he'll come."

"I will ask. I believe he is in Macon."

Ruth Anne called Larry. Yes, indeed he was interested. Ruth Anne told him that it could only be her and Larry, no one else - not yet. Dr. Roberts was not happy, but Ruth Anne promised to get back as soon as she could.

JANET TELLS A SAD STORY

Ruth Anne arrived first. The grill was a classic greasy spoon, the smell of burnt fries and burgers all around. The place was packed with highway travelers to and from Florida, as well as a few local workers, and waitresses in pink dresses with white hats.

"I'll be with you in a second, honey!" one of them said.

Ruth Anne didn't go to many places where waitresses in pink called customers "honey."

She asked about the side room and was quickly escorted to a table.

"What can I get you, honey?"

"Oh, just some iced tea with lemon."

"Sure thing! Be right back, sugar!"

Ruth Anne wondered if "sugar" was better than "honey." Has my status risen already?

The side room was small. A funeral home calendar and pictures of flowers hung on the walls. There was only one small window, which held a noisy air conditioner. A side door led to the kitchen, and Ruth Anne could hear an equally noisy dishwasher. The floor needed to be swept and mopped, but it was clear that wasn't going to happen anytime soon. Buck Owens played over the radio in the kitchen.

So much for a nice quiet back room at Tom's Grill.

It was only a moment before Janet came in. It was obvious

she had been crying, and she looked very tired. Her face was ashen, and her hair unkempt. Nurse Ruth Anne couldn't help but step in. She hugged Janet and quietly asked, "Are you okay? Are you sleeping well?"

"No and no."

Janet seemed to gain a little courage as she sat across from Ruth Anne. They were holding hands when Larry arrived. As he sat, the pink waitress came up and put her hand on his shoulder. "Well hello, honey! Can I get you anything?"

Larry smiled at the curvy young waitress and began to speak, but Ruth Anne kicked him in the shin under the table. "My sweetheart," she said, "will have some coffee, black!"

Ruth Anne smiled smugly and winked at Larry. Larry decided to jump right in and ask Janet to tell her story. She looked as if she might melt if she didn't start talking soon.

Larry had ordered a basket of fries. A soon as "Honey Lady" brought them in and topped off drinks, Larry stood and pulled the sliding shade door closed. He sat down and just nodded to Janet.

Larry wasn't expecting very much out of this. If anything, he thought Janet might have a little dirt on the sheriff, since she had been part of the office staff. He knew that Froggy was close to the sheriff. But Janet's nervousness seemed to indicate there was something very serious and dark here. Maybe she had a truckload of dirt.

For a few moments, Janet stared at her trembling hands. When she began to talk, there was a noticeable tremor in her voice. "I have a pretty good idea who killed Bert Andrews," she said. "In fact, the killer confessed to me."

Ruth Anne slid her chair to Janet's side and put her arm around her. Janet was softly sobbing, but it only took a minute for her to collect herself. As she began to speak, her voice became stronger. "Froggy did it. He told me on the phone as he left town."

This shocked Larry. Froggy? Why? And how did that drive

Big Bob to frame the Sanderson brothers? Janet smiled as she saw the confusion in Larry's face.

Ruth Anne was not as confused as Larry—she had heard the ugly rumors in the past, but she had never dwelt on them, and when Bert was killed, Ruth Anne hadn't even made the connection.

Janet went on to explain that Big Bob was an evil snake. She told the story of her affair with Bert Andrews, Big Bob's blackmail, how she tried to stop it and, mostly, of the many evil skeletons in Big Bob's closet. But what she didn't understand was why Big Bob had chosen to let Froggy know. Janet described her last conversation on the phone with Froggy and his confession to her. "I don't know where he is," she said. "I'm so afraid he may have hurt himself. Oh God, I couldn't live with that."

Janet softly sniffled as Ruth Anne held her. After a minute, Larry broke the silence. Already the wheels were turning in his mind. With the wizard in custody, things could now break quickly. "Janet, I have one question. Why are you telling me this? And why now?"

"Well, I can't keep it inside any longer. And I'm worried for Froggy. He needs to be protected. I'm sure Big Bob will kill him if he can. I feel like I've destroyed everything I've touched. I feel so dirty."

Ruth Anne held her tightly as Janet continued to sob. Even Larry wiped away a tear. "Okay, Janet," he said. "I want you to go to your sister's house here in Macon. Promise me that?"

She nodded.

"We'll find Froggy and I'll do everything I can to protect him. The sheriff will soon be behind bars. Later today I'll send for you and have you make a formal statement."

"I have enough dirt to put that fat son of a bitch away forever."

"I'll help you do that, with pleasure. Also, I advise you to get an attorney. You may need some good legal advice. But between you and me, I think we can keep you out of very much trouble."

As they left and then watched Janet drive off, Larry made a point to Ruth Anne that it wasn't necessary to kick him in the shin so hard.

"Sure it was," she said. "I did not like the way you looked at that pink harlot!"

"But it's the girl in the white nurse's uniform that has my full attention."

Ruth Anne batted her eyes at Larry to complete the joke. "And I just love a man in uniform!"

Both laughed. It was good to find a little joy after the gut-wrenching session with Janet.

"Well, I was going to ask you a really important question this weekend," he said. "Maybe if my shin quits hurting, I'll remember what it was."

"You better remember or I'll kick you harder!"

Ruth Anne and Larry held each other and kissed, lingering for a few minutes behind the diner. The spell was broken when one of the kitchen workers, carrying out trash, tripped and fell because he was watching the uniformed lovers. Cans clanked and rolled and the boy got to his feet, trying to apologize. "I'm so sorry, so sorry. Please don't let me stop you!"

Larry roared laughing at this; Ruth Anne was blushing. "Spilled trash, hell or high water will not stop me!" He kissed her again. He would remember the question. There were more happy tears—and sad tears—coming soon.

Amos Ross explains

The lunch crowd at the Lilac Road church was lighter than usual today. One of the assisting officers, Steve Taylor, came by a couple of times. He had also been to the high school a couple of times, and also to Coach's house to check on Mike and Lee. Steve checked in with Amos, called Macon with a report and headed to lunch and to see Sweet Momma. After he left, Amos found himself all alone at the church for the first time in several days.

He decided to take advantage of the quiet by catching up on some reading in his small office. He had just gotten started when he heard the side door open.

It was two members of his congregation, Brothers Bradley and Henley.

Amos escorted them to the table by the fellowship room and they sat. He offered them some leftover cookies, but they declined: they wanted to get right down to business.

Brother Bradley, a retired foreman from the docks, was wearing jeans and an old work shirt. He was a very powerful man, and had once been an outstanding baseball player, with even a couple of years with the Memphis Red Sox.

Brother Henley, a local farmer, was wearing bibbed overalls and holding his baseball hat. He started the conversation: "Brother Ross, several of the brethren in our church want to know what's going on in this church building.

There has been a lot of police here and it's very odd. It really seems funny, since Gone is still in jail. It seems like nothing is happening."

"Yes, I'm sure it does."

"Everybody knows the state police guys are holding Lee and Mike. It is almost like they're rubbing it in Big Bob's face. Who are they protecting?"

Amos answered, "The state police guys are also watching over Gone in the jailhouse. Big Bob knows that he doesn't hold all of the cards for once."

"So what's going on? Tell us!"

"Well, I can't talk that much about the case, not now. But this will all be public soon. I can tell you this: Officers Wayne, Taylor and Katz are working this and doing what's right. I'm sure Gone and Lee will be treated well and protected. Gone will probably be out of that jail cell soon. They needed a place to work and have meetings, away from town and away from the sheriff. I welcomed them here."

Brother Henley took a deep breath. He nodded and said, "Amos, I really want to believe you. But you know that this is very serious in our community. People are worried, and angry."

Brother Bradley added, "That's right! My grandson is the quarterback on the football team and he says that things are really rough in school. Some of them white boys are running their mouths, especially that Bobby Willet. That apple sho' enough fell close to the tree. We just want you to know that some folk think things are getting worse. We need this to end. We need some assurance."

Amos thought for a second. He replied, "Give me a few more days. I'll pass along your concerns. I hear you. If this doesn't change soon, I'll arrange a meeting for you and the state police guys. Please trust me just a little longer. And please let me know if you hear anything serious or bad." He paused. "And please pray for us all. Please encourage patience. Let everyone know they can come talk to me."

The two visitors sat silently for a minute, and then Brother Henley spoke up, "Okay, we'll do that. I hope this eases up soon. How is Sweet Momma?"

"She's doing as well as she can. You know this is very hard on her. Pray for her too."

"Amos, you be careful. Nobody wants to lose you or your family."

The men left quickly after shaking hands with Amos. This made Amos feel very good, but he knew this all needed to end soon or other folks would get hurt.

In his office he prayed, as hard as he ever had. "Lord, help me do the right things."

Where is Froggy?

As soon as Larry could get on a phone to Dale Katz, he explained what Janet had just told him. Soon there was a statewide manhunt for Froggy, but the state police were really clueless as to where to look.

Next Larry decided to make a call to Janet's sister. "Do you have any ideas where Froggy might have gone?"

"Not for sure, but I know he has a brother near Valdosta. They used to camp and fish in the swamps near there."

This information narrowed the search for the suspected killer. A deputy sheriff in Sumner County talked to a game warden who remembered seeing a pickup truck that sounded a lot like Froggy's. Froggy's brother hadn't seen Froggy, but he did tell the officers about some of their old favorite camping spots.

As the day came to a close, Froggy's hours as a free man were numbered.

He was hiding in the campgrounds where he had camped so many times. Froggy had a gun with him and he was deeply depressed - enough so that he was thinking of ending all of his pain - the hurt of knowing you had been rejected and then in response had destroyed other lives, including your own.

Supper at Becky's—
THE FEAR OF LIVER AND ONIONS

Mike and Lee recovered through the morning and began to work on geometry, English and Spanish homework. Mike worked hard. Lee worked hard copying Mike's work.

"At least do something different so it won't look like you copied everything."

"That's a good idea!"

They worked throughout the day. Around noon, Larry came by with burgers and fries from the Circle. After school was out, Suzy came home and told the guys the plan for the evening. "Becky's dad will come get us at about six. We're going to eat dinner there. Trooper Anderson will meet us there. Then we can go to the movie."

"Did Becky say what was for dinner?"

"No, she just laughed and said to tell you it was your favorite!"

"Oh, Lord, I hope that doesn't mean liver and onions!"

Mike spent the next two hours sick with remembrance of the liver and onions at Becky's house. "That girl is part devil" he said.

Lee had heard the stories, and he wasn't very happy either.

Becky's father picked up the kids and drove them to the Patterson house. Mike and Lee were very happy to see Ray's Chevelle in the driveway and Ray on the front porch, waiting.

"I hear you soft pukes got a workout this morning."

"You could say that," Mike answered as Ray laughed.

"I am saying that!" Lee added and laughed.

Suzy added, "You're going back to my house tonight, so you'll get another one of Daddy's training camp specials tomorrow, bright and early!"

Mike answered, "Well, that's just wonderful. I can't wait!"

Becky came outside with the call to the dinner table. She took Mike by the arm and gave him a she-devil wink. Mike knew it—liver and onions. But as he stepped in the door, he detected the distinct smell, the very good smell, of Southern fried chicken. Suddenly he felt very happy and relieved. Becky could see it on his face and she couldn't help but laugh. Mike grinned and asked, "It's not chicken gizzards and livers, is it?"

"No, sugar, no livers and no gizzards!"

It was a loud, noisy dinner, but the noises were happy ones.

CROWS' NEST

Soon after the chicken, gravy, mashed potatoes, biscuits and everything else was gone, the kids helped clean up and then went to the movie. The Starlight didn't have a big crowd on Thursdays, so they were able to slip right in. After the huge dinner, no one was interested in candy or popcorn, except for Steve Taylor. The entire crew slipped up the stairs to the balcony (known to the local black moviegoers as the crow's nest). Suzy, Ray, Mandy, Lee, Becky and Mike sat in a string on the second row. Steve sat a row behind them, with two other plainclothes officers. One of these was Officer Anderson, who munched on popcorn from the giant one-dollar box.

Before the movie started, the evening's attendant, a fellow student, was checking seats. When he recognized the fugitives, he lingered just a moment.

"Is everything okay, son?" Trooper Anderson asked.

"Sure, sir. Enjoy the movie!"

Just a little later that evening, the Starlight attendant would seek out and find Bobby Willet at the Burger Circle. Bobby Willet immediately began to make a plan.

As the movie began, Mike found himself very drowsy. Becky took his hand and very skillfully helped him lean on her shoulder. Before the cartoon was over, Mike was sound asleep. Steve Anderson thought it was both cute and funny. He spent most of the next hour tossing pieces of popcorn at Mike's head.

Some hit him, but none woke him.

Becky, however, was getting very annoyed. She picked up pieces of popcorn and when she had a full handful, she turned just enough to throw them at Officer Anderson. He laughed, but he also stopped tossing popcorn.

GIGGING A FROG

As Mike was settling into his long after-dinner nap, a small team of Sumner County deputy sheriffs descended upon Froggy, sleeping in his pickup near Devil's Gullet Swamp. He was dragged from the truck seat, frisked, cuffed and arrested. His truck was searched. They found his gun and a tire tool with encrusted blood and brain matter.

Froggy was dazed, partly from pure surprise and shock, but partly from a lack of sleep. As the officers began to transport him to Macon, Froggy began to feel relieved.

In a jail cell, in dirty clothes, hungry and thirsty, he would finally sleep.

Squeezing a Wizard

Paul Foss was kept in a solitary cell in Macon, locked away alone down a lonely hallway for several hours. He was moved to an interrogation room in the late afternoon and told he could contact a lawyer soon. He was left in that interrogation room for over two hours with little contact. The room had only a single small wooden table with three chairs. The floor was hard tile, dirty white. No mop had been seen in this room in a long, long time. The walls and low ceiling were a soft white, and there was a single, bare sixty-watt light bulb in the middle of the ceiling that gave a harsh yellowish glow. The heavy wooden door had no windows.

Paul Foss had heard the lock turn when they put him in the room. There was a small mirror by the door, and Foss was sure it was for observation. The room was warm, muggy and smelled of stale cigarette smoke.

The state police officers were letting the wizard stew for a while. Larry had meant to talk to Foss a bit sooner, but he waited on the report by phone from Sumner County. Once he was sure Froggy was securely in custody and soon to be on his way to Macon, he called Janet and then Ruth Anne. After this, Larry and Dale Katz headed for the interrogation room.

Dale was clearly excited. "This will be fun; I'll be the bad cop!"

"That should be easy!"

"Oh yeah, especially now. Let's go bust this S-O-B!"

Larry and Dale hit the door hard. The wizard was leaning on the table with both arms forward. He glared up as Larry sat down across the table and laid down a thick file. The file was merely a printout of unpaid speeding fines from every county in South Georgia, but Foss didn't need to know that. Larry waited a minute or so to say anything. First he picked up a clipboard and started writing on the legal pad it held. Every few seconds he would look up at the nervous wizard. Dale leaned against the door and said nothing. Finally, Larry placed the clipboard back on the table, upside down. He leaned back in the chair.

"Did you kill Bert?" he said.

"No," Foss said. "I have not seen a lawyer yet."

"You will, soon enough. I think you'll get to know a whole bunch of lawyers."

Again, Larry just waited. He leaned forward and drummed his fingers on the table. "How did you get your dirty little hands on the money bag and the other stuff from Bert's shop?"

Foss's eyes popped wide just for a minute but he calmed. "I will not answer any more questions until I talk to a lawyer."

Larry shook his head and said very softly, "Son, you are in a lot of trouble. This shit storm is just beginning."

Dale walked forward, placed both hands on the table and leaned very close to the wizard. Foss backed away in fear, noticeably shaken, his face pale.

"We just arrested the probable killer," Dale barked, spit flying. "But we know you were involved in this mess. We're gonna put you away, for a very long time!"

In a trembling voice, Foss blurted out a weak defense: "I can tell you things and I can prove them."

Larry laughed, stood and put his arm on Dale's shoulder. "Back off, boss! Let's get this piss ant a lawyer and then we can have some fun!"

Soon, two state police officers moved the wizard to

another room as bleak as the first. But it did have a phone on the table. Foss was scared, and could barely think. He first thought to call Big Bob, but Big Bob had a way of silencing his enemies and friends. On the table was a pile of business cards for local attorneys in Macon. The wizard picked one. Later that evening he conferred with the young lawyer. This lawyer advised him to wait until charges were filed before providing any information. Then they could try to make a deal.

But Larry and Dale really needed to ask only one question. They had a short talk with Foss's attorney and explained to the young lawyer why his client was in very deep trouble. This young, inexperienced attorney realized this might be too much for him, but he got a promise that Larry and Dale wouldn't ask any more questions... except one, and that one would be a yes/no question.

Dale, Larry and the lawyer entered the interrogation room.

Larry asked, "Paul, did Sheriff Willet give you that evidence? The bank bag and merchandise from the gas station?"

The wizard glanced around the room, perhaps looking for a sympathetic face. Not finding one, even in his lawyer, he sat upright, cleared his throat, nodded and answered: "Yes, he did."

There were still many things not clear to Larry. But he was sure Bob Willett was at the center of everything. Dale and Larry decided to press charges and further interrogate the wizard and the frog in the wee hours of the morning. But first, later that same night, they brought Janet and her lawyer in to make her statement with the District Attorney. The plan was to get just a little more corroboration from these key players with the DA and then press formal charges. This would provide the needed arrest warrants and that would get the rest of the main players arrested and off the street. Larry finally felt like they could get this murder-conspiracy case put away.

Larry realized that he needed to do so quickly, a cornered snake could be very dangerous. Larry was also getting a sense of a lot of very criminal activity that had been going on for a long time. This would take a lot of effort down the road but it would be worth the effort.

Sweet Momma's front porch

About the time Mike was waking up at the end of the movie, and as Dale and Larry had a chat with Paul Foss, Sweet Momma received a visitor. It was a very nice September evening and she was on the porch even after dark. She couldn't see the glowing eyes of the Andy-demon, but she certainly felt its presence. "Best go on now," she said. "You's not welcome here!"

"You haven't won, old lady. I have come to watch you suffer." Andy laughed lowly, an unearthly sound, and slowly walked to the porch steps. As he got nearer, his eyes glowed more brightly; the wind stirred the magnolias and all of the brush. If Momma could see, she'd have noted the same glow in the trees that was present in the grove the night she'd been in the hospital. As the spirit neared the porch, Momma grew frightened and backed deeper into her chair. She sat with a thump, short of breath. "You leave me now!"

"Very soon you'll be leaving me, you troublesome old hag!"

Andy lifted his once-broken arm and pointed under the porch. A bolt of yellow light flashed—towards the firecracker Paul Foss had planted under the porch, at the command of Big Bob, on instruction from Andy himself.

The timer started counting back from thirty.

Andy roared a laugh. "Time to say goodnight!"

Suddenly Zeke appeared on the porch and shouted, in a

voice that only Andy could hear, "Leave this place! Leave this place!"

In an instant, the smelly breeze, as well as the glow and the evil, were gone. Momma felt as if the sun had come up. She began to smile, sensing Zeke's presence.

Zeke pointed at the bomb. "Take it away!"

A cool breeze raced up the porch, lifted the bomb and carried it deep into the woods. It exploded harmlessly among the dewberry brambles.

As the noise settled, Momma thought she heard a dog bark, but she was not sure. "'Bout time you got here!"

"Well, Miss Ivy, you just stir up all sorts of trouble."

STRAWBERRIES AND CREAM

The gang left the movies quietly, some in Officer Anderson's cruiser and some in Ray's Chevelle. None noticed that they were followed by a red Charger, which hung well back.

The gang went back to Becky's house for a quick dessert. Becky's mother had placed bowls of strawberries and cream on the dining room table. The kids thought this was too fancy. As everyone sat, Lee asked, "Are we supposed to eat these or admire the beauty?"

Suzy said, "Well thank you, Lee! Mrs. Patterson worked hard to set these out."

Ray laughed. "I think Lee meant to say that the strawberries and cream in these beautiful china dishes are presented magnificently."

Suzy gave him a mock slap as all laughed. She said, "Ray, stop making fun of her!"

Ray recovered quickly. "No, these strawberries are magnificent!"

Another slap. Becky's mother jumped in and instructed, "Napkins in your lap, spoon in your right hand, and dig in!"

They did.

Soon the party migrated to the front porch to enjoy the night air. All were quiet and tired, and they sat without speaking, listening to the late-summer night sounds. Then they heard a faint boom in the distance.

Ray asked, "I wonder what that was?"

Lee answered, "Somebody's firecracker. Or cherry bomb, maybe?"

It wasn't long before Coach Carter drove up. Everyone gathered around him; they could clearly see he was very upset. "Lee, Mike, we need to go," he said. "Suzy, your mother needs you."

"What's wrong, Daddy?"

"Adam has been reported as missing in action. We just got the telegram."

Suzy collapsed, but Ray and Becky caught her.

When Coach Carter and the kids got to his house, there were over forty coaches and players waiting. Teams can be amazing.

Bobby Willet watched, hidden up the street behind a row of junipers. His big idea would just have to wait. Bobby had many big ideas, but most of the time he lacked courage to pull them off.

Part 14
Big Bob Busted—Friday

Confessions in Macon

Froggy Allen was delivered to the Macon County jail about 3:00 a.m. Friday. He could barely walk—not only was he very tired, but his feet were shackled. His hands were in cuffs and he was wearing the dirty clothes he'd had on for days.

Any infantry soldier on active combat duty would be proud of Froggy's four-day-old clothes; the amount of grime was impressive. Froggy hadn't slept for days, nor shaved in over a week. His dreams had been racked with visions of a Confederate soldier. This visage had threatened that he would hurt Janet if she or Froggy said anything. So, Froggy was tired, dirty, hungry and afraid. Very afraid.

As the interrogation began, Froggy was reluctant to speak. Larry and Dale had made sure the young district attorney and Froggy's public defendant knew the basics of the evidence. The young lawyer found himself defending a wizard and a frog on the same night. But Larry and Dale wanted to know only two things. The investigators and the lawyers had planned a simple, fast interrogation.

First, they put Froggy in the same room and chair where the wizard had been allowed to cook for a while. Even though Froggy was cuffed to the table and chair, he slumped forward and fell asleep. Larry thought the cuffs were ridiculous; Froggy couldn't run anywhere.

Dale laughed. "Even if he bolted and ran, any of us could

catch this guy!"

After the officers and lawyers conferred one last time, they all entered the small room.

Larry began the questions, but he had to shake Froggy's shoulders to wake him. Froggy was mumbling as he slept. The look on Froggy's face was a mix of fear and sorrow.

"Froggy, Froggy. Do you hear me?"

Froggy shook his head, squinting against the bright yellow light. Larry thought that Froggy looked barely alive. None of them knew how close Froggy was to a massive heart attack.

Larry made a note to himself to have a doctor look at Froggy. "Froggy, do you know who I am?"

"Trooper Wayne. I see you at the cafe."

"Froggy, do you know where you are?"

"Yes, this is the Macon jail."

Larry paused a moment and took a chair as Froggy began to slump again. "Stay with me, Froggy. We'll let you rest soon. Just a few questions."

Froggy shook his head, and tears rolled down his cheek. "I will never rest again. Is Janet okay?"

"She's very worried about you, but she's okay. We spoke to her late last night. Froggy, do you know why you're here and under arrest?"

Froggy took a deep breath and hung his head, sobbing softly. "Because I have ruined everything; Bert and Janet, oh God, how could I be so stupid."

Larry looked at Dale and nodded. Dale stepped to the table. Even Dale realized that this suspect was totally broken. "Froggy," he said, "did you kill Bert with your tire tool?"

"Yes."

Froggy's attorney had advised him not to answer such a question, but Froggy had no fight left and he did not care about the future. He was crushed.

"Did you take any money or things from the store?"

"No, I just left. Like that old ghost told me."

This made no sense, but the officers and Froggy's lawyer chalked it up as just something a tired, scared man might say.

Larry waved his hand to signal that this was enough. He felt very sad and also very tired. "We have enough," he said. "Get him cleaned up and let him rest. He'll be arraigned soon. Let's work on a warrant for Sheriff Willet. I don't think we have enough to arrest anyone else, yet."

Larry wanted formal statements from Sam Elkins and Fred Dobbs. He didn't think the deputies were involved in the frame job, but he wanted more insight.

The officers were getting Froggy out of the chair so they could book him. As he stood, leaning on the deputies, he looked at Larry and said, "Watch out for Janet. I'm afraid someone will hurt her. Tell her I love her, and tell her not to worry about me. I am not worth the effort."

Larry felt very sad and tired, but it would be a long time before he could sleep. While Larry waited on the warrant, he tried to question Paul Foss again, but the wizard wasn't talking now.

"Don't worry, Paul," Larry said. "We've got lots of time and so much to chat about!"

PHONE CALLS

Later that same Friday morning, Larry called Janet. He told her Froggy didn't look very good, that he was tired and dirty. But he was safe. Maybe in a few days she could visit. Larry told her that Froggy had said he loved her and wanted her not to worry, but Larry knew that was pointless.

Larry hung up the office phone and sat quietly for a few minutes, wiping away a tear. He called Ruth Anne at home, before she left for work. "I love you," he said. "This will settle soon. I want to spend time with you, away from this crazy situation."

"I love you, too. I'm open to any good ideas or other proposals!"

Larry laughed. He was feeling better now. "Can you get word to Sweet Momma that I found the lie and that I will chop the head off of the snake very soon, later today."

"How mysterious!"

"She'll know what I mean. Arthur will be out of jail and home soon."

"That is good to hear!"

"But don't tell anyone else. Not yet!"

"Okay."

"I'll be back in Hawkinsville in just a few hours. So, take care."

"Oh, Larry?"

"Yes."

"You should know that Coach Carter's son, Adam, was reported missing in Vietnam."

"Oh, that's very hard to hear. I am so sorry!"

"There's so much to worry about these days."

"That's true enough. But I'm going to close the book on some of those worries."

"Good."

"One more thing!"

"Yes, sweetie?"

"Tell her she picked the right girl for me!"

"She picked?"

"At least she thinks she did. I'll tell you the story someday."

"I can't wait!"

Ruth Anne was laughing as she hung up; Larry could tell it was a happy laugh. He felt recharged. He and Dale picked up the state court judge's warrants to put away the sheriff and headed to Pulaski County.

THE CIRCLE—
BIG BOB SPILLS HIS MALT

Like most weekdays, Big Bob had driven to the Circle about noon. But today was different. Big Bob was very worried. He should be. Things had been very quiet in the office all morning, except for one phone call. A lawyer friend and Klan member from Macon had called Big Bob to warn about the arrest of Froggy. Big Bob didn't know how much Froggy could tell the troopers, but he was afraid that with both Froggy and the wizard in custody, nothing good would happen, not for him, anyway. Big Bob was actually beginning to set up another frame job on the wizard and Janet, but he was too worried to think clearly. He couldn't figure out a story that made any sense. As he sat in his anger and worry at the Circle, slowly finishing a chocolate malt after two enormous cheeseburgers, he was totally unaware that two state police cruisers had pulled in behind him, blocking any escape.

Dale and Larry had met Steve and Amos Ross at the Lilac Road Church to make a very simple plan to arrest the sheriff. Amos was going to visit with Sweet Momma until Gone could be brought home. Dale and Larry were in the front car. Steve and two additional state police officers were in the second car. As soon as the troopers' cars pulled behind Big Bob, they turned on the bubblegum lights and turned off the engines. The two officers with Steve walked to the front of Big Bob's cruiser. In theory, they were blocking any attempt by the sheriff to run. In reality, Big Bob couldn't run anywhere anyway. As Larry and Dale approached the driver's side of Big Bob's car, the radio crackled and the old soldier's voice came through.

Only Big Bob heard his words: "Enjoy your time in torment!"

There really was not much drama. Dale commanded Big Bob to step out of the car. He was unarmed—his holster belt didn't even fit anymore. Larry quickly cuffed him and forced him to lean over, belly on the trunk. Dale read off the arrest warrant. The light lunch crowd milled around, watching. To a person, everyone felt that Big Bob had it coming.

As Dale got the sheriff into the rear seat of the cruiser, he could not resist saying, "Been a pleasure doin' business with ya!"

"Go to hell."

"Not today, thanks. But enjoy your trip there! You'll probably be staying longer than you would like!"

Dale and one of the officers were to ride with the sheriff to Macon. Larry and the others were headed to the Pulaski County Sheriff's Office and jail to break the news of the sheriff's arrest and to free Gone.

In just a few short minutes, the only thing left at the Circle was Big Bob's empty cruiser. Someone would have to clean the front seats; Big Bob had peed his Big Bob pants and spilled his chocolate malt. He was such a slob.

The Klan Spreads the Word

On most school days, school kids with cool cars would show up at the Circle at lunch. Bobby Willet was one of those kids. Since Bobby and Bert Jr. had quit the team, they hadn't eaten in the cafeteria. The football players usually would sit together, and it was usually a pretty loose, fun group. But since the murders, the arrest of Gone and the fact that everyone was looking for Mike and Lee, many of the school's social groups had splintered. The very fragile relationship among the black and white students was temporarily frozen. Anxiety and animosity were running high. It was inevitable that some release of tension would occur. There was a large group of people in town that didn't like where this story seemed to be heading. The townspeople were uneasy because a well-known white man and businessman had been savagely murdered. Dale Katz had called it a "caveman murder," and that statement had been quoted in newspapers all the way up to the Atlanta Constitution. A young black man had been arrested. Even though almost no one outside of law enforcement knew real details, most people—most white people, anyway—were sure that Gone Sanderson was guilty and should be hung. Most people knew that Bob Willet wasn't an honest person and that he'd often manipulate things for his personal benefit. But he did protect the white folks. So, most of the town's white people felt a mix of emotions and opinions about the sheriff's arrest. But it had been clear that Big Bob was losing control. The troopers had pretty much taken over the town to send a very quiet but powerful message: that they were there to restore order. This time, order just might include justice for a young black man.

There was one faction of the white culture that was very angry about the sheriff's arrest. Both Big Bob and Paul Foss were shining stars in the Klan and those friendly with the Klan. It was high time for a few cross burnings and bombs. Klan dragons from all over South Georgia, and even Alabama and South Carolina, would heed the call to come to Hawkinsville.

Or would they?

Bobby pulled into the Circle and saw his father's cruiser, unoccupied. Bobby and Bert Jr. walked over and investigated. Lisa, who'd been working the lunch shift, walked over and told Bobby and Bert Jr. of the arrest. Bobby was infuriated. He wanted to run to his car and race away from the Circle. He wasn't even sure where he was going—he just needed to get away from this ugly situation and the embarrassment. He would think of a way to get back at Lee and Mike. Bobby Willet was no dummy.

Even the old soldier was taking an interest in Bobby again.

Before Bobby left, Larry, as sort of an afterthought, returned to the Circle with Steve Taylor, looking for Bobby. Larry was aware of Bobby's threats and he wanted no further trouble from this angry boy. They found him and took him into protective custody.

Gone is Gone!

After the arrest, Larry and the other troopers headed for the sheriff's office, with Bobby in the back seat—his first time in cuffs. He was angry and scared.

They also had a judge's authorization to have Gone released. There were only two people at the sheriff's office when they arrived, Fred Dobbs and Sam Elkins. Neither looked surprised when Larry came in the door. Steve came in behind him, guiding the handcuffed Bobby.

"Fred, Sam," Larry said. "Do you know that Sheriff Willet has been arrested and taken to Macon?"

Sam just dropped his head and nodded, slowly.

Fred said, "Yes, we heard. We were going to just stay here until we were told what to do. I suppose the county board will meet soon. Sam is the chief deputy; maybe he'll be made acting sheriff."

Larry asked, "Sam, can you handle that?"

Sam perked up a bit. He was afraid he would go down with the sheriff. Sam had worked for Big Bob for many years and had participated in his share of dirty police work on Bob's behalf. But he had stayed clear of big trouble. "Well, for now I can."

"Sam, you and I will need to have a very serious talk," Larry said. "I don't know where that talk will go. But I think I can trust you. I need you to be in charge here. Do not make any big moves unless you talk to me or Dale Katz. Can you do that?"

"Sure, Larry. And thank you!"

"State police officers will establish radio contact with you and provide patrol. Let us know if you need help or need us to check something out."

"Okay. When can we talk?"

"Soon, but don't talk to the papers or any outsiders. Just say that the state police are assisting Pulaski County. Say that you cannot comment on an ongoing investigation. Stuff like that."

Sam was relieved that he had a chance to begin to right some of the wrongs. He realized that his wings had been clipped a bit, but at least Larry was using him.

"Fred, can you help us?" Larry said.

"Sure. What are we going to do with Bobby?"

"I just want to hold him here overnight for safekeeping. He's made too many threats. I don't want this to go from very bad to much worse. We'll stick him in a cell, and it's okay with me if you lose the key for a day or two. I'm charging him with threatening his fellow students. We'll get the paperwork done as soon as we can."

Steve and Sam led Bobby to a cell. They were hoping the fuse on this firecracker would just burn out, but for now, this firecracker was making a lot of noise, and the curses and threats just kept coming.

Larry turned directly to Fred, "Okay now," he said. "First, I have an order to release Arthur Sanderson. Can you get him out and bring him to me?"

"You bet!"

In less than a minute Gone came through the door, a huge smile on his face.

"Arthur, are you ready to go home now?"

"Lord, yes!"

"Well, I hope you're hungry. I think Sweet Mamma will

have something good on the table."

"You not playin' with me?"

"No, sir, you are released," Larry said. "The charges have been dropped by court order."

Gone smiled and asked, "Trooper Wayne, can we get the hell out of here?"

"Immediately!"

Before Gone disappeared out the door, he stopped and turned to Fred. "Thanks for bringing me food and talking to me."

As Gone and Larry left, Fred sat down at his desk. This was the best he had felt in many weeks. He surely deserved a victory cookie!

HOMECOMING

When Larry and Gone arrived at the Sanderson home, there was a big party going on—as much of a party as Ivy Sanderson would allow, anyway. Amos Ross and most of the Lilac Road Church congregation were there. Most of them had brought food. Dishes covered the counters, tables and every available surface in the dining room and kitchen, spilling over onto the back porch.

As Larry and Gone drove up, the crowd of people formed a welcoming line that stretched from the porch to the front drive. The line led to Momma in her rocking chair. She sat clutching her Bible and a handkerchief. As the car stopped, Gone turned to Larry and Larry nodded. "Go see your grandmother and tell her you love her!"

At about "Go see," Gone was already out the door. He ran to his grandmother. The people clapped and shouted many "Praise the Lord!" and "Thank you Jesus!" proclamations. Many tried to touch Gone or pat his back, but he moved way too quickly. He fell at his grandmother's knees and dropped his head in her lap. Ivy Sanderson placed her hands on his head and cried, sobbing loudly. "Oh thank God," she said. "Thank God."

All of the people gathered close to Gone and Sweet Momma. Many tears rolled down many happy cheeks. For a few moments, all of the food was forgotten.

Reverend Ross, standing on the porch behind Momma's rocker, nodded at Larry Wayne and gave him a smile and a salute. Larry just nodded back, blinking away his own tears. Sometimes you get to do something good.

As this was happening, there were two more late arrivals. One was Ruth Anne, who walked up to Larry and gave him a hug. She saw his tears and knew he was nearly exhausted.

The other late arrival was Zeke. He came from behind the house. He stopped briefly by the porch, then went directly to Larry.

Larry stood up straight and said, "Hello. Good to see you again."

"Yes, sir! I sho' am glad to be here with you today!"

"Are you well?"

"Okay enough. But you need to be careful yet. The evil is losing strength, but it can still do damage. Watch the boys, for just a little longer."

"Can you tell me anything else?"

"Nope, not now!"

"Figures."

"Just be careful. Mind them boys. You done good, real fine, but you ain't done yet. We need to finish up!"

Larry had begun to suspect that there was something unusual about Zeke. But he had no idea what it was. He just thought, Sometimes it's just best not to know everything.

Gone had been in the house and came back out with a platter full of fried chicken, mashed potatoes and gravy, biscuits, more gravy and a heaping pile of green beans. He sat at Momma's feet and began his well-deserved feast.

WHAT'S NEXT?

The afternoon moved along slowly as friends and neighbors came and went. The sight of Gone with his grandmother was a welcome sight to all. There were lots of laughs and big smiles.

Amos Ross was one of the very happiest. His dreams had been heavy with memories of cutting down Gone's father.

For a while, Larry just sat on an old stump in the shade. As they left, people would come to him and shake his hand, just smile and nod, or sometimes say thank you. Many would bring him another piece of pecan pie or some fresh tea. Larry was going to forever be known as the man who broke Big Bob and freed Gone.

Ruth Anne had been visiting with Sweet Momma, but when she noticed how exhausted Larry looked, sitting on his stump, she walked over to him, then simply hugged him and kissed his cheek. The hug broke as Mrs. Ross walked up with a one-quart mason jar nearly overflowing with crumbled cornbread and buttermilk, and a spoon.

"Momma sent this—but she wanted me to remind you not to clink your spoon. Set down and eat. I'll bring you another glass of tea."

"Oh, thank you!" Larry said. "There's nothing better!"

Amos carried a chair from the porch and placed it beside Larry's stump. "Ruth Anne, have a seat."

"Why thank you, Reverend Ross, sir."

"Can I get you something to eat or drink? It would be my honor."

Everyone laughed as Ruth Anne sat down. "Just some tea, please."

"Sure thing. Larry, when you finish feedin', Sweet Momma wants to see you. So, come on up on the porch when you're done."

Ruth Anne got up from the chair, instead scrunching up beside Larry on the stump. Again she put her arms around him.

Larry winked at her and said, "We are not supposed to participate in public displays of affection while in uniform."

"That didn't stop you in the parking lot at Macon. And this is not public; this is Miss Ivy's front yard. If you don't like me setting this close, just go ahead and arrest me!"

"I would have to put you in the back seat."

"I bet you'd like that!"

Larry squeezed her shoulders and stood. Holding hands, the pair walked up on the porch to visit with Sweet Momma.

Sweet Momma said to her grandson, "Arthur, help me to my feet!"

Gone jumped up and helped his grandmother stand. She stepped carefully over to Larry, wrapped him up in a big grandmother hug and immediately began crying great big happy sobs. There was not a dry eye on the porch.

"Thank you, thank you, thank you!" Momma said.

"You are very welcome. But I had a lot of help."

Again, there were many "Praise Gods" and "Hallelujahs." After a moment, Sweet Momma pulled back and raised her huge blind eyes to Larry.

"You cut the head off of that old demon snake!" she said. "You are a good boy, Larry Wayne. And you had better take care of this pretty girl or I will cut a switch and tear you up!"

"I will do that," he said. "We'll be talking about that soon."

"Good for you. Finally!"

Momma hugged both Larry and Ruth Anne. Everybody was enjoying the hug session, so they didn't hear the car drive up. It was Coach Carter with Mike and Lee. Mike and Lee ran up on the porch to greet Gone. The Hawks' starting backfield was finally reunited. For the first time Lee and Mike hugged each other, really hugged each other. Coach Carter hung back in the yard. Larry and Ruth Anne asked him if there was any news about Adam.

"No, nothing new," he said. "But we keep hoping."

Ruth Anne squeezed his hand and smiled. "We're all hoping and praying for you."

Very soon Gone and Amos Ross came down the steps and approached Coach Carter. Larry and Ruth Anne stepped aside slowly. Coach Carter shook Gone's hand and pulled him into a hug. "It is good to see you! Now we're gonna have to get you back in shape. We've got a game next week!"

As it had worked out, the team had a bye this week. But Coach Carter wasn't really worried about next week's game; not yet, anyway. He wanted these boys back in school and back to their everyday lives.

"Okay, Coach, I'll be ready," Gone said.

"We'll have a conditioning workout tomorrow morning. You be there!"

"That sounds fun!"

"I see a few days in jail didn't change you!"

"No, Coach, but I'll still smoke all of 'em!"

Coach laughed at this display of humility. Few of this little crowd noticed that Zeke had approached, very quietly, and stepped up to Larry. "Remember my warning," he said. "Be careful!"

Zeke turned to walk away, but he stopped and stood still for a few seconds. A puzzled Larry, Coach and the others stood around, as if waiting on something else from Zeke. He slowly turned, but he was silent. No one, not even Gone, said anything.

Larry noticed a very faint green glow in Zeke's eyes. All felt a cool rush of air in their faces. Ruth Anne thought she heard a laugh of a little boy. She turned her head as if to hear better just as Zeke moved, stepping up to Coach Carter.

Zeke smiled softly and placed his hand on Coach Carter's shoulder. "I know your heart is heavy," Zeke said, "but you'll see your boy again. He will be a great father, as you have been—to many boys."

Zeke turned and left, quietly as always. Larry sat back down and told Gone about Lee's escape and the need to keep Mike and Lee out of the public eye. "So, until we get the last of this mess straightened out," Larry said, "I guess we need to find a place to hide you fellows for a couple of days."

Gone had an idea. He shared this idea with Coach Carter and Larry. But he did not share everything he had in mind – not the fun part.

First taste of sin

Gone covered his real scheme very well. After dark, he was planning on heading to the Good Times Club. So, why not take Lee and Mike? Why not, indeed! Just so long as Sweet Momma didn't find out. Or Ruth Anne. Or anyone else!

So Gone explained, "We'll stay here with Momma. Reverend Ross and the troopers can check on us. Maybe Coach can pick us up first thing in the morning so that he can proceed with running our asses off."

At first Larry thought this was stupid, but soon he began to see the value of the idea. Larry, in turn, explained it to Amos. Amos wasn't real happy, but he did see some wisdom in the idea. Larry said goodbye to Ruth Anne and went to the church to make some phone calls. First, he called back to Macon and talked to Dale Katz. Dale thought the plan was okay.

After the feasting, as everyone began to leave, Larry spoke to Sweet Momma, Amos Ross and Gone. "You boys stay here, inside the house," he said. "We'll patrol the area around the house, the church and the Rosses' home through the night. Call us if there is any problem or anything suspicious."

Everyone agreed. Soon it was quiet.

Sweet Momma was in bed very soon. That night, Sweet Momma slept better than she had in many days. If she had only known what Gone had in mind, she wouldn't have slept so well. Gone had been taking such risks for a long time. It didn't seem all that dangerous to him. He knew that he could hide his young tagalongs. Gone needed to be at the club to celebrate with his friends. He was just not accustomed to thinking about others.

The three young men sat in the living room watching TV. About ten o'clock, Gone revealed his plan. It was simple, simply awful. "Let's go out the back porch and walk down to Good Times. We'll get back by early morning."

Lee was hesitant but curious. Mike was scared, afraid to say no but afraid to go along. Gone could see the fear in his eyes.

Gone pleaded, "Mike, this will be the greatest night you ever had. Be a man!"

Make gave in. Somehow, he knew he would regret this. They quietly slipped out and walked along trails that Gone knew all too well.

A very young man was leaning against the back door, smoking a cigarette. He stepped out and said, as he delivered a high five, "Gone, welcome back, brother! Let me go in and make a place for your boys; they better not be up front."

In just a few minutes he returned and said, "Come on in!"

He led them in quickly, past the beer kegs and stacks of empty bottles. He turned them down a hallway, pushing aside a heavy drape that served as a door. It was dark, just barely enough light to see. The heavy curtain dampened the loud James Brown song on the jukebox, as well as the party sounds from the club. The sounds were still there, just muted to where conversation was possible. Mike was bringing up the rear and his heart was beating fast and hard enough that he was afraid Lee would hear it. But Lee's heart was beating almost as loudly.

The young man stopped the three boys and explained, "We're going into the girls' dressing room. They've made a place for you." He was smiling, and noticed Gone stifling a laugh as he added, "You little boys do as you're told. You mind those girls!"

Even Gone hadn't been in this part of the club. There was a second curtain, and their escort knocked on the wall loudly. "Can we come in?"

"Come on in, sugar!"

Their escort had taken on Smokey's role as the girls' gofer. The Good Times was not a strip club, but the waitresses and dancers wore just enough to remain legal. In the dressing room they wore flimsy gowns. Many of these girls were no older than Lee and Mike; they had fled very bad lives with no future and had to make do the best they could.

It was quite a scene. A good half a dozen girls gathered around the boys, all giggling and trying to take Mike and Lee by the hand. Lee's eyes were big and he was smiling, a very happy boy. "This is way better than Coach Carter's basement."

Mike's mouth was hanging down to his chest. He couldn't say anything. When he did, it was something like, "Oh, oh, Lord have mercy!"

A tall, pretty girl with a large Afro smiled and winked at Mike. She took his hands and held them to her face. "Hello, sugar. My name is Candy! You are so cute and your face is so red! Lavonda, look at this boy's face!"

Lavonda was shorter, with big eyes and straightened hair, but also very pretty. "Yeah, them white boys with light skin and freckles do turn red."

Mike was finally able to speak, looking at Candy he said, "You're pretty. You look like the lead singer for the Supremes."

Candy laughed and replied to keep the comical flirting going. "No, I'm way more prettier than she ever was."

Mike and Lee both loved this kind of attention. But Gone wasn't happy—he was being totally ignored. The girls took the boys to their room. It was small; there was a bunk bed against the wall with bare mattresses, and a calendar from 1966 with pinup girls for each month. Lee thought he might take it home as a souvenir.

In the center was a battle-scarred card table. Upside-down beer cases served as chairs. All of this sat atop a creaky wooden floor. This was actually the poker room, where some of clubbers would come back and play cards for money. But not tonight. There were two decks of well-worn cards on the table. Candy and Lavonda quickly cleared off the empty bottles and ashtrays. Before long they were all playing blackjack and jokers-wild poker, using beer bottle caps as money. Plates of pulled pork and baked beans were served. Mike and Lee drank the first of many Blue Ribbons. This was a first for both.

Mike had a bad feeling. My mother and Becky will kill me, he thought.

Gone left for the club room before long.

They had great fun, all night. The girls took turns babysitting Mike and Lee.

Candy sat by Mike and laughed loudly every time he won a hand. "Mike is so sweet; he's gonna buy me a fur coat and a diamond ring!"

"After the Cadillac!"

"Whatever you say, baby!"

It was just innocent fun. It would go nowhere more serious. But both Mike and Lee were drunk. Somewhere before dawn, the party broke up. Around 5:30 a.m., Gone collected the two babies. Mike and Lee were both asleep, leaning over the table. Gone shook the table and both boys fell backwards with a loud crash. At least four girls were asleep on the beds. All were way hungover. All came awake.

Candy was not as sweet as she had been earlier. "Who the hell is waking me up? I'm gonna slap your stupid ass cross-eyed!"

"Shut up and go back to sleep!"

"Okay," she said, and went back to sleep.

Mike and Lee followed Gone out the back door. They traveled home the same way they'd come. The boys were drunk as the fabled skunk. It was a good thing Gone knew the way home.

When they got to the Sanderson house, they plopped onto the porch. Mike was beginning to sober, a little. "I have a feeling that I'm gonna pay for this. Oh Lord, what have I done to myself." Mike sat on the porch with Lee, waiting on Coach Carter. Gone lay on the couch inside.

When Sweet Momma woke, it didn't take long for even a blind woman to figure out that these boys were not feeling very good, and why. She had seen—or smelled—this before.

She began lecturing the three little children. It was quite a sermon. Gone had heard it before. Lee had heard it preached to Gone, and he was a little embarrassed, but mostly sick to his stomach. Mike was sure he was doomed to hell and a servant of the devil. His stomach felt at least that bad. So this is what it feels like to die and go to hell, he thought. But it was going to get worse.

When Coach Carter pulled up, Momma called him to the porch and let him know what was going on.

As they loaded into the car, he told the boys, "I hope you had a good time last night, because you're gonna pay for it this morning and all next week in every practice."

Gone fell asleep in the car on the way to practice. It wasn't a new experience for him to be on the bad side of a coach and looking at special running drills designed just for him.

They got into sweats and assembled with all of their teammates. All three had pounding headaches and the sunlight hurt. After a few stretches, the running commenced. Shortly thereafter, the puking commenced. Ray laughed at his friends and made fun of them until Coach Carter told him to shut up. By the end of practice, even Coach Carter felt a little sorry for them. Gone took it very well; even hungover he ran like a deer.

Mike and Lee took this lesson to heart. But there would be more consequences to come. Ruth Anne and Becky would also make him pay.

Saturday Really Has Arrived

Mike and Lee went to Mike's house after the Saturday-morning torture session. They both looked like death served on a cracker.

Sweet Momma had called Ruth Anne. She knew the score. When they arrived, Ruth Anne remarked, with sarcasm just dripping off her voice, "That must have been a rough practice!"

There was more to come on this Saturday, but Mike and Lee just wanted to sleep for a few hours. There would be consequences for sure. Gone eventually told some people about that Friday night, and the story, in various forms, spread quickly. Mike's mother was furious, Becky was furious and Coach Carter was furious. Mike felt like a lion tamer, surrounded by furious lions.

It seemed as if trouble was over: the snake had been beheaded. But there was more hate about. An angry young man and an angry old soldier-demon would try again. Their trials were not yet over, and Sweet Momma had a little more work to do. But Zeke and the good guys could maybe rest soon, very soon. Mike and Lee were about to learn just how thick blood can be.

PART 15
DOORS BEGIN TO CLOSE

Plans

Mike and Lee crawled out of bed around noon. They briefly considered going fishing, but it was just too hot. Both had begun to sweat already, just thinking about breakfast. Further, Mike knew immediately that his mother was angry. As Mike and Lee walked into the kitchen, Ruth Anne just stared at Mike. Lunch had been served: a jar of peanut butter, a jar of blackberry jam and white bread.

"There's lemonade in the fridge."

Mike wasn't sure which was colder, the lemonade or the delivery of the information from his mother.

Mike and Lee made sandwiches, filled glasses of lemonade and moved to the front porch. Both were beginning to recover somewhat, with food and the cool lemonade.

"I reckon your mother heard about last night," Lee said.

"I guess so; I haven't seen her this mad in a long time."

As soon as practice was over, Coach Carter told Suzy what the boys had done. Between Suzy and Ray, everyone learned the story of Friday night. Mike, Lee, Gone and even Larry Wayne would all suffer the wrath of angry mothers and grandmothers. But it had seemed like such a good idea at the time.

As Mike and Lee finished their lunch, Ruth Anne came out to check on them. She held a plate of warm chocolate chip cookies.

"Mom, I am sorry. I feel really dumb."

"You should. You are smarter than that!"

"Okay, Mom."

"I'm ashamed of you. Mike Thomas, drunk as a skunk. I hope Coach Carter runs you 'til your tongue falls out!"

"He tried! Actually he did."

Lee covered up a laugh.

Ruth Anne was still angry and said, "I hope he tries again!'

Lee couldn't keep from laughing any longer. But it came out as sort of a muffled giggle. He said, "Oh, he tries every day, believe me!"

"Lee Sanderson, stop giggling," Ruth Anne said. "This is not the least bit funny!"

Ruth Anne stood with a firm, angry hand on her hip. She was still holding the plate of cookies in her hand. She was waiting for something.

Mike finally said, "I am sorry, Mom. It will not happen again."

"If it does, I will throw you out, right on your skinny little white ass!"

Mike and Lee tried to stifle a laugh, but they failed after about five seconds of silence. Ruth Anne did not use the word "ass" very often. Even Ruth Anne laughed finally. She sat down the cookies and pulled up a chair. The cookies were fabulous.

"I need you boys to help me around the house," she said. "Amos, Sweet Momma and all of their folks are coming for supper. Larry will be here. Mike, call Becky and invite her; but fair warning, she is mad as a wet hen!"

"Why?"

"*Why*? Suzy told her about your indiscretions and poor judgment, of course! And she called me to see if it were true. And I confirmed the fact that you had indeed been a very bad boy."

"You did? Why would you do that? Gee, thanks, Mom!"

"Because you were stupid. And I am still angry.'"

Lee laughed again and said, "Oh shit!"

"Be quiet, Lee! I am angry with you also."

"This will be a fun phone call," Mike said. "Maybe I can just see her after work."

"Whatever. Just finish your chores first!"

As Mike began sweeping the kitchen he wondered how so many people could be so angry. He hadn't meant to be bad. But it had been kind of fun. What a Saturday! And it had been going since just after midnight.

THE GATHERING AT THE GROVE

After Big Bob was arrested and Gone released, word spread around the region and became the number-one topic of conversation. It was on the radio news and even the Macon television news. The news also spread among the Klan all over the state. A plan had begun to develop amongst the local Klan. It was not very organized, but it is always easier to cause trouble than to avoid it. As Sweet Momma would say: "Dumb is nearly always easy; smart takes a little work!"

The plan was to gather at the grove, march to the Ross home and burn crosses at the house and church. Bobby Willet and Bert Andrews Jr. were among the group. Bobby had been let out of his holding cell early that morning and Bert had picked him up.

This crowd would gather strength and numbers through the day. Alcohol-assisted courage would increase along the way. Dumb is really easy. Among the gathering, there was an old spirit. But even this old spirit was getting tired. Perhaps the sense of old anger and hatred were fading, maybe losing power. The old sergeant felt a need to rest.

Just to himself, he whispered, "I'll rest in the shade near the creek. It's peaceful there."

As the old shadow faded from the light into the shade, he realized that this Klan would not ever help him or anyone else. He felt tired. This game of hate never seemed to go anywhere.

Andy felt the weight of so much history and pain, but he felt trapped in the cycle. There was no way out. He had to drive this to a conclusion. But as he sat in the shade, he remembered spending good times with Betsy and Susannah and Bobby Jeff in the shade along the stream. The old spirit then looked around at this gathering in the grove, and said, "Let them scatter; they have no more substance than dandelion seeds. I will not be the wind to drive them."

But the seed of anger had already established itself. The events of the past few days had provided water and sun. It would grow in this crowd.

COMMON SENSE

Late that same Saturday morning, Sam Elkins thought it wise to let others know about the growing troubles at the grove. He called Trooper Taylor, who felt it wise to alert Reverend Ross. So, these three men met at the Lilac Road Church. Sam knew that Roy and Shorty Allen, Froggy's brothers, were right in the middle of the gathering at the grove. They and Bobby Willet were fanning the flames with false accusations and distortions of the truth. In their view, the real killer had been released. They would seek their own vengeance.

Sam had decided that those people in the grove needed to know some truth. Some would never believe, but they needed an opportunity to at least hear the truth. So, Steve, Sam and Amos loaded in Steve's state police car and headed for the grove. All three were nervous, but this had to happen.

The state police car pulled into the hospital parking lot—there was no available parking anywhere near the grove today. The three men approached the park, walking without talking. Steve was in uniform, crisp and professional. Sam was not in uniform, but most of the people gathered knew him. Reverend Ross was also in casual clothes, but he was carrying his black leather covered Bible. They walked three abreast, Trooper Taylor in the middle and Amos Ross on his right. As they first entered the park, they were hardly noticed. It was

Bobby Willet who saw them approaching. He and the Allen brothers stepped up to confront them. Most of the robed Klan also turned to look, and silence prevailed. Many of the Klan carried clubs, some were armed with guns.

Steve spoke first. "What are you planning to do, Bobby?"

Shorty Allen was the unofficial spokesman and he stepped up front. Bobby was silent. "We plan to let everyone know who is in charge in this place," Shorty said. "It seems you state fellers have forgot your place."

"I know exactly where my place is," Steve said. "Now the rest of you should go home and let things settle down. We do not need more violence. I do not want to see anyone hurt. This is not your place."

A voice from the crowd said, "You have released a murderer and destroyed good men. We cannot let this stand!"

All were quiet. It was deathly quiet. There was no breeze, and the trees were still. It was if the whole earth was holding its breath waiting to see who would blink. It was Sam who spoke next. At first his voice was muffled, but it gained strength as he gained courage. "It is time you hear some facts," he began. "It may be hard to figure, but what I am going to tell you is the God's truth.

"Froggy Allen, my old friend for most of my life, killed Bert Andrews. You do not need to know why. Froggy had some tough breaks and even I don't know everything, but he killed Bert—that I know for a fact. Sheriff Bob Willet set it up so as to frame Arthur Sanderson. Big Bob is a liar and a coward and a murderer. He will get what he has earned; he will die by the sword. His own deceit has destroyed him."

No one said anything in reply because they knew that Sam's words were probably true. Sam continued, "So, don't hurt anyone else. This just needs to end."

All were silent. Most of the group members lowered their clubs and looked down.

Trooper Taylor spoke up: "You heard him. Please just go

home."

Absolute silence followed.

The Bobby Willet stepped forward and screamed, "You lie!"

It was silent again. Trooper Taylor had had just about enough and was stepping forward to talk this smart-assed boy down. But Amos reached out and took Steve's arm, stopping him. Steve turned to Amos as Amos stepped forward. He began to speak after whispering a silent prayer, "Lord, help me be your prophet."

Trooper Taylor nodded in acknowledgment to Reverend Ross.

"My friends," Amos began, "I came today to ask you to consider choosing a peaceful path. I bear you no ill will. Most of the long strife between us is based on false beliefs and fear. But the anger must go. Truth cannot penetrate an angry heart. Whatever you believe the truth to be, please do not strike against the innocent. God bless you and may peace be with us all!"

With that, Amos Ross turned to walk away. Deputy Elkins turned and followed. The gathered Klan stood in silence, the energy of their anger quickly fading.

Steve Taylor stepped to Bobby and quietly said, "Go home before you get in real trouble. Your aunt and uncle are there; they want you to come home now. Don't make things worse for yourself."

Steve turned and also walked away. The silence was almost overwhelming.

An angry Bobby Willet stepped forward and hurled his club right at the trooper. It would have struck him smack-dab in the back of the head, but at the last second it veered, as if pushed by an invisible hand. Steve felt the breeze of the club and as he turned, he felt a definite cool breeze in his face. A defiant, still angry Bobby glared at him. The young trooper reached for his baton. He was going to put this pup on the ground.

But a soft, gentle voice whispered, "Let it go. It will do no good to fight him this way."

Steve stared at Bobby, eye to eye. It was Bobby who folded and turned around, cursing the day.

Steve turned and followed Amos and Sam. He shook Amos Ross's hand and said that his speech might have been the bravest thing he had ever seen.

They had won the day. Within an hour, the gathering had fallen apart.

Steve Taylor would always wonder, but would never know, who had spoken to him and kept him from going after Bobby.

Bobby Willet was hatching a new plan. He wasn't finished. It was so easy to be dumb.

MIKE EATS HUMBLE PIE
AT THE CIRCLE

As the crowd was dispersing from the grove, another confrontation was just getting started. Ray and A.J. had come to Mike's house. Both felt left out from the Good Times fiasco, and both would complain about it for a long time. Ray dropped Lee off at his house, A.J. at his house and Mike at the Circle.

Mike was hoping to maybe walk Becky home and try to beg forgiveness. It was just about time for her shift to end.

Ray let Mike out by the picnic tables in the back and, with a deep Ray-laugh, said, "Good luck, buddy. You're on your own on this one."

Becky had just delivered her last order and was heading inside the Circle. Her lone acknowledgment had been to ignore Mike's wave and thrust a defiant nose into the air as she walked nearby. In a couple of minutes she came back out with her purse and walked over to Mike.

"Hi, Becky," Mike said with a very soft voice—his sweetest voice—as he stood and tried to take her hand.

Becky folded her arms and scowled at Mike.

"Can we talk? I can explain this."

"I bet you can," she said acidly.

Mike began again, "Well, can we talk?"

"I'm listening, but you better talk fast, little Mikey."

"Can I walk you home?"

"No, Daddy is coming. Hurry up."

"Okay, before I forget, you are invited to our house for supper."

"I know, your mother invited me. I'm coming with Suzy."

"Okay, good."

"Anything else?"

"I am sorry. I really didn't do anything too bad, but it will not happen again."

"Just drunk as a skunk with dancing girls."

"Yes, I know."

"I heard it was really funny when you got sick at practice. Ray said you looked like a slobbering, drowned rat."

"That was how I felt and how I feel now."

"That is how you should feel."

"Everybody seems to want to be sure I feel terrible."

"Good! I hope you feel just awful!"

Becky said this with arms folded. Mike just sat back down.

"I feel awful. Message received loud and clear."

Becky let him soak a few more seconds. Slowly she let a smile creep in. "You are dumb as a post sometimes, but you are a cute little drowning rat." She leaned forward and kissed Mike on the forehead. "Go home and help your mom get ready. I'll see you tonight. If you ever do that again, it's liver and onions forever!"

"Yes, ma'am!"

Becky turned to walk away just as her father drove up. She turned back to Mike and asked with a laugh, "No go-go girls, right?"

"Never again."

"Mike, please don't ever do that again."

Mike nodded in acknowledgment. He would never do that again.

Mike hurried home. He didn't feel like he was out of the doghouse, but at least the door was open.

Saturday Evening at the Thomases'

As Ruth Anne prepared the house for company, she had a sense that many things had turned the corner towards good. She prepared several trays of treats and finger foods. The main course was going to be hot dogs on the grill with many simple fixins. She made coleslaw and sliced potatoes to roast. She had gallons of vanilla ice cream to go with Becky's cake.

Ruth Anne and Becky had been laughing about Mike's Friday-night adventure, but they agreed to keep Mike on the spit over the fire, roasting a bit longer. Ruth Anne had him mow the backyard and sweep the patio. He set up kitchen chairs, folding chairs and the patio furniture into a large semicircle. He cleaned the grill and got the charcoal ready. He also cleaned out the old green Coleman ice chest and made sure there was plenty of ice in the freezer. About midafternoon Ray and A.J. brought hot dog buns and more ice. Both declined the opportunity to develop new kitchen sanitation skills. So, Mike swept, mopped and cleaned the counters. Ruth Anne quickly set out bowls and trays of goodies and told Mike, sternly, "Hands off until tonight! Besides, little doggies in the doghouse do not get treats!"

"Mom!"

"Be quiet, doggy! Vacuum the living room and take a shower."

"Okay."

Mike finished up, cleaned up and sat in the living room watching the Georgia-South Carolina football game on TV.

Larry showed up around kickoff, and soon all four boys—or three of them, at least—were engrossed in the game. Glory, glory, Georgia Bulldogs! Larry and Mike sat on the large formal sofa, men of luxury. Ray grabbed two large, yellow flower-print pillows and stretched out on the floor. He too was in luxury. A.J. sat in the corner, took the Life magazine from the reading table by the chair, put his feet on the stool and said, "I refuse to watch this Neanderthal display of athleticism. You guys see a football and go into warpath mode."

Mike laughed and countered, "I have an old set of tinker toys upstairs if you want to play with them."

A.J. threw the magazine at Mike and began watching the game too.

By 6:00 p.m. everyone was there, the Sandersons—including Gone—the Rosses, Suzy, Becky and Steve Taylor.

The boys were determined to watch the end of the game. In the next few weeks, Gone, Lee, Ray and Mike would receive letters from Coach Dooley informing them that the Georgia Bulldogs football program had great interest in their progress. A.J.'s recruitment would be mathematics and physics at Georgia Tech.

But tonight, before dinner, the girls were on the patio and the boys were fixed on the television.

As the game ended, the guys began to head out back. A.J. had already torn himself away from the TV and started the charcoal, saying, "The little boys will be hungry when the game is over."

Just before they came outside, Sweet Momma said, chuckling softly, "Let's tell Lee and Mike we're worried about their upset tummies and that they can only have one hot dog, no chili and no sweets."

Everybody laughed loudly.

Ruth Anne followed up, "I know that is funny, but I worry about the boys. They cannot be involved with that stuff!"

Mrs. Amos added, "I'm pretty sure Coach Carter will put the fear of God in them."

Sweet Momma wished someone would put the fear of God in Gone.

A.J. had to say something; this was just getting too serious. "Well, it made me mad too!"

"What did?" Ruth Anne asked with raised eyebrows.

"They should have asked me to go with them!"

"And what would that achieve? You would have just been in the doghouse too."

"Short, fat white boys don't get many chances for trouble. I feel like I got left out. Poor me!"

Sweet Momma laughed at this. "A.J., you don't need that kind of trouble. And you know the boys in the living room like you very much. I am sure you will find ways to be naughty."

The boys and troopers came outside and the feast began. Mike and Lee ate too much.

GONE'S CALL

As supper moved towards dessert, Ruth Anne migrated back into the kitchen and was setting out bowls and spoons, preparing for cake and ice cream. Gone also left the patio and came into the kitchen. He had an important question for Ruth Anne Thomas; it would turn into two questions.

"Ms. Thomas, can I talk to you?"

"Sure, Arthur. Was the food good?"

"Yes, ma'am, wonderful!"

"That's good. There's more to come!"

"I'll definitely have some of that cake and ice cream!"

"What did you want to ask me?"

"I know that Momma isn't doing well. Since I got home, she seems much weaker. She doesn't fuss after me as much as she used to. I kind of miss that."

"That's sweet. You should let her know you love her."

"I will. I don't know if I've ever said that. But she's always been the only person I can trust."

"I understand. But many people are here for you."

"I know, but it's hard. So, how is Momma? She really won't tell me much."

"Well, Arthur, she is very sick and probably will not get better. Her heart is failing. She's lost her vision and is very weak. We must watch after her very closely."

"Is there anything I should do?"

"Just stay close. She adores you. Just be there. And behave yourself; she doesn't need any stress from extra worry. And remember, you can always talk to me!"

Gone turned to go back to the patio but had a second thought. "Have you heard any more news on Coach Carter's son?"

"No, and Suzy hasn't said anything."

"I hope he's okay."

"Me, too. I just can't imagine how that feels."

"I hope Coach is okay."

"Arthur?" A thought had crossed Ruth Anne's mind. She was going to teach Gone how to reach out; just a small step. "Why don't you call Coach Carter and ask him about Adam?"

This surprised Gone; he hadn't even considered doing that. But he quickly decided to.

Ruth Anne dialed the phone and handed the receiver to Gone. Ruth Anne watched Gone and followed his eyes.

"Hi, Coach, this is Gone." A pause. "No, I'm not in trouble again."

Ruth Anne noticed the smile on Gone's face. She sensed his confidence growing as the conversation progressed. Ruth Anne was always a mom first.

"I will. I'm at the Thomases' house. Everything is fine. Coach? Have you heard any news on Adam? I... I've been thinking about you and your family." There was another pause as Coach Carter answered. "Oh wow, Coach!" Gone said. "That sure is good news. Can I tell folks?"

Ruth Anne brightened.

"Okay, I will," Gone said. "I'll tell Suzy right now."

Gone handed the receiver to Ruth Anne and both smiled, really big.

"What did he say?"

"He said Adam is fine. Let's go tell everyone."

Coach Carter and Gone would both remember this evening and the simple gesture throughout their lives.

Gone Addresses the Supper Party

Ruth Anne and Gone walked out onto the patio together. "Dessert is ready, but Gone has something to tell you all!"

Gone cleared his throat and began slowly, "I talked to Coach Carter just now. Adam was found and is now in a hospital in some funky town in Vietnam. He has several wounds and a broken leg, but he'll be fine. He should be back in the States soon."

Suzy leaned on Becky and sobbed.

This news certainly made this a good evening. Dessert was good. Everyone settled on the patio. It was a very pleasant September evening. Lee and Mike made plans to fish on Sunday afternoon, after church, of course. Mrs. Ross and Momma wanted everyone to come over to Momma's house for homemade ice cream on Sunday evening. Everybody agreed that was a good idea. As the sun set, the charcoal glowed softly and things seemed peaceful. Sweet Momma spoke up: "Everybody, pay me some attention. I got things to say."

Momma Takes Charge of the After-Supper Program

The folks at the party had settled. Sweet Momma couldn't see it, but she sure could feel it. Mike was sitting in the grass, looking for a four-leaf clover before it got too dark. Becky sat beside him and took his hand. Ray, Suzy and Mandy sat on kitchen chairs that they'd moved beside Momma. Gone and Lee pulled up chairs beside them. The other adults sat on the other side. Thus there was a rough half-circle around Momma on the patio, kids to the right and adults to the left. A.J. was the last to sit. He was looking for a spot when Momma said, "A.J., set down; I'm gonna get tired soon."

Suzy jumped up and said, "Take this chair. Ray and I are going to set with Mike and Becky."

She took Ray's hand as they sat. She had called her mother after Gone's announcement. She felt as if all the cares and troubles in the world were gone.

First, Momma asked, "Larry Wayne, where are you? You have business to tend to."

"Here, Momma, by Ruth Anne."

"Have you got something to say? Finally?"

"Yes, ma'am!" He cleared his throat, twice. "Ruth Anne and I are planning to marry, around Christmas probably."

This brought everybody to their feet, with lots of hugs and congratulations. Mike was not at all surprised—Larry and his mother had already told him the news. Ruth Anne was glowing as she told everyone the story. After a few minutes, everyone began to settle back into their places.

Momma finally called the party back to order. "Y'all hush now. This makes me very happy!"

She was quiet for a moment. Gone stood and helped her wrap her hand-woven shawl around her shoulders. There were tears in Momma's blind eyes. "Y'all listen close. I have stories to tell. There are things you need to know, and I been carryin' this by myself too long. I'll only be able to tell this one time through."

She was quiet for a moment, and Lee said, "We're listening, Momma!"

She nodded and began.

PART 16
THE STORY OF SPIRITS AND SUSANNAH ROSS THOMAS

THE FAMILY STORY—
ALL THE FAMILY

At first Momma told the story about Andy Thomas in the Civil War. She told the story of the Thomases' good home on Fair Creek and the very happy Bobby Jeff. She told about Zeke, but she didn't draw the connection to the ghost Zeke that the boys knew. She didn't want everyone to think that she was just crazy, at least not right from the first. But as she told how Andy, Zeke and Bobby Jeff had died, her voice turned soft and she had to wipe tears. She remembered how her grandmother had told the story with tears on her cheeks.

She told of how Susannah Thomas helped her aging father- and mother-in law in their last days. She also told of the birth of Ezekiel Samuel Thomas, Mike's great-grandfather. Most of this story Mike had heard before.

But the rest of this story was a surprise to all. As Momma launched into it, the circle of kids closed more tightly. During the pauses, everyone was quiet, not making a sound. Even A.J. sat quietly.

"After the war and after the birth of little Sam Thomas," Momma said, "things changed around Hawkinsville and Fair Creek. People were poor and times was hard. So many families had lost sons and husbands. Many, many of the black folk moved up north or to the cities.

"Susannah Thomas struggled to keep the farm going.

About this time, she took on Ellie, a young black woman that had run away from a south Alabama plantation to get away from bad men and hard times.

"Susannah and Ellie became fast friends and Sammie soon called her Aunt Ellie.

"These two strong young women had developed a reputation and skill as midwives. For years they assisted with the birth of most children around Fair Creek.

"Susannah and Ellie knowed many a secret.

"During the years after the war, there were many Federal troops around the area, policing the territory. Many of the units had black soldiers. They would often patrol the area around Fair Creek. Some of the patrols would call on the Thomases.

"There was one tall, handsome young black man that took a shine to Susannah. Suzie would flirt with him and Ellie would fuss at her—'You best be careful, this ain't nothing but trouble! That kinda thing.'

"Before long, the two became lovers, Luke and Susannah. She would slip away to meet Luke, her secret boyfriend. In just a few weeks, Susannah realized she was very much pregnant.

"I don't know if Suzie ever told Luke, but for whatever reason, he was shipped away and never heard from again.

"For a long time, only Susannah and Ellie knew that Susannah was expecting. In fact, very few people ever knew— it was easier then to hide a pregnancy for a girl living on a farm. Both young women were terrified of what lay in store. But Ellie had an idea and she convinced Susannah to go along. Susannah really had little choice. Ellie set things up.

"When the child came along, Ellie took the little baby boy to a neighboring family, a black family by the name of Smith. They was good people, the Lord's people!

"Thus, Abraham Thomas Smith was also raised along Fair Creek.

"Susannah and Ellie created a story that Suzie's baby had

been delivered but passed away shortly after birth. They even made an empty grave with a fake headstone. No one ever questioned the story and no one cared about just one more black child being raised by the Smiths. But the Smiths did care. They raised Abe Smith, who had a daughter named Annabelle, my mother's momma, my sweet grandmother.

"So, you now see, Susannah Thomas was Mike, Lee and Gone's great-great-grandmother. You boys is all cousins!"

Everyone sat in stunned, amazed silence.

It was A.J. who broke the silence: "Holy shit!"

It had been more than fate that brought these boys together in 1965 on the creek. Under the watchful eyes of gentle spirits, including old Zeke, the fragile friendship had grown. It was pretty fast now; blood thick. Old family ties now a strong knot. But there were a few more things to take place. And there was a demon spirit not quite yet ready to quit.

Part 17
Giving Up the Ghost

☉N THIS SUNDAY

On this Sunday, the Sandersons, Thomases and Rosses, and many other families, were back in church, like any other Sunday. Darkness had turned to light and spirits were lifted. The air seemed fresh, the morning was bright. The last ten days had been amazing. Fear, anger and frustration had been almost too powerful. But there was peace in the simple return to normal life. As Mike sat in church, beside Becky, he thought about Momma's story. It was amazing. But Mike realized that it really didn't change how he felt about Lee or Gone. Mike was proud of his friendship because Lee was a good person, but the distant, though significant, family connection was neat nonetheless. At the Lilac Road Church, it was "dinner on the ground" Sunday. And it was an amazing feast among amazing friends, brothers and sisters.

FISHING

Early that Sunday afternoon Lee, A.J. and Mike met at the creek, ready to fish. But it was a slow, lazy afternoon. The fish were not biting. This usually led to some serious discussion.

Lee: "A.J., when will you stop farting in public?"

A.J.: "Mike, are you going to marry Becky?"

Mike: "A.J., how does it feel to be ugly and stupid?"

Lee: "Do you think Coach will make us run in practice tomorrow?"

Mike: "Do fish swim in the water?"

A.J.: "I'm hungry!"

Lee: "Now that's a surprise!"

Mike: "Well, I'm hungry too."

Lee: "No, you're bored. When you're bored you look for food."

Mike: "I guess I'm bored a lot. I'm glad we have a game Friday."

Lee: "Yeah, but I wish we didn't have to practice all week."

A.J.: "We have a geometry test Wednesday!"

Lee and Mike: "Wonderful!"

This continued nonstop for hours. As they left, they began looking forward to homemade ice cream at Sweet Momma's house that evening. It was to be the last celebration of this crazy weekend. But there were things happening in other parts of town.

As Mike walked with his friends, he felt a strange sense of something evil brewing. It was a warm, humid afternoon and storms were gathering to the west and getting ready to sweep in.

Bobby Jr. and Bert had been sitting in Bobby's Charger near the grove. It was quiet there, nothing going on. By lunchtime they had finished off a six-pack of beer. Bobby was fueling his bravery, trying to match the anger he felt. He wanted to strike, but didn't have a clear target. Everyone had turned against him. His hold on power had slowly dissolved. Somebody needed to pay for his losses. He needed to show everyone that he was still a force to be reckoned with. But nobody was paying any attention.

Poor Bert Jr. was just along for a very bad ride, listening to Bobby's cheap-beer rant.

"It seems so stupid that Mike Thomas is starting on the varsity," Bobby said.

"And it still makes me angry that those Sanderson idiots are even on the team. This town has just gone crazy. The stupid coaches let this happen. That Thomas kid has the state police, teachers, coaches and every black person in Hawkinsville as his own little army."

On an on Bobby went with this—everyone was against him and he was running out of opportunities to get the upper hand. A couple of times during his ranting, he reached under his seat and pulled out a pistol he had "borrowed" from Big Bob. It was a big, menacing, shiny chrome-plated monster.

Bert thought about just walking away, but he just did not have the courage. That would be a fateful decision; or rather a fateful choice to not make a decision.

Bobby headed towards the Circle. As he pulled in, he saw Becky working near the picnic tables out back. He had an idea: a really good, very bad, idea.

Bobby Just Cannot Help Himself

Things were very slow at the Circle. Becky actually felt good to be working again and not have so much worry. The afternoon was not very busy, especially for a Sunday. Trooper Steve Taylor had stopped by for a late lunch. He was on duty and had mentioned that both Hawkinsville and the Circle were "dead."

"That's okay," Becky said. "We all need a breather. Where is Mike?"

"He and Lee are fishing, I believe. I bet the fish are not biting; everything around here is asleep today."

"Well, I don't see the attraction of the nasty things anyway. Best leave them in the water."

"Well, it is a lot nicer to just drive up and order a burger. I have to get moving. See you later."

Becky waved as Trooper Taylor slowly pulled out. As he left the Circle, Becky noticed that the parking lot was completely empty.

"Don't see this very often," Becky muttered to herself as she began to change trash bags out by the picnic tables in the back.

After a minute, she heard a car pull into the lot. A knot formed in the pit of her stomach. She recognized the rumble of the Charger's big block engine and knew it was Bobby Willet Jr. without even looking. Becky thought she would head inside quickly and avoid him. But as she turned back to the building, she dropped the trash by the can when she realized that Bobby had already cut her off. Bobby stomped the gas and, with a big engine rumble, got the red dragon between Becky and the restaurant's back door. Bobby stopped the car, got out and walked around to Becky. Bert Jr. also got out of the car and just stood by the open door. He had a very silly grin on his face.

Bobby trapped Becky between himself and the car. He smirked and laughed and said in a high, silly voice, "Well, hello, little Miss Becky."

"Bobby, let me get back inside. I'm busy and I do not have time for your foolishness."

Bobby seethed at this rebuff, and his voice deepened to a low, angry rumble. Even Bert felt the change.

Bobby grumbled now in a very angry pitch, "No, let's talk for a minute."

"No, I just want you to leave me alone."

"Why? Would little Mikey get mad?"

"No—I would get mad."

"Maybe you need to cruise with me and Bert. We can have a good time."

"Not on your life."

Becky backed up slowly towards the tables, but Bobby and Bert also shifted, keeping her trapped.

"Bobby, you're scaring me!"

"No need to be scared—just get in the car. We'll have some fun!"

"Never."

Becky bolted to run but Bobby grabbed her arm and hair. Becky screamed but Bobby pulled her hair, hard. "Shut up or I really...will hurt you!"

Bobby forced her into the car, pushing her in from the passenger side. Bert slid into the passenger side, holding her down while Bobby got in. Becky was wedged between the bucket seats.

Bobby pealed out quickly. He opened up the Charger and they headed east down towards the river, by the old warehouses and the docks.

Lisa had watched this through the back door, but she said nothing to anyone.

It was almost fifteen minutes before anyone else noticed Becky was gone. It would be longer still until someone took action.

Down By The River

Bobby pulled the Charger into a narrow alley between two large abandoned warehouses near the old docks. Nobody would see them there, especially on a Sunday. It had been a hideout for Bobby's gang for a long time. Bobby turned off the engine and put his arm around Becky. She tried to lean away but Bobby roughly pulled her closer to him and held her tightly. "Set still," he commanded.

Bert was concerned, but still very afraid of Bobby.

Bobby reached under the driver's seat and pulled out the Colt .357 Magnum with its six-inch barrel. He waved it in front of Beck's face, barrel pointing to the roof of the car, back and forth. "We should have asked little Mikey to come along. I bet this would have tamed that tiger boy."

Bert gave a nervous laugh.

Becky was gasping for air, gulping down huge breaths. She was trembling and crying softly. She lowered her head and closed her eyes. "Bobby, please take me home," she pleaded. "I haven't hurt you."

"Oh yes you have, little princess. Oh yes you have."

For just an instant Bobby felt a little tiny bit of pity. But he had to be tough. He snickered at her soft crying. Bobby also briefly thought of the consequences of hurting Becky—she had many friends and this would get Bobby in even more trouble. That caused a brief flash of frustration and a little fear. But feeling the fear just made Bobby cycle back to anger—including anger at his own weakness. Bobby's power had been stripped away, and the fear of being shut down again was very real. Bobby's resolve to do something—something that was very bad—was building.

After listening to Becky sniffle and feeling her quake with fear, Bobby decided to have a bit more fun. "Becky, let's go for a little walk, here along the riverbank. It is so nice here."

Bobby opened the door and got out carefully, pulling Becky behind him. They walked towards the riverbank, which was anything but pretty. It was just an ugly, dead-fish-smelling mudflat. Bobby walked Becky close to the water, gun in one hand and firmly gripping Becky's arm with the other. "How about a swim?"

Bobby pushed Becky, but it was just a feint, making her stumble and scream. She pulled away from Bobby for just a second, but Bobby grabbed her again and pushed her back towards the car. As they struggled, Becky lost one pink tennis shoe in the mud. When they got to the car, she tried to pull away again. Bobby slapped Becky hard across the face and then pushed her into the car. "Let's find a better place to have some fun with Becky."

MIKE AND THE GANG JOIN THE CHASE

As Mike, Lee and A.J. were leaving the woods and Fair Creek Park, Mike heard the rumble of Ray's Chevelle. Ray pulled up in the parking lot and leaned out of the window. "How about let's cruise down to the Circle?"

Fishing gear in the trunk, the boys were starting to get in when Zeke approached the passenger side of the car, out of nowhere. Mike was beginning to climb in but Zeke stopped him, holding his shirt sleeve. "Bobby has taken Becky," Zeke said. "They're in his car on the east side of town somewhere. Call the lawmen and head that way. You need to be there. But be very careful."

Ray and Lee also heard Zeke's message. Ray reached for Mike and pulled him into the car. Lee and A.J. had fallen into the back seat. Before the door was closed, Ray was already letting off the clutch. The Chevelle roared.

Ray roared, "I am going to smash that worthless little piss ant!"

Ray stomped the gas, slinging gravel everywhere. They headed for Mike's house—it was nearby and there was a phone there.

Mike called the state police office, and within minutes Trooper Taylor was out looking for the Charger.

Ray and the gang also headed out to join in the search.

431

Mike's heart was racing and he was very afraid. But he was also very, very angry. Lee was also very angry.

MIKE AND ANDY

Ray knew that Bobby sometimes hung out at Grove Park. He headed there first. But there was no one there. They headed east of town by the old warehouses; again Ray knew this was a beer-drinking hiding spot.

"Hurry, Ray!" Mike said.

But Ray needed no encouragement. There was almost no traffic in town on this lazy Sunday afternoon. They were quickly by the warehouses and down the old gravel lanes to the river's edge. There was not a car or person in sight. It was deathly quiet; just the sound of the water flowing by, dark, muddy—angry. Mike stood by the water, looking around, and that's when he saw the shoe. He recognized it immediately and his heart sank. Ray and Lee rushed over.

"This is Becky's shoe," he said. "I know it. Her initials are on the back."

Mike feared the very worse. He was sinking fast. Ray and Lee headed downstream along the riverbank, looking for some sign. A.J. followed. Mike, trailing behind, wiped tears from his eyes.

Mike was suddenly forced to the ground by a sudden wind. The wind was warm and foul. As he rose to his feet, the old soldier was standing there, blocking his path. "Hold on, boy, you need to listen to me," Andy Thomas said. "I can protect that little girl. She is still in the red chariot with that scared little fool."

Mike was scared for Becky. He was afraid to listen to Andy, but afraid not to listen. "I can make sure that Bobby doesn't hurt Becky," Andy said. "I can make sure that she gets home safely. If you don't listen to me, it'll already be too late."

Mike was shaking, torn whether to run or stay.

"I'll have Bobby go after the old lady, the one you call Sweet Momma, and in turn Gone will kill him. The old woman is almost dead anyway. You will not intervene in any way. If you let this happen, I will save Becky. Ignore me, and they all die."

This was the devil's bargain. The tired old spirit had just presented a chance to hurt Sweet Momma or hurt someone else. There seemed no way out.

Mike collapsed to his knees.

Saving Becky was all Mike wanted, and all he could think about.

Her face filled his mind. Then he remembered her hug on the night Coach brought Lee back to his house. He remembered the tear in hear eye and the smile as she said, "We cannot abandon our friends."

Mike pulled away and jumped to his feet. He pushed Andy back and yelled,

"No! you are a liar. I do not need you to save Becky."

Ignoring the screams of anger from the old soldier, which only he could hear, Mike yelled to his friends, "Let's go! She's not here."

As the gang loaded in Ray's Chevelle, AJ asked,

"How do you know?"

"I'll explain later - or, try to anyway."

Bobby Tries to Hide

As the Charger motored back into town, Bert was trying to hold a handkerchief on the cut over Becky's eye. She took the rag from his hands and held it herself. Bobby took back roads to avoid being seen, working his way back to the Macon highway.

This was happening just as Mike and his friends arrived at the warehouses.

"Don't worry, Becky, we're going to have some fun in the country!" Bobby's voice was pure evil. Becky desperately tried to think of some means of escape.

Bobby laughed loudly as the Charger hit eighty. With the windows down, it sounded like the car was inside a tornado.

Trooper Taylor was coming south on the Macon highway just out of town when the Charger blasted by. As he turned on his bubblegum light and siren, he said, "Damnation, boy; you just cannot let things be."

Steve had much ground to close, but he was doing it, and Bobby soon realized the chase was on. He continued to laugh, and in a creepy, high-pitched voice, yelled, "Becky, are you having fun? Are yoouu having fuuuuuun?!"

Becky closed her eyes and prayed that Bobby would stay in control of the flying car. "Princess, you just wait till we get to the party spot!"

The car was on the edge of control, barely making the

turns, dodging oncoming cars and making dangerous passes. Becky was still stuffed onto the floorboard, with Bobby and Bert holding her down.

Trooper Taylor kept Bobby's car in sight and called for help. He was trying to get a roadblock set ahead.

As Bobby rounded a curve and lost sight of Trooper Taylor, he rapidly downshifted and turned onto a dirt road. It was an escape he had used before. He quickly pulled into a mimosa grove and shut down the car.

Trooper Taylor flew by. It took a few minutes for him to realize the Charger had disappeared. He turned around and began to search back towards town. Other officers were closing in to assist.

Mike Approaches

Things were quiet at the Thomas house. Too quiet. Ruth Anne was almost sick with grief and worry. Mike had told his mother what he knew before the crew left to look for Becky. Ruth Anne made some phone calls, one to Larry and one to Amos Ross. But all they could do was wait. She was in agony.

As Trooper Taylor flew past the now-parked Charger, Ray was also closing ground. They could hear the screaming siren ahead. But Ray also knew of the mimosa grove and the hiding place for kids and cars on the north side of town.

"I have an idea," he said.

THIS MUST END

After Trooper Taylor whizzed past, Bobby said, "Let's go for a walk."

"Bobby, please let me go," Becky said.

"I will, in time."

Bobby took off his belt and strapped Becky's hands behind her back. He was standing behind her, holding the belt in one hand and the .357 in the other. He led her in to the woods, well out of sight from the road. They were walking along a fence row, with Bert following.

Becky was limping with only one shoe. "Bobby, please don't hurt me." She was crying softly and was very scared, with tears and blood running down her face. "Please, Bobby."

Bobby forced Becky to the ground, without another word. His large, angry eyes did the talking. But there were now other witnesses—an angry old soldier watched, but this sickness was exhausting. He only watched. The little idiot Bobby needed no coaching now.

Bert Jr. was also just watching, too scared to move, afraid to stop Bobby and too scared to run. As Becky hung her head and sobbed, Bobby forced her onto her back. Just as he did, a cool breeze hit him in the face like an ice hammer and pushed him back. He stumbled and almost fell, and he dropped the pistol. Bobby sprang up and stepped towards Becky again. His anger was exploding. He grabbed a stick and raised it to hit

Becky.

Finally Bert sprang into action. He picked up the pistol and stepped towards Bobby. Bert reached for the stick and cried out, "Bobby, no!"

As those words rang out, another old figure materialized out of thin air, just in front of Bobby. Zeke's eyes flashed red and he growled, "Stop this!"

Becky scrambled to her feet and stood behind Zeke.

Bobby and Bert froze, and the command was repeated: "Stop this!"

Bobby and Bert backed away slowly, gaining some distance. Bert dropped the pistol.

As this was happening, the Chevelle pulled up behind the Charger. Before Ray had even stopped the car, Mike was out the door, running towards the noises and voices he heard coming from the woods. Lee was close behind, but this time, on this day, Mike was faster than Lee.

Mike ran straight to Becky and she collapsed into his arms, sobbing. Mike glared at Bobby and Bert. Only his great love and concern for Becky kept him from charging them.

Bobby and Bert were finally moving, scrambling to get to the Charger.

As Lee approached, he saw the gun on the ground. No one, not even Zeke, was watching Lee. All of his anger towards the Willets and the hurt they had inflicted on the Sandersons just erupted from Lee. Lee grabbed the gun and ran straight at Bobby, Bobby and Bert came to a sudden stop – cut off from the Charger by Lee. Leveling the barrel right between Bobby's eyes, Lee was shaking but his aim was steady enough. He gritted his teeth and pulled back the hammer, but then he hesitated for just a split second. It was enough time for Zeke to step in front of Lee. "Young Lee," he said, "it ain't good and it ain't worth it. This will just bring on more hate. You will destroy yourself, not Bobby. He is already gone."

All stood in absolute silence, watching Lee, waiting for his next move.

Finally, Becky said softly, "Lee, put the gun down. Everything is okay now. I'm fine."

Lee looked towards Becky, but he turned back to Bobby and stepped towards him again, shoving the pistol closer. Bobby tried to back up but he fell. Lee kicked at him and reestablished his aim. Lee's hand was shaking as he squeezed the gun tighter than ever. Lee screamed in anger, "You should die! Now!"

Ray walked up behind Lee very carefully and quietly. He reached past Lee's shoulder and gripped the gun. He placed his other hand on Lee's shoulder. Ray said, very calmly, "Lee, let me hold the gun. You don't need a gun to stomp this little piss ant."

Lee dropped his gaze to the ground and released the gun. Ray hurled the gun into the weeds across the fence. Ray turned Lee around, to walk back towards Mike and Becky.

Bobby and Bert jumped into the car and were back on the road quickly. Once again, Bobby opened up the Charger. But it would be the last time.

Zeke walked to Mike and Becky and removed the belt from her wrists. "Don't be afraid now."

"I... I'm not afraid of you," Becky said. "Thank you so much."

"You are mighty welcome. Now go on and take care of yourselves. Hurry up, now."

Becky and Mike walked to Ray's car as quickly as she could on shaky legs. Tears and sweat were stinging her eyes; her wrists hurt and her hands were numb. She almost fell twice. But as she stumbled along to the car in Mike's arms, she felt a cool breeze in her face. She didn't really understand what or why, but it was comforting. Mike picked her up and carried her the rest of the way.

When they reached the highway, they saw Trooper Taylor on his way back towards town, lights still on. They flagged him down. Becky was safe, but he needed to get Bobby locked up. He once again took off in pursuit. He would find them, but not in the way he hoped.

Bobby was scared and angry. He fled south. But he didn't get far. He was shaking, barely in control of the car.

A voice that sounded very much like Big Bob's boomed through the stereo speakers: "You really are a no-good quitter!"

The message was like a farewell curse. Bobby's hands seized and he lost control of the Charger. He hit the gravel on the right shoulder of the road, tried to recover too quickly and then skidded across the road and rolled off to the left. The red Charger was almost split in half as it crashed into a telephone pole. Both young men were ejected.

Anger claimed two more lives. Maybe now it would be sated—for a while, at least.

ICE CREAM

Mike got Becky home while Trooper Taylor and other officers worked the scene of the Charger crash. Mike stayed with Becky throughout the afternoon. Trooper Taylor dropped by to check on things and ask Becky a few questions. Suzy came over and stayed with her through the rest of the afternoon. Becky did not want to go to the doctor. "I'm tough enough to take a black eye."

Maybe so, but Mike would not let her get more than three feet away from him.

Becky also insisted that they all go to Sweet Momma's for ice cream. She had a feeling there may not be all that many more chances to visit with Sweet Momma. Becky's family came along. Becky looked like she'd lost a prize fight, but she was finally beginning to relax a bit. But still, Mike wouldn't let her out of his sight all through the evening.

Pretty much the same crowd that had been at the Thomases' the evening before were now at Sweet Momma's. People were scattered around the front porch and sitting in the front yard. Lee, A.J., Gone, Larry and Amos sat out front, talking about the events of the afternoon. The same went for the girls on the porch—well, the girls and Mike, who stayed right by Becky's side. It was a terrible fate for Bobby, but it felt like the last act of the play. Almost. Maybe work, school and family really would return to normal soon.

Zeke quietly walked out of the woods and waved to the men and boys. Even though Ivy could not see him, she sensed him.

Zeke looked at Becky and smiled. She smiled back and nodded. Only the boys and Becky knew the role Zeke had played that afternoon. Becky hadn't told anyone about Zeke's rescue: when she'd talked to the police, she'd left that part out of the story.

To a person, Mike, Lee, Becky, Larry, Ruth Anne and Amos Ross had begun to suspect that Zeke was not just a kind-hearted old man. It was impossible to explain his sudden appearances and his ability to see what was about to happen. But just like Sweet Momma had learned to do, they just accepted it for—well, for whatever it was. There was something about his presence and his talk that was just soothing to the spirit. No one worried about what he was.

Zeke quietly said, "Are you all ready? Storm's coming."

Sweet Momma answered, "I reckon, but I'm gonna have me some more ice cream first!"

And that she did.

A STRANGE STORM

In just a few short minutes, the sky turned gray and dark. The wind began to blow in angry gusts that made the old oaks groan in displeasure, their limbs creaking as if in pain. A stinging, cold rain began to fall and lightning began to pop nearby. Momma stood with her cane and went inside. "I'll be back in a minute," she said. "Stay on the porch. I'm just going to get my sweater."

True to her word she returned with her pink sweater and sat down in her old rocking chair. Amid the chorus of rain on the tin roof and the thunder, she hummed "Rock of Ages."

This was an unusual storm. The lightning was strange shades of green and yellow, and the trees seemed to glow with the same colors. Larry asked the question that all were thinking: "I've never seen lightning like this. What is happening here? Maybe we should go inside?"

Zeke was the first to see the glowing eyes. The misty image in the rain of an old Confederate soldier slowly appeared in the front yard and then approached the porch. The wind and the rain seemed to go right through him.

Zeke said, calmly, "Andy, it is good to see you."

It was very quiet; even the thunder subsided a bit.

A.J. muttered, "Holy shit, who is that weird son of a bitch?"

Reverend Ross smacked A.J. on the back of the head.

Momma added, "A.J., hush your dirty mouth!"

Momma stood, with her cane in hand, and said to Andy, "Leave my house!"

No one said a word. Only Momma and Zeke really knew who the soldier was. Mike only knew that he was bad, whatever he was.

The soldier took one step up the porch, but Momma threw up her cane. "Stop!"

"Old woman, you are done," Andy said. "You come with me."

"You done caused too much trouble," Momma said. "I think I'll stay here."

Andy looked at Mike, pointed and said, "I gave you a choice. You chose the little girl. Now I'm taking the old lady."

Mike shook his head and said, a little shaky but with authority, "I rejected your offer. You had nothing to give except pain. You get nothing. Do what Sweet Momma says and get out of here. You'll take nothing!"

Momma took one step forward and pulled a very old, dirty flag rag from underneath her sweater and held it up for all to see. Even the Andy thing took wide-eyed note—of the sling he'd made from the tattered flag from the battlefield at Gettysburg.

"I know who you is!" Momma said. "Andy Thomas was a good man; you need to release him and let him rest. You need to release him in God's holy name."

The wind settled, the trees became still and the rain ceased. Andy relaxed his arms; he smiled, and nodded. The old soldier was tired. Distant and buried memories of happy, long-ago things came back. For a very brief moment, his visage shifted. The old Andy, before the hate and destruction, before the war, returned. He had a soft smile, but looked tired—like he'd just been through a big battle.

Mike felt the storm roll out and peace settle in.

And then old Andy simply faded away.

There was dead silence.

Then Zeke said, "It's almost time to go." He turned to Sweet Momma, nodded and said, "I'll see you soon. We are almost done, these boys will have to finish, take it to the end."

Slowly he walked back into the woods and out of sight. As Zeke disappeared into the trees, Mike once again heard a faint dog bark.

A.J. said, "Can anybody tell me what just happened?"

Larry answered for all: "Not really."

PART 18
MOVING ON—MONDAY

Mike and Amos Sing Again

Sleep hadn't come easy for Mike that Sunday evening. Things had come to some ending, he knew, but he had a nagging sense that more was to come—that the story was just not over, that there was still some important revelation to come. But Ruth Anne had made sure that Mike was up and ready to go to school. It seemed like it had been ages since Mike had walked to school, but the reality was, it was only a little over a week.

When Ruth Anne left for work, she gave Mike a quick kiss, and some advice: "Be careful. Remember that most people just don't know the whole story and what really happened. Turn the other cheek and be peaceful."

Mike rolled his eyes, but he knew she was right. Mike left the house just as his mother backed out of the drive. She waved and pulled away.

Mike realized that this was one of the very few times he had been alone in about a week. It seemed a little odd. He stood on the sidewalk and looked around. All was quiet. He turned and headed for his shortcut, towards the Lilac Road Church. It wasn't long before Mike was humming. He wasn't conscious of the song, but he moved to its rhythm.

As he approached the church, Reverend Ross was raking the flower beds by the front sidewalk. Mike crossed the street and approached him, still humming.

Amos began to snap his hand in time with Mike's step. He also began to hum along. It was a good song, one of the Temptations' best. They broke out in lyrics together:

"'Cause so badly I wanna go outside

Such a lovely day

But everyone knows that a man ain't supposed to cry.

Listen, I got to cry, 'cause cryin', ooh, eases the pain, oh yeah!

Even this hurt I feel inside

Words could never explain,

I just wish it would rain

Oh how I wish that it would rain!

Oh yeah, yeah, yeah."

Both men laughed, shared a high five and separated.

"Keep singing, Mike!" Reverend Ross said.

"Okay. How about 'Ain't Too Proud to Beg' tomorrow?"

CALL ME

Even the events of the past few weeks could not alter the superficial flow of everyday life at the high school. Mike, Ray and A.J. talked in the hall before geometry class. As the bell rang and they took their seats. Becky turned and smiled at Mike. Again, Mike was senseless. He was smitten, still, but beginning to recover the ability to think a little bit more quickly and clearly. Through the day, Mike noticed only a few glances and whispers. Mike noticed that Lee was missing from their first-period class, and he began to worry. But Lee showed up before second period. A.J. saw him first and greeted him as he approached in the hall. "We thought you'd decided to run again!"

Lee answered with a smile and shook his head. "Gone and I stayed with Momma," he said. "She's not feeling good; she didn't sleep well. I sat up with her most of the night. I need to check on her later."

This worried Mike.

Lee continued, "She wasn't breathing well, not talking much."

Mike said, trying to lift Lee a bit, "I bet she'll be talking our ears off soon."

Lee just shook his head, clearly very worried.

Mike added quickly, "I'll call Mom and have her check on Momma."

Lee smiled; it was obvious he liked that idea.

After the call from Mike, Ruth Anne and Amos Ross dropped in to check on Momma. She just rocked in her chair and softly chuckled. "Goodness gracious, bless your sweet hearts," she said. "I'm just fine. Get on back to work now!"

In science class, Lee and Mike were both very happy to see that Mr. Penner would be the new teacher. A.J. liked it, too. He sat in class with a big grin, following Mr. Penner's every word.

Mr. Penner realized quickly that this was a form of respect and he tried to have a little fun with A.J. "A.J. Wright, what are you so happy about?"

Everyone laughed and A.J. blushed.

Class was over, the bell rang, and Mr. Penner closed with, "I appreciate your attention to me. This will be a good class from now on."

Mike and Becky, Ray and Suzy, and Lee and Mandy all were walking together before the boys had to head for practice. As they parted, Becky squeezed Mike's hand and smiled, giving Mike some parting orders to call her that night.

"And don't let one of those nasty linecrackers damage that cute face and pretty nose!" she said.

Mike laughed. "I think you mean linebacker," he said. "I'll tell Coach Carter that my face has great value!"

Becky laughed, and just had to add, "I don't understand why you like this silly game so much."

"Coach will run us like dogs, and then I'll be asking the same question!"

They parted with smiles; they would talk later.

But neither knew how serious their talk would be.

Coach Carter talks

Practice moved along smoothly. Everyone was glad to be back out there, including, clearly, Coach Carter, who offered instruction at every opportunity:

"Don't jump till you see the ball move!"

"Come on, Gone, you're faster than that. Granny is slow, too, but she's old!"

"Do you know the difference between two and one?"

"You guys look like old ladies!"

"Wrap your arms! Roll him up!"

"That was one sorry attempt at a block. Were you trying to scare him?"

"Do you think your ugly face will scare somebody so much that you don't have to block them?"

"Lee, come on. Catch the ball! You're a wide receiver, not a wide dropper."

"Mike, good Lord, hit him like you mean it! Don't take it easy on him!"

It was never fun to be the target of Coach Carter's wrath. But when he was picking on someone else, it could be funny. All of the players would do anything for him.

When practice was over, Coach gave a short speech about how good things could be when everyone got a fair chance. What Mike would always remember was how Coach talked about how very special it is to be a member of a team.

Supper—Hard to Square

Larry came to supper that evening. Ruth Anne had made a simple meal of leftovers. But it was fine. Mike realized that Larry was more relaxed and smiling. Mike and Larry were planning to watch Monday Night Football, new to ABC. Mike loved to hear Dandy Don Meredith and Howard Cosell. A.J. could do a pretty good Cosell imitation, especially when picking on Ray: "It was an amazing display of physical prowess, Big Ray demolished four—not three, but four—hot dogs! An amazing example of athletic hoggery!"

Larry got the recliner and Mike stretched out on cushions on the floor. Ruth Anne brought in some cookies. Larry and Mike had cleaned the kitchen while she made calls to check on patients.

"Mom, did you check on Momma?"

"Yes," Ruth Anne said. "She was very weak, but just refused to come to the clinic. We gave her some stronger medicine. I'll check on her later and tomorrow."

"I'm sure Lee and Gone are there, watching the game. Lee loves the Steelers."

During the game, Larry and Mike talked about what would happen to Big Bob and the others. Mike said, "It's hard to believe Sheriff Willet would do all of those things."

Larry answered, "Yes, but some people are never held accountable for what they do. They really think they're entitled to hurt others. It makes no sense, and if not for strange coincidence—or maybe fate—he would have continued to hurt people. Hatred and bigotry can become normal thinking to some. It starts small and just grows out of control. But it sure is hard to square all of the things he's done. We're just scratching the surface."

Mike added, "And it sure is hard to square many of the things we've seen!"

"Sure is. But Big Bob and his gang will never see life outside of prison. The prison doc told me that the news of Bobby's crash hit him hard. His heart is failing. He won't last long."

LEE CALLS

Just before halftime, the phone rang. Ruth Anne was reading the paper and just about to get ready for bed when she answered. It was Lee. She noticed at once that he seemed very distressed.

"Mrs. Thomas, I think Momma is gone. I don't know what to do."

"What do you mean, Lee?"

She heard Lee take a very deep breath, which he released in long, broken sighs, almost like sobs.

"Lee, take your time. I'm here."

"She went to bed early and said her eyes were hurting. I helped her get in bed. I checked on her just a few minutes ago. She's not breathing and didn't respond to me."

Ruth Anne swallowed a sob. "I'm on my way; I'll be there in a minute."

Lee called the Rosses, and Larry called for an ambulance. All quickly converged on the Sanderson home. But Lee had been right; Sweet Momma was gone.

Friends and members of the Lilac Road Church began to come by, gathering once again on the porch and in the living room.

Mike had called Becky and told her. Soon Coach Carter, Suzy, Becky, Ray and A.J. arrived. Mike was sitting in the same chair at the kitchen table where Sweet Momma had fed him that feast after fishing with Lee.

He was crying softy when Becky walked in and sat in his lap. She cried as she hugged him closely. Gone sat beside them. He had a pitcher of tea and a stack of Tupperware glasses. He smiled at Mike and reminisced about one of their first conversations. "You had any transgressions today?"

They all laughed, wiping a few tears away. One thought that would stay with Mike long after this night was that family trumps everything.

New Home

Sweet Momma's funeral was on Friday morning. Mike sang with the Lilac Road Choir. "We Are Climbing Jacob's Ladder" would always have special meaning and bring a tear. Mike stood between the Walker sisters while they sang. After the funeral, all went to the Sanderson home for lunch. Mike would always remember the elegance of Reverend Ross's sermon honoring Sweet Momma, and how pretty Becky was in her black dress. Her black eye was fading – and all of their hearts were healing.

It was a difficult and long day. But Gone, Lee, Mike, Ray and everyone else had decided the Friday night game would go forward. It was a home game. No one played their very best, but it was a good release. Gone was still much better than everyone else. Very soon, Lee moved into the Thomases' house. Gone stayed at the Sanderson home, but the following fall he would be a Florida State Seminole, and eventually a Heisman finalist.

Life moved on, but despite so many big changes, Lee and Mike would always find the time to get a line in the water.

PART 19
ZEKE'S LAST FISHING TRIP—SATURDAY

Sore again

By the middle of October life had settled into normal. The Hawks were winning, the band marched, each class progressed. On a very normal Saturday, Mike and Lee both woke up with very sore shoulders and necks. They passed a lazy Saturday breakfast with Ruth Anne. Larry dropped by, in uniform, a reminder of things recently past. But breakfast ended with a list of Saturday chores. Mike and Lee hustled though the tasks and the house cleaning, mowed the yard and watered the flowers. They had plans—they were heading to Fair Creek. They were overdue for a fishing trip.

"Just don't bring the slimy things home!" Ruth Anne Thomas, soon to be Ruth Anne Wayne, meant what she said.

Sitting in the Sun

By early afternoon Mike and Lee had lines in the water. Lee had once again given Mike a lesson in knot tying. They had brought along a small transistor radio and tuned it to the Georgia-Mississippi State game. But both were just enjoying the sun and not worrying about anything.

UNDERSTANDING

Both Mike and Lee were drifting off to sleep in the warm sun. There was just a little breeze. It was halftime in the game and "Leonard's Losers" with Leonard Post Toasties was playing on the broadcast. Neither Mike nor Lee paid attention to anything going on around them.

Zeke slowly walked out of the woods and smiled at the two lazy boys.

Mike saw him first and startled awake. "How long you been standin' there?"

"Just a minute or so," Zeke said. "Calm down. You look like you seen a ghost!"

Lee also sat up, shaking his head. "What's up, Mr. Zeke?"

"Not much. Gettin 'any bites?"

"No, it's really slow. Might pick up later."

"I just wanted to see if you boys was okay."

"Yeah," Mike replied. "Things seem okay now. How are you?"

"I's just fine and dandy!"

They were all silent for a minute, enjoying the cool breeze in their faces. Mike had a question for Zeke. "Have you ever seen anything like all this?"

"You mean like the murders and lies?"

"Well, yes, and the person that came to Sweet Momma's in the storm?"

"Yeah, I seen plenty of that stuff."

"Well, I sure don't understand much of it."

"There' s not much I can explain," Zeke said. "I just know that nothin' is gained by clinging on to old hates."

Lee said, "I know Sweet Momma liked you. I know you helped her and she liked talking to you. I know you helped Larry, too. How did this all happen?"

"When people trap themselves in hate and lies, bad things happen until good folk step up!"

"Well, you stepped up."

"I had help!"

THE HELPERS

Zeke turned from the boys and motioned back to the trees, as if beckoning someone or something from the shadows. "Come on out now. Slow down a little for us."

Lee and Mike felt a cool breeze in their faces again. The breeze picked up and then Mike saw a brief, bright-blue flash. The cool breeze in his face was very familiar.

Zeke said, "Come on now, come on. These boys here are our friends, and, your cousins."

A shy, young boy in old bibbed, home-cut overalls walked forward with his head down. His red-blond dirty hair and freckles stood out. This boy was clearly a Thomas. He was carrying a stick. Slowly a small terrier showed up behind the boy and let out a soft bark, just a soft little growl that said, "I'm nervous!"

The little boy reminded Lee of Mike from when they'd first met on the creek.

Zeke introduced the shy sprite: "Boys, this is Bobby Jeff Thomas and Shady!"

It didn't make sense—it was crazy!—but both Mike and Lee remembered their manners anyway.

"Hi, I'm Mike."

"And I'm Lee."

"Bobby Jeff did a lot for us," Zeke said.

Mike and Lee were speechless. They all just stood quietly.

Mike sensed this was an event marking the end—of what, he wasn't sure, but it was a point of passage for something? Zeke answered that unspoken question. "It's time for us to go," he said. "We can rest now. I'm glad this worked out. I have waited for both of you, and this time, for a long time. I watched you grow. You is both fine people. Remember that. You are step-up men."

They all stood in silence for a minute. Zeke finally said, "We're going now. I hope the sun always shines on you. Keep those lines in the water." Zeke added one more thought, something that was very important.

"You still have work to do in this struggle, finish!"

Zeke and Bobby Jeff turned and began walking to the trees, slowly fading. Bobby Jeff threw the stick and Shady barked and gave chase. Bobby Jeff followed his dog, laughing, and both faded. Then Zeke was gone.

Lee and Mike were speechless and stunned. Finally, Lee said, "Let's not tell anyone about this."

Mike just nodded in agreement.

Time Moves ⊙n

Neither Mike nor Lee would ever speak of this to anyone else. Larry did ask Mike if he ever saw Zeke again, but Mike just answered that he thought the old man had moved on.

The events of the early fall of 1970 would fade, but Mike never forgot the gentle old man. Life would have its struggles, but there was always time for lines in the water. Sometimes Mike would look into the trees to see if Zeke was watching. He was never there, except in Mike's heart.

EPILOGUE

A FRIDAY NIGHT IN THE SOUTH

Fifteen years later, Mike and Lee stood on the sidelines as assistant coaches. It was Coach Carter's last season. In the stands, Larry and Ruth Anne Wayne sat with Becky Thomas and her triplet daughters, now six years old. They were bored little girls and would soon be playing in the grass by the bleachers. But they loved the marching band.

When the game ended, Larry and Ruth Anne walked out holding hands. Larry steered Ruth Anne toward a Georgia state trooper who had been watching the game along the sidelines. Larry tipped his hat and said, "Good evening, Trooper Sanderson!"

The trooper tipped his hat too. "Good evening, Trooper Wayne and Mrs. Wayne."

"Gone, don't call me that! I am Ruth Anne to you."

"Yes, ma'am!"

"Can you come by for coffee?"

"You bet!"

After a brief NFL career, Gone Sanderson was now one of the best—and fastest—state troopers in all of Georgia.

Good things happen when people share their lives with each other in very safe, fun places. Hate and anger can never overcome friendships that grow strong over lines in the water.

About Atmosphere Press

Atmosphere Press is an independent, full-service publisher for excellent books in all genres and for all audiences. Learn more about what we do at atmospherepress.com.

We encourage you to check out some of Atmosphere's latest releases, which are available at Amazon.com and via order from your local bookstore:

A Book of Life, a novel by David Ellis

It Was Call A Home, a novel by Brian Nisun

Grace, a novel by Nancy Allen

Shifted, a novel by KristaLyn A. Vetovich

Because the Sky is a Thousand Soft Hurts, stories by Elizabeth Kirschner

Stronghold, a novel by Kesha Bakunin

All or Nothing, a novel by Miriam Malach

Eyes Shut and Other Stories, by Danielle Epting

Say Hello, a novel by Katy Stanton

Stay North, a novel by Shelli Rottschafer

A Pressing Affair, a novel by Eleanor Kelley

Swept Away, a novel by Arnold Johnston

The View From My Window, a novel by Patricia J, Gallegos

Wake Up, a novel by Alejandro Marron

About the Author

With a background in medicine, science, and technology, author Scott McVey drew from his interest in the history and culture of small-town America to evoke the rich landscape of the American South in his debut novel, *Lines in the Water*. Showcasing his sharp eye for detail and a knack for individual voice, the story is resonant with McVey's commitment to making sense of the connections between our past and present and his affinity for a classic crime-mystery sensibility.

As a young man, McVey was an avid sportsman and National Football Foundation and Hall of Fame award-winner, an experience that informs his writing about the boys on the Hawkinsville High School team in *Lines in the Water*. Earning his Doctor of Veterinary Medicine degree at the University of Tennessee in 1980, McVey went on to complete a PhD in Veterinary Microbiology following three years operating a dairy practice in southern Tennessee. After completing his doctorate in 1986, he joined the faculty at Kansas State University, securing a promotion to Associate Professor in 1992.

Through the 1990s, McVey worked in both the university and the private sectors as a scientist and researcher, culminating in a position as a Senior Research Investigator at Pfizer Animal Health in Lincoln, Nebraska. Since then, he has been a professor at the University of Nebraska, served as president of the American College of Veterinary Microbiologists, and worked in the Senior Science and Technology Service on arthropod-borne animal disease for the USDA. He is currently the Director of the School of Veterinary Medicine and Biomedical Sciences at the University of Nebraska Lincoln and Associate Dean of the Iowa/Nebraska Professional Program of Veterinary Medicine. He has published numerous research papers and was an editor and co-author for the 3rd edition of *Veterinary Microbiology* (Wiley-Blackwell, 2013).

In recent years, McVey has turned to writing fiction, bringing to the page a life of travel, keenly observed characters, and memorable voices and locales. *Lines in the Water* is his first complete work of fiction.

CPSIA information can be obtained
at www.ICGtesting.com
Printed in the USA
BVHW071051110821
614085BV00004B/364